by

Diane E. Lindmark

Stand up for yourself

Diane E. Lindmark

Text and cover copyright © 2018 Diane E. Lindmark

All Rights Reserved

This book or any portion thereof may not be reproduced or used in any manner whatsoever without the express written permission of the publisher except for the use of brief quotations in a book review.

All characters appearing in this work are fictitious. Any resemblance to real persons, living or dead, is purely coincidental.

2022-10

If you enjoyed this book please check out these other books by Diane E. Lindmark

The Stone Family Series

A Solitary Stone Book 1 of the Stone Wall Trilogy
A Stone Falls Book 2 of the Stone Wall Trilogy
The Stone Wall Book 3 of the Stone Wall Trilogy
Heart of Stone Part 1 Passage of Stone
Heart of Stone Part 2 A Stone Divided
The Measure of a Man
Lady Huntsman
Founding Fathers
Hidden Stories

The McLoughlin Family

Safe Haven
Any Port in a Storm
The Eye of the Storm
Storm Bringer

The Crosses

The Christmas Hitchhiker
The Christmas Breakdown
The Christmas Derailment
The Christmas Avalanche
Dukes and Plumbers

One Off's

Second Age of Darkness
The Kith
Land and Treachery
One Man's Wife
Legacy
An Accident of Faith
The Wrong Life
For Family Honor
Rough Road

I

Wednesday, October 25

"Miss, Miss, you need to wake up. All passengers have to disembark."

Lenore opened her eyes and looked around. She murmured, "Sorry." She got to her feet and picked up her backpack. She grimaced at the sight of it, it definitely needed to go. She walked down the narrow aisle and exited the bus. She slung her backpack over her shoulder and looked around. She shivered, the morning was just a little cool.

A man unloading the luggage from the bus compartment asked, "Do you have any luggage, ma'am?"

She shook her head and asked, "Is there a diner, or someplace to get something to eat nearby?"

He pointed. "Down the street four blocks, hang a right, two blocks on your right."

She nodded. "Thank you." She looked at her wrist. She sighed. She needed to get a new watch. As she walked out of the bus station, she stopped a man. "Excuse me sir, do you have the time?"

He looked at his watch. "Eight oh five."

She nodded. "Thank you."

When she hit the street, she looked around and laughed at herself. "What the hell am I doing in Phoenix, Arizona?" She shook her head. She was not even sure how she had gotten here. Beyond the bus, of course, everything seemed to be some kind of a haze. Granted, the last couple of years of her life had been a haze. She walked slowly, telling herself, *There's nowhere you have to be anytime soon. Stop and smell the roses. Enjoy the view.*

When she entered the diner, a waitress looked up, coffeepot in hand. "Anywhere you like, Hon."

She nodded and chose a corner booth. She slid in and grabbed the menu. She began examining it, asking herself, *I wonder if they have anything for under three hundred and seventy-five calories.* She sighed and shook her head. *No, no, no, stop that. You can have whatever you want to eat.* Her thoughts were interrupted by the waitress appearing.

"What can I get you? Do you want some coffee?"

Lenore hesitated. "Yes, I would like coffee with cream and sugar, and I want a pancake and a banana, if you have them."

She poured her the coffee. "Cream and sugar's on the table, and one banana and one pancake. You want whipped cream on that?"

Lenore started to shake her head. "No ... Yes, yes, I would." She smiled.

The waitress smiled back. "Coming right up."

The waitress returned a few minutes later and set the plate in front of her. Lenore asked, "Is there a grocery store around here near a hotel? I need to pick up a few things."

The waitress nodded. "Sure, there's Bertram's Hotel, and they're right around the corner from a twenty-four-hour Walmart."

"Where would I find them?"

"You can look it up on your phone, should pop up on the GPS."

Lenore laughed. "I don't have a phone."

The waitress looked surprised then shrugged her shoulders. "I can't survive without my phone. I'll draw you a map, be back in a couple minutes."

Lenore was just finishing eating her breakfast when the woman reappeared with a piece of paper. "Here you go, Hon."

Lenore took it, folded it, and stuck it in her pocket. "Thank you. What do I owe you?"

"Seven dollars and fifty-six cents."

Lenore got to her feet and pulled some crumpled bills out of her pocket. She straightened them and set a five and then five ones on the table. "Thank you. Keep the change."

She hurried out of the diner telling herself firmly, *Keep your head down and don't stay anywhere too long.* It was a long walk to the grocery store, but she did not mind. When she arrived, she went straight to the pharmacy department. She paused by the reading glasses rack. She glanced at herself in the little mirror. She looked like hell. She sighed and shook her head. She moved on to the hair dye department. It took her a few minutes to find the best match. She read the label, sounded easy enough. She threw it in the cart and grabbed a bag of hair clips, then headed for the luggage department. Along the way she grabbed a hairbrush and a pair of scissors. She found a small carry-on duffel bag and threw it in, along with a new backpack, making sure to get plain, nondescript looking things. Then she went to the men's department and found a zip up gray hoodie. She tried on the small, decided she liked it and threw it in, then she went to the juniors' department. She grabbed a pair of size five boot cut jeans and went into the fitting room. They were way too big, but she decided to get them anyways. She grabbed another pair along with a man's belt and wallet. She threw them in the cart, then she grabbed a package of socks, some underwear, and three new bras. She hesitated. It was getting cold. She grabbed a plain wool cap and a pair of gloves, and then went back to the men's department. She got a blue and a gray long sleeved T-shirt and threw them in. Then she went to the home department and grabbed a towel. When she walked past the jewelry department, she grabbed a cheap watch. Deciding it was not safe for her to eat out again, she went to the food department and got two TV dinners and a box of granola bars, then she checked out, and exited the store.

She pulled out the little map, then headed for the hotel. It looked kind of run down, probably the perfect place. She entered the office. "Can I get a room for the night?"

The clerk frowned and looked at his watch. "It's well before check-in, I'd have to charge you for two days."

She shrugged her shoulders. "That's fine."

"Can I see some ID, and how would you like to pay for this?"

She pulled out her ID and handed it over. "Cash."

"If you don't use a credit card to pay for the room, I have to take a fifty-dollar cash deposit just to cover any damages. You get it back when you check out."

She nodded. "That's fine."

Five minutes later, key in hand, she headed for her room. She liked the fact that the door opened onto the street. No hallways. She entered and dumped everything on the bed. She dumped out her backpack and made sure it was empty, then she set it aside. She put the TV dinners in the little fridge, then stripped out of her clothes and put everything on the bed. She wrapped her towel around her shoulders and went into the bathroom. She brushed her hair and then tossed it from side to side, examining it. It took her a few minutes, but she finally decided on how to cut her hair. Once this was done, she opened the box of hair dye and proceeded to apply it. When she was done, she used one of the hair clips to secure her hair up on top of her head while she waited for the dye to soak in. She cleaned up all the hair, making sure there were no traces left. She flushed it down the toilet. When the time was up, she showered thoroughly, being sure to rinse out all the dye, and then went back to the bed. She examined everything laid out in front of her. She put on her new clothes, then she packed all the clothes into her new bag. She examined what little was left on the bed. She rubbed her face. She felt like crap. She pulled out a necklace and a ring and dropped them in her old backpack, then she put the rest of her jewelry away in her small jewelry box, pausing only briefly to look at the photo, then she added it to the jewelry box. When she was finished, she put the box in her new backpack. Picking up her new wallet, she removed all of the tags and excess junk, then she put her ID and money into it before throwing it into her new backpack. She sighed, then began examining the pill bottles. She decided to wait on a sleeping pill until tonight after dinner, but for now she needed something to keep her going. She was also discovering she was prone to panicking, and she was also hurting like hell. She knew she should put it off a little longer, but she did not want to. She grabbed the bottle of oxycodone and poured two into her hand. She looked into the bottle. There were only four pills missing out of this bottle, which meant there was a hundred and sixteen left, and she had a whole other one hundred and twenty count bottle. She closed her eyes and momentarily contemplated taking them all, then she shook her head, put the lid back on, and threw them in her backpack. She laughed at herself and shook her head. She said to herself, "Well, if you can't stay on the wagon, at least have a good time falling off of it." She grabbed the bottle of Concerta and took one out, then she grabbed a Zoloft and threw the rest of the bottles in her backpack. She went to the bathroom and poured herself a glass of water, then she downed all four pills in a single gulp. She put on her shoes, then she grabbed her new backpack and her old backpack, and went in search of a pawn shop.

It did not take her long to find one. She entered and looked around. She tried to remember the last time she had been in a pawn shop. It had been a really long time. She paused in front of a television that was for sale. It was on mute, but the news was running. She watched for a couple of minutes. There had been a police involved shooting, a fatal car crash in the early hours, a pop star had gone missing – suspected kidnapping – and President Trump and the media were again at odds. She sighed and shook her head. "Same shit, different day, and that is why I don't watch the news." She crossed to the counter.

Doug looked the girl up and down. He sniffed. He could smell the fresh hair dye, and if her eyes were any indicators, she was stoned out of her mind. He asked cautiously, "Something I can help you with?"

She nodded and set the backpack down. She unzipped it and pulled out the ring and the necklace. "Yeah, I was looking to sell these things."

He picked up and carefully examined the Gucci backpack. It looked brand-new, it did not have a mark on it. He pulled out his gold testing kit and examined the necklace and ring. He stepped over to his computer and typed in a description of all three items, none of them were listed as stolen. He asked, "You want to sell them, not pawn them?"

She nodded. "Yeah, there's no way I will be able to afford to get them out of hock."

He nodded and refrained from asking if it was going to go up her nose. He shrugged his shoulders. "I don't know if I've much of a market for that backpack. I mean, I'll take it off your hands, but not for near what it's worth. Best I can offer you on that is three hundred. Nice necklace, nice ring, seven hundred for both."

She nodded and pulled out her ID. "I'll take it."

Doug took the ID and examined it carefully, expecting it to be a fake, but unless he missed his guess, it was real. He was not quite as familiar with California IDs as he was Arizona's, though he did find it interesting that it was an ID and not a driver's license. He filled out his receipt book and flipped it over to her. "If you'll sign here, I will get your cash."

She signed, and he counted out a thousand dollars. She put two hundred in her wallet, wadded up the rest, and dropped it in her backpack. She went back to the hotel. By the time she arrived, she was starving. She fixed one of the TV dinners, then decided to treat herself to a sleeping pill, undressed, and went to bed.

II

Thursday, October 26

Lenore groaned and rolled over. She did not want to get out of bed. She did not want to face the day. She shook her head and told herself firmly, *You can do this. You can do this without chemical aid.* She got out of bed, showered, and got dressed. She had the other TV dinner for breakfast, then she cleaned up and packed her room, making sure she did not leave anything behind. She even pulled out the trash liner and tied it shut. She had seen a trashcan outside by the office. She momentarily contemplated sacrificing the fifty dollar deposit, not wanting to answer any awkward questions, but she decided since she had no idea how long her money was going to hold out, she could not afford to lose it. But maybe if she pulled her hoodie down low, she could avoid any awkward questions about the change of hair color, and maybe she would even get lucky and there would be a different desk clerk. She grabbed her backpack and her small duffel and headed out of the room. She disposed of the trash along the way. To her relief, there was a different clerk at the desk. She checked out and got her fifty dollars back. She exited the office and looked around. She had no idea where she was going or what she was doing. She chose a direction at random and started walking. She had been walking and thinking for a long time and finally she realized she was starving. She started looking around for somewhere to eat. Finally, she came across a small diner. She entered and sat down at the bar. It was very busy. The waitress at the bar asked, "What can I get you to drink?"

"Water with lemon in a to-go cup."

The waitress, Janet, raised an eyebrow, but nodded and returned a minute later. Lenore was looking at the menu. She was having a hard time focusing. She felt like her teeth were going to vibrate out of her head. Her whole body felt like it was trembling and shaking. She knew she could not go any longer, she had to have some pills. The waitress was staring at her expectantly. She tried to look at the menu, finally she just said, "I'll have the special with broccoli."

Janet nodded. "Coming right up."

Lenore got up and went into the bathroom, relieved to see it was single occupancy. She locked the door and opened her backpack. She hesitated and then decided to take the prescribed dose of everything except the oxy. She decided to only take one oxy. She stared at the handful of pills. She was rocking herself back and forth. She told herself weakly, *If you had any guts, you'd flush them all down the toilet.* She turned on the water and grabbed a handful and took the pills one at a time, then she grabbed a paper towel and dried off, closed her backpack, and went back to her seat. She picked up her glass of water and sucked it down.

Janet returned with the plate only a few minutes later. Lenore picked up her fork and began playing with her food. She told herself she needed to eat it, but she just could not seem to bring herself to. It was some kind of white meat covered in brown gravy with mashed potatoes dripping in brown gravy. It did not look very appetizing. Finally she forced herself to actually eat the broccoli, then she nibbled at the potatoes. The waitress approached and asked, "Something wrong?"

Lenore started laughing. "More than I can even begin to convey, but as far as the food is concerned, no, it's not. It's me."

Janet smiled. "You're far too young for it to be that bad."

Lenore shrugged her shoulders. "I'm sure there are plenty of people in the world who have it way worse than I do, but as far as I'm concerned, it's terrible."

Janet nodded and frowned. She shrugged her shoulders. "Well, you could do what I always do. Go home, pull the covers over your head, and pretend like today doesn't exist, and start anew tomorrow."

"Home. Now there's a foreign word if I ever heard one. I don't think I've ever known what a home was. I didn't exactly have the best mother in the world."

Janet frowned. She was not used to having to deal with stoners in the afternoon. Usually you had the stoners in the evening and the early hours. That was one of the reasons why she preferred the afternoon shift, less troublemakers, but as she continued to stare at the girl, she was starting to think she was not a troublemaker, maybe just troubled. She shrugged her shoulders and said, "Maybe go back to your roots. Maybe look at how far you've come, might help you know where you're going."

She sighed and shook her head. "You are very determined. Well, my mother was not good at laying down roots and we never lived anywhere longer than six months."

"What about Dad?"

She sighed and shrugged her shoulders. "According to Mom, he took off before I was even born. His name's not even on my birth certificate, but that probably has a lot to do with the fact that Mom didn't even know his name. It's complicated." She decided she did not want to continue this conversation. She got to her feet and indicated the plate. "What do I owe you?"

"Six fifty."

Lenore pulled out her wallet and threw a ten dollar bill on the counter. "Keep the change." She grabbed her backpack and hurried out. She started walking as fast as she could. She walked as long as she could, until she needed to catch her breath. She paused and looked around. The road she was walking along had a metal guardrail. She paused and sat down on it. She set her backpack on her lap, unzipped it and began digging around for her jewelry box. Finding it, she pulled it out and she opened it. She picked up the photo that consisted of all she knew about her father, other than of course what her mother had told her, which was that he had taken off before she was ever born. Lenore always found it difficult to believe anything her mother ever told her. At least half of her mother's stories were always lies. Her mother was a pathological liar, of that she had no doubt, and of course she was the kind of person who always tainted things in her favor, and it was always someone else's fault. She was always the innocent victim. Whenever she thought about her father, she always had more questions than answers. She examined the photo. The two men in it both looked like respectable, good looking, good natured men. She shifted her attention to the woman, her mother. Now there was a tramp if she had ever seen one, even back then. She thought about it. Why did her mother not know his name? Had she just forgotten? Did you forget the name of your child's father? Well, if you were her mother you could, especially if you had only heard it once. Maybe that was it? Maybe he was not to blame at all. Maybe it had just been a one night stand? That was exactly what she would expect from her mother. She stared into the photo, examined it. There was a crowd of people around her mother. Mom was standing in the middle, turned to face the camera. She had a good looking guy on each arm. They were both leaning in close. All three were smiling and laughing. They were standing outside, and a sign in the background read 'Leaf County Fair'. She could also see several Texas flags. She examined the face of each man. It was hard to really tell anything about either one of them, and her mother had always flatly refused to point out which one of them was her father. Lenore considered that maybe her mother did not know. She shuddered. She did not want to think about her mother being involved in a threesome. She considered that for a minute, maybe it was less sinister. Maybe her mother had been stoned and could not remember which one she had gone to bed with? That made more sense. She closed her eyes and told herself firmly, *I will not become my mother.* She sighed several times and shook her head. "Well, sweetie, then you better get your shit together, because you're already well on your way."

She was startled from her contemplation by the sound of brakes hissing. She looked up to see a big rig coming to a stop. The window was lowered and an older man shouted, "Hey girl, you shouldn't be sitting there, that's real dangerous. I go by here every couple of weeks and at least three or four times a year that guardrail's taken clean out. They'll take you with it. You know, it's a really dangerous stretch of road. You shouldn't be walking along it. Why don't you hop in and I'll give you a ride to the next town."

She hesitated only a moment. She did not want to walk anymore. She closed her backpack, got up, opened the passenger door of the big rig and asked. "You sure it's not an inconvenience?"

He chuckled. "I spend so much of my time talking to myself, it'll be nice to have somebody else to talk to."

She nodded, got in and closed the door. He got the truck moving, then offered her his hand. "I'm Thomas."

She shook his hand. "Lenore." She looked back at the photo in her hand, then at Thomas. She asked, "How far is Leaf, Texas?"

He considered for a minute. "Well, if memory serves, that ain't too far from Amarillo, which puts it about eleven hours. Why?"

She shrugged her shoulders. "Somebody suggested I go back to my roots. I don't have any roots to speak of, but I do have a photograph to trace."

He held out his hand. "May I?" She shrugged her shoulders and handed it to him. He examined it, then he shrugged his shoulders. "Doesn't look familiar. I've never been there. I've been to Amarillo on numerous occasions, and that's why I know about it. Seen the signs, but it's one of those puny little towns if you blink, you'll miss it. Farming community, ranch community, somethin' like that. This Fair is probably their big claim to fame every year." He handed the photo back.

She unzipped her backpack and stuck it back in her jewelry box.

Thomas had not been trying to snoop, but it was impossible not to notice the half-dozen pill bottles in her backpack. Beyond the fact that they were right on top, they rattled. He discreetly observed her out of the corner of his eye. She was a pretty thing, though far too skinny for his liking. What his wife would call a twelve pounder, which meant she was tall and skinny like a supermodel. She had longish auburn hair and looked tired and strung out. After a long minute he decided to ask, "So why are we tracing a photograph?"

She shrugged her shoulders. "Nothing better to do, I guess."

"Who's in the photo?"

She hesitated a long minute, trying to decide. "Do you remember a flash in the pan folk rock performer from about twenty years ago, Evanjalevn?" He nodded. "Well, my mom was at this concert, though I'm sure concert is a stretch, with her two buddies and I was born nine months later. Mom has always maintained that Dad was just a loser who didn't stick around."

He nodded and held out his hand. "Can I see the photo again?" She shrugged her shoulders, pulled it out, and handed it to him. It took him several minutes of glancing from the road to the photo, back and forth. Finally he handed it back. "I'm no expert, but they look like decent kids. I mean, I'm assuming Dad is one of these two. They look like ordinary hard-working cow hands." He chuckled to himself. "Listen to me calling them kids. They gotta be about my age now."

She looked at him in surprise, then she examined the photo. "They look like everybody else in the photo, what makes you say they're cow hands?"

He pointed. "Look at their hats. Look at their boots. Look at their jeans with their belt buckles. Those are cow hands."

She examined their hats. They looked old and beaten up. She looked at their jeans, they looked a little worse for wear. She examined their boots, they were square toed, muddy and did not look new. She shifted her attention to their belts. "Okay, I'm clearly missing something. What?"

"Any city slicker who wanted to dress up for a Western concert is gonna have on shiny boots and pristine hats. Look at the sweatbands around those hats. Those had to have been worn outdoors a couple of seasons. They're misshapen, they're not pristine. Look at those boots. Those boots were worked in. They weren't put on for a concert, and those belt buckles? Those are rodeo belt buckles. They earn those. I would say that the only thing they changed for the concert was they got out their good belts, probably didn't have time to change clothes or get cleaned up. Trust me, those are cow hands."

She looked at him dubiously. "And what makes you so confident?"

He chuckled. "I grew up on a ranch. I'm from down in West Texas and that's still where I make my home. Trust me, I know the difference between the dudes who are playing at being cowboys, and real cowboys. Those are real cowboys, which means chances are you can still find them around Leaf."

She considered for a long minute, then asked, "Are you headed back to Texas?"

He nodded. "My load is going to Fort Worth. How old are you? No bullshit. I ain't gonna go to jail for taking a minor across state lines."

She laughed. "I'm eighteen." He looked at her dubiously. She held up her right hand. "My hand to God, my eighteenth birthday was October 11th."

He nodded. "Barely eighteen, that was only two weeks ago."

"But legal."

He nodded. "All right. I can drive for seven more hours before I have to stop and rest for an hour, that's usually when I grab my dinner. If you promise not to give me any trouble, I'll let you stay with me to Odessa, Texas. There's a bus station there. You can catch a bus to Leaf."

She smiled. "Thanks. I promise I will be no trouble at all. I'll buy your dinner, your drinks, whatever. You're the best."

III

Thomas had been driving and thinking for almost an hour. He pointed to his backpack. "In there's a laptop. Pull it out and turn it on."

Lenore did as she was told. "Okay, now what?"

"Go to the web browser and look up the bus station in Odessa, and then check tickets from Odessa to Leaf."

She did as she was told. She frowned. "There are no tickets to Leaf. Apparently if you want to get to Leaf, you have to go to Amarillo."

He nodded and sighed. "I'm not surprised. Look up from Odessa to Amarillo."

She sighed. "You said it was ten hours to Odessa. You have to take an hour lunch break, that's gonna put us in Odessa sometime after eleven, right?"

He nodded. "Somethin' like that, why?"

"The bus for Amarillo leaves at nine thirty. There's no way we can make that bus, and the next ones not till nine thirty the next day. That's gonna be fun."

He nodded and sighed. "That's what I started worrying about. Odessa's such a small area. Check from Tucson to Amarillo."

She smiled. "Hey, that's much better. There are buses leaving every four to six hours." She looked at her watch. "And I think I should be able to make the three fifteen out of Tucson and that gets in at a very reasonable ten AM, instead of the one AM the Odessa bus gets in."

He nodded. "Well then, kiddo, looks like you and I are going to be parting ways in Tucson." He looked at her out of the corner of his eye and demanded, "Can you afford a bus ticket?"

She nodded. "I've got a little money. It says the ticket's two hundred dollars. I figure tax and any extra fees they stamp on should be two fifty, I've got that much cash."

He nodded and glanced at the screen. The two earlier buses were sold out. "Let's go ahead and make sure you have a seat on that bus." He pulled out his wallet and handed her his credit card. "Use my credit card to get you a ticket and then you can give me the cash."

"Are you sure you want to do that?"

He nodded. "It'll be fine. Let's get you a ticket."

Twenty minutes later she handed back his credit card. She dug around in her backpack and found her cash. She pulled it out and counted out three hundred dollars and handed it to him. "Here this should cover everything."

He offered her back eighty dollars. "The ticket was only two twenty."

She shook her head and zipped up her backpack. "Two twenty-eight and you are giving me a ride to Tucson. You let me use your computer. I think it's fair."

He shook his head. "The difference is, kiddo, I got a job and you don't."

She shrugged her shoulders. "I'll get a job. It'll be fine, and besides I still have a few things left I can hock."

He looked at her quickly and demanded, "What are you running away from?"

She glared at him. "I am not running away."

He nodded. "Right, you are not running away. You only have a backpack, a little duffle and you're hocking your stuff, but you're not running away. Right, makes perfect sense."

She shifted and looked out the passenger window, crossed her arms over her chest, and ignored him. They did not speak again until he pulled up outside the Tucson bus station. She started to get out, but he gripped the sleeve of her sweater. "Look kid, I don't know what you're running from, I don't know what you've done, but just remember, eventually you have to face the music. If you've done something wrong, you're still young, you can make it right. But if you're running from somebody's who's hurting you, never forget the cops are your friends, not your enemy, and you're eighteen years old. They can't make you go home. Don't spend the rest of your life on the run because of people who can't make you do anything. You're an adult. You make the decisions. Don't let them make 'em for you."

She frowned. "I'm not sure that's true, but it sounds nice. Take care yourself, Thomas. It was nice meeting you." She grabbed her stuff and climbed out of the truck. She closed the door and headed into the bus station to redeem her ticket. She did not have long to wait before she could board the bus. Once they were on the move, she sighed with relief. She could not explain why, but she felt better when she was not sitting still. She knew it was irrational, but she was afraid they were going to find her, and she did not want to go back. She would rather die than go back. She was glad she was able to get a window seat. She adjusted her stuff, stuck her leg through her backpack strap, pressed her duffel up against the window as a pillow and tried to get some sleep. She had twenty long hours ahead of her to think about what she was going to do next, which was a good thing because she had no idea. She did not even know why she was going to this little town in search of a potentially fictitious father who might not have ever even been in the town. The photograph she had could just be a couple of random guys her mom had latched onto for a photo op. She sighed and shrugged her shoulders. It did not matter, Texas was a really big place. She was sure she would be able to find a place to hide. She fell asleep.

IV

Friday, October 27

Lenore sat looking out the window. They would be pulling up at the bus station any minute now. When they came to a stop, she grabbed her stuff and disembarked with the rest of the passengers. She went to the information desk. When it was finally her turn, she approached the clerk and asked, "How can I get to Leaf, Texas."

The woman made a face and begin typing away on her keyboard. "No buses or trains go that far out of town. You can download one of the rideshare programs, create an account, and get a ride out."

She shook her head. "I don't have a phone."

The woman's eyes widened. She demanded, "How do you live?"

Lenore smiled. "Rather easily, actually. You breathe in, you breathe out. Occasionally you eat and drink. It's very easy. You should try it sometime."

The woman rolled her eyes. "Ha, ha, very funny. Then I guess a cab is your only bet, but you'll have a hard time convincing any of them to take you out there to begin with. They're gonna charge you double, so you're looking at like four hundred dollars, and that's only if they agree to take the ride. A lot of the cabbies won't. Not really sure what your options are. I guess the best I can suggest is you take one of the city buses as far as it will take you South and see if maybe you can pick up a ride from there. Don't you have a friend you can call to come and get you?"

She shook her head. "Can you tell me what city bus will take me the furthest South?"

The woman shrugged her shoulders and clicked some more keys. "Bus number two fourteen. You can pick it up right down the street at the corner in about twenty-five minutes and that goes as far south in the right direction as any public transportation can take you, but that's still gonna put you like sixty or seventy miles from Leaf. I'm not sure which side you're aiming for. But I can give you a Texas map and an Amarillo map, and I can print you off a map and highlight some of the best routes to get to Leaf, if that might be of help."

Lenore nodded. "Yes, thank you. I'm sure that will be of assistance, and then I can figure something out from there." It only took the woman a minute, then she handed her a stack of information. Lenore took it and headed for the bus stop.

Fortunately, she did not have long to wait. The bus arrived only a few minutes later. She boarded it and settled in to wait for the last stop.

Lenore stepped off the bus and looked around. She pulled the little map the information lady had printed her out of her pocket. She took a moment to orient herself, then she shivered. It was a lot colder in Texas than it had been in Arizona, and according to the map it was an eighteen hour walk to Leaf if she followed the route given to her by the information lady, but that looked like back roads. She thought she stood a better chance of hitching a ride if she stuck with more major thoroughfares, even if it probably added a few miles. If she got a ride it could be better, but she still needed to plan for the worst case scenario, which meant she was probably going to have to find a place to camp for the night, because something told her out in the middle of nowhere there was not going to be a hotel. She started walking, keeping an eye out for somewhere to buy a sleeping bag. She had been walking for a little over an hour when she ran across a large store that said 'Hunting and Fishing'. She detoured and headed for the main entrance. As she entered the store, an employee by the door smiled at her.

He said somewhat apologetically, "I'm sorry ma'am, but you can't bring the duffel in. You have to leave it at customer service."

She stared at him for a moment confused, then she understood. She nodded. "No problem." She approached the customer service counter.

The lady behind the counter smiled. "Can I help you, ma'am?"

"Yes, the guy at the front door said I had to leave my duffel here."

She smiled apologetically. "Yes, sorry. We have had some incidents with shoplifters lately." She slid a small piece of paper across to Lenore. It had a twist tie on one end and reminded her of a luggage tag. "If you'd please just write your name and phone number, we'll hold it back here for you."

Lenore smiled. "I don't have a phone."

The woman looked a little surprised, then shrugged her shoulders. "That's fine, just your name. But don't forget it."

Lenore nodded. "I won't." She quickly filled out the card and then headed into the store proper. She stared. She had never been in this kind of store before. It was huge. It appeared to have everything from skiing and rock climbing equipment to hunting and fishing, gun ranges, and lots of pretty things to look at. Right now, the thing that caught her attention most was the large concession stand. She approached and appraised the menu. The man behind the counter said, "Whenever you're ready."

Her eyes continued to flick over the menu as she said, "Thank you, just a minute." Everything seemed to have beef or bacon on it. A man got in line behind her. She gestured for him to go ahead of her. "I'm still looking, please go ahead."

He nodded and smiled at her. "Thank you, ma'am."

She found it difficult not to smile. He looked like something out of a movie. He was in cowboy boots, jeans, a jean jacket, underneath was an unbuttoned plaid flannel shirt and a blue T-shirt. He also had on a cowboy hat. His boots and jeans were covered in mud and well used. The jacket, too, looked like it had seen better days. He approached the counter and said, "Large cup of coffee, black."

The young man finished helping the gentleman, then looked back at her. He did not say it, but Lenore could feel his judgmental eyes saying, 'Are you ready yet?' Finally she decided. She stepped up to the counter. "I would like the baked potato with only cheese, sour cream, and butter please, and the largest soda you have."

He rang her up and handed her a cup. He indicated the soda machine. "Please, help yourself, ma'am. If you'll have a seat, I will bring you your potato as soon as it's ready."

She nodded and took the cup. "Thank you." She approached the machine. After a long minute, she filled the cup full of ice and then got herself some unsweet tea. She sat down and removed her hoodie. It was a little warm in here. She had been sitting there for a couple minutes sipping her drink when she realized somebody was watching her. She glanced around discreetly. The old cowboy, well maybe not old, fifty she guessed, was sitting at another table drinking his coffee, playing on his phone, but every few seconds he glanced in her direction. She did not like that, it made her nervous, but after a few minutes he got up and got a refill on his coffee and headed into the store. The young man brought out her potato. She ate it and got a refill on her tea, then headed into the store. It did not take her long to find a sleeping bag. She also decided it would be a good idea to pick up a bag of dried fruit and a bag of trail mix. She was enjoying looking around the store.

She paused at a knife display. They were all in a glass case. The clerk appeared in front of her and said, "If you'd like to see something, I would be glad to show you. I just have to see an ID first."

She looked at him in surprise. "Why an ID?"

"You have to be eighteen or with a parent in order to handle the knives, company policy."

She nodded, pulled out her wallet and showed him her ID. She pointed to one of the knives. "Is that a good knife?"

He nodded and opened the case and handed it to her. "It's a very good knife."

A voice from behind her startled her. "That is a matter of opinion." She looked over her shoulder. It was the cowboy from earlier.

He made her nervous, but she asked anyways, "What do you mean?"

He took the knife from her, closed it, and then handed it back to her. "Open it."

It took her a minute or two of fiddling with it before she figured out how and she discovered it was very stiff and hard to open, and it hurt her fingers. It was equally difficult to close. "You're right. I don't like that one at all." She handed it back to the clerk.

The cowboy pointed. "Show her that one."

She looked at the case. The one she had just been looking at was priced at a hundred and twenty dollars. This one was only priced at twenty-five dollars. She took it and opened it.

"That does open much easier, but isn't that more dangerous?"

The cowboy chuckled. "That depends. If you're gonna use it to save your life, you want it to open pretty quickly, but you're still doing it wrong." He took it and held it in his hand. He put his thumb on the little knob. "See, you're supposed open it like this." He flipped it open only using his thumb. "Now see, if you're carrying it for protection, that's the kind of blade you want, but just remember, the problem with a knife or gun is they can take it away from you. I personally would rather have my daughter rely on a gun instead of a knife."

She shook her head. "I don't think I could stab somebody or shoot them. I just thought it might be useful."

He nodded. "I'm sure you would find many uses for it, ma'am." He nodded his head and wandered off.

"I'll take this one."

The clerk nodded. "Are you done shopping and ready to check out altogether, ma'am?" He indicated the other things in her cart.

"Yes, thank you." A few minutes later she was all checked out. She stopped by customer service and retrieved her duffel bag and went outside. She put the two bags of food in her backpack, opened the knife, cut the tag off the sleeping bag, threw them and the bags in the trash, and then stuffed the sleeping bag in her duffel. It barely fit, but at least she only had to carry two things. She started walking again.

She had been walking for about ten minutes when the cowboy pulled alongside her in a pickup truck. He lowered the window and asked, "Need a ride?"

She hesitated. "You're probably not going my direction."

He laughed. "Where you headed?"

"Three eighty-five."

He raised an eyebrow. "That's an odd destination, but I pass right by there on my way home. Why don't you let me give you a ride?" She hesitated. He added, "It'll save you thirty miles of walking."

She nodded. She definitely liked the sound of that. She turned to face him and asked, "Are you sure it's not a bother?"

He shook his head. "Like I said, I go right by there." She got in the truck. "Buckle up."

She buckled her seatbelt and they drove on. "So since clearly three eighty-five is not your final destination, where is your final destination?"

She shrugged her shoulders. "Would you believe I don't have one?"

He laughed. "That depends, is it the truth?"

She shrugged her shoulders. "I guess so, since I don't know where I'm going or what I'm doing, it has to be the truth, doesn't it?"

He shook his head. "Look sweetie, you seem like a real nice kid, let me offer you a little advice. Go home. You keep going on like you are, somethin' real bad is gonna happen and that'll be a real shame."

She laughed and shook her head. "I find it interesting that you assume that there is a home to go back to, and I find it interesting that you assume the home that I allegedly left is better than living on the streets. I also find it interesting, I bought food, bought other things, and yet you think I'm homeless."

He nodded. "Simple logic. Dry rations, sleeping bag, knife, and walking. Conclusion, homeless."

She shrugged her shoulders. "I guess I can see your logic."

"So, is home really that bad?"

She shifted a little in her seat so she could better look at him. "And you're interested exactly why?"

"I told you, I have a daughter. I don't like the idea of her on the streets. When you become a parent, you tend to look at other people's kids as offshoots of your own."

She shrugged her shoulders. "I wouldn't know anything about that. My mother barely cared about me. And she sure as hell didn't care about anybody else's kids."

He sighed and shook his head. "Some assholes just weren't meant to be parents … How old are you really?"

"Eighteen, you saw me give him my ID."

"IDs can be fake."

She laughed. "I wouldn't even begin to know how to go about getting a fake ID. Well, actually, that's probably not true. I probably could've asked my mother, but that would've involved talking to her, which would have defeated the purpose of ditching her."

He shook his head. "Sorry, kiddo, sounds like your mama is a piece of work."

"I believe that would be an understatement."

He nodded. "Let me give you a little good parenting advice. Stop taking rides from strangers. It's gonna land you dead in a ditch. The next time you get to a town, go to the church and ask for help finding a job and getting a place to live. Try to put down some roots before you really get stuck in this life."

She laughed. "I'm starting to find it very interesting how everyone has suggestions for what I should do with my life, waitresses, truck drivers, and now a cowboy." She shook her head. "Very interesting."

He nodded. "Very interesting, all three professions that see a lot more of life than you would think, and I would say they all get a front row seat to life at its worst."

She considered that for several minutes. She had not thought of it that way, but he was probably right.

He pulled his truck over to the side of the road and pointed. "That's three eighty-five right there, which is kind about the middle of nowhere. You sure I can't take you on to the next town? Be a lot safer."

She shook her head. "No, I'll be fine."

He nodded, leaned on the steering wheel, staring straight ahead of him as he said, "Just remember, when the kick to the nuts doesn't work, sternum, throat, nose, eyes, and ears."

She looked at him very dubiously, then she shook her head. "I'm sure you're being kind, but that won't be necessary." She got out of the truck, turned back and smiled. "Thanks for the ride." He nodded and drove off. She looked around, then headed south.

V

Despite the cool day, the sun was beating down on her. That combined with the walking made her feel very hot. Lenore stopped walking and sat down her backpack and her duffel bag. She took off her hoodie and tied it around her waist. She pushed the sleeves of her T-shirt up past her elbows. She ran her fingers through her hair, then pulled it back in a ponytail, grabbed her backpack and duffel, and started walking again. She had been walking for nearly an hour and she was getting tired. At this rate she was going to have to find some place to camp on the side of the road. She did not like the idea of sleeping outdoors. She had never gone camping and she certainly did not want to think of what strange nasty creatures could be found in the Texas countryside, but she had put herself on this road, she was going to see it to the end. She contemplated trying to hitchhike, every few minutes a car would drive by, but she did not like that idea. It was not just the cowboy's warning. So far, all the times she had been picked up, it had been by people offering her rides out of the goodness of their heart. She preferred to keep it that way, it was a little less like begging. She hoped not to have to fall that far. Hopefully she would be able to find a job and could earn her keep. She did not like the idea of having to beg. A shiny tricked out pickup truck pulled up in front of her. She started to walk around it, the driver lowered the passenger window and asked, "Need a lift? Where you headed?"

She hesitated, remembering what the cowboy said, but he looked like a nice guy. "I'm headed for Leaf, Texas."

He smiled. "That's where I'm headed too. Jump in, I'll give you a ride."

She got in. "Thank you."

He pulled back onto the road and continued on. He asked with a laugh, "Car break down?"

"No, I don't have a car."

He looked at her in surprise. "So you're just walkin' to Leaf? Where from?"

"Amarillo."

He laughed. "That is a really long walk, not one I'd want to make. I'm Jace, by the way, and you are?"

"Lenore."

He made a face. "That's a stuffy sounding name."

She shrugged her shoulders. "I don't know, I always kind of liked it."

He nodded. "I guess it's good to like your name. I'm not too crazy about mine, but I've heard worse, especially around these parts."

She considered that for a long minute, then asked, "Such as?"

He laughed. "Bubba Cartwright. You know, with a name like that you think he'd be fun, but he ain't. He's a sanctimonious asshole."

She considered that, then nodded. "Yeah, I don't think I'd like to be called 'Bubba'."

He laughed. "I would think not since you're a girl, but you probably wouldn't like 'Sissy' any better, and we got one of those in town too."

"Definitely not."

"So what brings you to Leaf?"

She shrugged her shoulders. "Work. I heard they do a big winter fair. I thought maybe they could use some extra help."

He looked at her confused. "Fair? We don't do any fairs around here."

She looked at him with concern. "But I saw pictures. It said Leaf Fair, and there were winter decorations in the background, and I thought I saw a Ferris wheel."

"Oh, you mean the rodeo. Yes, we have a rodeo. It starts right after Christmas and goes for four weeks. You must've seen photos of the fairground sign because it says Leaf County Fair, but it's the fairgrounds. You know, 'Win a teddy bear'. Stupid shit like that."

"Rodeo. So like do people come from all over for this?"

He nodded. "Texas, New Mexico, some from Oklahoma, just depends on who's competing on the circuit, things like that, but depending on your skills, some of the ranches are hiring around here." He turned his truck off onto an old dirt road.

She looked around. "Where're we going?"

"Leaf, it's a shortcut."

She jerked her thumb in the direction they came from. "But there was a sign that said 'no through traffic and no trespassing'."

He nodded. "Yeah, Mr. Cartwright would definitely start shooting at any strangers or troublemakers who trespassed on his land, but he doesn't mind the locals who are coming from Amarillo cutting across this section of his property. Like I said, it's a shortcut, saves about twenty miles."

Lenore was starting to get a bad feeling about this.

"So where you from originally?" he asked.

"Los Angeles."

He looked at her and grinned. "No shit! Really? Man, I want to get the hell out of this town. I would love to go to Los Angeles. I wanted to go to school there, but Dad wouldn't let me. Wellll, that ain't strictly true, he'd let me, he just wouldn't pay for it. He said I wanted to go to school in Los Angeles to party and he wasn't paying for me to party. He was paying for me to go to school."

She nodded. "Sounds reasonable."

He pulled his truck over and put it in park. He reached under his seat and pulled out a bag. He dangled it between them. "You want to party?"

She stared wide-eyed. Inside the bag was three little vials of white powder. She shook her head. "No, I'm not into partying, thank you."

He opened the bag, grabbed one of the vials, and poured a little on the side of his hand. "Aw, come on, live a little. We're young, we're supposed to have fun." He offered it to her. She shook her head. He shrugged his shoulders, brought it to his nose and snorted it. He shook his head and yelled, "Yeah! Now that's what I'm talking about!" He licked the side of his hand.

Lenore reached for her duffel bag deciding it was a good idea to get out of the truck right now. "I think I'll walk from here."

He grabbed her arm and pulled her towards him. "Why would you walk thirty miles when you can get a ride from me?" He grabbed ahold of her ponytail and pulled it loose. She struggled.

"Let me go!"

He got a good hold of her hair and jerked her head down. "Hey, if I'm giving you a ride, the least you can do is suck my dick." She punched him in the ribs. He let go of her. She turned and tried to get out of the truck, but he grabbed ahold of her and he was a lot bigger and stronger than her. She found herself on her back, lying across the seats. She tried to get her knee between him and her, but he pushed it out of the way, and then backhanded her. "What the hell did you have to hit me for? I'm giving you a ride! I think you owe me a ride!" She continued to struggle against him. He grabbed the collar of her shirt and ripped it. She was hitting and kicking him. He tried to kiss her, and she bit him. He pulled back and punched her in the ribs. She squirmed and struggled and kneed him in the side, then he punched her in the face. He pulled her beneath him, she remembered what the cowboy had said. When he moved in to kiss her again, she punched him in the sternum. He reared back holding his chest. She reached up and pushed open the passenger door. She rolled over and tried to scramble out, but he grabbed ahold of her right leg and pulled her back. She kicked him in the sternum with her left leg. He let her go and she slid out of the truck, barely managing to grab her backpack and duffel on the way out. She was face first in the dirt with her feet still in the truck when he grabbed ahold of her ankle and yanked off her shoe. She scrambled to her feet and ran along the barbed wire fence until she came to one of the posts. She threw her stuff over it, put one hand on the hip high post and easily leapt over the barbed wire. She grabbed her stuff and ran into the cover of the trees. Once she felt like she was well concealed, she dropped down on the ground and caught her breath. She sat there breathing heavily, she had heard his truck peel off. That was good. At least he was not going to chase her. She looked down at her stockinged foot. Well, maybe he threw her sneaker out. In a couple of minutes she would go look. When she felt calm, she went to investigate. No such luck. The creep had held onto it, not strictly surprising. For the moment she felt safer on this side of the barbed wire. She hesitated, unsure of where she was and where she should be going. Finally she decided it was better to continue in the direction they had been going. She started walking along the fence.

She had been walking for well over an hour. The sky seemed to be getting prematurely dark. This was making her nervous. She also realized she should have bought a flashlight back in town.

Oh well, hindsight was always twenty twenty, right? That was what they always said. Then it started drizzling. She stopped and pulled on her hoodie. She shivered. She was cold, scared, alone, and soon to be in the dark. She hoped desperately it would only drizzle for a couple of minutes, but the drizzling turned to a soft rain. After an hour she was soaked to the bone and felt frozen through. She laughed at herself. She had never been a religious person. God had never been evident in her life, which is why she thought she must be a hypocrite. She kept finding herself asking him for help. She had asked for help back in the truck, now here she was asking to be out of the rain. She shivered and kept walking. She had been walking for about ten minutes when she saw off in the distance what looked like a shed. She knew she was trespassing, but she did not care. She shifted directions and headed for it. She sighed. When she got closer, she could see it had a lock on it, but there was a window, a very small window. She walked up and pushed it open. She opened it as far as it would go, then forced her backpack and her duffel through it. She was sure she could fit through the window. She was very slender and delicately built, though surprisingly tall. She could easily reach the window but she lacked the strength to pull herself up and into it. She examined the window, trying to figure out how she was going to get through it. She walked around the shed. On the other side was a large log, about twelve inches wide and about eighteen inches tall. It took all of her strength, but she was able to roll it over to the window, then stand it up. She carefully climbed onto it and then stuck her arms through the window. It took a little finagling and squirming, but she got her shoulders through, then she was able to push on the inside of the window and get her torso through, followed by her hips, then with some more finagling she was able to turn so that she was now sitting in the window. She groped around above her and found one of the rafters, then she pulled herself the rest of the way through the window. Now she was dangling there. After a minute she dropped to the ground. She landed on something which caused her to stumble, fall and hit the ground hard. She lay there groaning, but at least it was dry and out of the wind. She pushed herself to a seated position. Her left foot was killing her. She was sure she had blisters and other cuts and irritations from walking in her stockinged foot for so long. She dug around in her backpack and found a bottle of water. She had not taken any pills since yesterday, and she needed to. She needed to badly. If she shifted a little and held up the bottles to the dim light coming through the window, she could just make out the pills. It took her a couple of minutes to find the one she wanted, then she took them, got the sleeping bag out of the duffel, and wrapped up in it. She knew she should change out of her wet clothes, but she was too tired, hurt, and scared to give a crap. All she wanted to do was sleep.

VI

Saturday, October 28

Bubba pulled up outside the line shack. He got out of his truck and was halfway to the door of the shack when he realized the window was open. He narrowed his eyes and tried to remember the last time he was out here. No, the window had definitely been closed and he did not think the wind could have blown it open, then he glanced at the chopping block which he knew for certain was supposed to be around back. He considered for a minute. The window was about six and a half feet off the ground, give or take, and was so small he could not imagine anybody but a child being able to crawl through it. He debated for a moment about going back to his truck and radioing the Sheriff. He shook his head and murmured to himself, "Now you're just being paranoid." Nevertheless, he switched the key to his left hand and pulled his Glock out and automatically flipped the safety off. He quietly unlocked the door and pushed it open. He raised an eyebrow at the purple sleeping bag lying in the middle of the floor. He backed up just a little and pointed his gun at the ground as he whistled. The sleeping bag moved. He whistled louder. He reached over and flipped on the battery-operated lamp as he said, "Probably a good idea if you go ahead and wake up." The figure started and sat up. Catching sight of him, she scooted away on her backside. He raised an eyebrow. Her hair was a mess and her clothes were covered in dirt. He hesitated a moment, then decided yes, it was definitely a her. He backed up a little more and beckoned her with two fingers. "Why don't you come on outside so we can have ourselves a little chat. I got a coffee thermos in my truck."

She shook her head frantically. "Look, I'm sure I'm trespassing. I don't want any trouble. Please, just let me be on my way. I'm not on your property by choice. I kind of ended up here." Lenore had just finished speaking when her eyes finally adjusted to the light and she realized he was holding a gun. She screeched and put her hands over her face. "Please, don't shoot me! I didn't mean to trespass!"

Bubba looked at the gun in his hand. He nodded, flipped the safety back on and stuck it in his holster. "I'm not gonna shoot you, but come on out."

She grudgingly got to her feet and walked out slowly and awkwardly. She shivered and still felt damp. Once outside, she hugged herself. The wind was cutting through her damp hoodie like a knife and she hurt all over.

Bubba looked her up and down. His eyes finally came to rest on the missing sneaker. He scratched the back of his head. "What happened to your shoe?"

She shook her head and she groaned and put her hand to the side of her head. "I don't want to talk about it. Can I just be on my way, please?"

He looked around. "You're like forty miles from the nearest town. Exactly where do you think you're going anytime fast, let alone with only one shoe? Let's not forget that."

She shook her head. "But he said this was a shortcut to town."

Bubba nodded, crossed his arms over his chest, and said with extreme sarcasm, "Right, and who would he be?"

Lenore frowned. She took a deep breath and looked the man up and down. He was young, not much older than her, and rather good looking if you went for the country boy look. In the early morning light, she was not one hundred percent sure, but it looked like he had blonde hair and blue eyes, kind of a lean athletic body, and like everybody around these parts, was wearing well-worn boots and jeans, though he was wearing a T-shirt with a long sleeved flannel shirt unbuttoned over it, and of course, the requisite cowboy hat. She rubbed her hands up and down her face. "Look, I don't want to cause any trouble. Can I please just be on my way?" She shivered again.

Bubba wished he could laugh. She had just rubbed more dirt all over her face. But he was getting the distinct feeling this was not a laughing matter. He shook his head and mentally apologized to the Sheriff as he said, "Look, right now as I see it, your options are: we can stand here in the cold and wind and wait for the Sheriff; or you can grab your stuff, get in my warm truck, and I can take you to talk to the boss, and he can decide whether you're trespassing or just passing through. But just a suggestion, I wouldn't put my faith in the Sheriff right now, because the way you look, he's gonna throw you in jail, whereas the boss will probably take pity on you."

Lenore hugged herself tightly. "What do you mean the way I look?"

He stepped back a few steps and jerked his thumb in the direction of his truck. "See for yourself."

She hesitated a moment, then she approached and looked in the driver's side mirror. Her eyes widened and she leaned forward as she stared at herself in horror. She looked like she had been covered from head to toe in a mud mask. She pulled off the hoodie, turned it inside out, shut her eyes, and started rubbing her face. She was surprised at how much that hurt. She stopped and looked at herself again. She looked even worse, and now her hoodie was even dirtier. She sighed and looked back at the man. He had looked amused, now he looked really unhappy. She asked a little nervously, "What?"

Bubba pursed his lips together. The collar of her shirt was torn, she had scratch marks on her neck, and now that some of the dirt had been removed her lip looked bruised, and he was starting to think her eye was a little puffy as well. He shook his head. "Nothing, get your stuff and get in the truck."

She shook her head. "I don't relish the idea of getting in a truck with an angry stranger."

He held out his hand. "Bubba Cartwright, and you are?"

She stuck her hands in her pockets. "Lenore."

He nodded. "Nice to meet you, Lenore. Now please get your stuff and get in the truck, and let's go talk to the boss."

She did not like it, but she did not see that she had any choice. She limped into the little shed and got her stuff. When she turned to head out, he appeared in the doorway and took her stuff from her and jerked his head in the direction of the truck. "Get in." He went to the rear of his truck and put everything in, then he went back to the shack, turned off the lamp, closed the window and latched it, then he locked the door and headed for his truck. Getting in he said, "Buckle up, the roads can get kind of rough after a rainstorm."

Lenore sat pressed up against the passenger door shivering. She buckled her seatbelt. "I really am sorry. I didn't want to be any trouble."

He shrugged his shoulders, then he gave her a smile. "Hey, you're getting me out of work." He turned the heater up a little. He frowned and kept looking at her out of the corner of his eye. Finally he demanded, "How on earth did you end up in the line shack?"

She shrugged her shoulders. "I was walking along the road and it started raining and then I saw the building and I just wanted to get dry. Didn't look like I damaged anything. If I did, I'll pay the damages."

"You didn't cause any damage, but that conveniently doesn't explain how you ended up on the property."

She shrugged her shoulders. "I don't want to get into it." He sighed and looked annoyed, but did not ask any more questions. She kept looking at him. She wondered why Jace said he was a sanctimonious asshole. He did not look like one. He looked like a nice guy; then again, Jace apparently was a creep, so maybe that is Jace's way of saying nice guy. She shivered.

Bubba gestured to the thermos at her feet. "Coffee's in there. Lid turns into a cup. Help yourself. It's black, but it's hot. If you want any cream or sugar, you have to wait 'til we get to the ranch house."

She started to decline, then she decided she was too cold to care what it tasted like. She unscrewed the lid, then removed the cap and poured herself some. She carefully put the cap back on. She held the cup with both hands, breathing in the steam. She took a sip. It tasted awful, but felt wonderful. She was on her second cup when they pulled up outside a huge house. He put the truck in park, smiled at her and said, "Time to face the music, or the boss, depending on how you want to look at it. Come on, can't put it off all day." He reached over and grabbed the thermos. It did not escape his notice that she cringed away from him, then got out quickly, probably to put more distance between them. He forced himself to smile as he got out of the truck. He did not want to look angry, he was afraid of frightening her. He said gently. "Leave your stuff for now." He gestured to the front porch. "Ladies first." She grudgingly went up the steps. He reached around her and opened the door. She entered and he followed her in. He hollered, "Pop, you in here? You are never going to believe my morning."

A voice from somewhere in the distance yelled, "It takes forty-five minutes to get to line shack number twelve and here you are back an hour and forty-five minutes, so it better be really good!"

Wayne entered the living room and raised an eyebrow. He looked the woman up and down, then he said with amusement, "That, boy, has to be the sorriest catch you ever brought home. Where did you pick it up?"

He laughed. "Asleep on the floor of the line shack. Can you believe she can fit through the window?"

Wayne shook his head. "The hell you say. Can't be nothing but skin and bones, and how did she get so filthy?"

"She says it was raining and that's why she climbed through the window, so I'm guessing dirt floor, soaking wet, equals mud."

He nodded and shook his finger. "That makes sense, and does she have a name?"

She grudgingly extended her hand. "Lenore." He took it and shook it. She backed away just a little under the guise of glancing around the house.

Wayne resisted the urge to wipe his hand on his jeans. He asked with a smile, "Wayne Cartwright, and how old are we, and do we have a last name?"

"I'm eighteen, and I don't see that last names are mandatory. I get that I was trespassing. I'm deeply sorry. If I caused any damage I will pay for it, but if I'm not in trouble can I please be on my way?"

He pointed down at her foot. "And exactly how far are we going with only one shoe, and when did that happen?"

Lenore rolled her eyes. "Why are the two of you obsessed with my missing shoe? If I'm not worried about it, why should you be?"

Wayne nodded. "Are we running away or to?"

She sighed. "Apparently nobody in this day and age minds their own business. I'm eighteen, I can do what I want. If I want to walk away and never look back, that's my prerogative, and if I want to do it with only one shoe on, that's nobody's business but mine."

He nodded. "Fair enough, but you are trespassing on my property, so I got a right to know who I got trespassing on my property. That way I can decide can I let you go, or should I call the Sheriff? Would you have a problem if I called the Sheriff?"

She sighed. "If that's your way of asking if I have a criminal record, the answer is no."

"I was more of trying to ask if people were looking for you."

She sighed. "Highly probable, but that's none of my affair. They can keep looking. I'm eighteen. It's none of their business what I do."

He nodded. "All right, your decision. So where are you headed?"

"I was headed into Leaf to see if maybe I could find work."

He cocked his head to the side and looked dubious. He looked her up and down again. If she weighed ninety-five pounds he would be surprised. She was about five feet nine and all skin and bones. Even her clothes hung on her, and he did not like the implication of the torn shirt or the bruises on her face, and clearly she was in no mood to convey information or confide in anyone. He shrugged his shoulders. "Can you ride a horse?"

"No."

"Can you cook?"

"Kind of."

"What does that mean?"

She considered for a minute. "It means when I was a kid, if I wanted something to eat I had to make it myself, but I'm not sure I would classify that as real cooking. I can make macaroni and I can follow a recipe, at least I used to be able to."

He pursed his lips together and nodded then asked, "Can you do bookkeeping?"

"No."

He sighed. He did not know why he was finding her more interesting by the minute. He asked, "And what exactly do you know how to do?"

She considered that. She could not think of anything she knew how to do that he would consider useful. Finally she sighed and shrugged her shoulders. "I don't know how to do anything, at least not anything I think you'd find of value, but I'm willing to learn, and I'm hard-working. There's nothing I consider myself above doing."

Wayne nodded. "Right, so you'd shovel shit out of the stables?"

She replied without hesitation, "Yes."

Wayne cocked his head to the side, smiled, and raised an eyebrow. He glanced in Bubba's direction. Bubba looked equally surprised. Wayne held out his hand palm up. He gestured with his fingers for her to come to him as he said, "Give me your hand." She held out her hand. He took it and turned it over and examined it, then he examined her nails. They had clearly been manicured, but they had also clearly been cut off by an amateur. He took her other hand and examined it, same thing. Her hands were soft and delicate. "It's hard work. You gonna probably get a lot of blisters and a few calluses along the way."

"I used to be on a dance team. I've had to perform with my feet covered in blisters and bleeding. I've also had to keep going with sprained ankles, bruised hips. I've hit the ground hard time after time and had to keep getting back up and trying again and again. I'm not afraid of hard work. If you're willing to give me a job, I promise you I will keep it."

He nodded. "I don't pay people under the table."

She smiled. "Lenore Stevens."

He smiled. "It's very nice to meet you. The job comes with room and board, though I do have to say you pose a bit of a dilemma for me."

"Why's that?"

He laughed. "The bunkhouse is off-limits to women."

Bubba shrugged his shoulders and suggested, "Servant's quarters. The house maid's room is small, but it's got a private bath and a good lock on the door."

Wayne nodded. "That's a real good idea. Show her to the room, get her clean linens, and show her where the laundry room is." He looked at his watch. "I'll head on out to the line shack and I'll take care that business for you." He pointed at Lenore. "You have exactly forty-five minutes to get showered, changed, put your clothes in the washer, and then you and the boy can go to town and pick up supplies and get you a pair of boots and a hat, and if you take one minute over forty-five minutes, he'll be leaving you in town."

She nodded. "Yes sir, Mr. Cartwright, that's perfectly understandable."

Bubba nodded and jerked his head. "Let's get your stuff out of my truck and then I'll show you to your quarters."

VII

Lenore had run through the shower and was now frantically drying off. She went into her bedroom and got her cleanest dirty clothes. She was glad to have access to a washing machine, she would do laundry when she got back. She picked up her hoodie. She grimaced. She would just have to freeze today, she was not wearing that. She threw it on the floor. She grabbed two clean pairs of socks, stuffed one in her pocket and put the other on her feet. She hurried back to the entryway.

Bubba was sitting in his favorite comfortable armchair reading a book when he heard her come in. He stuck his bookmark in and set it on the table, then he looked up at her. His eyes flicked down the jeans. The ones she had been wearing earlier were baggy, these were snug fitting and they made her look even skinnier than she had before. The T-shirt was just a little baggy, and to his surprise, she was incredibly beautiful. Her hair was auburn, though he thought the color looked a little fake, and she had soft gray eyes. Now that she was all cleaned up, he could tell that her left eye was just a little bruised and puffy, and the right side of her mouth had a busted lip. He frowned. He got up, picked up a jacket off the coffee table and a pair of boots from next to it. He crossed to her. "You're a lot smaller than my mother, but I think these will at least do until we can get you a pair of boots in town, and here, this is an old jacket of mine."

She looked at the floor and murmured, "Sorry. I know I'm being a lot of trouble, but I promise I'll make it worth it." She took the boots. They were fur-lined rain boots. She set them on the floor and stuck her feet into them. They were a bit big, but they were warm and dry, huge points in their favor, and anything was better than walking barefoot. She took the coat, expecting it to swallow her, but to her surprise it fit her rather nicely.

Bubba chuckled at the confused look on her face. "Perhaps I should've said I outgrew it. That's from middle school. My mother never got rid of anything. Looks good on you." He crossed to the intercom and pressed a button. "Alejandro, I'm heading to town. Do you need anything?"

"Actually, Bubba, if it wouldn't be an inconvenience, if I call in an order to the grocery store, can you pick it up for me?"

"That's why I'm asking. Let me know when it will be ready."

"Will do, sir."

He jerked his head in the direction of the door. "Let's get out of here before Pop jumps my ass about taking all day." He started to walk away, then he looked back and pressed the intercom button again. "Did the old man tell you there was going to be an extra person for dinner from now on?"

"No sir, he failed to mention that. Hearty eater?"

Bubba chuckled. "I doubt it seriously. She can't weigh more than a hundred pounds."

"I'm sorry, sir, must not heard you right. Did you say she?"

"Don't be difficult, you heard me fine."

Lenore waited until he turned around to say with indignation, "And for your information, I weigh a hundred and twenty pounds, thank you very much."

He snorted. "I doubt it." He headed for the door and opened it for her. He gestured her out. She headed for the truck. He unlocked it and they both got in. "Now, pay attention to the way into town in case we have to send you to pick up supplies."

She laughed. "I wouldn't recommend that. I don't have a license and I've never driven a car."

He stepped on the brakes and turned to look at her. "You are shitting me! You're how old?"

She rolled her eyes. "Eighteen. I'm sorry, in Los Angeles there's this wonderful thing called the public bus system."

He nodded. "I knew there was a reason I didn't like California."

She snorted. "Something tells me there's a lot more than just that."

He started moving again and chuckled. "Oh shit, you're probably a Democrat. Man, Pop is just gonna love you. Well, do yourself a favor. If you intend on keeping this job, don't ever argue politics with Pop. He believes you're entitled to your opinion, but he's still the boss, so don't argue with him."

"How is it you manage to say Democrat like it's a swear word."

"This is Texas. It is, or did you not notice that we're pretty red here."

She rolled her eyes. "I had noticed that, but fortunately I don't consider myself anything. I don't involve myself in politics."

He sighed and shook his head and chuckled. "Pop won't like that either."

"Sounds like your dad is not going to like me. I guess I shouldn't get used to having a job."

He shrugged his shoulders. "Do your job, get out of bed on time, make it to the table fully dressed on time, and don't call him a stupid old fart, and you'll get along just fine. He's a reasonable man." After a couple of minutes, he said, "Despite your lack of a driver's license, you should still pay attention so you know how to get off the ranch. You never know when it might come in handy."

"You mean when your father fires me and makes me walk back to town?"

He chuckled. "He'd never do that. Threaten it, but not actually do it. I seem to recall me cutting up a dust at the rodeo and Pop told me if I didn't knock that shit off, I'd be walking home. I straightened up pretty quick. Granted, there were probably fifty people who would've been willing to give me a ride home, but I'd have gotten an earful the whole way."

She sighed and shook her head. "That is beyond my comprehension. Guess it's the difference between growing up a huge city and a teeny tiny little town where everybody knows everybody."

He nodded. "True enough. So who slapped you around?"

She sighed and rolled her eyes. "I took care of the situation. I don't need any help. I'm a big girl."

He nodded. "Right, and how many shoes did you have when I met you?"

She rolled her eyes, reached over and shoved him in the shoulder. "Will you let that go?"

He laughed. "Never, not as long as I know you. I will always remember that."

Lenore had greatly enjoyed the drive into town. In fact, she had enjoyed the Texas countryside very much.

Bubba parked his truck outside the store. "Now I should warn you, this place only carries the basics. If you're looking for anything fancy or frilly, it's probably not your best bet. They just carry enough to get us by so we don't have to go into Amarillo all the time, but they'll have a decent pair of boots and a good hat for you."

She nodded and they both got out and headed in. A gentleman in his sixties came out of the back. He was staring at her in surprise as he offered his hand to Bubba. "Ain't seen you in here in a while, boy. What brings you here, and who's this pretty little filly you got with you?"

Bubba jerked his thumb in her direction. "Nice to see you, Sam. This is Lenore. Pop just hired her, but as you can see, she's not exactly equipped for our way of life. He wants her to get a pair of boots and a hat and charge them to him."

Sam looked her up and down. "Tiny little thing, bet she wears a six-and-three-quarters. What size shoe do you wear?"

She smiled. "Five and a half."

He nodded and gestured for them to follow him. He examined the wall of hats. "Got a specific color you're looking for?"

She replied, "Durable."

Sam smiled and looked over his shoulder at Bubba. "I like her already." He pulled off a dark brown hat and handed it to her. "Try that one. Tell me what you think."

She put it on and wiggled it. It seemed to fit funny. "I don't think it's quite right. It seems a little tight on my forehead, but it seems loose on the sides."

He nodded, reached over and fiddled with it for second. "Sure does, but it's the right size." He reached over and flipped on a steam machine. "It'll be a few minutes. Let's go get you a couple pairs of boots to try on." He led the way back to the boot aisle as he asked, "Square toe, round toe, pointy toe?"

"I'm sorry, what?"

"Your boots. Square toe, round toe, or pointy toe?"

She shrugged her shoulders. "Whatever."

Bubba said with exasperation, "Not whatever. These are your feet we're talking about. What are you gonna be comfortable in?"

She looked at him. "I already told you I'm a dancer. I'm used to not being comfortable. It does not matter. I can wear any of them."

"Well, you're not a dancer anymore."

She rolled her eyes and demanded, "Which would you recommend?"

"I think square toe are more comfortable, but Pop don't like nothing but stupid old pointy toed boots."

Sam asked with annoyance, "Bubba, have I smacked you recently?"

He laughed. "Not since I got taller than you."

She sighed and said, "Fine, square toe." It only took her a couple of minutes to find a pair she liked.

Sam headed back to the hats. She watched in amazement as he reshaped her hat and by the time he was done with it, it fit perfectly. "Now, I can fix it as long as you don't do something stupid like run it over with a truck or let the dog eat it."

Bubba said with annoyance, "One time, one time." Sam started laughing.

She looked from one to the other and back again. "One time what?"

"One time I run over my hat with my truck, and he never lets me hear the end of it."

Sam said still laughing, "Well, it was a first. I never had anybody run over their hat with a truck before."

"Ha, ha, ha, very funny. Put them on Pop's account."

She shook her head. "No, I have money."

Bubba looked at her dubiously. "This ain't a twenty-dollar pair of sneakers we're talking about."

"I know. I can read, count, add, and subtract. The boots were a hundred and fifty and the hat was a hundred."

Sam rang her up and she paid for it.

Bubba raised an eyebrow when she opened her wallet. He saw it was full of cash. He was going to seriously have to reevaluate his opinion of the situation. They were just walking out of the store when his phone chimed. He pulled it out. "Our grocery order's ready. Let's stop by City Hall, and then we can pick up the groceries and head back to the house."

She asked a little nervously, "Why are we stopping by City Hall?"

He smiled. "All government services are there, including the Department of Motor Vehicles. You need a Driving Manual. Though come to think of it, the Sheriff's office isn't there, it does have its own building."

She sighed and asked, "Is this a condition of my employment?"

"Yes, yes it is." A few minutes later they pulled up outside City Hall. "Driving manuals are just inside the door on the right with all the other brochures. Be sure to get the one in English, unless, of course, you can read Spanish."

She smiled, "Read, no. Speak, yes." She hopped out of the truck, hurried in, grabbed the driving manual, and hurried back. As she climbed in, she asked, "You can call in your grocery order?"

He laughed. "Yes, it's a courtesy the store owner gives to the ranches. That way whoever's in charge of the kitchen can call in an order and then Joe Schmoe idiot can pick it up. That way I don't have to actually know what I'm doing, I just pick it up for Alejandro, someone who knows what he's doing."

She smiled. "So have you like never had a girl work for you? He seemed pretty surprised by that."

He scratched the back of his neck as he drove. "I'm sure we have at one point in time, I just don't remember. Most ranch hands are men, and I don't have any sisters, so …"

She looked at him. "So you have brothers?"

He sighed. "Had, he died of leukemia when he was eight. He was younger."

She closed her eyes and shook her head. "I'm so sorry."

He shrugged his shoulders. "Don't be. I had him for eight years. They were eight really good years, and before you ask, Mom died two years ago. Started out as flu, became pneumonia, and before we knew what hit us, we're sitting in a hospital going 'This is the twenty first century and people still die of pneumonia?' Mom's health was never great."

She sighed again. "I'm so sorry."

"I try not to dwell on the bad. I try to focus on the fact that I had her for twenty-one years. A lot of people don't have that."

She nodded. "Tell me about it. My dad was gone before I was ever even born, not dead, just gone."

He shook his head. "Now that's something I can't understand. No matter how I may or may not feel about a woman, I will never abandon my kids. Granted, I hope to have the good sense not to make any with a woman I don't want to keep." They pulled up outside the grocery store and everything was loaded in just a few minutes, then they were on their way back to the ranch. They were both very quiet when they arrived. She helped unload the boxes and got her first look at the kitchen. It was huge and beautiful, very rustic. She liked it. She thought it would be wonderful to sit at the table and drink tea. She was surprised at how peaceful she found the kitchen.

Alejandro waited until they were done unloading the truck before he looked the girl up and down and said firmly, "Let me explain a few rules of my kitchen to you, girlie, before you go ruining any of my stuff. If the hands come in here to make themselves something, they better clean up every last crumb or I will make them lick it up. That cupboard over there, that is the only pots and pans you can touch. You touch any of my good pots and pans, I will beat you to death with them. Everything in the refrigerator is labeled and dated. The date is the do not consume after date. This is a real date, don't play with it, and I clean out the refrigerator every morning after breakfast. So if you're being sent off on the ranch and you come in here at four o'clock in the morning to make yourself a sandwich, check the damn date on the ham. It's not my fault if you poison yourself. Are we clear?"

She laughed. "Yes, sir. Check dates, don't poison myself. You will not take the responsibility for it. Don't touch your pots."

He nodded. "Good. And one more thing, the dry erase board over there, go write your name on it. If Mr. Cartwright tells you at dinner time you're going to be out on the property, you need to know that that means you're gonna need a lunch. I know to make ya'll's lunches by placing checkmarks by your names. No checkmark, no lunch. If he tells you at breakfast time that he needs you to go out on the property with someone, you look at me and tell me you're going to need a lunch so I know to get up right then and make your lunch. Everybody has their own lunchbox. I will decide which one you get and then show it to you. So don't screw up and take somebody else's. Any questions?"

"No, sir."

VIII

Lenore was in the process of cleaning out one of the stalls when Bubba approached. He looked around. He nodded with approval. "Not bad for a greenhorn. Well, it's getting late, let's knock off and go get something to eat. This will be waiting for you tomorrow."

She looked over her shoulder. "I'll be just a couple minutes. I just want to finish up, it's not quite right."

He nodded. "All right, but don't be too long, and a word to the wise, Alejandro gets real pissy if you show up at his table without washing your hands and face first. The hands always come through the back door and there's a wash sink, soap, and towels, everything you need to clean up right there. There's also a boot scraper, don't forget to use it."

"Yes, sir, Mr. Cartwright, I'll remember."

He chuckled. "Mr. Cartwright is my father. Everybody just calls me Bubba."

She shrugged her shoulders. "If you say so."

She finished cleaning out the stall, then checked to make sure everything was right before heading to the sink. She took off her jacket and tossed it on the cabinet and carefully pushed her sleeves up, trying not to get them dirty. Then she began scrubbing her hands to the elbows as she read the sign over the sink. It was a large, weather-beaten sign and the letters were in red.

'Soap is a requirement as is the nail brush,

when you are finished washing your hands, dry them thoroughly.

Please examine the hand towel.

If it is filthy, throw it under the sink in the bucket and wash your hands again.

Clean hand towels get hung to dry.

I do not allow dirty cow hands at my table.

<u>The Boss' Wife</u>'

She smiled and picked up the nail brush and scrubbed her hands, then washed her face and neck. She dried off and neatly folded the hand towel and hung it back up to dry, not that she thought it was going to as cold as it was. She grabbed her jacket. Finding the boot scraper, she cleaned her boots and headed inside. The long table she had seen earlier now had a half-dozen men sitting around it in addition to the three she had already met. They all started to get to their feet. Mr. Cartwright said, "As you were gentlemen, Lenore here is one of you. She started work today. That's why I asked Stewart and George to join us for dinner tonight." They all nodded as they reclaimed their seats. She moved towards one of the two empty seats. As she hesitated, Mr. Cartwright laughed and said, "Now see, Sweetie, around here if you're shy you ain't gonna eat, so sit down."

She nodded. "Yes, sir." She noticed that all of the men had removed their hats and hung them on the sides of their chairs. She removed her hat and placed it on the little knob there, then she sat down.

He smiled at her. "Now usually we don't wait supper on anyone because people kind of stagger in, but since Bubba said you'd be just a minute or two we waited. Now at my table when dinner is served, I say grace. If you're here when grace is said and you are not religious, I do ask that you please be respectful to those of us who are, but you are not required to take part."

She raised an eyebrow and watched as everyone bowed their heads, and with the exception of Mr. Cartwright and Bubba, they all crossed themselves. Then he said, "For what we are about to receive may the Lord make us truly grateful. Amen." Everyone murmured, 'Amen', then crossed themselves again and began helping themselves to something to eat.

She hesitated a moment, then got herself some mashed potatoes, two dinner rolls, spinach and green beans. She suddenly realized everyone was staring at her. She looked up and opened her mouth to speak.

Bubba demanded, "Oh, please tell me you're not a vegetarian. You can't work on a cattle ranch and be a vegetarian, it just doesn't work."

She shrugged her shoulders. "I'm not a vegetarian based on any belief systems, such as killing animals is wrong, it's just my nutritionist felt that it was better for me to … never mind. You don't care. Don't worry, sir, I have nothing against hunting, fishing, or eating animals, or skinning them and using their hides. I kind of like leather actually."

Alejandro said with annoyance, "So it's just my meat you have something against." One of the guys snorted and almost spewed his drink. Alejandro rolled his eyes, picked up his napkin, and threw it at the other man who started snickering.

Wayne rolled his eyes. "I should warn you, the only women these guys have ever gotten close to is their sisters."

Alejandro laughed and pointed at the beverage spewer. "He got you good."

The man replied, "Ha, ha, ha, that only shows what you don't know. I don't have a sister."

Bubba whistled. "Can you try not to scare away the new hand, and before this dinner totally goes downhill, Lenore, let me introduce you to this bunch of idiots." He jerked his thumb to his right. "This young pup right here is Aaron. He's the son of a former hand, but he's only sixteen and still in high school, so don't lose sight of that. He's the nicest and most corruptible, but if we corrupt him too much before he turns eighteen, his mama is gonna kill us, and she's a crack shot. So watch it. He only works for us on the weekends and during school holidays. Justin and Travis are twins, even though they don't look like it, and if they decide to try to murder each other, just stay out of it. And of course, Alejandro you've already met. The empty chair's if we ever have guests, which most people are smart enough not to come and dine with us. And then there's the big boss at the other end of the table. Then we got Benny, he claims his English isn't so good so he uses that to get away with saying inappropriate things with the 'oh is that what that means, I didn't realize it.' So just watch out. George is pretty quiet, you don't have to worry about him …"

He started to skip over her, but Wayne added quickly, "And gentlemen, Lenore is from California and she knows nothing about ranch life, but she says she's willing to learn. So please, no dirty tricks, and no greenhorn hazing, at least for the first week. Give her a chance to find her feet before your blow her off of them."

They all grumbled but said, "All right."

Bubba chuckled and went on, "Next to you we've got Ramon ..." the beverage spewer. "... Now he fancies himself a ladies' man. And last, but most certainly not least, is Stewart. He's the only sane one of the bunch, which probably has a lot to do with why Pop made him foreman."

She smiled and nodded. "It's very nice to meet all of you."

Ramon leaned over and asked, "Would you like some water or tea to drink?"

She looked up. At either end of the table was a pitcher of water and a pitcher of tea. He was closer than she was. "Some tea would be nice, thank you."

She picked up her glass and he picked up the pitcher and poured her some. "Don't worry, we're not as bad as they make us out to be. We just like messing with each other. We're like a big family."

She smiled. "I'm not worried. I promise you, you can't be as bad as dancers."

Bubba said quickly, "Don't challenge them, please, I'm begging you."

She smiled. "Yes, sir."

She listened as they all chatted over dinner, discussing everything from issues on the ranch, to the news, weather, and politics. Fortunately, they all seemed to agree, which actually made it a pleasant dinner conversation. Ramon was the first to finish. He got to his feet and asked, "Is there anything else you need me to handle before I turn in for the night, sir?"

Wayne shook his head. "Not tonight, but first thing in the morning I'd like you to look at my truck. It was making a funny noise."

He nodded. "Yes, sir, I'll look at it right away, and I just finished overhauling the engine on number seven. Is the girl gonna use it from now on?"

Wayne opened his mouth to reply 'yes', but Bubba beat him to it. "Not until we teach her how to drive."

They all stared at him in astonishment, then they all looked at her. Wayne was the first one to find his voice. "Oh, delightful. She don't know how to drive. Ain't that gonna be fun. Remind me to add that to my list of questions before I hire somebody."

Lenore said a little apologetically, "I'm sorry. If my not knowing how to drive is an inconvenience, Mr. Cartwright, if that's a deal breaker for you, I do understand. I'll leave first thing in the morning, if that's all right with you."

Bubba said quickly, "No one said it's a deal breaker. It just means we have to think a little differently when we're giving you jobs. Don't worry, there are plenty of times we send three guys out together. You just have to ride with somebody or you'll be stuck dealing with the stables, which believe it or not, ain't such a bad idea."

Wayne raised an eyebrow and shook his finger in his son's direction. "Say, that ain't such a bad idea. Back when your mama was alive, we didn't have to leave somebody behind in the stables because she could look after the animals, and one of the guys just had to clean them out when she was too busy. I say that's a good idea. We'll make her responsible for the stables. It'll keep her right here, she doesn't have to go out on the property, which makes me feel a lot better, because something tells me she don't know how to use a gun either."

Alejandro added helpfully, "And you were discussing hiring some part-time help around the house since Mrs. Davenport can't handle the work anymore."

Bubba nodded. "That sounds like more than plenty of work. She'll be plenty busy and that frees up the rest of us to do stuff that requires more experience."

Wayne nodded. "Sounds like a plan. Well, tomorrow's Sunday, so Bubba, just show her the basics that need to be done, our usual Sunday workload. Then on Monday you take her over every inch of the stable, make sure she knows what she's supposed to be doing. If you feel she still needs a chaperone, Stewart can babysit her on Tuesday, and hopefully by Wednesday she won't need a chaperone. As soon as she's finished working in the stables on Wednesday, Alejandro can start showing her what she can do around here. Any questions?"

She shook her head. "No, sir, Mr. Cartwright. That sounds great."

He raised an eyebrow. "No whining that it's sexist? That we're going to be keeping the girl around the house?"

She shook her head. "No, sir, how can I complain? You're bending over backwards to keep me employed. You could easily fire me. If I have to do five part-time jobs to stay employed, I'll do that. I told you I wasn't above hard work. You want me to scrub the kitchen floor, I'll do that."

He nodded. "Good to know."

She was the next to finish. She got to her feet and asked, "Is there anything you'd like me to do before I turn in, Mr. Cartwright?"

Wayne shook his head. "No, get some sleep, but be sure that you set that alarm clock early enough that you will be at this table for breakfast at six AM. Even my married hands show up for breakfast. That's where we discuss the events of the day, and any changes that have happened since dinner."

She nodded. "Not to worry, Mr. Cartwright. I will be at breakfast on time." She went into the kitchen and saw that there were no dishes in the sink. She washed off hers and opened the dishwasher. It only took her a moment to decide how they were supposed to go and she put them away, closed the dishwasher, and headed to her room. She closed the door behind her and locked it. She leaned against it, rubbing her head. She felt terrible. Every bone in her body ached. She tried to tell herself that she did not need to take any pills, that she could put it off till morning, but she knew she could not. She unpacked her stuff and put it into the second drawer of her dresser, then she hesitated a moment deciding on what pills to take. She decided on a pain pill, a muscle relaxer, and a Zoloft. She would take a sleeping pill right before bed. She looked at her dirty clothes. She had to do laundry or she would not have anything clean to wear tomorrow. She was startled by a knock at the door. She crossed to it, unlocked it, and opened it. Bubba was standing there with an open cardboard box. "Can I help you, sir?"

"Well, it occurred to me you can't have much in the way of clothes, and like I said, my mama never threw anything away. So I went on up to the attic and I found some boxes from middle school. There are some long sleeved T-shirts in here, a couple of hoodies, and some jeans I think will fit you. Also, some pajama bottoms and other stuff. I'd wash it all before wearing it, it's been up there while. If you're not interested, just push the box in the hallway and I'll pick it up tomorrow."

She stepped back and held the door wide. She indicated the floor. "Thank you, that's great. I have to admit I was trying to sort out the clothes dilemma when you knocked. You can just drop it anywhere."

Bubba nodded as he looked around the room trying to remember if he had ever been in here. He saw a small pile of clothes on the floor. He sat the box down next to them and scratched the back of his neck. "Don't take offense to this, but do you have anything to sleep in? I mean clean?"

She blushed deeply. She cleared her throat and shook her head. "No."

He nodded. "I'll be right back." He was back only a couple minutes later. He held out a T-shirt and a pair of pajama bottoms. "They're probably way too big, but they're clean and they have a drawstring. That way you can do all your laundry."

She smiled. "Thank you, sorry to be so much trouble. I'll get them washed and back to you."

He shrugged his shoulders. "If you're gonna be taking over Mrs. Davenport's work, that means you will be doing Pop's and my laundry, which I have to say I really hope you are. I hate doing laundry, so you can just return it with the rest of my stuff."

She smiled. "I have no objections to doing laundry, so I will gladly take over that chore."

"Well, in that case, good night, ma'am, and I will see you at breakfast." He started to walk out, then added. "Do I need to show you how to use the washer?"

She shook her head. "I'm sure I can figure it out."

IX

Saturday, November 11

Lenore was working on cleaning out the stables with Aaron. She liked him. He was a nice guy, not like the ones she was used to working with. They were always hung up with themselves and their conversation was usually limited to themselves. Aaron could talk about lots of things, as could any of the other hands. They were all fun to work with.

Aaron paused in what he was doing, took off his hat and wiped his forehead on his shoulder. He stuck his hat back on his head and then demanded, "So, got any plans for Saturday night?"

She considered for a minute, then nodded, "Yes, when I am done cleaning out the stables, I'm going to go soak in a really hot tub and refuse to get out for at least an hour until I have feeling back in my toes. How is it my feet are freezing and the rest of me is sweating?"

He laughed. "I wondered that on many occasions myself. Sometimes I feel like my hands and feet are gonna fall right off, and yet I've got sweat dripping down my forehead, but a hot bath does not sound like much of a Saturday evening."

She shrugged her shoulders. "I think it sounds wonderful. So, Mr. Party Animal, what do you have planned for tonight?"

He chuckled. "I am not a party animal. I just think that does not sound like what someone our age should be doing on a Saturday night. It's like something my mother would be doing on a Saturday night, not an eighteen year old fox, but to answer your question, Jace and a bunch the guys are gonna go fishing by the lake, probably a little underage drinking. You want to come?"

She stopped what she was doing and turned and stared at him. "Isn't Jace a little old for you to be hanging out with? He's what, twenty-five?"

"Hey, I'm not just some kid, you know."

She frowned and shook her head. "Look, I'm not trying to be a killjoy, and it's not like I'm some grown-up telling you it's a bad idea. We're what, two years apart? I'm just telling you I think Jace is bad news and I think if you have the sense that I think you do, you won't go get yourself tangled up with him and his friends, but I know when you're sixteen years old getting the attention of older people is awesome. Trust me, I've been there, but that one scares me. I'd watch out." She went back to what she was doing.

Aaron frowned, looked up from what he was doing, and asked, "I didn't think you'd been off the ranch since you got here. How'd you meet Jace?"

She shrugged her shoulders. "I don't see that we need to get into it."

He stopped what he was doing. "So you're not so grown-up that I shouldn't feel that an adult is telling me what to do, but you're too grown-up to talk to me. That don't make sense."

She sighed and stopped what she was doing. "Age has nothing to do with it. It's just something I'd really rather not get into, okay?"

He shrugged his shoulders and went back to what he was doing. "Fine, I thought we were pals, but apparently you think I'm a rat who can't keep his mouth shut."

She sighed. She was going to have to remember that Aaron was very good at manipulating people. After a long minute she said, "Okay, but it's just between you and me, because if Mr. Cartwright finds out, he'll can me."

He stopped what he was doing and looked at her. "Now you got me worried. What's going on? I won't tell."

"Okay, so I wanted to come down this way from Amarillo. The buses don't come this far, so I took a bus as far south as I could go and then I started walking. Jace pulled over and offered me a ride, and come on, let's be honest, who wants to walk sixty miles when they don't have to. Everything was fine and then he turned off onto the road that comes onto this property, some side road, I still don't know exactly where it was. He pulled over and reached under the driver's seat and pulled out a bag that had three vials of cocaine in it. He offered me a snort. I said no thank you. He took a snort and I got out. That shit is nothing to play with."

He whistled. "Dude, I fully expected you to tell me that Jace did a little weed, but seriously? coke? That I did not expect. Oh, I don't like knowing that."

"Just remember, you said it would stay between us."

He groaned and rubbed his hands up and down his face. "Yeah, well, this puts me an awful spot."

She went back to work as she asked, "How so?"

He chuckled. "Right, you probably don't know."

"Know what?"

He laughed. "The Sheriff is my dad."

She swallowed hard, stopped, and turned to look at him. "You won't tell him, will you?"

"No, I won't, because I told you I wouldn't. You should though. My dad would flip his wig if he knew that anybody in town was dealing cocaine. Granted, that's probably what Jace was doing in Amarillo because, believe me, if anybody in town was selling anything stiffer than weed, Dad would know about it. He's not like some small town Sheriffs who just want to skate by and keep things to a minimum. He actually gives a shit about this town." He shrugged his shoulders and went back to work.

"So, since your dad is the Sheriff, does that mean I can rest easy tonight knowing you're not going partying with Jace?"

Aaron was lost in his own thoughts. Something about her story just did not seem right. Not Jace doing cocaine, that he could believe. It explained his tendency to violent mood swings. He considered a minute longer, then he realized what else had happened that night. When he had worked with Ramon her first Sunday, Ramon had speculated on how she had gotten the bruised cheek and busted lip.

Lenore said with annoyance, "Planet Earth calling Aaron. Earth to Aaron."

He started. "Sorry, I was thinking about something else. What did you say?"

"I said, so I don't have to worry about you partying with Jace tonight?"

He shook his head. "Definitely not." He focused on what he was doing for several minutes, then he said, "Look, I'm pretty sure you're gonna tell me to stay the hell out of it and it's none of my business, because that seems to be your patented response for anytime people actually show that they're interested in caring about you, but umm … Jace didn't get overly friendly, did he?"

She focused on what she was doing. "No, I told you. As soon as he snorted the cocaine, I was out of there."

Aaron frowned and focused on his work. He did not believe her. He wondered if he should confront Jace. He did not like the idea of Jace getting fresh with Lenore, and he certainly did not like the idea of Jace smacking her around. He would have to think about it. Maybe he could find a way to discreetly talk to his dad about it, or maybe he would ask one of the guys for some advice, but whatever he did, he would have to be really careful.

Lenore finished cleaning the last stall. She stretched her back and put away her tools. She liked Saturdays, all she had to do was clean the stalls and feed the animals and with Aaron's help, it took half the time. Aaron finished what he was doing and came to put away his tools. They were just heading out of the stables when Mr. Cartwright entered.

Wayne looked around. He said, "Well, Lenore, you've gotten really good at this. You even do a better job than the kid, so I think this will probably be your last Saturday cleaning the stables, Aaron. From now on, you go out with one of the boys, or have your own list of chores to do on the weekend. I don't want to cut your pay because you only have half a day's work; besides, I can use you elsewhere."

Aaron smiled. He was thrilled to be getting out of the stables. That was considered a kid's job. He wanted to do a man's work. "That's great, Mr. Cartwright. Lenore's got this covered. She don't need me."

"Good, why don't you go into the kitchen, have yourself some lunch, and then take truck number five on down to the fence that divides our property and the farmers' market road. Some big rig took out a huge section of the fence last night. George and Ramon are already over there working on it. Go give them a hand."

"Yes sir, Mr. Cartwright. I'll grab me some lunch and be on my way."

Lenore hesitated a moment as Mr. Cartwright stared at her. After a long minute she asked, "Is there something special you need me to do, sir?"

Wayne considered as he looked the girl up and down. She was a handsome filly, a bit on the scrawny side for his taste, but definitely appealing, and he had never been one for noticing clothes, but lately she sure had been wearing a lot of clothes that looked familiar to him. On an impulse he asked, "Those wouldn't happen to be Bubba's clothes, would they?"

Lenore blushed. "Yes, Mr. Cartwright. He was kind enough to notice I didn't have much in the way of clothes, and he said he'd outgrown these, and I should make use of them. Is that a problem, sir?"

He shrugged his shoulders. "That depends on whether you have any plans of being the next Mrs. Cartwright."

She shook her head. "No, sir, I … I have no interest in getting involved with anybody, ever. And I certainly don't have any interest in settling down and having a family … I wouldn't have the first idea what to do with a kid." She squirmed uncomfortably as he continued to bore holes in her. She felt like he could see straight through her.

He slowly nodded. "Well, if you're not interested in having a family, then stay away from my son, but he's right about the clothes. No sense in them sittin' in a box, rotting. Just don't get any ideas about the previous owner." He hesitated a moment, then added. "I don't have anything else for you around the ranch, so why don't you go get cleaned up, have some lunch, and enjoy the rest of your day. You haven't had a break since you started here."

She nodded. "Thank you, sir, have a good evening." She hurried away.

Wayne turned and watched her go. He crossed his arms over his chest. He had to admit he felt a little disappointed. He liked Lenore. He liked her a lot and for a city slicker, she was really taking to ranch life. He sighed and shrugged his shoulders. He was a big believer in God helps those who help themselves, but he also knew sometimes there are things you just cannot handle on your own. Maybe this was one of those things that needed to go into his God box. It was a difficult thing for him to do. He had a hard time letting go, but sometimes you just have to put your faith in God and walk away.

X

Lenore entered the house and went straight to her room. She locked the door, but did not bolt it. She did not know why, but she did not like the idea of being bolted into her room. She was sure someone somewhere had a key if she were to fall and hurt herself. She undressed and put her dirty clothes in the hamper. She sighed and inhaled deeply. She headed for her dresser. She opened the second drawer of the dresser and reached for the bottle of oxycodone. Her hand froze halfway. She squinted. When did she take her last pill? She had taken two last night and one this morning. She looked at all the bottles of pills. Was that better or worse? She rubbed her face as she tried to think, but she could not. She could not concentrate. All she could think about was taking the pills. She shut her eyes and forced herself to think. When she had left home, she had had a sixty-day supply of her regular dose, which was four a day. That would be two hundred and forty pills. She had been gone from home for eighteen days, eighteen times four was seventy-two. Two hundred and forty negative seventy-two was one hundred and sixty-eight. She found the two bottles of oxycodone and dumped them out on top of the dresser. One hundred and sixty-four, there were only one hundred and sixty-four pills left. She was not getting better, she was getting worse. She was never going to be able to stop. Tears started down her cheeks. She gathered up all the pills. She looked at the handful of pills. She told herself firmly, *If you want to be done with this, there are only two options, swallow the damn pills, or flush them down the toilet. It's the only way you are ever going to be done with it.* She grabbed a black magic marker and all the pill bottles. She went into the bathroom. She wrote the name of each pill on the bottle and the milligrams and flushed them down the toilet before she had a chance to change her mind. She looked at herself in the mirror. "You know, come tomorrow he's gonna fire you." She nodded. She took a long, hot shower, put on a T-shirt and a pair of pajama bottoms, then she unlocked the door and crawled into bed and tried to sleep. Around midnight she could not sleep anymore. She was going to be sick. She went into the bathroom and spent the rest of the night throwing up.

XI

Sunday, November 12

Bubba was in an incredibly good mood as he rolled out of bed. Despite the fact that almost one hundred feet of fencing had been taken out, they had gotten most of it fixed. George and Aaron were gonna go back today and finish up. He washed up, got dressed, and headed down for breakfast. He paused and poured himself a cup coffee and headed for the table. He raised an eyebrow. He sat down and indicated Lenore's untouched plate. "Did she ever come in for supper last night?"

Everybody shook their heads. Bubba looked at his watch. He was late for breakfast, it was fifteen after. In the two weeks she had worked on the ranch, she had never been late. He would give her a little more time. He helped himself to some breakfast, but he was finding he no longer had the stomach for it. He did not like this. He was getting a bad feeling about it. He waited until everyone else had filed out, then he got up and went to her room. He knocked on the door. No answer. He knocked louder. Still no answer. He tried the door and it opened. He entered the bedroom. The lights were out, the bathroom door was open, and the light was on in there. The bed was empty, and he saw her feet and calves through the open bathroom door. She was clearly lying on the floor. He charged forward as he yelled, "Pop!" He peeked into the bathroom, she was lying on her side, soaked in sweat and shivering. He glanced around the bathroom. Sitting neatly on the bathroom cabinet was a row of empty medicine bottles. He stepped into the bathroom, one leg on either side of her. He reached down and grabbed her by the shoulders, pulled her to a seated position, and shook her as he shouted, "Lenore, how many did you take?" She groaned and her eyes fluttered open. He shook her again. "Dammit, woman, how many did you take and what did you take?"

Lenore groaned and murmured, "Nothing, that's the problem." She closed her eyes.

Bubba shook her again. "What do you mean you didn't take anything? What did you take?"

Alejandro said from the doorway, "I think she might mean this is withdrawal, not an overdose."

Bubba shook her again. She opened her eyes. He demanded, "Are you going through withdrawal? Is that what this is?"

She groaned again. "Yes ... no more pills ... I think I'm going to be sick."

Bubba shifted her quickly as she began gagging. He grimaced as she dry heaved over the toilet. He sighed several times, then said, "Call an ambulance, Alejandro."

Lenore's forearms were resting on the seat of the toilet. She rested her forehead on the back of her hands. She groaned and said pleadingly, "Please, no doctors. They did this to me. No doctors. No more pills."

Wayne leaned in the doorway. "That sounds ominous."

Bubba nodded. "No shit."

Alejandro hesitated, then asked, "What are we going to do? Withdrawal is very dangerous. She could die of dehydration. Detox can take days."

Wayne raised an eyebrow and asked, "Speaking from experience?"

He shrugged his shoulders. "I told you when you hired me I had a colorful past. You said it wasn't my past you were interested in, merely my future."

Wayne nodded. "True enough, but right now that could be useful information."

Alejandro shrugged his shoulders. "Yes, I've gone through detox before. Detox from liquor, detox from pills, but not for so many. I count five different pills, two of them I recognize, most of them I don't. Zoloft and Oxy, those are the only ones I know what they are, and the dose for the Oxy, that is very high."

Bubba squatted down and rubbed her back. "Lenore, why were the doctors giving you the pills?" Her eyes fluttered, but she did not speak. He gave her a shake. "Lenore, why were the doctors giving you the pills?"

She murmured, "Keep me quiet. Make me happy. Dancing monkey, just a dancing monkey, puppet on a string."

Bubba looked up at his father. He swallowed hard, then asked, "Does that worry anybody else?"

Both men nodded. Wayne patted Alejandro on the shoulder. "Go get her a bowl, and a glass of cold water with a straw. Then get a bowl of cold water and a washcloth, and see if we can get her cooled off. Bubba, get her into bed and I'll go call Doc Baxter."

Lenore groaned and started crying. "Please ... no doctors. No pills. I'd rather die."

Bubba pushed her hair out of her face. "Doc Baxter's an old family friend. He's not going to give you anything you don't need, and I'd really rather you didn't die, so why don't you focus on getting this shit out of your system and then we can argue over everything else later." He stood up and got a washcloth. He ran it under the cold water, then wrung it out. He wiped her face and her neck. He sighed and shook his head. He tossed the washcloth in the sink, then he grabbed a hair band and her brush. He carefully brushed and braided her hair. She seemed oblivious. Then he grabbed the washcloth and rinsed it off, wrung it out again and laid it on the back of her neck, picked her up in his arms and carried her to her bed. She hardly weighed anything. His father pulled the covers aside and he lay her on the bed.

Wayne patted his son on the shoulder. "I'll be right back." He went into his office and sat down contemplating. He pulled out his phone and pressed the Doc's name.

Baxter picked up on the third ring. "Gee, Wayne, how nice of you to call so early on a Sunday. I mean, I mean it's not like the rest of the world sleeps in on Sunday."

"Well, if it's not something I ever do, then you should know it's important."

The mirth Baxter had been feeling suddenly dissipated. He sat up in bed and asked, "Somebody hurt?"

"Not exactly. Look I'm sorry to do this, but I have to call in a solid you owe me."

Baxter ran his hand up and down his face. He wished he could plead ignorance, but he knew exactly what Wayne was talking about. After a long minute he said, "I'm listening."

"This is one hundred percent off the record. The cops can't get involved. You can't ever write anything down about it, understood?"

He chuckled. "Like I'm gonna rat you out."

"I have an eighteen year old female going through drug withdrawal. Bubba and I just found her on the bathroom floor. She's in a bad way. She said something a little disturbing."

"I'm still listening."

"She said, 'No doctors. No more pills. Doctors did this to me.'"

"I wish I could say I'm surprised, but I'm not. I'm assuming you need me to come up there and take care of your patient with the flu."

"Is this something we can take care of here, or do we need to get her into a rehab center or something?"

He got up out of bed, went into his office, and shut the door. Pitching his voice low, he said, "It's dangerous, but yes, we could handle it there. The two major dangers in this situation are dehydration and suicide. Somebody's gonna have to be with her at all times." Baxter did not even bother bringing up any options about taking the girl to rehab or to the hospital. Clearly Wayne was unwilling to do that, so he was not going to waste his breath.

"We can handle that, but I don't want to involve any more people than I have to until I know what's going on."

"Okay, try to see if she can keep any water down, nothing but water. I will be there as soon as I can and will cover it from there. I'm gonna have to run some labs, but I can do that under Jane Doe. I'll be there as soon as I can." He hung up.

Wayne tossed the phone on his desk and got up and went back into her room. Bubba was sitting on the edge of the bed running a cold cloth along her cheek. She was soaked in sweat, but shaking and shivering. He rubbed his hands together and paced up and down the small room. He kept looking at Bubba, who to his surprise was far calmer than he was, but then again, he seemed to have something to do. Wayne did not have anything to do except wait. Finally, the Doc arrived.

Baxter looked around. He pointed to the wall at the head of the bed. "Bubba, can you find a stud and put a three-inch nail in that wall."

Bubba hopped to his feet. "On it."

"Wayne, can you find me a metal coat hanger."

Wayne turned around and opened the closet. He grabbed one of metal hangers out, pulled the shirt off of it and threw the shirt over the closet rod. He crossed to the Doc and held it out. "What do you need a hanger for?"

Baxter was in the process of starting an IV. He pulled out the saline bag and handed it to him. "See the little hole in the top."

Wayne did not need further instructions, he slipped the top of the hanger through it, then held it up. Bubba reentered at this time, nail and hammer in hand. It only took a moment, then the IV bag was hanging at the head of the bed. "There, now that I have an IV started, we can relax a little, though that will probably empty really quickly." He patted her cheek several times. "What's her name?"

Bubba responded, "Lenore."

Baxter snorted. "Or so she claims."

Lenore opened her eyes. "It is Lenore. It wasn't a fake ID, Doc."

He frowned, clearly not believing her. "So what were you on?" She shut her eyes tight, then her chest started convulsing. He scooted back and grabbed her shoulder as he fumbled for the bowl. Bubba got it first. She barely got her head over the bowl before she started throwing up. Everyone but Lenore was quiet for several minutes.

When she was finished being sick, she tried to push herself up on her elbow, but she could not quite manage it. She just squirmed a little more off the bed, fumbled for the glass and rinsed out her mouth. She started sniffing and crying. "I'm so sorry. I'm so sorry."

Bubba rubbed her back. "It's okay, everything's gonna be all right." He got the washcloth and wiped off her face. "There you are. Bet the cool cloth feels good. Here, let's get you back on the pillows." He adjusted her back against the pillows, then he rinsed off the cloth and lay it across her forehead.

Baxter leaned back and raised an eyebrow in Wayne's direction. Wayne held his hands out and shrugged his shoulders, clearly indicating he did not know either. "Well, now that that's over, can you tell me what you were on?" Her eyes were shut and she seemed out of it. He gave her a gentle shake. "Come on, I need to know what you were taking." She groaned and tried to roll onto her side.

Bubba offered, "There's a whole row of pill bottles in the bathroom. The labels have been torn off, but she wrote on them, what they were, and how many milligrams."

Baxter got to his feet and went into the bathroom. He groaned and rubbed his face. He stood there shaking his head. "I need to draw some blood." He went back to the room and got everything he needed. When he was done drawing blood, he gave her shake. "Lenore, I need you to answer me. Was that all you were taking? If you were taking something else, I need to know. Any cocaine, heroin, ecstasy, crystal meth, any of that?"

She groaned and shook her head. "No, just what the doctors gave me."

He shook her again. "Why did the doctors give you them? Was it the same doctor, or different doctors?"

She groaned. "Sometimes the same, sometimes different. If one doctor's prescriptions expired, my mother would just get a new one to give her a new prescription. They never questioned it, just gave out prescriptions like they were candy, anything to make the monkey dance."

Baxter raised an eyebrow. He looked up at Bubba and asked, "Monkey dance?"

Bubba shrugged his shoulders and indicated he had no idea. "She said something real close to that earlier, something about happy, quiet, puppet on a string, dancing monkey."

Wayne added, "When I hired her she said she used to be a dancer."

Baxter looked at the IV. The bag was empty. He switched to a fresh bag. He got to his feet and picked up the blood samples. "If that runs out before I get back, just slide this little thing over and unscrew it. I only had two at the house and have to go back to my clinic and get some more. That one should last longer though, and gentlemen, I do not like the sounds of any of this. Maybe it's just my overactive imagination, but young girl on the run, with that many pills, saying doctors did this to me, Mom got them to do it. Sounds like an underage sex ring to me. I think you should call the Sheriff."

Alejandro said from the doorway, "I hadn't wanted to say it, but I was thinking that too."

Wayne shook his head. "All the more reason to keep the Sheriff out of this, at least right now. We don't know anything, and I'd rather not do anything to put this girl at risk until we are able to know more. As soon as she starts clearing up, we can ask some questions. Until then, let's just focus on treating her and not worry about anything else."

Bubba nodded. "I'm with Pop. For all we know her mom's just one of those horrible parents who feels that pills fix all of their kid's problems."

Baxter nodded. That was equally likely. He was lucky being a country doctor, most of his patients' parents were of the opinion that they just needed to work more. "All right, I'm going to head into town and get these to the lab in Amarillo. We should have a response in a couple hours. Right now she seems to be in the sleep it off stage, but that can change at any minute and she can go to the slit her own wrists stage, so let's not leave her alone."

Bubba nodded and sat down on the edge of the bed. He dumped the cloth in the water and wrung it out. He rubbed along her neck. "I'll stay with her. The chills seem to be dissipating."

Baxter nodded. "For the moment, but they're gonna come and go. With the dosages that are on those bottles, we're looking at a good two to three days of this, maybe even more, and just in case there was any confusion, this is not the worst of it. The worst is yet to come. This is just the initial withdrawal."

XII

Wednesday, November 15

Bubba dozed in the armchair he had brought into Lenore's room. He had scarcely left her side since Sunday. He had thought Sunday was bad, and he had foolishly thought that they were over the worst of it because Monday had not been so bad. She just slept, then Tuesday rolled around. That had been like Sunday all over again. Sometime around midnight, things had gone from bad to worse, and the next twelve hours were the longest of his life. He had seriously considered taking her to the hospital, but she had made it through it. Then around noon today she had seemed a little better and had gone and taken a shower. He had stripped the bed and put fresh sheets on, then she had curled up in bed and had slept. He had sat down in the armchair covered up with a blanket and fell asleep, but something had awakened him. He was not quite sure what it was. He did not really want to wake up, then shouting from somewhere in the house brought him into full consciousness.

Wayne snapped angrily, "Dammit, Diego! I don't give a shit if you are the Sheriff, you got no business here!"

Diego snapped back. "Dammit, Wayne! I don't want to cause any trouble for you or your family, but somebody called in a report saying that they were being held prisoner in your ranch house, and my dispatcher was on the phone with her when somebody in the background shouted 'What are you doing?' and the phone went dead. We've known each other all our lives. I know it's a bullshit call, which is why I didn't go get a warrant first, which is what I should've done, but now you're being a stubborn ass, and won't let me just look around. You're starting to make me worry."

Bubba sat up and rubbed his face. He got up and laid the blanket over the armchair. He headed into the living room. "Evening, Sheriff."

Diego raised an eyebrow. "Bubba, you look like shit."

He chuckled. "I feel like shit. Scarcely slept in four days."

Diego raised an eyebrow and asked, "Troubles?"

"In a manner of speaking, new ranch hand's got the flu. Baxter was worried about her getting dehydrated, falling and hurting herself, so I been keeping an eye on her."

Diego nodded and looked thoughtful. "Dehydration can cause hallucinations. Any chance she got ahold of the phone?"

Bubba shook his head. "There's no phone in the servants' quarters, and I think my phone's probably dead in the dining room. When I went to check on her on Sunday morning, I'm pretty sure I left it on the table. So there's been no phone near her. I say you got a prank call."

"Well, it was a woman who called. Can I talk to her, then I can leave y'all in peace?"

Bubba shrugged his shoulders. "She's been pretty sick. It ain't pretty in there."

"I'm sure I've seen worse. I do have four children."

Wayne laughed. "No joke. Kids can make a mess faster than anybody, especially as closely as you spaced them."

He shrugged his shoulders. "What can I say, gets cold around here and I like my wife."

They all laughed. Bubba led the way down the hallway. Diego cocked his head to the side as he followed. He did not think he had ever seen Bubba in anything but boots. Now watching him walk down the hall in his stocking feet was a bit peculiar. As he approached, he noticed the door was open. He had intended to just peek in, but his policeman's eyes scanned the room. It was a small room, only about ten by ten with a twin bed to the left of the door, the closet and dresser to the right. On the opposite wall was the bathroom door which was standing open and he could see sitting on the counter a whole row of pill bottles. He went straight for them.

Bubba cursed under his breath. He forgotten they were sitting there.

Wayne smacked Bubba upside the head. He whispered, "Dumb ass, I thought you had the sense to throw those away or hide them when you heard us yelling."

Bubba shrugged his shoulders and whispered back, "I was asleep. I wasn't thinking clearly."

Diego shook his head as he read the bottles. "As long as we've known each other Wayne, I would've thought you would not lie to me. Flu my ass, withdrawal is more like it."

Wayne said quickly, "Those are all prescription. There's nothing for you to worry yourself about, Sheriff."

Diego gestured to all the bottles. "Not a damn label in sight, Wayne. I understand she's your hand and you want to protect her, but clearly from the amount of drugs we're talking about, she had to be dealing."

Bubba snapped angrily, "You don't know her. You don't know anything about her. Don't go judging her, and I don't believe for a minute that she would ever sell drugs. She wants to get off the pills, not get back on them. She said doctors gave them to her. I believe her. She had no reason to lie, not to mention as miserable as she was at the time, I don't think she could've lied. I don't think she would've had the foresight to lie."

Diego sighed and rubbed his face. "Look, if she's a good kid, I don't want to give her any trouble. Let me run her ID. If it comes back clean, maybe we don't have a problem."

Wayne considered that for a minute, then he nodded. He looked around. He did not see her backpack anywhere. He opened her top dresser drawer, nothing. He opened the second drawer. He saw her wallet and a jewelry box. He opened it and raised an eyebrow. He picked up the photograph and looked at it. He turned it over, stenciled across the back by the photo lab was 'January 1999'. He swallowed hard and held the photo with both hands. He leaned forward and rested his elbows on the dresser as he stared at three people in the center of the photograph. "Diego, New Year's Day, nineteen ninety-nine. My daddy took you and William to task about the truck. Daddy didn't want any drinking and driving done on New Year's Eve, so he had ordered all the trucks to be parked at the ranch house by ten PM. You and William had taken one of the trucks out, but the truck wasn't back until about four AM. Which one of you hitched a ride with another one of the hands, and which one of you stayed out?

Which one of you didn't come back until morning?"

Diego replied quickly, "That was twenty years ago. I don't remember."

Wayne turned around and held out the photo. "It wasn't twenty years ago. It was almost nineteen years ago."

Diego took the offered photograph. He staggered back and bumped into the wall. "Where the hell did she get this photo? I've never even seen this photo. It was taken by ..."

Wayne supplied, "That damn singer's promotion crew. I remember William was talking about it for days. He thought it was fun that y'all had been asked to take a photo with her. She was hot stuff then, pretty too. Tell me you or my brother didn't do something stupid."

Diego put his hand over his mouth. He started shaking his head. "It's just a coincidence."

Wayne reached back and grabbed her wallet. He threw it at Diego. "Is that a damn coincidence?"

Diego opened up the wallet and stared at the date of birth on her ID. He pulled out his phone, went to his web browser and begin typing. He shook his head. "Says very clearly, due date September 27."

Wayne jerked his thumb in Bubba's direction. "He was a month late, and how late was Aaron?"

Diego looked down at the floor. "Ten days ... William caught a ride back. I got drunk with the stupid singer and spent the night with her."

Bubba almost sagged with relief. He murmured, "Thank God for that. I don't think I could handle her bein' my cousin."

Diego started shaking his head. "Let's not go getting ahead of ourselves. Do you think I was the only guy that that singer was screwing, and we don't even know if she's related to the singer? You guys are just filling in blanks here. There's no evidence."

Bubba walked over to Diego and took the photograph. He sat down on the edge of the bed and gently shook Lenore. Her eyes fluttered open. "Lenore, who's this in the photo?"

Lenore groaned. She reached up and pointed. "Stupid bitch in the middle's my mother." She shut her eyes and looked away.

He gently shook her again. He held the photo a little closer. "Who are the guys in the photo with her?"

"Just some guys. Mom said one of them was my father, but she couldn't remember which one she'd slept with. That was typical for her." She closed her eyes and rolled over to face the wall.

Bubba reached down and gripped the bandage on her arm from where the doctor had drawn blood last. He yanked it off. She did not even murmur. He got up and crossed to the door and shouted, "Alejandro, can you bring me a sandwich bag!" Alejandro appeared a moment later and handed over the bag, then he left. Bubba shoved the bandage in the bag and handed it to the Sheriff. "I'm sure you have a lab that can figure that out for you."

XIV

Diego sat in his truck staring at his garage. He had been sitting there for twenty minutes. He was not sure he could face his wife right now. Finally he told himself, "It does not get easier the longer you wait." He nodded, then he sighed. "Maybe I should wait till I actually know something. Right now I don't know shit." He laughed at himself, got out, grabbed his rifle, locked the doors, and headed into the house. He crossed to the gun safe and put both guns away neatly, then he went into the kitchen, sat down at the table, put his elbows on it, his face in his hands.

Natalia raised an eyebrow. "You're home early, honey. Rough day? Want some coffee?"

He shook his head and looked at her. "I think a little liquid courage would go a lot farther."

She sighed, crossed to the liquor cabinet, and pulled down a bottle of Jack and a glass. She crossed to him and set them down in front of him. He reached out and grabbed her hip. He looked up at her and smiled. "I love you."

She smiled back, bent down, and kissed him. "I love you too. You want to talk about it?"

He shook his head. "No, but I have to. Maybe not today, but tomorrow. That's what I keep asking myself. Should I go ahead and talk to you about it now, or should I wait? Right now I'm only guessing. Tomorrow I should have facts."

She pulled out a chair and sat down next to him. She reached over and squeezed his hand. "Hey, I thought we were partners. I thought we talked about everything, real or imagined."

He nodded. "This is different. This could be a major fuck up."

She rubbed his hand. "Then I definitely think we should talk about it now, so come on, out with it."

He sighed several times. "You know this is one of those, there's just no easy way to break it. I might have a daughter ... another daughter ... a daughter you didn't give me."

Her eyes widened. After a minute she asked, "Older than Aaron?"

His shoulders slumped. "Baby, I have never cheated on you. Two years older than Aaron."

She laughed nervously and squeezed his hand. "Then I don't see why you're so worried. We'd never even gone out on a date. When was this?"

He sighed and rubbed his face. "New Year's Eve, nineteen ninety-eight. I'd just broken up with the charming Samantha."

She nodded. "Oh, right, the one who you found out, after you'd been home for like eight months from college, that she had been cheating on you the whole time you were gone."

He nodded. "That would be the one."

"Diego, that was six months before you and I ever even thought about going on a date. I was still at school. You didn't ask me out until the middle of June. You have nothing to feel sorry about, or guilty about, at least not as far as I'm concerned, and if you didn't know about it until just now, then she really doesn't have any room to be mad at you. She should be mad at her mother."

He nodded. "It's complicated, but I don't think she is mad at me. Granted, right now I don't think she's gonna remember our brief conversation. It's complicated."

"Who's the mother, if I can ask?"

"Remember that big flash in the pan folk singer, or folk rock, whatever. She called herself Evanjalevn."

Her eyes widened. "Oh, who could forget her, especially right now."

He shrugged his shoulders. "What do you mean right now? Is she doing some relaunch of her career, some kind of come back?"

She rolled her eyes and smacked him on the arm. "I know a lot of Denise's music grates on you, but there are a few performers she listens to that you actually like. I would've thought you would have remembered Persephone is one of your daughter's favorite performers."

He struggled to remember. "Oh, yes, I like some of her music, but I don't approve of my thirteen year old daughter watching her dance around stage half naked with a bunch of skeevy looking guys hanging all over her, doing what looks like having sex on stage with their clothes on."

She started laughing. "Oh, my darling, I think you are going to have a very, very bad day."

He shrugged his shoulders and held his hands up to the side. "How could this day get any worse?"

She pulled out her phone and started typing, shaking her head. "Oh darling, you should never have asked that question." Finding one of the articles she was looking for, she tapped on it and handed her phone to him.

He took it and started reading.

'Pop performer Persephone was reported missing yesterday by her mother. It is still unclear as to whether Persephone has walked out, or whether there has been foul play. The performer's mother, once known from coast to coast as Evanjalevn, is adamant that her daughter would not walk out in the middle of shooting a music video. She must have been kidnapped. Police, however, are not convinced.'

He looked at his wife and said, "Oh please, tell me you are kidding me. This is an older daughter, right?" He handed the phone back to his wife and went to his computer. He began typing away. Ten minutes later he banged his head into the keyboard. It was undeniable. The hair color was different, Persephone was a blonde and Lenore had red brown hair, but it was clearly the same girl.

Aaron crossed through the living room, raised an eyebrow in the direction of his father, then shifted his head to look at his mother. He jerked his thumb in his father's direction as he mouthed, 'What's wrong with him?'

Natalia shrugged her shoulders. "Being a father is not always an easy thing, Sweetie."

Aaron opened his mouth to speak, but his father lifted his head off the keyboard and banged it into it again. He put his hands on the back of his head and shook his head face first on the keyboard. Aaron could not help it, he chuckled. "So I guess this is not a good time to ask Dad for help with my homework."

Diego lifted his head off the computer and asked, "When is it due and do you want to fail?"

"It's not due till next Friday. Seriously, Dad, what's wrong?"

Diego turned around in his chair. He looked at his wife and raised an eyebrow. She nodded, saying gently, "I'm thinking you are, so I think you should at least go ahead and tell him."

Diego sighed and rubbed his hands up and down his face, then he asked, "How upset would you be if you discovered you were not my oldest child?"

Aaron raised an eyebrow. "Whoa, that was not what I expected you to say." He shrugged his shoulders. "Like, before Mom oldest child?"

"Yes."

He shrugged his shoulders. "I guess I'd be cool with it. I mean it just depends. Is the guy an asshole?"

"It's a girl, and you would be better able to answer that question than I would, because there's a very strong possibility that your coworker Lenore came here looking for her father. And by father, I would mean me." He pointed at himself.

"Shit."

Natalia slapped her son in the arm. "Language! I let the first one slide, I'm not letting the second one."

"Sorry, Mom, that just poses a serious dilemma for me. Something that was already a major dilemma, and I was trying to figure out how to have a discreet conversation with Dad about it anyways."

Diego got to his feet and demanded, "You've seen Lenore do drugs."

Aaron made a face and shook his head. "No, why would you ask that?"

"It's complicated. What's your dilemma?"

"Okay, so on Saturday I was working with Lenore and I told her I was gonna go hang out with somebody. She was kind of weird and kind of warned me off. She told me some things that I'm not supposed to repeat, and then I got to thinking about it, and I remembered some other things. So on Sunday I was working with George alone, and I asked him, and so he gave me like the total 411, and so I kind of like formed some conclusions in my head, and I don't like them, and I didn't know what to do about it, and I still don't know what to do about it, but like if she's my sister, it kind of changes everything. I mean, I want to keep my promise to her, but I feel like it's also my job to look out for her. That's what you and Mom always taught us. That you know secrets can be poisonous, and not to keep dangerous secrets, and this just really feels like a dangerous secret."

Diego said firmly, "Aaron, you're a smart kid. You have good judgment. Use your good judgment. If something is making you feel concerned about any of your friends, whether it's a sibling or not, it doesn't matter. This is a person you care about and a person you are concerned for. You need to do what you feel is right, and if they can't forgive you for doing what you thought you had to, to look after them, then they're not worth your time."

"I think Jace either tried or did ..." He opened and closed his mouth several times. Finally he blurted it out, "... rape Lenore."

Diego's mouth formed an 'oh'. Natalia gave a little gasp and put her hand to her mouth. Diego took a deep breath and let it out slowly, then he asked gently, "You said you formed these conclusions. Start to finish, tell me what made you come to this conclusion."

"Okay, so I was working in the stables with Lenore. We're talking about what our plans were and I said I was gonna hang out with Jace that night. She stopped what she was doing and looked at me and told me she wasn't an adult, she wasn't trying to like be a killjoy, but Jace was trouble and

I needed to stay away from him. We kind of talked back and forth a little, and she finally admitted that he picked her up on the side of the road when she was coming out here. She was hitchhiking and she got in his truck. He turned down the ranch road. She said he stopped the truck, reached under his driver's seat and pulled out a bag that had three vials of cocaine and he offered her some. She said no, then she says he snorted some and she got out of the car. That's her story. But when she showed up for dinner the first night, she had a busted lip and a bruise on her cheek and Ramon was even making guesses the next day about how she got them. So after we had a little chat, when I was working with George, I asked him where Lenore came from. He said he didn't really know, but he heard Bubba talking with Stewart, and you know Stewart's been on the ranch for like twenty years so he's like family. And Bubba told Stewart that he found her in one of the line shacks soaking wet, covered in mud, with only one shoe, and her shirt was torn."

Diego got to his feet and headed for the front door. Natalia shouted, "Where are you going?"

"To have a conversation with a little shit." He grabbed his keys off the hall table.

She shouted, "You're not taking a gun, are you?"

"Conversations use words, not bullets." He yanked open the door and slammed it shut.

Aaron looked at his mother and asked, "Did I say something wrong?"

She walked up to her son and hugged him. "No baby, you did just right. Your dad is just doing what dads do. Let's just hope by the time he gets to Jace's parents' house, the cop is more in control than the dad."

XV

Diego was halfway between the front door and the driveway when he stopped. He glanced from his work truck to his personal truck. He stood there shifting back and forth as one thought after another ran through his mind. There was no doubt in his mind that Jace had hit his daughter. He laughed at himself. He had already accepted that she was his. He knew that he had only been fighting the inevitable since he had heard because he did not want to hurt Natalia, but now that hurting her was not on the table, all he wanted to do was protect his daughter, and of course, beat the ever-living shit out of Jace, but fortunately his cop brain was taking control. Then he realized he did not want to just flatten the little shit's face, he wanted to make sure he did not have an opportunity to ever hurt another little girl, and if he went storming in there fists flailing, he would screw any case they had. In fact, if he got involved in it at all, he could screw the case. He had to merely be acting in an advisory capacity. He hated it, but it was the right thing to do. He shifted from foot to foot as ideas continued to race through his brain. The easiest course of action would be to wait and catch Jace speeding, but that could take a little while. He was impatient. The second easiest course of action would be to simply ask Jace's parents for permission to search the truck and the house. They were good people. He thought there was easily a sixty percent chance that they would agree to it, but there was always that forty percent chance that they would decide to stupidly protect their son at the cost of anyone else's child. Parents could be unpredictable, which only left a warrant. Did he have enough information to get a warrant? He did not know. That would be left up to the judge. He headed for his work truck. He did not like the idea of being out without a gun, but if he went back into the house Natalia would knock him over the head before she let him take a gun. He got in his truck and pulled out his phone. He called his second in command, Neil Baxter.

Neil picked up the phone up on the second ring. "Thought you said you were going home for the day, Sheriff?"

"Yeah, well, shit spilled over. You at the station?"

"No, but I'm like two minutes from it."

"Good, I don't want to explain just this second, but I need you to do a couple of things for me. To begin with, I need you to take the lead on a case that I will fill you in on after I talk to the judge. Two, I need you to swing by the station and pick me up a spare handgun and rifle."

Neil hesitated on the other end. After a long minute he said, "Sure thing, Sheriff. Where do you want me to meet you?"

"Five miles east of town on Farm to Market 1782."

"Will do, Sheriff. See you then."

Diego hesitated. He did not want to make this next call. Finally he sighed, hit the judge's name. A cheery voice picked up on the first ring, "Diego, I haven't heard from you in forever. You, Natalia, and the kids need to come over for dinner again."

He forced himself to sound cheery as he replied, "You know I don't schedule events. That's Natalia's job. You girls work that out, and I'll show up."

She laughed. "You always say that, so what are you calling for?"

"Unfortunately, Marylou, business. I need to have a word with the judge. Is he around?"

"Yes, sir, he just got home. Give me a minute. I hope it's nothing too terrible."

A moment later Tex came on. "Afternoon, Sheriff. What's the problem?"

"One big cluster and a serious conflict of interest for me. I've already told Neil he has to take the lead. I hope you'll say I can still at least be an observer if I promise to keep my mouth shut and not flatten somebody."

Tex sighed several times as he dropped into an armchair. "That bad?"

"Pretty bad."

"And exactly how? Is it personal?"

Diego laughed, but it was a bitter sound. "That's where it gets unpleasant and complicated. Let's just say there's probably an eighty-five percent chance I have an illegitimate daughter I just found out about."

"I don't like dealing in percentages. What's your gut telling you?"

"She's mine."

"All right, if that's what you think, I believe you. Does Natalia know?"

"Yes. I just told her and Aaron. That's where things get messy. Aaron's been working with the girl out at the Cartwright place. She told him in confidence that Jace Whitaker picked her up when she was walking to town. He took that turn off onto the Cartwright place, pulled over and pulled a bag of cocaine out from under his seat and offered her some. She told Aaron she turned it down. I've actually not really spoken to the girl. I don't know if I can believe it. She told him she got out of the car when he started snorting coke. Aaron didn't believe her. He asked questions of the other guys and it turns out she showed up to the ranch beaten up. Aaron thinks Jace either tried to, or succeeded in raping her."

Tex was leaning back in his chair thinking. "Besides the fact that she was beaten up, was there anything else that made Aaron think that?"

"He said that George overheard Stewart and Bubba talking. Bubba found her early in the morning in one of the line shacks, sleeping. She was covered in mud, her shirt was torn, she was bruised up, and she was missing a sneaker."

Tex started tapping his hand on his desk as he listened, then he rubbed his chin. "So you would like a warrant to search Jace's truck, and you are looking for drugs and a sneaker? Do we know what the sneaker looks like?"

"No, but I could call Bubba and ask him to look around."

"Why Bubba, and why haven't you talked to your daughter yet?"

Diego hesitated a long minute. "She's detoxing right now. She says the doctors gave her drugs to keep her quiet and happy, whatever her mother asked them to give her."

"Do you believe that?"

He considered, going over everything in his mind. "I think if she was a stoner, one of the guys on the ranch would've noticed. She's been at their place for two weeks now. All the pills that she was taking, they all support that they were all prescription narcotics, not recreational stuff, though a lot of people use it for recreation, and no there were no prescription labels on the bottles, but I think she removed them to protect her identity, and given who her mother is, I can see her doing it. Lenore apparently kept making remarks about a dancing monkey, puppet on a string. I don't think the kid's had an easy life. Her mother's a piece of work."

"I have to say Diego, I find it very hard to believe you got yourself involved with that kind of woman."

"I was twenty-two years old, out drinking with my buddy. I just found out my girlfriend of six years had been cheating on me the whole time I was away at college, and she was smoking hot and hitting on me. The epitome of young and dumb, but what twenty-two year old guy wouldn't be stupid and get himself involved with the hot new folk rock singer of the hour? She was a rising star then. Tickets for her concerts were impossible to get. I wouldn't have even gotten to go except William got the tickets."

"This former lover of yours wouldn't happen to be a washed up singer who has a very famous daughter right now who's currently MIA?"

"Please do not glorify a one night hookup by calling her my lover, and whatever you do, don't repeat that, Judge. Lenore wants to hide. I don't think she wants to go back to that life, and quite frankly. I'd rather she didn't. Clearly it's not a good life for her."

"I won't say anything. Do you think when she's over this, she will swear out a complaint against him?"

Diego considered for a minute or two. "I think she will. The only reason she brought it up was she didn't want Aaron associating with Jace. I think she would do it if it was presented to her as protecting others."

"You're the Sheriff of this town. I don't see any problem with you being an observer, and I don't see a problem with you talking to people, being involved in a verbal capacity, but you do not look for evidence, you do not search, and you certainly don't touch Jace. Swing by my place, I'll have a warrant ready for you. I'll have all the bases covered, Jace's truck, his bedroom, and any common areas. I don't think he's stupid enough to store drugs in his parents' room or his siblings' rooms."

"Agreed. If his daddy found it, he'd shoot him."

"You can contact Bubba, tell him to send the information to Neil to forward on to me."

"Will do." He hung up then texted Bubba and Wayne.

'Look around Lenore's room. See if you can find her solo sneaker. If possible send a photo of it, size, description, brand, anything of that nature to Neil Baxter. Tell him to forward it to the judge. If it's not there tell him whatever you remember about it.'

When Neil pulled up next to the Sheriff, he got out and headed for his truck, holding the rifle and handgun. He handed them over as he demanded, "Why did Bubba Cartwright send me a photograph of a sneaker?"

Diego sighed and rubbed his face and carefully explained everything he knew to Neil, only leaving out anything to do with Persephone. When he was done, he said, "So when we get there, you're gonna serve the warrant, and you're gonna search Jace's truck. You are looking for drugs, and you are looking for that sneaker. There's no point in going through the kitchen trash, any of that kind of stuff. Chances are, if it was thrown in that, it was gotten rid of over a week ago, but I'm betting that the idiot completely forgot it was in his truck. It's probably under the seat. Whatever you do, do not mention rape or attempted rape right now. All we are looking for is arresting him for possession. Maybe we'll upgrade it to possession with intent to distribute. Right now I just want to lock him up. Once we have him, we can always increase the charges."

Neil nodded. "Yes sir, Sheriff."

They both got back in their trucks and headed for the Whitaker place. They both had barely gotten out of their trucks before Sammy came down the front steps. He headed straight for Diego, extending his hand. "Diego, what brings you out this way?"

Diego shook hands with him and indicated Neil. "Neil's got something he wants to say to you. I'm just here in an advisory capacity."

Sammy raised an eyebrow and shifted his attention to Neil. "Neil, what's going on?"

"Mr. Whitaker, I have a warrant to search your pickup truck with license plate 1001012. The warrant also gives us permission to search Jace's bedroom, and all common areas of the house."

Sammy took the warrant. He read down through it. "Narcotics and a sneaker?" He's shifted his attention to Diego and demanded, "Why a sneaker?"

Neil cleared his throat and said a little uncomfortably, "Right now we're just collecting evidence and information. We'll know more after we complete our search. It would go a lot faster if you cooperate. Could I have the keys to Jace's truck, please?"

Sammy did not know why, but he found the drugs less disturbing than a sneaker. He gestured to the truck. "I don't think he ever locks it in the drive."

Neil headed for the truck, putting on a pair of rubber gloves as he went. He was just putting his hand on the door handle when Jace came out of the house demanding, "What the hell you doing? Get away from my truck!"

Sammy said firmly, "Just stand back. They have a warrant."

"I don't give a damn what they got! They don't have no right to go through my truck!"

Sammy turned on his son, crossed his arms over his chest, and said with annoyance, "Actually, they do. That's exactly what a warrant does, it gives them the right to go through your truck, and they don't get a warrant without probable cause, so why don't you explain to me why they have a warrant to search your truck and my house for drugs, or should I be asking you about the sneaker, because I'll tell you right now, my mind is going over a lot of unpleasant ground about that sneaker they are looking for."

Neil shouted, "Sorry to interrupt, Mr. Whitaker, but the truck is locked."

Sammy pulled his keys out of his pocket and tossed them at Neil. "There's a spare key on there." He turned back to his son and demanded, "I'm waiting."

Jace growled and shouted back, "This is horse shit! I don't know anything about any drugs and I certainly don't know anything about …" His eyes widened, and he suddenly looked stricken. He closed his mouth, then opened it, trying to recover, but he could not. He could not think of anything, and the longer his father stared at him, the worse it got. Finally he cracked and looked at the ground.

Sammy stepped forward and pointed at his son. He shouted angrily, "Boy, you had damn well better tell me right now why they are looking for a sneaker, because you know."

He swallowed hard and tried to meet his father's eyes, but he could not. Neil whistled. They all turned to stare. He came out with a sandwich bag with six glass vials and they were full of white powder. "Look at what I found right under the driver's seat. Sheriff, what do you want to bet that ain't powdered sugar, and though I can't reach it, I did see a sneaker under the passenger seat."

Sammy glanced at his son. Jace had his hand over his face and he had gone as white as a sheet.

Neil finished bagging and labeling the vials, then went around to the other side of the truck. They all watched in grim silence. He came out a minute later holding up a sneaker. He said with irritation, "Looks a little small to be yours, Jace." He shifted his attention and asked, "What size is that sneaker we're looking for, Sheriff?"

Diego replied, "Five and a half."

"Bingo, right color, right brand, right size, and a whole lot of cocaine to go with it. Definitely a trifecta."

Diego glanced at the stricken look on Jace's face. He decided to see what happened if he gave him just a little nudge. "You know, boy, things'll go a lot easier if you just tell us what happened."

"Nothing happened. I don't even know where that stuff came from. I had this hitchhiker in my truck a couple weeks ago. The bitch had some cocaine with her. She offered me some. I said no …" He started stumbling over his words, trying to figure out where to go with his story now. His dad walked up to him and slapped him upside the head.

"You stupid little shit, you were never a good liar. Why are you even trying?"

Diego was staring at the sky. He desperately wanted to say something, but he knew he should keep his mouth shut right now.

Neil said just loud enough the Sheriff could hear, "Sorry, Sheriff." Then he moved towards Jace and demanded angrily, "So this allegedly female hitchhiker offered you some cocaine. Was that before or after you slapped her around?"

Sammy had turned to look at Neil. Now he turned back to his son and reached out and slapped him upside the head, and kept slapping him upside the head as he demanded angrily, "Did you attack a woman in your truck? Slap a girl around …" Jace brought his hands up to try to protect his head, but his father kept getting around them and hitting him.

Neil looked at the Sheriff. "We should probably stop him."

Diego shrugged his shoulders and looked helpless. "I'm under strict orders from the judge. I can't get involved in anything."

"Don't try lying to me, boy! You tell me right now, did you hurt that girl?"

Jace shouted, "Sheriff, get him off me!"

Sammy slapped his son several more times. "I knew I spoiled you growing up. I didn't want you to have to work hard like I did. That's where I went wrong with you."

Jace interrupted his father and shouted, "Please Sheriff! If you get him off me, I'll say anything you want me to! I'll tell you where I got the drugs! I'll tell you about the stupid little bitch, whatever you want! Just get him off me!"

Neil did not need to be told twice. He charged in and pulled Sammy back, saying firmly, "That's enough, Sammy. I can't arrest him if you're beating the shit out of him."

Sammy jerked free and turned towards the house. "Get him off my property. I don't want to see him right now. When I calm down, I'll come talk to him."

Neil turned to Jace as he pulled out his handcuffs. He handcuffed him and read him his rights, then loaded him the back of his truck. He retrieved the two evidence bags from where he dropped them and threw them on the passenger seat. "I'll take him down to the station and book him. Sheriff, you gonna come in and oversee his interrogation?"

Diego shook his head. "No, you do the interrogation. I'll be behind the glass."

"Roger that, Sheriff."

XVI

Thursday, November 16

Lenore groaned as she came back to consciousness. She struggled to a sitting position. She looked around her room. There was an armchair that had not been there before, in addition to a lamp which was on, casting the room in a dim glow. She felt horrible and was starving to death. She pulled her T-shirt out a little, stuck her nose in and smelled. She stunk. She struggled to her feet, then she discovered she had an IV stuck in her arm. She sat back down and picked up a tissue. She used the little locking clamp she had seen the nurses use to close the IV. Then she carefully removed the tape that was holding the IV on. After a moment's examination she carefully pulled on the IV and it came out. She pressed the tissue to the now vacant hole. She got back up and staggered to the bathroom and turned on the sink. She splashed water on her face, then brushed her teeth thoroughly. She hesitated and decided if she tried to use her mouthwash, she was going to puke again. She stripped out of her clothes and turned on the shower. She got in, holding onto the walls. She did not care that the water was freezing, she stood under it until it got warm, then she grabbed her loofa, applied soap liberally and started scrubbing. Finally finding one thing to be grateful to her mother for, her mother had forced her to get electrolysis on her underarms and bikini line when she was fifteen, so at least she did not feel like a woolly mammoth. When she was finished, she got out, dried off, and exited the bathroom wrapped in a towel.

She started when she saw Bubba standing there with his arms crossed. "In what world was it a smart idea to take a shower without somebody around?"

She wanted to say several angry remarks, but realizing she was still here and not in the hospital or a jail cell, she told herself she should be really nice. She said apologetically, "I'm sorry. I woke up and felt disgusting. I felt like I smelled, and all I could think about was a nice hot shower, and you'll forgive me, but I'm not used to having men watch over me while I shower."

Bubba was certain he was blushing. He cleared his throat. "Clearly you don't remember Tuesday, but I do understand your point, but it would've been nice to know you were in the shower, that way we could check on you, but I'll be in the hall if you need me. I'll let you get dressed. You hungry, want something to eat?"

"Yes, actually I'm starving. I feel like I haven't eaten anything in days."

He sighed and scratched his stubbled cheek. "Probably because you haven't, and just in case you were curious, it's about nine o'clock on Thursday."

Her eyes widened. "I thought those were all bad dreams. There really have been a bunch people in and out of this room, haven't there?"

He nodded, finding it very difficult to maintain eye contact, his eyes kept wanting to drift down to her bare legs, and the knowledge that there was nothing but a towel between him and bare skin was not making it easy. He cleared his throat and said, "Doc Baxter, Pop, Alejandro, the Sheriff."

She swallowed hard. "What did the Sheriff want?"

He shrugged his shoulders. "Somebody made a call saying that we were holding them prisoner, a woman. We know it wasn't you doing it when you were out of your head, which by the way, you were never outta your head, just really sick."

She stared at him in confusion. After minute she asked, "Has that kind of thing ever happened before?"

"Nope, that was a first, but I'll go on and get out here so you can get dressed." He turned and walked out, closing the door behind him.

She finished drying off, got dressed, and then opened the door. She felt very unsteady on her feet as she walked to the supply closet. She opened it and found the disinfectant spray, then she returned to her room.

Bubba asked, "What are you doing?"

"Cleaning my room. It needs it."

"Don't you think food first?"

She shook her head, then held her head and realized that was a really bad idea. After a minute she said, "Since I expect your father to let me have breakfast and then fire me, I'd really like to leave the room clean." She reentered her room and started stripping the bed. She threw the dirty linens on the armchair, then sprayed the entire bed and pillow. She propped the pillow up so that it could get some airflow around it. Bubba leaned in the doorway, watching her, drinking a cup of coffee. She cleaned the bathroom, then picked up the dirty linens and went to the laundry room. She threw them in the washer, returned the disinfectant spray, and grabbed a broom. She swept the bathroom and her bedroom. He just quietly moved out of her way as she came and went.

She was just finishing sweeping the floor when Wayne appeared in the doorway. He nudged his son with his shoulder and said, "What is she doing?"

Bubba shifted his head to look at his father. He shrugged his shoulders. "Apparently she thinks you're going to fire her."

He nodded. "I can see how one would think that, but if I was gonna fire her, I would've dumped her butt in an ambulance and fired her already."

Bubba nodded. "I know, but it seems to make her happy, so I figured I'd just stand here and watch. Doc said to expect some strange behavior once she got over the physical part. He said the mental part would take about two weeks, and then she should only have some relapses, but a lot depends on personality, and since she wasn't exactly taking them of her own free will, I think probably a week, two weeks, she should be mostly fine."

Lenore stopped what she was doing and turned to stare at them. "Exactly what did I say when I was not exactly myself?"

Bubba narrowed his eyes trying to remember. "You kept calling yourself a dancing monkey. You said, 'Just a puppet on a string.' You called your mom 'the evil bitch' or 'crazy bitch', I don't remember which. Guess it amounts to the same thing, and you kept saying not to call a doctor because they did this to you, and you cried begging for no more pills."

She emptied the dustpan into the trash, then washed her hands and rubbed her face. "I guess you guys want some answers." She almost laughed.

They gave identical facial expressions, shrugged their shoulders, sighed, and replied simultaneously, "Only if you want to."

She crossed her arms over her chest and stared at them. She asked with curiosity, "So after the past almost week, you're perfectly willing to keep me on without any questions answered? So it's kind of like it never happened, just go back to things the way they were?"

Wayne laughed. "Oh, not exactly like they were. Doc says you can't exactly be trusted to be left alone for a couple weeks, so one of the lads is gonna have to be babysitting you, and since Bubba and I don't feel it's right to not explain to the guys what's going on, that means you're gonna be stuck with me, Bubba, or Alejandro for the next two weeks. Where one of us goes, you go, and trust me, we'll make sure you get all the shit jobs." He took a big swig from his coffee, then smiled and added, "Sometimes literally." To his surprise, she smiled, and looked very happy.

"I can do that, and I won't complain, I promise. I just don't want to leave. I like it here."

He nodded. "Good. Well, I got some work that needs to be done out in the north forty, so I'm gonna head-on out and take care that. Boy, get the girl some breakfast, and then drag her out to the stables and see how much work she can get done."

She grabbed her boots and stuck her feet in them, then she went into the kitchen. Bubba started to follow her. Wayne grabbed the back of his shirt.

Bubba took a step back and looked over his shoulder at his father. "Yes, sir?"

"I hadn't wanted to ask over the past few days, but is something going on between you two?"

"Yeah, she's my employee and I'm her boss."

Wayne shook his head. "Don't make me smack you, boy."

He shrugged his shoulders. "No, there's nothing going on between us, but under the right circumstances I wouldn't mind if there was. I like her. She likes the ranch. She's a good worker. I think she'd fit in around here nice on a permanent basis."

Wayne mulled that over for a minute. "As long as you ain't letting your dick do your thinking. I just want to make sure you're not letting your need to score outweigh your head. You gonna tell her about Diego?"

He smiled. "I'm never looking to score, Pop. I thought you knew. You taught me better than that, and as far as the Sheriff is concerned, that's none of my affair. He's gonna have to man up and handle that one himself, but I ain't worried, he will.

Known him all my life, ain't never known him to take the coward's way out."

XVII

Diego looked at his watch, it was five thirty. He should have long since left the office, but he just could not seem to pry his eyes away from his monitor. He had spent the last hour researching into the infamous Persephone. He had not seen a single word that give him comfort. When Evanjalevn had first started out, she had a good girl reputation, but then she fell off the planet for about six months in nineteen ninety-nine. She had tried to make a comeback, but not as a good girl, as a wild rocker, she had not done too bad. She had been in the business for about four years when her career was ruined by throat polyps, which permanently damaged her vocal cords. She fell off the radar for almost ten years, then she emerged as the mother of the up-and-coming star Persephone, an oversexed, half naked, wild rock star. Just like so many of her contemporaries, she had the super hot, muscular dancers, who in his opinion got way too friendly with an underage girl. Even were that underage girl not his daughter, the cop in him did not like it any more than the father. In the past six months, the rumors had been running rampant with sex scandals, threesomes, wild parties where the cops got called, involving drugs and alcohol. He finally could not look at it any longer. He switched off his monitor, grabbed the papers off the printer, folded them and stuffed them in an envelope, then headed out. He waited until he was in the truck, then he switched on his Bluetooth and called Natalia. She answered and said with a laugh, "Let me guess, stuck at work, not going to be home for dinner?"

"Do I do it that often to you, Love?"

She laughed. "Actually, very rarely, only a couple times a year. You're usually pretty good about being home when you say you're going to, but something told me you weren't going be home early today, so I already fed the kids."

"Good. I don't know when I'm gonna be home. I'm on my way out to the Cartwright place."

Natalia was silent for a long time, then she said, "Are you sure you want to do that by yourself?"

"My responsibility, I did it. No sense dragging you into any unpleasantness."

"Remember, we're a team, and I don't think there's going to be any unpleasantness. I think she came here looking for something real in her life, something normal, and I think she wants that to be her father. Little girls like having Daddy around."

He smiled. "I know, I have two."

"No, you have three."

"One of them is not so little, and she's got herself into a lot of big girl trouble."

Natalia said firmly, "You don't know anything about the real girl. All you know is what's splattered all over the Internet, that's not the same thing at all. Aaron likes her. He says she's nice, and let's look at this honestly, would she be cleaning out stables if she was that girl that's splattered all over the Internet?"

He sighed several times. "I love you so much. You're right. I hadn't even been looking at it that way, but you're right, that doesn't make sense. That girl all over the Internet does not fit with the girl who's been here working in the stables."

"Good, glad I was here to help you. Just remember, when you look at her, don't see Persephone, try to focus on Lenore, and let Persephone go. Don't worry about her. I don't think she's gonna exist anymore. I don't think Lenore wants her to exist."

He could not help it, he was smiling from ear to ear. "God, I love you, woman. I don't know what I'd do without you."

"I'm sure you'd manage."

"Well, do me a favor, don't ever make me test that theory."

She laughed. "I have no intention of it."

He hung up the phone and thought about everything he needed to say, tried to put his thoughts in order. When he pulled up outside the house, he got out slowly, not sure he was ready for this, but knowing he had to do it whether he liked it or not. He finally mentally kicked himself in the butt and headed for the door. As was typical around a ranch, he did not get the chance to knock. The door was opened by Wayne. "Evening, Sheriff, not surprised to see you here. Hungry? We were just sitting down to dinner."

"If I wouldn't be imposing, dinner sounds great."

Wayne stepped back and gestured for him to enter. "There's always a place at my table for you, you should know that."

He took off his hat and hung it on one of the hooks, then he looked back. "Even after yesterday?"

Wayne patted him on the back. "Always." He squeezed his shoulder tightly. "We all have our skeletons." He laughed and added as he leaned in close, "Though Alejandro's been trying to work on fattening yours up."

Diego snorted with laughter. "Thought she looked a bit scrawny."

They both headed into the dining room and sat down. Wayne gestured. "Lenore, I don't think you've met our Sheriff. This is Diego Mendoza." They both seated themselves.

She smiled at him. "Nice to meet you, sir, I have heard a lot about you. Aaron is very proud of his father."

Diego was glad he was spared from having to answer by Ramon demanding, "So what brings you out this way, Sheriff?"

Alejandro got up and went into the kitchen. He came back with a plate and silverware, set them down in front of the Sheriff, then smiled and said, "Here you go," before reclaiming his seat.

"I just have a few things I need to talk to Wayne and Bubba about, but it can wait until after dinner."

Lenore had been a little nervous when she had come in to dinner, and then when the Sheriff had arrived, her nervousness had increased. Nobody had asked her where she had been, though they had all commented that they were glad she was feeling better. She was going to have to ask Bubba later what he had told them. The Sheriff seemed quite comfortable conversing with everybody, and very knowledgeable. He even contributed to some of the discussion about ranch problems. She tried to focus on her eating, but she found she was just feeling terrible.

Alejandro reached over and stuck his fork in a piece of chicken. He got up and walked around behind her and dropped it on her plate. He leaned in and whispered in her ear, "If you don't start putting some meat into your stomach, you'll never get better. Those veggies and starches are only gonna get you so far. You need some solid meat in your stomach. It's the only way you are going to improve. Now shut up and eat it."

Diego raised an eyebrow, but he was not given a chance to ask. Wayne said with amusement, "She's from California and fancies herself a vegetarian. It's been galling him for weeks, and since she looks like death warmed over right now, I think he probably just told her that mashed potatoes weren't gonna get her anywhere. Though I could be wrong."

She could not help it, she laughed. "No, that is almost word for word what he said, though he did say vegetables and starches." She cut a small piece of the chicken and took a bite. She realized everyone was staring at her. "Ah, so is this the new hazing, watch the Valley girl eat her chicken."

They all shrugged their shoulders, but it was Travis who said, "I'm just waiting to see if you like break out in a rash, turn red, or start frothing at the mouth."

She picked up her napkin and threw it at him. "God, you guys are such jerks." They all roared with laughter. He picked up her napkin and threw it back at her.

Wayne said quickly, "Whoa, whoa, before this escalates. Just remember, if anybody starts a food fight, they are the one who gets to clean it up, and nobody has to help them."

Lenore nodded. "That is a very strong discouragement. He who throws it first, cleans it all." She was only able to eat about half of the chicken breast before she felt like her stomach was going to explode. Not strictly surprising, she was the last hand at the table. She picked up her plate and got to her feet.

Diego said, "Before you go wandering off, I need to talk to you, ma'am. Wayne, is there somewhere she and I can chat privately?"

Lenore sat back down. "No, they can stay. I think I know where this conversation is going. They might as well hear it too."

Bubba said gently, "Perhaps you two should talk alone."

"No, like I said, I know where this conversation is going. You might as well hear it, and then you can decide whether you'll fire me or not."

Wayne shook his head. "We're not gonna fire you. Stop worrying about it."

She laughed. "Oh trust me, you will probably change your mind, because I'm pretty sure the Sheriff is here involving a missing persons' report."

Diego chuckled. "That does come into this conversation, but it's not the beginning. I'm fine with them staying too. Wayne has always been like an older brother to me. I'm the oldest of six, so it was always kind of nice knowing Wayne was around to jerk me up short, keep my head from getting too big. His brother William was my best friend growing up, and we used to work this very ranch together. In fact, we went to college together, and when we came back from college, he and I were together when I found out that my long-term girlfriend had been cheating on me the whole time we were away at college with a lot of different guys. So being my best friend, he decided it was New Year's Eve, and since I didn't have a girl to kiss, he was gonna take me out to the Fairgrounds, get me drunk, and we were gonna have fun whether I liked it or not." He chuckled remembering. "Never mind the fact that his daddy had told everybody their butts had better be in bed by ten o'clock. He wasn't having any drunk driving in his trucks. William being William, said no problem, I'd be the one doing all the drinking. He'd be the one doing the driving, and he'd argue with his daddy in the morning. He was the youngest."

Wayne cleared his throat and chuckled. "He could charm the rattles off a rattlesnake. Shit, I would've gotten my ass fried over that, he would just get a slap on the wrist. He was really good at that."

Diego nodded. "Given how last minute it was I don't know how he managed it, but he got us tickets for the big performer at the rodeo that year. She was pretty hot stuff, sexy too, and the girls always chased William, but this girl wasn't chasing William. She was going after me. That was unusual. I wasn't used to that. I guess that's why I got stupid and I spent the night with her in her trailer." He pulled the papers out from under his seat. He slid them across to her. "I got called out here on a prank phone call, but some information came to light along with a photograph. A photo of me and William and your mother. It's in your jewelry box, which you're familiar with. I ran a DNA test, you're my daughter."

Lenore picked up the papers. There was a lot of stuff she did not understand, but she understood the results, positive for paternity. She stared at them for a long time, then she set them down. "Okay, that was unexpected."

He nodded. "You showing up and me finding out you are my daughter, that was unexpected, but once you told me … once you told us … I mean we were all there for it … that the woman in the picture was your mother, and that she said one of the two guys was your father, I knew it was me, even though I was in a little bit of denial. What I don't understand is given the life you had, one would think that was ..."

She interrupted him. "That it was the dream life? It's not, it's hell. Nothing you do, nothing you say is private, and half of what gets printed isn't real anyways, and the people who print it and spread it don't care what it does to your life. I was miserable there. I'm a hell of a lot happier here. Look, you got your life in order, Sheriff. My intentions in coming out here was not to cause any problems or disharmony in your life, and believe me, the last thing you want is that she devil's eyes on you. Any association with that other horrible person will only cause heartache and despair for you. So don't worry about it, you go on with your life, please, exactly as it is, and whatever you do, don't create any association between yourself and me, because that's only going to end badly for you."

Diego shook his head. "Look, I've spent a ridiculous amount of time on the Internet over the past twenty-four hours, and all of the digging I've done, there was never any association between Lenore Stevens and your other life, but like it or not, you're my daughter, and I want to be there for you, and you clearly need somebody here for you. Bubba and Wayne are great, and I'm eternally grateful to them for what they've done for you since you showed up, but you are my daughter.

That's my responsibility, and there are some other unpleasant things we have to discuss, because there's a little bit of a file that was created here."

"What does that mean? I've been flying under the radar."

"You've done a pretty good job of it, but you ran into Jace, and I know all about it."

She sighed and rubbed her face. "That little weasel told you after he promised me."

Bubba demanded, "Whoa, whoa, whoa! What does Jace have to do with this, and what did he promise you?"

She sighed and rolled her eyes. "Jace did not promise me anything, the little weasel is Aaron."

Diego nodded. "Yes, and when your little brother – or younger brother, he's not your little brother – when your younger brother learned that you were his sister, his slight issue of conscience became a very big issue, and he wanted to make sure you were protected. That's what brothers do, whether they're older or younger, they look after their sisters. Maybe not out in California, but that's how they behave out here, and given the fact that your brother was convinced that Jace either raped you or tried to rape you, I think he did the right thing in telling his father the Sheriff, your father the Sheriff."

Bubba shot to his feet. "I will kill him!"

Diego leaned his chair back on two legs and pointed to himself with both hands. "Bubba, hello, Sheriff. Come on. I don't want to have to arrest you for shit like that. Now sit your ass down and keep your mouth shut." Bubba grumbled, but dropped back into his seat.

Wayne said with a laugh, "Four on the floor, Diego."

Diego chuckled and dropped his chair back down. "Sorry."

Lenore said, "Look, I have no idea where Aaron got these strange ideas.

Diego cut her off. "Don't even try lying to me, young lady. I have Jace sittin' in one of my jail cells with a written confession. He confessed to having the drugs. He confessed to selling them to some specific friends." He swallowed hard and looked at the table. "And he confessed to trying to rape you."

She blushed and put her hands over her face. After a minute she said, "So now what? What am I supposed to do? You want me to what?"

Diego was surprised at how scared he was. He cleared his throat. "Under normal circumstances we would require a full written statement from you to verify, but since he gave a full confession, all that is being asked of you is to read his confession and verify its accuracy." He pulled an envelope out of his jacket pocket and pulled out an ink pen. He slid them across to her. "If you would open it and read it, if it is accurate you just have to sign it. If you disagree with something, you may handwrite in the corrections and mark out anything that you feel is inaccurate, then sign it."

She reluctantly took them, but before she opened it, she closed her eyes and very carefully went over everything in her mind, then she opened it and read it. She read it twice. She was surprised at how accurate it was. She uncapped the pen and signed it. She started to slide it across when Mr. Cartwright said, "I know, it's probably ridiculously nosy of me but ..." Lenore did not give him a chance to finish, she shifted directions and slid it in his direction.

She sighed and rubbed her face again. "So that's all I have to do?"

Diego said with irritation, "No, next time you report it. He slapped you around, tore your clothes, and you were just gonna let him get away with it?"

"I didn't want to draw attention to myself."

Wayne finished reading the confession. He did not look happy. He slid it across to Diego. Diego merely placed his hand on it, and slid it to the other side of the table. Bubba picked it up and started reading it.

"I get that, but you let a man get away with it once, then they think they can do it again, and again, and again, and how would you feel in six years if it was your little sister?"

Her shoulders slumped and she stared down at the table. "I'd feel terrible that anybody got hurt because I didn't do something."

"Good, then remember in the future, it's not just about you, but it's about their next victim."

She nodded. "You're right. I'm sorry."

Bubba finished reading it, slid it back to the Sheriff and demanded, "So what's going to happen to shit head? Please tell me he's not just getting probation."

Diego frowned. "He's getting off a lot lighter than I would've liked, but for his cooperation and full confession he was offered a reduced sentence. The judge has agreed to let him off with thirty days in county lockup, which believe me, it's a cakewalk, it's not like San Quentin. It's practically a country club. And for his cooperation he doesn't even have to report until the Monday after Thanksgiving. He's on parole until then. He has to do a thousand hours of community service, then he has to attend two anger management classes, two drug rehab classes. Plus, the little creep admits to getting one of the girls he knows to make that prank phone call. Apparently he learned that you were working on the ranch and he thought it would be funny to cause trouble for his favorite person, namely Bubba. They hate each other by the way."

Bubba grumbled, "I absolutely hate it, but if it's best we're gonna get, then I guess I just have to deal."

Diego grumbled and nodded. "I feel the same way, but now that that's cleared up, let's discuss that missing person's report. It has been filed as an abduction, though local LEO's do not feel that way, but nevertheless, manpower is being wasted. I feel that the only appropriate thing to do is for me to contact the lead investigator and inform him that I have seen and spoken to the person in question. The person in question wishes their whereabouts to remain unknown, but to call off his dogs."

She was frantically shaking her head. "No, if that happens, she'll be here. I don't want her here."

Diego chuckled. "Oddly enough, I would love to run into her again. She wouldn't like it though. However, I cannot in good conscience allow people to continue to think that you have been abducted. I can put a stop to it, and I can make sure that the investigating officer does not inform her of your whereabouts. You are an adult. He has to respect that. The worst thing that he might do, which I don't think he's going to, is demand to talk to you on a video chat just to make sure you're okay, you're not being coerced or anything like that, but I don't think he's gonna do that because there's really no evidence suggesting you were kidnapped."

She rubbed her hands up and down her face, and sighed several times.

Wayne finally spoke. "All right, I can't contain my curiosity any longer. What the hell is going on? What is this other life that you keep hinting at? And I'm assuming 'the her' you keep referring to is Mommy Dearest, though she does not sound like a darling."

Lenore sighed several times. "Okay if I don't explain a few things to you, you're going to end up thinking I'm some spoiled rotten little bitch who couldn't put up with her charmed easy life any longer. I mean, come on, how hard is it, dancing and singing? Well, I will tell you this, it's a hell of a lot harder than it sounds, but I think in order for you to fully understand, you need the whole of the story, or at least the real guts of the matter, which I guess the problem really started coming to a head about three months ago …"

HELL

Monday, August 28

Lenore tried to focus, but she was finding it very difficult. Her irritation was at an all time high. She had just arrived back in LA yesterday after a six month domestic and international concert tour. She was actually looking forward to taking a few days off when she had been awoken at four o'clock this morning and told she had to get dressed and down to the lobby where a car was waiting to take her to the studio so she could get her makeup done to be ready by eight to start shooting a new music video. Why was she shooting another video, a video she did not want to be shooting? In fact, right now, the only thing she wanted to be shooting was her mother. And of course, as was usual, Jane – Lenore refused to think of her mother as Evanjalevn, she may be forced to call her that on occasion, but she certainly was not going to glorify her by thinking of her as that, and in reality she tried as much as possible to call Jane 'Mom' or 'Mommy'. It drove her right up the wall, she did not like people thinking she was old enough to have a grown daughter. Jane had yet to make an appearance. She was probably still snug in her bed. Jane did not like to rise before noon. Lindsay, the choreographer, approached. "Persephone, sweetie, do we need to rehearse this again? You seem a little confused about the steps."

She sighed and shook her head. "I'm not confused about them, I just don't like them. There's a difference."

"What don't you like about them? Maybe we can fix them ..." She snapped her fingers and did a little jiggle as she was talking, "... I mean if it's not hot enough for you, not sexy enough for you, we could do a different wardrobe. We can change your boots. What if we spritzed Davey down so he looks hotter and sweatier, would that do it for you? What can we do to make you happy?"

She said with annoyance, "Put a shirt on him. I mean, seriously, why do all my dancers have to be half naked steroid junkies? Can't we just once do something classy and elegant, and not like every other bimbo on a stage, doing nothing to set ourselves apart, and look just like the rest of them?"

Cam, the director, charged forward. "But sweetie, sex sells, and with your body we can sell a lot of sex! After all, we're all in this to make money, and half naked gorgeous guys make a lot of money, just like half naked blonde bombshells make a lot of money."

She said with annoyance, "I'm not really blonde."

Rita, her manager, surged forward. "Cam, I think we need to take, you know, like a thirty minute break. I think Persephone just needs to get a little peace, to sit down for a min and then she'll be back and good to go. Why don't you and Lindsay go look at those pages and see what you can do." She took Persephone by the arm and maneuvered her to her dressing room. She waited until they were behind closed doors before she said firmly, "Persephone, doll, I thought your mother and I had gone over this with you a thousand times. Whatever you do, don't admit to not being a real blonde. You want your fans to be guessing what your real hair color is? That's why we changed it six times in the past five years. We go with what's hot. We go with what's popular, and who really thinks Marilyn Monroe was a real blonde?"

Lenore dropped into her chair and started to rub her hands up and down her face.

Rita said quickly, "Don't! You will mess up your makeup."

Lenore took a deep breath. She desperately wanted to get up and wash her face and say she did not care, but she was too much of a coward. Instead she said, "You know, one of these days, Rita, you're gonna push me, and I'm going to say I quit. I just got back from a six month tour with you guys dragging me all over the place, and I said I wanted to take two weeks off, and yet here we are the next day, shooting a music video. Don't I have any say in my life?"

"Sweetie, you have to strike while the iron is hot. Right now you're popular, you could be unpopular tomorrow. So let's make you as much money as possible right now. You can take a break when you're not popular."

Lenore bit her tongue and counted to ten. She was not just tired. She was tired of all of this and she just wanted to walk away. She asked, "So I do this music video, and then I can take two weeks off?"

Rita laughed and started shaking her head. "No, no, no, we already have you booked into the recording studio to record that new album. I mean, what's the point in doing a music video for this song if fans can't buy this song?"

Lenore thought in her head over and over, *I quit. I quit. I quit.* Then she sighed with frustration several times, once again cowardice won and she said angrily, "Fine. Let's just get this over and done with." She got to her feet and headed back to the stage.

Lindsay surged forward and handed her the new pages. "Just a few minimum changes, and they really don't require you to do anything different."

Lenore flipped through them, then wadded them up and threw them on the floor. "No way! Absolutely not! We have been over this time and time again, my butt and my breasts are off limits, and if you think I'm kissing him, you're out of your mind!"

Lindsay rolled her eyes. "Sweetie, I understood that when you were sixteen, but you're seventeen, about to be eighteen. Get over it, it's part of the job."

Lenore smiled. "Fix it, or come the morning of October eleventh, you'll be looking for a job, because you're right. I will be eighteen then, and that means Mom will no longer be the one calling the shots, and I will decide who works with me, and who doesn't. Decide which list you want to be on!"

Lindsay blinked. "Man, somebody is extra bitchy this morning. Did she not get her wheatgrass this morning?"

Rita glared at Lindsay. "Not appropriate, we'll stick with the original routine."

Cam sighed then yelled, "Back to one, everybody, and we're going with the original routine."

Ten hours later, Lenore was exhausted and fed up. Despite her having begun firm this morning, she as usual had backed down, and backed down, and had now shot some scenes she really was not happy with. Why did she always do that? As soon as her mother got involved, she always found herself knuckling under. The only thing she never compromised on was where they could put their hands, and that she was not kissing them, and they had to keep their tongues to themselves. Unfortunately she was now in a different pair of boots, shorts that barely covered her butt, and a jewel encrusted bustier, all of which made her feel like she was dancing around in her underwear. She sighed several times, then consoled herself with the knowledge that she just probably had one more day of shooting. It was rare for a video to take longer than two days, then she could put this whole nightmare behind her. Lindsay approached. She groaned. "What now?"

"Cam wants to try shooting the stair scene a little differently. He wants you to run up the stairs, when you hit your mark, he wants you to be standing on your right leg. He wants your left leg bent in front of you just a little. He wants you to toss your hair over your left shoulder and look back at the camera as you reach for Davey, then Davey is gonna grab you. You're going to lean back for just a moment, and then he's going to yank you into his arms."

Lenore wanted to say no, but she knew if she said no, her mother would be up here and then they would be discussing it; which would mean she would be browbeaten into doing it anyways, so she might as well just save time and go ahead and agree. Could she fire her mother? She would have to think about that. She sighed as the makeup girl powdered and primped her.

Cam yelled, "Places everyone!" She went and stood on her mark. Then he yelled, "Action!"

She charged up the stairs as directed, however, not like directed, when she reached out, Davey made the grab too late. She was already moving to toss her hair over her shoulder. She lost her balance and fell backwards down the steps. She hit them hard, then rolled, slid, and landed at the bottom. Marty, one of the lighting guys, appeared over her immediately. "Persephone, are you okay?"

JC, her head bodyguard appeared a moment later. "Hey, girl, do we need to call an ambulance?"

She groaned and pushed herself to a sitting position. "No, I think everything's intact."

Cam yelled, "Where's Doctor Todd? Isn't he supposed to be here?"

A minute later she heard Todd saying, "Excuse me, let me through." He appeared at her side a moment later and knelt down. "Well, Persephone, that was very graceful of you. Where do you hurt?"

"Graceful of me? He missed the grab and you're blaming me?"

Todd replied calmly, "I was not trying to establish blame, I was merely saying that I thought you were more graceful than that."

"Well, excuse me, Doctor, but it's a little difficult to be graceful standing on one leg, leaning backwards with your head over your shoulder. You try it sometime. I would love to watch you fall down the stairs."

Todd stood up and indicated her as he said, "Gentlemen, why don't you help her to her feet? Clearly she's not in that much pain. Let's take her over to a chair where I can examine her properly."

Marty and JC each gripped an arm and carefully helped her to her feet, then they escorted her over to a chair. She said, "Oww, oww, oww. I think I sprained my ankle, and my bad knee is really hurting."

Todd nodded. "Let's go ahead and get the boots off."

She tried to remove them herself, but found she just could not manage it. It required twisting her body in a position it really did not want to twist right now. Debbie from wardrobe came over and took her boots off for her. Todd dropped down on one knee and began examining her ankle and knee. She had to grip the arms of the chair not to scream in pain, then he worked his way up to her hips, finally her arms, neck, and spine.

Jane finally appeared and demanded, "Is she going to be able to go back to shooting or should we go ahead and dismiss everybody?"

He hesitated a moment. "I don't think there's any way she's going to be able to continue today. However, I think if we ice everything down, pump her full of anti-inflammatories and painkillers and keep her off her feet and still for the rest of the day, I think she'll be able to return to shooting tomorrow. She'll be in a lot of pain, but we can manage that with more painkillers. There may be a need for some additional makeup, she's going to have some scrapes on her arms, back, and I think there's going to be a nasty bruise here on the side of her thigh, but I'm sure makeup can handle all that."

Jane sighed. She turned to Cam. "Will we be able to get it finished tomorrow?"

He shrugged his shoulders. "Hard to say. We were pretty slow today. I was already concerned we weren't going to make it tomorrow, but if she's going to be injured, she's probably going to be moving slower and she's just going to slow us down even more than she already did today. A lot's just going to depend on how cooperative she chooses to be tomorrow."

"All right. Well, I guess we had better just go ahead and plan on it taking three days to shoot this video. Todd, can she walk to the car and then into the building and up to her penthouse, or should we just carry her?"

"It would probably be better if JC just carried her."

She sighed with annoyance. "JC, Todd, why don't the two of you go ahead and take her back to the penthouse. We'll wrap up here and see all of you later."

JC bent down and scooped her up in his arms. "Hold tight, Miss P."

She wrapped her arms around his neck. He was the one man she did not feel every time he touched her, he was just trying to cop a feel. He carried her out to her car, and then he carried her into the hotel and up to her penthouse, all through backdoors, of course, avoiding the press. Fortunately, there were none to be had today. JC carried her into her room and set her on her bed. He asked, "Which pajamas?"

She shivered, just thinking about all the ice. "The purple flannels, with the purple long sleeved T-shirt."

He smiled. "Let me guess, and the purple socks."

She laughed and picked up her pillow and threw it at him. "Got a problem with that?"

It landed about two feet from him. He looked down at it and smiled before he finished retrieving her clothes, then picked up the pillow, and brought it back. He set it where it belonged and set the pajamas down on the bed next to her. "No, but I do have a major problem with the way you let them push you around. Girl, when you gonna learn you're the one who pays the bills around here. They're all just a bunch of has-beens trying to ride on your coattails. Put your foot down. Do things the way you want to do them."

She shrugged her shoulders and groaned. "I know, I know, but I don't have a say in the matter, not yet."

He sighed and shrugged his shoulders. "No, you don't have a say because you always back down. If you would've stood up from the beginning, you'd be in control, not Mommy, but I know, your day is coming, and you need to start standing firm now, or nothing's ever going to change."

"I know. I know."

"If you need anything, I'll be just outside. You want to hide in your room, or do you want to go somewhere else after you've changed?"

"I was thinking I want to go downstairs to the media room and watch a movie or two, but I can walk. I don't need you to carry me."

He reached down and grabbed her calf and gently lifted her leg. "Have you seen the size of this ankle yet?"

She winced. It was black and blue and appeared to have doubled in size. Her knee also was quite swollen. "Oh, damn. That looks bad, and I'm supposed to put a boot on that tomorrow. That's not gonna happen."

He snorted. "Yeah, that's what you say now. And come tomorrow morning you will be crammin' that foot into a boot because you will back down."

She sighed and her shoulders slumped. She knew it was true. "You're right." He left the room and she changed into her jammies. She barely made it to the bathroom to wash her face. Every step was agonizing. She tried to walk to the door, but she had not made it very far before she gave up and yelled, "JC!"

He came in shaking his head. He walked up and poked her in the side of the head. "Stubborn, the only times you ever choose to be stubborn is when it's stupid." He picked her up in his arms and carried her down to the couch. Todd was waiting with a bucket full of ice bags. He proceeded to pack them all around her, then he started pouring pills into her. She spent the rest of the night swallowing pills on demand and having ice packed onto her twenty minutes on, thirty minutes off, twenty minutes on, thirty minutes off, even when she was trying to sleep. Somewhere around three AM she decided she could not take it any longer. She eased out of bed and walked slowly to her mother's room, her night bodyguard, Bobby, following behind her. Expecting to find her mother asleep, she opened the door to her room without knocking. Her eyes widened and she stared in horror as she saw her mother on all fours in the middle of the bed wearing one of Persephone's costumes with Davey, the annoying dancer from earlier, on his knees behind her holding her by the hips. Clearly they were in the middle of some sick, twisted, sex scene. Lenore shouted with annoyance, "Oh, you have got to be kidding me!" She slammed the door and stormed back to her room. She sat down on her bed and put her hands over her eyes. She said, "I feel like I need brain bleach."

Bobby replied, "That makes two of us. I could have gone an entire lifetime without ever seeing your mother dressed like that. Even though your mother does have a great body, it's still just ... eww."

She could not help it, she started laughing, then looked up at him. "That explains why I have that particular incompetent idiot dancer. How long do you think he's been screwing my mother to get jobs?"

"Given the fact that your mother changes men like she changes underwear, probably only a couple times. They probably met when she was doing the casting the other day for the dancers, and she's probably just screwed him a couple of times since then."

Her bedroom door opened. She immediately put her hands over her eyes. She addressed her remark to Bobby. "Please tell me she has a robe on?"

"She doesn't, but at least she has her pants on, or your pants."

She opened her eyes, reached up and slapped him. He started laughing.

Jane said with annoyance, "Bobby, get the hell out." He nodded and exited the room. "That, young lady, should teach you to knock before you walk into somebody's private bedroom."

"I thought bedrooms were always private. Does that mean you have a public bedroom?"

Jane glared at her daughter. "Don't be sassy. You're the one who walked in on me. You're the one who should be apologizing, and what are you doing out of bed at three o'clock in the morning? You're supposed to be resting."

"And that's exactly what I was coming to discuss with you. I am not shooting a music video today. I'm going to stay in bed and I'm going to rest. I hurt all over. I don't want to be dancing, and I'm sure as hell not going to be dancing with the guy you were just screwing, in my costume by the way. And while we're on the subject of that costume, I will never wear it or anything like it again, and let's not even discuss the sick twisted meaning of you screwing someone half your age in one of your daughter's costumes. Can I just say, eww?"

Jane snapped with annoyance. "You will be at makeup at six o'clock in the morning. You will continue shooting this video because you are not going to be holding us up any more than we have to because it costs a fortune every minute you delay, and we cannot reshoot. So you are going to continue to shoot with Davey, so just get used to it!"

Lenore started shaking her head. "No, no, no, no! I will not! I will not work with that man! I will not continue to shoot this video, right now. I will not, you cannot make me. I'm taking a sleeping pill. I am going to bed and I'm going to sleep until noon, and if you try to get me down to make up, I'll lay on the stage floor and sleep, and when I decide we're going to reshoot this video, Davey will not be involved in it, and I will not work with any guy you're sleeping with ever again! So get used to it! If you want me to work with somebody, you better not be screwing them! Now get out of my room!"

Jane turned red in the face and slapped her daughter. "Don't you argue with me! I made you! I made you famous! I made you rich! I made everything around you happen and the only reason it happened is because you did what I told you to do! If you want to keep all of this, you better keep doing what I tell you to do, and if I tell you you're shooting in the morning, you're shooting in the morning! If I tell you you're shooting with Davey, you're shooting with Davey!"

Lenore had her hand to her burning cheek. She reached over and calmly picked up the bottle of sleeping pills. She unscrewed it, poured two into her hand, and popped them in her mouth and swallowed them. She pulled back the covers, crawled into bed, and turned her back to her mother.

Jane screamed in frustration, "Don't you dare turn your back on me! Listen to me!" After a long minute Jane stormed out, slamming the door behind her.

*****

Friday, September 1

Lenore was sitting in the media room having her yogurt for breakfast. For the first time in her life, she had stuck to her guns and refused to go back to shooting the video. They had tried all day Wednesday to persuade her, she had not yielded. By Thursday morning, they had given up and decided if she would not shoot the video, at least they could get her in the recording studio. So she had spent all day yesterday in the recording studio and she was supposed to be there at eight o'clock this morning, but recording was vastly superior to shooting. Katie, her press agent, came bursting in, laptop in hand. She looked horrified. "Oh this is bad! This is bad! This is really, really bad!"

Lenore raised an eyebrow. "I guess it's bad."

JC started snickering and added. "Really, really bad."

Katie glared at him. "This is not funny, this is bad."

Lenore smiled. "How bad is it?"

Katie sat down next to Lenore on the sofa. She shifted the laptop. JC leaned over her shoulder. He whistled. "Oh shit, that's bad."

Lenore put her hands to her cheeks. She was staring at a naked picture of herself sitting on her bed. "Where did they get that?"

Katie shrugged her shoulders. "I don't know. There's no security cameras in your bedroom or your bathroom, and yet they have photos of you walking around your room wrapped in a towel, walking around your room drying off without a towel on, and lying naked on your bed, and showering, and I wish I could say that that was the worst of it, but it's not." She clicked over to another tab and pressed play.

Lenore put her hands over her mouth as she watched a scene from the video that she had shot on Monday, but it had been severely altered. In the original video that she had filmed, she was standing a little to the side of a baby grand, tapping her foot, with her elbows resting on the baby grand, looking to her left, staring at the camera while singing. In the original video, Davey had been standing behind her, holding her waist, trying to get her attention, but it was like he did not exist. Finally in his frustration he had grabbed a handful of her hair and forced her to look at him. In the altered video, Davey grabbed a handful of her hair and forced her to look away from the camera then he dropped his pants, and gripped the woman's hip and adjusted her while he started getting it on. Only for the first few seconds where she was looking at the camera was it actually her, and Davey had even blown one take where he had made her look the other direction, but for the rest of the vile sex scene it was another woman, and they never showed her face again. Lenore stared at it dumbstruck. At the end of the awful seven minute long video, Davey stepped back and pushed her skirt down, then started pulling up his pants. It cut back to the real footage of her, where she had stretched out her arms across the baby grand, leaned forward and pressed her cheek into it, but whoever had edited had been an expert. It was so seamlessly done you could not tell where one woman changed to the other. The only reason she knew was because she knew what she had done. She started shaking her head. "No-no-no-no-no-no-no! How did they get that footage? That footage was done by the actual cameras! That that wasn't somebody's cell phone recording, and they had to have access to the stage to do that! And my bedroom and bathroom, how do they have access to my bedroom? I mean, this is a secure penthouse! This hotel offers state of the art security!" She sniffed several times and tears started down her cheeks as she realized the answer. There were only two ways they could have gotten a hold of this and gotten into her room. She wanted to scream. She wanted to tell Katie to get it down, but she knew from past experience, once it was out there, there was no stopping it. It would just spread like wildfire. She got to her feet and slowly walked to her mother's bedroom. She knocked on the door.

Jane called, "Go away, I'm sleeping."

Lenore walked in. "Why did you do it, Mother? It could only have been you or Rita, and Rita would never do anything like that, unless of course, it was on your orders. So any way you look at it, you were involved! Why did you do it? And don't pretend like you don't know what I'm talking about!"

Jane sat up and rubbed her face. "Oh, that. Well, since you weren't going to develop a bad girl reputation on your own, I thought I'd help you out. Don't worry, sweetie, it's only going to make record sales skyrocket, and the next big scandal will sweep it under the rug."

"No, it won't! Every time my name pops up, that's the first thing the media is going to run! It will forever be out there! It will always be popping up!"

Jane laughed. "You're crying like a baby. It's nothing, Persephone. It goes with the business, get used to it. I bet you your record sales go up by ten percent today."

"All you care about, Mom, is the money. That's all you ever cared about. You don't care what it does to me, you don't care what it does to anybody else." Not waiting for a reply, she turned and walked out. She spent the rest of the day locked in her bedroom, watching the news, checking her laptop. The hits just kept on coming. Now three of her former dancers had all given interviews about their flings with the rock star Persephone. The things they said, they made her sound like a nymphomaniac who could not get enough.

Finally she could not take it any longer. She went into the bathroom and chose a bottle at random. She knew anyone of them would get the job done.

ESCAPING HELL

Saturday, September 2

Lenore groaned and rolled on her side. She blinked and looked around. She was in some kind of hotsy totsy hospital room. JC was standing to the back, looking furious. He moved forward. "What the hell were you thinking?"

She groaned, grabbed the pillow, and put it on top of her head. "I'm not in the mood for a lecture right now."

He yanked the pillow off her head. "In the mood or not, you need it. What were you thinking? You're just damn lucky it was the bottle of sleeping pills! Had I come in ten minutes later, you would be dead!"

"Since that was the entire plan, you'll forgive me if I don't thank you."

He shook his head. "Why are you letting them get to you? If you're this miserable, just walk away. You don't have to do this. You don't have to be her meal ticket. Let her take care of herself for a while. It might be a rude awakening. You are smart, funny, successful, and sweet. You will bloom where ever you land. She is a weed that sucks the life out of everything around her."

She rolled onto her back and stared up at him. "If you hate my mother so much, why do you work for her?"

"I do not work for her. I work for you, and I'm one of the only people around here she can't just fire. I still have three years left on a four year contract. She can't fire me without probable cause, and fortunately for you, stupid little girls trying to end their life by swallowing a handful of pills doesn't count. Because believe me, right now there's nothing she would like better than to fire me."

"Now you're contradicting yourself. You just said I was smart, and now you're calling me stupid. Which is it?"

"You're right, my mistake. Lonely, miserable, little girls who do stupid things don't count. You're just lucky you didn't do any permanent damage to your body."

She groaned and stared up at the ceiling. "I'm glad she can't get rid of you. Life would be even worse without you."

He chuckled and reached over and rubbed her cheek. "Yeah, I know. You're like the bratty little white sister I never wanted, but I'm kind of glad I have her anyways." He tilted her chin up and shifted her head from side to side.

She tried to push his hand away. "What are you doing?"

"You know, sometimes the light hits you just right and I always think about something my granddaddy used to say, 'That one there, you can look at them and tell there's little mix in the batter.'"

She pushed herself up on her elbows. "What?"

He laughed. "That was my granddaddy's way of saying that somebody wasn't pure something, pure white, pure Asian, pure black. A little mix in the batter. I just can't for the life of me figure out what it is in you. It's not black, at least I don't think so, unless we're talking your daddy was like a quarter."

She pushed herself to a sitting position and examined her hands and arms. She had never thought of it, but he was right. She did have an unusual tint to her skin. Covered in makeup and under stage lights, she looked white, but in normal lighting, without makeup, there was something else going on. "What do you think it is?"

He shrugged his shoulders. "No idea, except like I said, I don't think it's black. I mean, look at me. Both my parents are half white, half black, and I'm darker than either one of them, and then you look at my sister, and even though we got the exact same parents, she's so pale she could almost pass for white but once you really look at her, you notice there's a little mix in the batter."

She leaned back against the pillows. "I feel like crap."

"Well, swallowing a bottle of sleeping pills will do that to you."

She looked around the room again. "What is this? Rehab? Am I going to spend like thirty days here getting in touch with my inner selfness?"

He snorted. "Oh, please. Do you think your mother would let them take you to a rehab center? No, you were taken to a private hospital where stars can come and relax and rejuvenate themselves, which is code for detox off the radar, and get back to work before they should be. The Doctor said that you could leave twelve hours after you woke up. They just want to make sure that all your organs are functioning properly, then you're back to the grind."

She groaned. "Which means I'm back to the recording studio with a long lecture about delays. Is today Saturday?"

He looked at his watch. "For about eight more miserable hours."

"I'm stuck here for twelve hours."

"That's what the doctor said."

She sat there thinking. She hated this world and everything about it, but if she tried to walk away and live a quiet life, at least for a while, nobody would leave her alone, but if she could disappear quietly, and stay hidden, after a year or so nobody would give a crap about her. She sat up and adjusted the pillows, then leaned back against them. How could she get from where she was, to nobody giving a crap about her? It was going to take careful planning and a little patience. She compiled a mental to do list.

1. ID for Lenore Stevens

2. Talk to my lawyer / get control of my money

3. Compile some cash

4. Get out of the penthouse without anybody seeing me

5. Get to a thrift store / get old crummy clothes / buy cheap sneakers

6. Bus station / first available bus out of town

7. Change bus / go farther afield

8. Get a hotel room

9. Pawn some jewelry

10. Go to store / get hair dye / buy new clothes

She went over the list carefully in her mind, making sure she had not forgotten anything. The hardest part was going to be getting the ID. She could not have it sent to the penthouse. Her mother would find out about it. She would have to get a PO Box. She re-evaluated her to do list and created a new number one, pushing everything back. Then she went over it again and again. There was no way she was going to be able to do this without JC's help, but it was best if he did not know what she was up to. She looked around, then she asked softly, "JC, the next time I have a little free time to do what I want, would you help me do something without telling anybody?"

He frowned. "That depends, what am I helping you with?"

"I want to get an ID in my real name."

He nodded. "Probably a good idea. I will help you with that, but what are you using for an address?"

"I can't use the penthouse, and they're going to want proof of address, aren't they?"

He nodded and considered. He pulled out his phone and typed away for a minute. "You don't have any credit cards, so there's no way we can get you to do a utility bill. You don't own any property, so we can't do that. Everything is printed in your mother's name, so we can't use that. Only leaves an employer pay stub."

She supplied, "And we can't do that, great."

He shook his finger at her. "Not so quickly. I have a friend. He kind of owes me and he works for a payroll company. I can have him work me up a fake paystub, using my address and your name. They don't verify the employment, so it's basically just for show as long as it looks real, and he can use a legit company too. No one will ever know. Nobody in the company will ever know, because they're not actually being billed for your employment. Nobody at DMV will ever know, because it's a real company."

"Couldn't he get in trouble if he gets caught?"

He shook his head. "There's no reason for him to get caught. He works one up, he emails it to me, I print it off, delete it, he deletes it on his end, we use it, we shred it. Nobody ever knew it existed, then your ID will be sent to my apartment. When I get it, I slip it to you. Nobody even knows it exists."

She nodded. "Thank you."

"Anytime, baby girl." She sat there reevaluating her mental checklist.

*****

Wednesday, October 11

Lenore entered her lawyer's office. The secretary got to her feet. "Good morning, Miss Persephone. How are you doing today?"

"It's a wonderful day. I believe I have an eight thirty with Mr. Sanderson."

"Yes, ma'am, he's waiting for you. Please go on in. Would you like me to bring you some coffee, tea, soda, anything to eat?"

Lenore smiled and shook her head. "No thanks, I'm good, but JC might want something." She gestured to a chair. "JC, why don't you take a load off."

He sat down and picked up a magazine. He smiled at the secretary. "Coffee would be great."

"Of course, sir, right away."

Lenore went into her lawyer's office. Hector got to his feet. "Good morning, Persephone. You look beautiful today. What can I do for you?"

She shook hands with him and they both sat down. "Well, I just want to make sure of a few things. You are my lawyer, right?"

He nodded. "Yes, ma'am."

"Do you work for me, or do you work for my mother?"

"As of today, I work for you. When you came into your money, you became my client."

"So anything I tell you is attorney-client privilege, correct, and you cannot repeat it?"

He smiled, hoping desperately he knew where this was going. He could not stand Jane or the way she used her daughter's money. "Correct."

"Good. So as I understand it, effective this morning, I now actually control my estate, so I thought we should have a conversation about that."

He nodded. "Absolutely. As you know, our firm has been handling your investments, your finances, paying your bills, all of that for the past three years, since your mother asked us to take over that. Your wealth has continued to grow, and of course, you have continued to earn more money. What do you want us to do with it? Do you want us to continue as we are? Do you want us to change how we are doing things?"

"Well, to begin with, I would like to make sure that all of my money and all of my investments are in my name, and in my name alone."

"Of course, I totally understand your concern, but under the laws that have been established to protect underage performers such as yourself, your mother only receives an operating allowance for your care and education. She can, of course, always request additional funds for additional needs, but now that you're eighteen, she will no longer be able to do that. In fact, really, as of November first, she won't even be receiving an allowance anymore because you have become of age. She still received her monthly allowance on October first, because you were not of age yet. It's one of those gaps in the system. Hopefully, you don't feel that we have allowed your mother to mismanage your funds?"

She shook her head. "No, I just wanted to make sure going forward that I actually control my life."

"Absolutely, and if you would like to have a more hands-on approach with your investments, please tell us what you need from us. We are very encouraging of our clients' full input."

She shook her head. "No, you have all been doing wonderfully with my investments so far. I have no interest in altering that whatsoever; however, I do feel that my mother is owed something for everything she has done to help me get this far. Since you've been paying all the bills, what is required for her to have a residence and living expenses?"

He shrugged his shoulders. "That depends largely on the type of residence we're discussing. I mean, she could have a very, very nice apartment for three or four thousand dollars a month. I guess a little has to do with ... forgive me for putting it this way, but I guess a lot has to do with the lifestyle you wish your mother to live going forward."

"As of right now, if nothing were to change, what are her monthly expenditures for housing, food, car?"

He sighed. "Right now, I would say your mother's operating expenses for food and lodging are extravagant, and on average, she's spending about a hundred and twenty thousand dollars a month. That penthouse suite that you are living in is not cheap."

She smiled and nodded. She could tell from his attitude he did not like her mother. "I know this sounds a little bit cowardly, but I don't want to deal with my mother, so I would like you to create an account for my mother in her name and her name alone, that your firm will deposit on the first of November, one hundred thousand dollars. Along with that deposit, I would like you to send a letter to my mother notifying her that that's all she gets for the month, and that she has officially been put on notice. I would like you in this letter to lay out that come the first of December, she will only receive fifty thousand dollars, and come the first of January and every month after that for the year of twenty eighteen, she will receive ten thousand dollars, and on the first of January twenty nineteen she will never receive another penny from me."

Hector was quite surprised by his own feelings. He desperately wanted to stand up and cheer. "I will, of course, have to draw up some papers that I will need you to sign. These will take a few days, and since I don't have the authority to act on behalf of your mother, but I do have the ability to act on your behalf, what I would suggest is the current joint account that you and your mother hold, which is the account we have been using for your living expenses, I suggest we remove your name from that account and then leave that account as the account she has access to funds. That way she doesn't have to change any auto pay she already has set up."

"Sounds like a plan. You let me know when you need me to come back and sign those papers and I will be glad to do it."

He nodded. "Of course, and if it is inconvenient for you to come into the office, I can always have one of my paralegals come to you, and if you don't want your mother to know, all she has to know is that it's papers you have to sign as a result of turning eighteen, which we will have other papers you do have to sign. There's no reason for her to be suspicious about it."

She smiled. "Sounds like a plan. However, there are a few employees that I would like to continue to be paid in accordance with their contracts."

He picked up a pen and paper. "Of course, their names?"

"I'm not sure of their last names, but my bodyguards, JC, Bobby, Sonny and Mickey. All of my other employees, I believe the contracts I have with them have expired, or are about to expire, apparently something to do with my eighteenth birthday. I couldn't have contracts that went over it by too much because of my age, because they were contracts my mother had to sign, I don't understand. I'm sure you understand. And I don't understand why the bodyguard's contracts are different."

He nodded. "Yes, that is correct, your bodyguards were employed by us on your behalf; however, everyone else was hired by your mother, and you don't want to renew any of those contracts?"

"No, and it shouldn't come as a surprise to any of them."

"Very good. I'm assuming you don't want me to use your mother as a go through, so may I have your cell phone number?"

She dug in her pocket and pulled out a piece of paper. "I actually don't carry a cell phone, however, this is my head bodyguard, JC's number. You can call him and get me."

"Excellent, is there anything else you would like to discuss?"

She got to her feet and extended her hand. "No, I think that covers everything."

"Well, I actually do have one thing I would like to discuss with you, ma'am. You do not have a will. If you were to die tomorrow, your mother would get everything."

She sat back down. "Oh, no. How long would it take to fix that?"

"That depends on how complicated your will is. We could draw up a temporary will in about half an hour, but you really should have something more permanent, especially given your vast wealth."

"Well, let's go ahead and get a temporary, accidents happen." She sat there for a minute struggling, trying to decide what to do with her money. "You know, when I was a kid, I would've starved to death if it wouldn't have been for the local food bank. I think that's what I want done with the money. I want to divide it up over food banks, but somebody has to oversee that, right?"

"Yes, ma'am, and considering the amount of money we're talking about, I would recommend at least two executors to make sure that there is no embezzling. Three is usually better."

"All right, for now why don't we make JC an executor, and you. I want my three bodyguards to get one million dollars each and then one percent of the royalties for their lifetime, and I want everything else to be divided up amongst the United States food banks. It's too much money to give to any one food bank."

He nodded. "I couldn't agree more. If you give me about half an hour, I'll get this all written up and we'll have something you can sign before you leave the office. I do have to go find out what your bodyguard's real name is."

*****

Tuesday, October 24

Lenore told herself it was now or never. If she waited any longer, her mother was going to be receiving the letter from Mr. Sanderson. She had everything taken care of, all of her legal ducks were in a row, she had a small stash of cash, she had managed to print off a map that told her where the nearest bus stop was, what buses to take to get to the bus station, where a thrift store was along the way, and right next to the thrift store was a cheap shoe store. Her mother was out on a date tonight. It really had reached zero hour. So the last thing she had to do was get rid of JC for ten minutes. She hesitated, mulling over all of her options, then she nodded. She grabbed her backpack and began throwing things in it, her jewelry box, pills, MP3 player, headphones. She put on socks, jeans, and a T-shirt, then she set her backpack on the other side of the bed where there was no chance JC would see it. She opened her bedroom door. He smiled at her. "Dude, I'm dying for a real cup of coffee, but I just don't feel like seeing anybody. Would you run down to the lobby and get me the biggest decaf French Vanilla ice coffee they sell?"

He smiled. "Soymilk?"

She wrinkled her nose. "Not today. Tyler can drop dead. I want real milk and then I think I am going to sit on the couch and watch a movie, so would you bring it to me in the media room?"

"Sure thing, girl, but don't leave the penthouse while I'm gone. I'll lock you in."

"Do I ever go anywhere without you?"

"No, but there's a first time for everything."

She waited until she heard the door close and lock, then she grabbed her backpack, sneakers, and headed for the media room. She opened the coat closet. There was always a bunch of random abandoned coats lying around. She found a thick black hoodie, pulled it on and zipped it up. She inhaled and coughed, whoever had worn it was a

heavy smoker, she pulled a letter out of her back pocket and stuck it on the coffee table. All that was written on the envelope was 'JC'. She looked around, convinced she had forgotten something. Seeing a bag of trail mix on the coffee table, she grabbed it and threw it in her backpack, then she exited the penthouse through the servants' entrance. Fortunately, being a famous star, she had entered this way so many times she knew how to get to the freight elevator and how to take it to the basement where the loading dock and the dumpsters were. Arriving, she pulled the hoodie down low, slung her backpack over her shoulder, stuck her hands in her pockets, and headed out the loading dock doors. No one noticed her. No one spoke to her. She headed for the street, keeping her head down. She arrived at the bus stop and got on the first bus. As luck would have it, it went right past the thrift store. She got off the bus at the little strip center and, went into the thrift store and quickly selected a pair of jeans and a man's shirt. She also decided she could not take the smell of this hoodie. She found a different one, purchased them without trying them on and then went next door to the shoe store. She found a pair of inexpensive sneakers, tried them on and then paid for them without taking them off. She left before the clerk realized she had also left her eight hundred dollar pair of Jordan's behind.
Fortunately, as she was approaching the bus stop, so was a bus. She checked her map. Hallelujah, her stars were aligning. It was a bus that would take her straight to the bus station.

She could scarcely sit still for the thirty-five minutes to the bus station, but as soon as she arrived she got off and hurried to the ticket counter. When a grumpy man yelled, "Next," she surged forward.

Fortunately, her ten minutes in line had given her time to peruse the board. There was a bus leaving for San Diego, California in twenty minutes. "One ticket for the bus to San Diego leaving in twenty minutes."

"Twenty-two dollars and some ID."

She handed over the money and her ID. He typed away and then she heard the printer a moment later. He handed over her ticket and her ID. "Have a nice trip, ma'am."

"Thank you, sir, I intend to." She went and sat down, removing the smelly hoodie. She laid it over the back of the chair next to her. When she got up, she conveniently forgot it, then she boarded her bus. When she arrived in San Diego three hours later, she went straight to the ladies' room. She changed into her thrift store clothes. When she came out of the stall, she wrapped her designer jeans around her T-shirt and left them on the counter, label up. She washed her face, then dried her hands and face. She went to the ticket counter and examined it. There was a bus leaving for Phoenix, Arizona in ten minutes. She quickly bought a ticket and ran for the platform. She barely made it. She sat down and sighed with relief. She had done it. She had gotten away. She was free.

XVIII

Thursday, November 16

Lenore sniffed, shrugged her shoulders, and held her hands up. "Well, there you go. Now you know what the rest of the world knows about me, or at least what they believe about me, which I guess is the stereotypical rocker who drinks, does drugs, sleeps with her dancers, and has wild parties." She sniffed several more times, then tears slid down her cheeks. She wiped them away.

Wayne stared. He could not even begin to imagine what it must been like to have a mother like that.

Diego was struggling to come to terms with everything he had just heard. His mind was running down two different tracks. One of them, the Dad, could not seem to stop thinking about the fact that his daughter was made so utterly miserable in her life by her mother that she believed the only way she was ever going to be free was to swallow a bottle of sleeping pills. Fortunately, his cop's mind was far more productive. It was dashing over laws, trying to figure out a way to at least repair some of the damage. Her press agent was right, those images would be out there forever. There was really nothing they could do to stop it. They could reduce it, but not stop it, and probably everything that could be done in terms of reducing had already been done, but he had some very interesting ideas on dealing with her public image. He could not and would not allow people to think that she was a tramp.

Bubba glanced from his father's stunned face to the Sheriff's contemplative one. He had no idea what was going on in the Sheriff's mind, but something told him somebody somewhere was going to end up paying for it. He decided it was best to let the Sheriff sort it out. He would probably like the results, but Lenore started crying. She buried her face in her hands. He got up and moved to her side. He pulled out the chair next to her, turned it sideways and sat down. He reached down and gripped the legs of her chair and pulled her towards him. He reached up and squeezed her shoulder. To his surprise, she leaned towards him just a little. He wrapped his arms around her and pulled her into his embrace. She buried her face against his chest and sobbed uncontrollably. He rubbed his hand up and down her back. "It's okay, girl, it will be all right."

She shook her head. "No, it won't. Everybody thinks I'm a whore. I mean, this is not like those films where you can tell that one of the people had no idea they were being recorded. I was actually looking right at the camera. I winked at the camera, and he was obviously playing to it. I mean, come on, if you came across that, wouldn't you think it was just some horrible porn film? I mean, it's not even cheap quality, it's not even grainy. I mean, this was professional equipment. Equipment I had rented on my video stage." She pulled free and tried to wipe her eyes. Bubba reached over, picked up a napkin, and handed it to her. She wiped her eyes and blew her nose. "I know I need to just let it go. I know the truth. What does it matter what, you know, fifty million people think?"

Bubba opened his mouth to reply, but Wayne got there first. "Oh, hell no! Perception matters, and I mean I'm sure that you released all kinds of statements saying that it wasn't you, but it's your word against their word, and you probably only played right into their hands and there's nothing you can do about that. What they did was wrong on so many levels, and you have every right to be hurt, angry, and devastated. Frankly, in my opinion, this has to be one of the ultimate betrayals. I mean, that woman fully admitted to being involved in it. I refuse to ever call her your mother, and I, for one, do not blame you a bit for walking away. I just hope you have found a little bit of peace and happiness here. I mean, you've seemed pretty happy lately. Well, until the other day." He hesitated a long minute. "And while we're clearing the air, I'm really hoping our little conversation didn't have anything to do with ... that."

Bubba and Diego both looked at him and demanded, "What conversation?"

She sniffed again. "Nothing, it was just between Mr. Cartwright and myself, not important, and if it impacted my decision to flush all the pills down the drain, in my opinion it was a good thing. I was never going to get off them easing myself off of them. It wasn't working. I had become too dependent on them, like a crutch, and yes, Mr. Cartwright, I like it here and I hope you'll let me stay. I know I've been a bit of trouble lately, but I promise I will make up for it. I know I probably cost you and Bubba both a lot of work, and I will pay you back, make it up to you, whatever. I'm sure some of the other guys probably have had to work extra hours because of me. I will make it up to all of you."

Wayne snorted. "Stop it. You don't have to make anything up to anybody. First off, as far as anybody else knows, you were sick, and it's the truth. Only myself, Bubba, and Alejandro know the truth about your illness, and I'd like to keep it that way. It's none of anybody else's business, and all the work got done. There's nothing to make up, nothing for you to feel guilty about, but if we're having an open and honest discussion, Diego, and especially Bubba, deserve to know. I commented on the fact that Lenore was wearing your clothes, Bubba."

Diego shifted his attention from his daughter to Bubba and narrowed his eyes, and said, "Oh, really."

Bubba glared at him. "Don't you start. There's nothing for you to go 'Oh, really' about. They're from middle school. Does she look like she could wear my clothes? They're outgrowns from the attic."

Diego looked at him dubiously, but decided to shift tacks. He looked at Wayne and asked, "And why would you think discussing the fact that she was wearing Bubba's outgrowns, because you would know that they were outgrowns, upset her?"

"It wasn't exactly the outgrowns we were discussing, it was more of whether she and Bubba were keeping time."

Diego shifted his chair, crossed his arms over his chest and said, "That must have been some conversation, because you are tap dancing all around the point."

She sighed and stared up at the ceiling. "Oh, for heaven sakes! For some reason he doesn't want to tell you that I told him not to worry, Bubba was just my boss. I didn't want to be involved with him or anybody, because I don't ever want to have a family. Because he told you his whole side of the conversation, so clearly it's my response he doesn't want you to know, though for the life of me I can't understand why." She shut her mouth. Clearly Mr. Cartwright had known something she did not, because the Sheriff looked furious and Bubba sighed, pursed his lips together, and shrugged his shoulders. She looked from one face to another, then shrugged her shoulders and demanded, "What did I say?"

Diego tried to force a smile. He reminded himself she was only eighteen years old. She had plenty of time to change her mind fifty times over. He said, "Wayne's just worried because he knows I come from a very large Hispanic Irish Catholic family. To me, family is everything."

She sighed and stared up at the ceiling. "Well, sorry to disappoint you, but I'm an atheist, liberal, and until tonight vegetarian, and tomorrow I'll probably go back to it. So clearly our lives don't mix. It was nice to meet you, Sheriff. I'm sure we'll see each other around. You have your nice orderly life, and right now I have my little bit of peace and quiet here, until, you know, somebody figures out who I am. I'd like to enjoy it, but when somebody figures out who I am, any association you have with me is only going to give you and your family no end of trouble. So it's late, I have to be up early. Good night." She got her to her feet and picked up her dishes and headed for the kitchen.

Wayne opened his mouth. Diego reached over and squeezed his shoulder and shook his head. He waited until she was out of the room. "Wayne, I would think you would know teenage rebellion when you see it. I would say probably not even half of that statement was true. It was just said to get under my skin. Her mom, who's been there her whole life, betrayed her in almost one of the worst possible ways. I'm the dad who was never there. She's not going to trust me, not right now. It's okay. I'm not worried about it."

Bubba rubbed his hands up and down his face. "Really, Pop?"

Wayne snorted. "Don't 'Really Pop?' me. This is a big piece of property and it would not be the first time an employee has tried to angle themselves or their children into the family, and before you go getting all uppity, boy, I wasn't against it. I was just asking, but I won't lie. When she told me she never wanted to have a family, I told her if she didn't want a family to stay away from my son. And you can get pissy, boy, if you want to, but you want a big family. Don't let having the hots for some girl make you lose sight of the bigger picture of what you want out of life …" He shifted his attention to Diego and said, "No offense."

"None taken."

Bubba snorted and got to his feet. He murmured, "Stay out of it, Pop. I got it under control." He picked up his dishes and went to the kitchen.

Diego smiled. "If you and I aren't planning a wedding before summer, I'm gonna be amazed. That is, provided they don't elope."

Wayne shifted in his chair, crossed his arms over his chest, and demanded, "And exactly how do you figure that? She doesn't want a family and he wants like a dozen kids. Those two don't mix."

Diego patted him on the back. "Like Bubba said, he's got it under control, and he's always had a good head on his shoulders. He was always like you. He was never anything like his uncle. He knows what he's doing and he's smart enough to know she's all talk."

"And what's that supposed to mean?"

"That means I've been a cop for eighteen years. I know how to tell when somebody's lying, and I know how to tell when they're scared, and she's both. I would say, based on life experience, she's terrified to have a family, and given her mother, can you really blame her?"

Wayne nodded, finally catching up. "So you think a little more time around here, and maybe seeing what a nice normal family life you have, she might realize she's not genetically cursed?"

"Somethin' like that."

Wayne nodded. "Well, I'm willing to entertain the possibility; however, what are you gonna do about those horrible people, because I know you. You ain't gonna let it stand."

He snorted and smiled. "To quote Bubba, 'Don't worry, I got it under control.'" He got to his feet and reached for his dishes. Wayne smacked his hand.

"You ain't a cowhand around here no more. You're a guest. I got it. Get home to that pretty wife of yours."

He nodded. "Thank you for supper. Thank you for looking after my girl. You need me, you know where to find me. I will see you around."

XIX

Friday, November 17

Lenore wondered what was wrong. This morning's breakfast was unusually quiet. Maybe it was just her, but everybody seemed incredibly occupied with their breakfast. She studied each one of them carefully. When she got to Bubba, she raised an eyebrow. He actually seemed very watchful, like he was waiting for something to happen. She continued on around the table. George looked a little off, and he was mostly playing with his food. She asked, "You feel all right, George?"

He shrugged his shoulders. "No, I don't. I just feel under the weather today. Wonder if I got your flu."

She shrugged her shoulders and felt a little guilty as she said, "Anything's possible."

Bubba paused, fork halfway to his mouth, considered for a minute. He was quite certain he could smell a set up, but he decided why fight fate. "Weatherman says it's gonna be an unusually warm day. I had planned on you and I painting line shack number sixteen. It's in desperate need of it, but if you're not feeling well, you shouldn't be messing with paint."

Alejandro suggested, "Why don't you take Lenore with you and he can stay here, work in the stables, and be close to the bunkhouse. If he can't finish, you guys can finish when you get back, and I can keep an eye on him."

Bubba nodded. *Definitely a set up.* But since in truth, he preferred Lenore's company to George's, why not. "Sounds like a plan. You know how to paint, Lenore?"

She shrugged her shoulders and smiled. "Is it really that hard? I mean you dip the brush in the paint, you stroke it up and down, or you run it up and down with a roller, right? It's not rocket science. I'm sure I can figure it out."

Bubba nodded. "I'm sure you can, but if you've never worked with paint, just a word to the wise. Despite your best efforts, it seems to end up everywhere, so I highly recommend putting your hair in a ponytail, I've got a ball cap you can use, and I'd change into clothes you're not attached to and hurry up, cause I want to get out there early so we can get it done and it have plenty of time to dry."

She nodded. "Yes, sir." She finished her toast and got up to clear her place.

Alejandro said quickly, "I'll make you a lunch."

She looked at him in surprise, then said, "Right, we won't be coming back here. Thank you." She hurried into her room and changed her shirt. When she reentered the kitchen, Alejandro handed her a large lunchbox and a thermos.

"I just went ahead and put it in one big box. Be sure to grab yourself a cup, though. I'm sure Bubba's got one in the truck, probably hasn't been washed in six months. Cowhands don't worry about such things."

She cringed and shook her head. "I did not need to know that."

He laughed. "Why do you think they're so hearty? Germs steer clear of them cause they probably kill the germs."

She laughed and shook her head and gave him a little shove. "You're terrible." Then she poured herself a cup of coffee.

"But it's true."

She hurried out and found Bubba standing by his truck, holding a baseball cap. She threw everything but the thermos in the back. She saw it was full of paint supplies. He whistled. She looked up. He tossed her the cap. "Try that on for size."

She tried it on. It went down past the bridge of her nose. She took it off, adjusted it and then tried it on again. "I thought Cowboys always wore cowboy hats, and you're still wearing yours."

He got in the truck and closed the door. She climbed in. He said firmly, "Buckle your seat belt." She buckled her seatbelt and he started up the truck and backed out of the drive. He waited until they were down the road a bit before he said, "I got a cap in the back." He jerked his thumb in the direction of the truck bed. "But why would I risk getting paint on one of my favorite hats? I'll change when we get there. I just ain't comfortable in anything else."

She nodded. "I can understand that, though I'm surprised you're so adamant about buckling my seatbelt, or are you afraid that I'll try to jump out while we're driving down the road?"

He laughed and shook his head. "No, I ain't afraid of that, however …" He brought the truck to a stop and threw it in park. He got out. "Slide on over here and buckle up." He closed the door, walked around the rear of the truck and opened the passenger door. "Scoot on over."

Lenore shook her head. "No, I don't know how to drive."

He rolled his eyes, reached over, and unbuckled her seatbelt, and shoved her across the bench seat. He got in and buckled his seatbelt. "Buckle up, and that's the point. You're gonna learn. You learn best by doing. You can read books all day about it and it ain't gonna teach you how to drive a truck."

She grudgingly buckled her seatbelt. "Fine, but I think this is a really bad idea."

"Noted. Can you reach the pedals all right?"

She was surprised to discover that they were just a touch out of her reach, despite the fact that he was about six inches taller than her. "Not comfortably."

"There's a lever under your seat. Pull the lever up and we'll scoot the bench forward just a smidge." It took them a minute before they had the seat adjusted right. "Now, all the trucks on the ranch are a little different, depending on our needs. I went with the heavy duty diesel engine, four-wheel drive, unfortunately, that means it's an automatic transmission. Nowadays the bigger trucks don't come with manual transmissions; however, all of the two door trucks on the ranch are all manual transmissions. I should probably be teaching you how to drive in one of those, because once you learn how to drive one of them, driving this thing is easy, but I wasn't thinking when I loaded my truck today. Next time I take you out, I will take one of the smaller trucks, but for now, let's focus on you getting a feel for being behind the wheel. As I said, this is an automatic, so really easy. Put your left leg back against the seat and don't plan on using it any time soon. You only ever use it if you drive a manual. Put your right foot on the brake. Now grip the gearshift and pull it towards you, then slide it over to the D for Drive, take your foot off the brake and switch it over to the gas pedal, and gently press down. Don't stomp on it."

Lenore was surprised that she only had a few little hiccups. Once she got used to the idea, she found it quite easy. She had been driving now for over half an hour. On an impulse she asked, "Okay, I'm curious. I thought out here on your private property, you didn't have to wear seatbelts, but you're very persnickety about it. Why? Insurance?"

He sighed. "No, my Uncle William."

She smiled. "Oh, yes, the charmer. Where is he?"

"Dead, when I was five. I don't even remember him. No one's exactly sure what happened. We guess he was working late on the water pump out in our West pasture. Started raining cats and dogs that night. Apparently from the tire tracks, he was already headed home when it started raining, and he liked to drive fast, and he was probably driving way too fast, especially on muddy dirt roads. Either he dodged to miss an animal, or took a corner too fast, but it's one of those we will just never know, he lost control and went into the trees. He wasn't wearing his seatbelt. He kissed the windshield. He didn't go through it, slammed back against the seat, slid over and died of internal injuries, bunch of broken ribs, skull fracture, you get the idea."

She sighed. "Sorry I brought it up."

He shook his head. "If it makes you buckle up every time, I'm not. Like I said, I don't remember the guy. Sadly, when I think of him, I think he was an idiot. Two seconds, it takes two seconds to buckle your seat belt, and had he been wearing it, he would be alive today, minimum injuries. I wouldn't bring it up to your dad if I were you."

"Why?"

"It was the first fatal car accident he ever had to investigate, and he and William had been buddies since kindergarten. Grandma used to say that they were as thick as thieves."

She sat thinking for several minutes. "So this line shack that needs to be painted, is it about the size of the other one?"

"You mean the one I found you in?"

She reached over and shoved him. He laughed. "Yes, that's what I mean."

"About the same, maybe even smaller, why?"

She shrugged her shoulders. "Well, I was just thinking if it's an all day affair, why should you stick around? I mean, if it's not very big, I can paint a bedroom by myself, and it's about the size of a bedroom. So why don't you just leave me here and come back for me later? I'm sure there's other work you could be doing."

He pointed. "Slow down, flip your turn signal up, and take that road right there."

"Why do I need use my turn signal?"

"Because we spend so much of our time driving around the ranch, if we don't keep in the habit of using our turn signals, we'll forget in town and cause an accident. I think it's best to just use them, better to keep the habit of using them than end up in the habit of not."

She nodded. "Makes sense." She slowed down and made the turn.

"Nicely done. You're getting the hang of it, and to answer your question, I am not leaving you out here by yourself."

"Why, because the doctor says it's dangerous to leave me alone?"

"Don't get uppity. I wouldn't leave any of the guys out here without a phone, without a truck, and without a gun."

"You didn't say no."

He sighed. "You're right. I didn't because you're right, Doc says we need to keep an eye on you for a couple of weeks, just to make sure you don't hit a low point."

She laughed and shook her head. She started to say something, then realized she did not need directions. She could see the shack. She made the turn off onto the little road and pulled up outside. She put the truck in park and turned it off. They both got out and started unloading their equipment. "Look, Bubba, you don't have to worry about me. If I was going to end it all, I would've done it back in LA."

"Well, you did try and fail back there. I don't want you to get the idea of succeeding here."

She shook her head, stopped what she was doing, and turned to face him. "Not going to happen. You see, that's what I realized. I could try again. I knew what I was doing this time. My mistake was only taking the sleeping pills that time. If I would've taken two things, or even three things, I wouldn't be here now, but I want to be here. That was what I decided. I wanted to live. I wanted a life. I didn't leave LA to end it all. I didn't leave LA to die. I left LA to live. That's why knew I had to get off the pills. When I was a kid, I was happy. Wasn't until I became Persephone that I wasn't happy. I was always pretty happy being Lenore. I mean, yeah, sure, life had its problems, but I was a hell of a lot happier dealing with those problems, and I know it's not going to last. Eventually somebody's going to find out who I am, but hopefully that won't be for a year or two. Hopefully things around here will stay the same and I can stay here that long. I've never been in the same place a long time. Jane was always changing hotel rooms. She was never happy anyplace long. She liked the go, go, go."

He smiled. He took off his cowboy hat and threw it in the truck. He put the ball cap on backwards. "Well, I'm really glad you have decided you wanted to live and I'm really glad you came out here. I think the Sheriff will be good for you."

She could not help it. She smiled. He looked ridiculously good that way. He looked good anyway, but there was just something about the hat on backwards. She shook her head and forced herself to say, "He probably would be, but I don't think I'd be very good for him. I mean, I can't see his wife wanting his daughter by another woman hanging around."

He shook his head. "Natalia is not like that. You'll like her."

"Yeah, I guess I forgot, you probably do know her pretty well."

He nodded. "Yep, my English teacher for third, fourth, and fifth grade." She looked at him in surprise. He laughed. "Remember, small-town. She taught English, social studies, and writing. Our school still teaches penmanship."

"Wow, a teacher, and you like her."

He nodded and tossed her a scrub brush. "We have to scrub all the old loose paint and any dirt or other things off before we can repaint. Yes, she was actually really cool. One of those teachers you enjoyed having, though I never had any problems in school, except college. Wasn't so crazy about college. I think I put my nose to the grindstone and worked so hard to get it done so I could come home. I mean, I just went to school in Amarillo, so any long breaks I could come home, but it's just not the same."

She sighed. "I would've loved going away to school. I had private tutors, but I didn't go to college. You know it occurred to me, do you have another name? I just find it difficult to believe teachers calling you Bubba."

He laughed. "Well, some of my teachers called me lots of things, but for the most part, everybody's always called me Bubba, except Mom. She hated it. She didn't want me to be a Junior, so she called me by my middle name, but Ethan, that was my little brother, well he was born eleven months and one week after me. He came six weeks early. I was a baby so I was barely walking and everybody started calling me Bubba, and it stuck. So for the most part, even my teachers called me Bubba, though there were those who remembered my dad and my uncle, so sometimes I got called one of their names. Apparently, I'm very charming just like Uncle William, so usually when I was called William, it was not a compliment."

She laughed. "So, Wayne?"

He shook his head. "No, I only ever got called that by mistake, and I won't answer to it."

"So does that mean you're not going to tell me what your middle name is?"

He smiled. "That depends, are you planning on using it?"

She laughed. "Oh, so you don't like it?"

He shrugged his shoulders and focused on scrubbing the shack. He knew it was weird, but he had a reason he did not want her using it. It was not that he did not want her to call him that, he did very badly, but for now he just rather she did not. At least, not until he knew he could keep her. "Like I said, everybody calls me Bubba."

Lenore had been discreetly watching him out of the corner of her eye. He looked a little sad. She decided maybe he did not want her calling him that because it reminded him of his mother, since only she had ever called him that. She could understand. She let it drop.

They finished in good time and started loading everything up. When they were finished loading the truck, she looked herself up and down. Bubba said with a laugh, "I warned you it gets everywhere."

She laughed and reached over and brushed his cheek. "I know. You have it on your cheek, your forehead, and your neck."

He laughed. "I ain't the only one. You've got it everywhere too."

"Well, I guess I'll take a shower and scrub it off when we get back to the house."

He chuckled and tossed her the keys. "I wouldn't get too attached to that shower idea if I were you."

"Why?"

"You'll see. Take us home."

When they pulled up in the drive, she saw the front porch had been decorated with streamers and balloons and a big happy birthday sign. She looked at it for a moment, then glanced at him. "Is today your birthday?"

He shook his head and got out of his truck. She got out and they started putting everything away. "Wednesday."

"Wednesday is your birthday?"

"No, Wednesday was my birthday."

She stopped what she was doing and stared at him. "Oh no, I ruined your birthday."

He shook his head. "I wouldn't call it ruined. I got to see a really pretty girl wrapped up in a towel. Dripping wet, by the way." He smiled, then realized she might not be amused by that. To his relief, she laughed and gave him a shove.

"Really?"

He shrugged his shoulders. "Hey, you were the one who left your bedroom door open and your bathroom door open and took a shower and came out wrapped in a towel. You're just lucky I didn't see more. I think had I come in about a minute sooner, I would have, and that would not have been my fault."

She sighed and shook her head. "What is it about men and enjoying looking at naked girls? I don't like looking at naked men, and I mean really, you've see one you've seen them all."

He laughed. "Oooh no, so not true. Believe me, there are way better and way worse, you're definitely in the way better department ... So does that mean you don't like guys?"

She hesitated a moment, then slowly turned to look at him. "If that's your way of asking if I harbor same-sex tendencies, the answer's no. I appreciate the male form, I just prefer it fully clothed."

He smiled. "Good to know."

Lenore did not know why but after a minute she said with irritation, "And besides, if you wanted to see me naked, all you had to do is look me up online."

He turned around and stared at her. She was reaching for a paint can, looking really ;unhappy. He grabbed her arm and turned her to face him, she looked down at the ground, he tilted her chin up. "Hey, look at me. I would never do that. You know that, right?"

She shrugged her shoulders and looked away. She could not bear the thought of any of the guys looking at naked pictures of her. "I'm sure eventually curiosity gets the better of everybody."

He said softly, "Hey, look at me." She grudgingly looked back at him. "I guarantee you I will never look it up. I have too much respect for you to do that. And as far as any of the other guys go, they won't either, not if they know that there are naked pictures of you out there, okay?"

She smiled and nodded. "Thank you."

He smiled back. "Anytime." They finished what they were doing, and he gestured to the porch. "Well, let's get this torture over with."

She laughed and bumped her shoulder into his. "So, Old Man, how old are you?"

"Twenty-four, thank you."

She smiled. "Well, I guess I'll have to come up with something appropriate for your birthday."

He barely stopped himself from telling her exactly what she could give him for his birthday. He shook his head. That was not like him. Normally his mind was not in the gutter, but all of a sudden, he could not get the thought of her in the shower out of his mind. After having seeing her in nothing but a towel, it was pretty easy to fill in the blanks and he kept telling himself he should not be doing this, but he still was. Finally he cleared his throat and said firmly, "You don't need to get me anything. You can just help me eat the cake, because if there's cake left I will eat it, so you can help me eat it."

"Sorry buddy, you're on your own. I don't eat cake."

He leaned over and whispered in her ear. "No, Persephone didn't eat cake. I'm pretty sure Lenore does."

She thought about that for a minute, then she smiled and nodded. "You know what, I think you're right."

XX

Saturday, November 18

Wayne scanned the breakfast table. "All right, lady and gentlemen, I just want to double check what everybody's plans are for Thanksgiving, so we'll start with you, Benny. Have your Thanksgiving plans changed?"

Benny shook his head and replied in Spanish, "No, Mr. Cartwright. As long as it's still all right with you, the family and I, we're going to leave here on Tuesday morning and we'll be back late Saturday evening, and I will be here at breakfast on Sunday. Which of course means I will be here for all of Christmas."

Wayne nodded and shifted his attention to George. "And you?"

"Luanne and I are having Thanksgiving dinner at our house. Of course, anyone not going away is always welcome at our table, and then we're going away for Christmas. We leave on the twenty second of December after the kids get out of school, and we'll be back here sometime on the twenty ninth."

Wayne smiled. "I'm sure everybody appreciates the offer, but I will be grilling steaks and corn and baked potatoes, and I laid in a supply of Hawaiian rolls for Thanksgiving dinner for anyone who wants to join me. I know it's not traditional Thanksgiving fare, but it's what I know how to cook. Just be sure before you get up from this table, you tell whoever you're dining with. Don't you dare wait till the last minute. And that brings us to you, Lenore. Any holiday plans?"

She shrugged her shoulders. "Work. I figured on a ranch it was just like any other day. I mean, animals still need to be fed and cleaned up after, right?"

"Yes, but people like to go home and see their family, so we try to split the workload and alternate years."

She smiled. "Well, I don't have any family, or any home to go home to, so I'll be around. I guess you can sign me up for a couple of dinner rolls, a baked potato, and corn."

He frowned, but decided not to argue with her. He shifted his attention to Ramon. "And what about you?"

Ramon shrugged his shoulders. "You know me, Mr. Cartwright, I don't got nowhere to go neither, and steak sounds real good. I've never been much of a turkey person myself, so sign me up for an extra thick medium rare steak, but be sure to tell Luanne I really appreciate the offer."

Wayne moved on down the line. "Stewart?"

He smiled. "Betsy and I are having Thanksgiving dinner at our house, and of course anyone who wants to join us is always welcome. Susan is coming in and she's bringing her latest boyfriend, so I'll probably be here working as much as possible to avoid whatever mess she brought home. But we're going to go visit Roger, his wife, and the grandkids for Christmas. We'll be leaving on the nineteenth and will be back on the twenty-ninth, so I'll be working the eighteenth and the thirtieth."

Wayne smiled. "Why don't you drag the flavor of the month on out here for a day's work? We'll test his mettle for you."

Stewart laughed. "I'll see if I can get Susan to let me get away with that. That would be fun."

Wayne was still laughing when he looked at the other end of the table. "Well, boy, you got any plans I don't know about?"

Bubba smiled. "No, I think my plan is the same as last year, eating too much, drinking a little more than usual, and maybe trying to sleep in on Friday, not that that ever works, but it's fun to try."

George said quickly, "Why don't you get yourself a girl? You'd find that sleep in thing a lot easier."

Bubba laughed and shook his head. "If I had me a girl, the last thing I'd be thinking about was sleep."

They all laughed. Wayne shook his head and moved on around the table. "Well, Aaron, you going to join us for a steak dinner, or do you think your mom's turkey's better than my steak?"

Aaron considered for a long minute. "Truth be told, if it's a choice between steak or turkey, steak's gonna win every time. If it's all right with you, Mr. Cartwright, I think I'll check to make sure my parents won't kill me and I'll just stay here for dinner. I mean, I'll be sleeping in the bunkhouse anyways. I don't see any point to go home and come back since I will be working all that week. And as far as my Christmas is concerned, I'll spend Christmas Eve at home to go to Midnight Mass with the family, get up, have Christmas morning, have breakfast with my family, and then I'll probably be out here by noon. If that's all right with you, sir?"

Wayne smiled. He did not think his steak dinner had anything to do with it. Aaron had glanced at his sister. "That all sounds good to me, and you know there's always a place for you at my table. The food might not always be that great, but there's always plenty of it, and you're always welcome. All right, Travis and Justin, what are you boys up to?"

Travis replied, "We are leaving here Monday late afternoon and will be back Friday morning. Hopefully we won't run into too much traffic, because everybody's gonna be shopping or sleeping in, so we think we should be here around ten o'clock."

"Good, so you boys will only not be workin' three days and y'all are working over Christmas, right?"

"Yes, sir."

Wayne nodded. "Now that just leaves you, Alejandro. I'm assuming you're still planning to fly home to Florida for Thanksgiving?"

"Yes, sir. Bubba is takin' me to the airport on the twenty second after lunch, and I will be back Friday morning on the red-eye. Ramon has agreed to pick me up and there are frozen dinners – my frozen dinners, not store-bought frozen dinners, just so everyone's clear on that – in the freezer. Lenore will be handling meals in my absence, except, of course, Thanksgiving dinner, and I have already run through all the cooking instructions with her, and she has written instructions and my cell phone number in case she runs into any trouble, but she'll be fine. I have complete confidence in her. And I will make sure that there are pies in the freezer so there will lots of dessert."

"And Alejandro, you're not going away for Christmas either?"

Alejandro snorted. "I chose to go away for Thanksgiving because the evil older sister is coming to visit Mom and Dad for Christmas and I really don't need to be around her drama."

Wayne frowned. "Well, I have always been fortunate and not had to have any dealings with family drama. Sorry to those of you who do have family issues. I will pray that they are resolved. Is there anything else we need to discuss before we break up for the morning?"

Alejandro nodded quickly. "Yes, I am making my last grocery store order before I come back from Thanksgiving. So anything y'all need, it needs to go on the list, because I will be calling in the final draft after breakfast, and then I'll be picking it up after I clean up from breakfast."

Lenore said quickly, "Actually, Mr. Cartwright, if it's all right with you and Alejandro, can I ride into town with him? There's a few things I could use."

Wayne shrugged his shoulders. "Fine with me."

Alejandro nodded. "Some company would be nice."

She nodded and got up. "Well, I'm going out to the stables and get to work. Whenever you're ready to go, just give me a holler."

XXI

Alejandro pulled up in front of the grocery store and put the truck in park. "I hope you don't mind, but I wanted to go do a little Christmas shopping. After all, my parents and I exchange Christmas presents at Thanksgiving, and there were a couple of things I wanted to get my mom. Meet you back here ..." He looked at his watch. It was just a few minutes to ten. "Say at noon, then we can load the truck and head back to the ranch."

She shrugged her shoulders. "Sounds fine to me as long as Mr. Cartwright's not going to be mad."

He laughed. "Girl, stop worrying about making the world mad. I sent them all off with lunchboxes. Nobody's expected for lunch at the house. I told him, you and I'd probably grab a bite to eat in town. He said that was fine. I told him I was gonna do a little Christmas shopping, he said that was fine. As long as the work gets done, he doesn't care how long it takes you to get it done. He pays you by the week, not by the hour. I mean, if this is your first job, I understand you being nervous, but you've been here for almost a month. Relax, you would think by now you would have learned the lay of the land."

She laughed. "It's not my first job. I'm just used to working for my mother, and well, she pretty much had every minute of my life planned. So if I wasn't where she expected me to be when she expected me to be there, believe me, I heard about it."

He nodded. "Yeah, working for family can be great, or be the biggest nightmare of your life. Usually there is no middle ground."

She nodded. "I can see that. See you at noon." She got out of the truck, then turned back. "Are we eating together, or just grabbing a bite to eat here and doing our own thing?"

He shrugged his shoulders. "Do our own thing." He dug something out of his pocket and tossed it to her. "Mr. Cartwright told me to give you that just in case. It's the key to the back door at the ranch house, and I put the spare key for my truck on there just in case you wanted to put anything away while you are shopping. Tonight when you're done, hang the key on the rack next to my name."

She nodded and stuck the keys in her pocket and replied, "Will do." She turned and headed into the grocery store. She picked up a hand basket and decided she had time. She wandered up and down the aisles. When she arrived at the tea, she selected a couple of boxes, then moved on. She debated over hot cider and hot chocolate. She decided against them both and moved on. When she reached the pharmacy department, she got all the things that she needed. She found it interesting how many things she had left behind in her quick escape, simple things you would not even think about, like lip balm, all those little bathroom supplies that you always had around. On an impulse she decided a thermometer would not a bad idea, and a bottle of acetaminophen and ibuprofen just in case. She knew the ranch had a large first aid kit, but she went ahead and made up her own little first aid kit. She smiled and decided she was going look at the hardware store. Maybe she would get a little rug and a new blanket for her bed, something to make the room look a little less austere and feel a little more like hers. She smiled. She liked that idea. Deciding she was done in the grocery store, she headed for the register. There was an older, grandmotherly looking woman in line in front of her. The woman was unloading her basket. She kept looking at Lenore. Lenore smiled back at her. Lenore wanted to laugh. The woman clearly wanted to demand to know if she knew her. She was sure it was the fact that she was in a small town, and the woman was used to knowing everybody.

Natalia was just entering the grocery store when she heard Beverly Adams demand, "Are you visiting our town? I've never seen you before." Natalia glanced at the register. There was a tall, very slender young woman in line behind Mrs. Adams. Her boots and jeans clearly indicated cowhand, and there was something very familiar about the jacket she was wearing.

The girl emptied her hand basket onto conveyor and placed it underneath. She extended her hand. "No, ma'am, I'm not visiting. I just started working at the Cartwright place. My name is Lenore Stevens."

Beverly stretched up to her full five foot two and looked down her nose at the girl. "Oh, you? I thought it had to be you."

Lenore raised an eyebrow. "Did I do something wrong?"

Beverly laughed and looked at Merle the cashier and said, "She tries to ruin my grandson's reputation, and she has the audacity to ask if she did something wrong."

Lenore was starting to have a bad feeling about this. "I'm sorry, ma'am, you must have me confused with somebody else."

She shook her head. "No, apparently there's only one tramp in town named Lenore. Though I for the life of me, can't understand what Wayne Cartwright is thinking, employing a little tramp like you. I would think he had better sense than that."

"Look lady, I don't know who you are or what you're talking about, and I really don't care, but I don't like you calling me a tramp, so why don't I just go back to what I'm doing and you leave me alone."

Natalia stepped forward and smiled. "Good morning, Mrs. Adams, how are you doing?"

Beverly snorted with disgust and said, "I hope you'll forgive me, but I'm not particularly pleased to see you." She shifted her attention back to the girl. "So I take it that means you spend so much of your time ruining young men's lives that there are just too many for you to even begin to fathom. Well, I strongly suggest you pack your bags and move on, because I intend to make your life in this town a personal hell. I will not allow you to soil the good name of my grandson with your accusations of rape, and I will make sure that everybody in town knows what a little liar and a tramp you are, and that you seduced my grandson and then decided to cry rape."

Natalia's eyes widened. She knew she should say something, but she was so stunned she had no idea what that should be. She had always thought Mrs. Adams was a nice old lady, apparently she had been sorely mistaken.

Lenore stared wide-eyed. All she could think about was it was happening all over again. Tears started into her eyes. She hesitated, looking at all the stuff on the conveyor, then she looked back at the woman. She knew she should not give ground, she should stand and fight it out, but she could not bear it. She turned, burst into tears, and fled the building.

Merle, however, was not short of words. He snapped angrily, "Mrs. Adams, I have no idea what's going on here, but I will not have you speaking that way to any customer of mine. And don't act like Jace is a saint or a little angel. That boy has always been a hellion and a half. And if you can't be polite to my customers in my store, you can find somewhere else to shop."

Natalia finally found her voice. She stepped in close and said coldly, "Let me make something very clear to you, Mrs. Adams. Lenore did not accuse Jace. Evidence was brought to light that Sheriff Mendoza had no choice but to investigate into. Evidence that was strong enough to elicit a warrant to search Jace's truck, bedroom, and common areas of your son-in-law's house for drugs, and based on some other information, the judge felt he was well within his rights to add another item to the warrant. That item was also found. Everything was done perfectly legally, and your grandson had legal representation when he filled out his statement where he pled guilty to felony drug possession, assault and battery, and attempted rape. I know Merle will not repeat any of this, and if you repeat any of it, you will end up crosswise with me and Diego, and that's not something you want to do. If I hear any whisper against that girl, I will make your life in this town a living hell. And believe me, when it comes to your grandson trying to rape an eighteen year old girl, the town is gonna take my side. So you don't want it spread around anymore than I do."

Beverly said angrily, "She's nothing more than a drifting tramp, and you're taking her side? She's an outsider. Jace is from here."

"Yes, she's not from here, but she also told my son to stay away from Jace because Jace tried to get her to do drugs. She protected my son when she had no reason to, and that is what led to your grandson getting caught with cocaine. And before you get too uppity, that little girl who you just made leave here in tears is Diego's oldest daughter, so you're lucky he didn't shoot Jace. And you better make sure that he stays away from Aaron, because Aaron's not exactly thrilled with him either. After all, Lenore is his big sister. This is very personal for me, don't cross me."

Beverly stared open mouthed for a long minute, then she looked back at Merle and said with irritation, "Are you done ringing up my groceries yet?" He nodded. She paid and left.

Merle waited until they were alone, then he asked gently, "Natalia, are you all right?"

Natalia shook her head. "No. Those things, are they Lenore's?"

He nodded. "Yes, ma'am."

"Please ring them up so I can pay for them. I'm assuming since she's still here in town and she doesn't know how to drive that the ranch has an order of groceries in back?"

"Yes, ma'am, they have a big pickup order."

"Then I will pay for these things, and will you please write her name on the bags and put them back with the ranch groceries so that they can make it back to her. Here's my credit card. I need to go call Diego. I'll be ... I'll be back in a minute. I have some shopping to do."

"Of course, ma'am, and take all the time you need. I'll hold onto your credit card for you."

She nodded, turned, and pulled out her cell phone. Heading out of the store, she called Diego.

Diego was sitting, watching the road the teenagers liked to speed down, waiting to catch someone speeding, when his phone rang. Seeing Natalia's picture, he smiled and picked it up, and answered, "Hey beautiful, I thought you were going to the grocery store this morning."

"I did, and I am, but I ... I got a glimpse of your daughter. Unfortunately, it wasn't a very good one. She was standing at the register being badgered by Mrs. Adams. It got ugly and I stupidly didn't interfere soon enough. Lenore ended up running out in tears. I think she headed west down Darren Street ..." Diego switched to his Bluetooth, then he headed back into town. "... Oh Diego, what was wrong with me? Why didn't I interfere sooner?"

"What happened?"

"I have never seen Mrs. Adams so ugly. She called Lenore a tramp repeatedly. Accused her of seducing Jace and then crying rape."

He growled and demanded, "Please tell me there was nobody else in the store."

"The only other person in sight was Merle, and you know he ain't talking."

Diego nodded. "Well, we don't have to worry about Merle, he's had several little run-ins with Jace himself over shoplifting and vandalism that Mrs. Adams doesn't know about. That will definitely put him on our side. Right now I'm just worried about Lenore."

"Me too. I thought I should go after her, but then I thought she doesn't know me from Adam, and I kinda got the feeling she wasn't the warmest to us right now anyways, so I figured it was better to let you handle it. I went ahead and paid for her groceries and I had Merle put them with the ranch's stuff."

He chuckled. "Something tells me she's gonna love that."

Natalia sighed several times. "If you need me to do something, just tell me."

"Love, you're already doing it. I can't imagine another woman on the planet not screaming her head off at me over this."

"Then any other woman would be wrong. I have nothing to complain about. It was before my time. So what are you going to do?"

"Right now, I'm trying to find my daughter. Once I find her, I have no idea. I don't think she likes me. I mean, she made it pretty clear that she wanted me to stay out of her life, though of course, she used the pretense of it was for my own protection."

"Well, why don't you ask her to come home with Aaron tomorrow and have Sunday supper with us. I know she'll say no, but we can try anyways, right?"

"I don't deserve you. I love you. You're the best wife on the planet."

"Oooo, keep telling me things like that and maybe I'll try on that black silky negligée you like so much."

He grinned. "You mean the one that looks really good on the floor."

She laughed and shook her head. "You are unbelievable."

"But you love me anyways. Gotta go, I just found her."

XXII

Lenore turned right going out of the store and ran about a block till she came to a small alley. She ducked down and sniffed several times and wiped her eyes on the sleeve of her jacket. It took her a minute to pull herself together. She stood there trying to decide what to do. She glanced at her watch, she had an hour and twenty minutes before she had to meet Alejandro. She contemplated the situation. "Well, it doesn't seem to matter where I go, I always end up getting labeled a tramp. If it doesn't matter where I go, then I guess I should stay where I'm happiest, and if Mr. Cartwright doesn't care about employing a tramp, then what does it matter to anyone else? I really only have to come to town every couple of months. I'll get what I need and leave. I don't have any problems on the ranch and nobody bothers me there. I'll endure an hour of misery every couple months." She nodded. She exited the alley and started wandering down the street, looking at the shops. A couple of blocks down she discovered a music store. She stood in front of the large window admiring the instruments. It was mostly band instruments, probably their only customers were the kids from school. She was considering going in and trying out one of the guitars. She missed her guitar.

"Do you play an instrument, or just sing?"

She jumped and turned around. The Sheriff was standing there. She sighed and said with irritation, "Let me guess, that nasty old bat called in a disturbing the peace complaint on me?"

He chuckled. "No, she didn't think of it, thank goodness. Look, I have to apologize about that. I will talk to her and I'll talk to Sammy as well. Trust me, Sammy will put her in her place. He's on your side."

"Who's Sammy?"

"Jace's father, he's a good guy. You'd like him."

"No offense, I'd rather avoid them all."

He nodded. "Probably the better idea."

"But don't go talking to anybody. There's no point. Doesn't matter. I don't come into town very often, and I don't care what people think. I'll stay at the ranch. They'll stay out here. It's all good."

He shook his head. "No, it's not, I'm not gonna let her terrorize you, and I'm not gonna let her make you feel unwelcome in this town. If anyone should feel unwelcome, it's Jace. And I'm not saying that because I'm your father, I'm saying that because I'm the Sheriff, and I know this town. If word gets out, he's the one who's going to be unwelcome."

She shrugged her shoulders, then a thought struck her. "If she didn't call in a complaint, why are you here?"

He smiled, pulled out his phone, and opened it and went to his photos, finding one of Natalia's photos. He turned it so she could see it. "Because she's my wife, Natalia, and she told me to come find you. She was really upset. She thought about coming after you herself, but she figured you wouldn't have anything to do with her since you don't seem to want to have anything to do with me."

She sighed and looked back into the shop. She stuck her hands in her pockets, took a deep breath, and let it out slowly. Her shoulders slumped. "It's not that I don't want to have anything to do with you, you just seem to have a really nice life. I don't want to screw that up."

He tentatively placed his hand on her shoulder. She did not pull away. He squeezed it. "You are not going to screw that up. Natalia wants me to invite you to Sunday supper. Why don't you come home tomorrow with your brother? We can have dinner, introduce you to the other kids, and then Aaron will take you back to the ranch. He'll be sleeping there until next Sunday so it's no skin off his nose. If you prefer, you can just be there as Aaron's friend, but I think that's a bad idea."

She considered that for a long minute. "Because you mean the others will get mad when they find out, because this is a small town and eventually everyone is going to find out?"

"That's about right." He gestured to the window. "But you didn't answer my question. Do you play an instrument?"

She nodded. "Guitar, acoustic. I've owned a couple of electric guitars over the past couple years, but was never as attached to them as I was my acoustic."

He frowned. "I'm surprised you didn't bring it away with you if you were attached to it."

She looked very sad and turned to face him. She crossed her arms over her chest and said mournfully. "Mom smashed it about two years ago, maybe three."

He sighed and shook his head. He stuck his hands in his pockets and looked back into the shop. He smiled when he saw Mrs. Newton watching them. He pulled his right hand out of his pocket and waved at her. "Smile, you're on candid camera."

She turned back to the window and smiled. "Ten cents says she thinks you're stepping out on your wife."

He laughed. "No bet." As they stood there in silence, he had to bite his tongue to not make a comment about the weather. He chuckled and shook his head. "This is awkward." Remembering her remark about the guitar, he asked, "Why did your mother break the guitar?"

She rubbed her hands up and down her face. "Look, Sheriff, I don't want to get into it. I shouldn't have even brought it up."

He nodded, grabbed a hold of her jacket sleeve, and turned her in the direction of the store. "Come on, I'll introduce you."

"No, that's a bad idea."

He shook his head. "No, standing here looking guilty, that's the bad idea." He wrapped his arm around her waist and pulled her in the direction of the store.

Mrs. Newton opened the door. "Diego, what are you doing?"

He laughed. "I'm trying to get this stubborn woman to come on in and look at guitars, but I guess if she's not going to, I'll just pick one. You have a pretty pink one? I bet she loves pink."

Lenore stopped struggling and turned to glare at him. "Pink, really?"

"I'll special order a hot pink one if you don't choose one of your own accord."

She laughed. "Something tells me you are not going to spend three hundred dollars just to spite me."

Mrs. Newton asked, "Acoustic or electric?"

They both replied simultaneously, "Acoustic."

Mrs. Newton replied quite honestly, "Actually, there is a very nice hot pink one in the magazine for two ninety-nine. It also has a matching hot pink case."

Lenore snorted, "Ha, called it."

Diego ignored her and asked, "Hard sided or soft sided?"

She looked thoughtful. "I think it was soft, but I'll have to double check."

Lenore said quickly, "I'm coming. I'm coming." She walked past the older woman and headed for the guitars. She pointed at the one for thirty-nine ninety-nine. "Can I take a look at that one?"

Diego shook his head. He pointed. "Uhuh, how about that black Yamaha instead?"

Lenore shook her head. "I don't need a three hundred dollar guitar. That one would be fine. Actually, I don't need a guitar it all."

He sighed. "And I thought Natalia was difficult to buy presents for. The black one. I'm not gonna buy somebody who already knows how to play a guitar a cheapo. That's what you buy for a kid you don't know if they're gonna stick with it, not something you buy for an adult who already knows how to play well."

She smiled. "What makes you think I know how to play well? I might suck."

"I doubt it seriously."

Mrs. Newton pulled the Yamaha down and handed it over, though she gave Diego a clearly disapproving look. "This is very nice guitar. It will last you a long time."

Lenore knew she should not, but she could not resist. She took it and began fiddling with it. It was very out of tune. She quickly tuned it by ear, then began playing the first song that came to her mind. She had to bite her tongue not to sing along.

Diego smiled and pulled out his wallet. "I'll take it along with a hard case for it, and she'll need some extra strings, picks, that little thing that goes on the neck they use to adjust …"

Both women said simultaneously, "Capo."

He snapped his fingers and pointed at Mrs. Newton. "Yeah, one of those things, and a strap, a nice one, a pretty one, not the plain one it comes with. Clearly she doesn't need a tuner."

Lenore stopped fiddling with the guitar and handed it back. "No, I don't need it."

He smiled and reached out and brushed her cheek with the back of his knuckles. "The only thing that would've made me happier right now was had you sung along."

Mrs. Newton cleared her throat. "Diego, really?"

He turned back and snapped, "Really. By the way, Lenore, Mrs. Newton is the high school music teacher, and I mean my high school music teacher, Aaron's high school music teacher, Bubba's high school music teacher. She's taught high school music for thirty years in the town. And Mrs. Newton, this is my oldest daughter, Lenore." He gave her a moment to stare stunned, then he added, "We just met."

She opened her mouth several times, trying to find words, but her mind was full of questions, questions she knew she should not ask.

Lenore sighed and shook her head. "Really, Sheriff?"

"Yes, really. I thought we just established outside that the whole town is gonna find out anyways, so why not just get it out there in the open. You are my daughter."

"Yes, and I'm already making enemies in this town."

He shrugged his shoulders. "And your point? I have enemies in this town, but I promise you, you will have a lot less of them if you and I aren't having clandestine meetings and I'm not buying you presents in secret."

"Well, I don't want you to buy me presents. I certainly don't want you to spend all this money on me. I mean, I'm sure your wife is really gonna appreciate you dropping seven hundred bucks on your …"

Diego cut her off. "Daughter. Don't use any other word, and Natalia will be fine with it."

She snorted and crossed her arms over her chest. "I find that really hard to believe."

Mrs. Newton said, "Actually, I'm on his side. Natalia will be fine with it. Natalia is a big supporter of the music programs in this town. She has fought to keep them for the past eight years."

Lenore turned to stare as she demanded, "What do you mean, fought to keep them?"

"Well, especially the high school music program. There's a huge argument, has been for the past several years, that it doesn't bring enough money or prestige to the town to make it worth keeping the program. That we should put that money into the football program which ensures more scholarships for our students."

Lenore shook her head. "Oh, hell no! What kind of idiot dreamed that up? Don't they realize that not everybody is meant to be an athlete, and for some kids music is the only thing that gets them out of bed in the morning, and besides, what can a high school music program possibly cost a year, a hundred thousand dollars?"

Mrs. Newton shook her head. "The estimated cost for the high school music program is fifty-four thousand dollars a year, that includes my salary, which I have not taken a pay raise in ten years to keep the program. I actually took a pay cut four years ago. It's not about the money to me, it's keeping the program. That is the most important thing. I just don't know what else we can do to keep the program."

Lenore opened her mouth and then bit her tongue. "Aww."

Diego had to look away not to start laughing. He did not know why, but he had a very strong suspicion she had almost said something to the effect of 'Who do I write a check to?'

Lenore coughed and put her hand over her mouth. "Aww, that hurt."

Mrs. Newton reached out and touched her arm. "Are you all right, sweetie? What happened?"

Diego could not help it. He bumped his elbow into his daughter and said, "See how quickly you go from scarlet woman to sweetie when people know what's going on?"

Lenore ignored him and replied, "Yes, ma'am, I'm fine. I just barely stopped myself from saying a swear word."

"Well, in future, just stop, don't bite."

"Yes, ma'am. I will remember that."

Diego decided to change the subject. "Is there anything else she needs to go with that?"

"No, I think you covered it all. Nowadays you can learn to play your favorite songs online. I really don't even carry sheet music anymore."

He smiled. "Good, ring me up."

Lenore decided to stop protesting. Mrs. Newton bagged up her things. "Here you go, dear. If you have any problems, it comes with a one year warranty. All the information is in the bag, but if you have any problems, you can always come down here and I will help you sort it out. The music shop is open Monday through Friday during the school year from four to six, and on Saturday from nine to three. We're closed on Sunday."

"Thank you, ma'am, I'm sure I can manage. If not, one of the guys at the ranch will probably be able to help me."

Diego waited until they were outside. "Why don't you let me give you a ride back to the grocery store. I'm assuming that's where you're going to meet your ride back to the ranch."

"It is, but I don't know if I can go back there, at least not today. I mean, if I wait by the road back to the ranch, Alejandro will just pick me up there."

He chuckled. "I'm sure he would, but I promise you, Merle is a good guy. You don't have anything to worry about. I'm sure he'll let you sit in the back of the store waiting for Alejandro."

She nodded. "All right."

They put her stuff in the backseat of his patrol truck, then to her surprise, he walked around to the other side and opened the door for her. She hesitated a moment, then gave him a hug. "Thanks for the guitar. It's really cool."

He hugged her tightly. "Anytime, baby girl."

XXIII

Sunday, November 19

Lenore had sped through her chores. She could not for the life of her figure out why she had agreed to go to dinner tonight with the family. She could not remember the last time she regretted something as much as she regretted this. She hurried from the stables to the house. She stopped at the boot scraper and scraped and scraped her boots, then she ran them through the boot brush several times. When she decided they were as clean as they were going to get, she hurried into the house, sat down on her bed and pulled off her boots, then looked at her watch. She had forty-five minutes before she had to meet Aaron at his truck. She pulled off her watch and tossed it on her bed. She went into the bathroom and twisted her hair up into a bun, then scrubbed her face, arms, and neck. She looked at herself in the mirror then shook her head. She still looked and smelled sweaty. She stripped naked and jumped in a cold shower and rinsed off her body, being careful to keep her hair dry. She knew she was being ridiculous, she was a dirty cowhand, not a rock star diva. What did it matter if she was a little sweaty and dirty? But it did matter, she wanted to give off a good impression. She finished up quickly, dried off, then she went to her closet and analyzed her wardrobe. She pulled off the pair of

black jeans that Bubba had given her. She had yet
to wear them. She examined them, they were
actually in pretty good shape. She tossed them on
the bed, then she shifted her attention to her shirts.
Most of them were graphic tees, but there were a
few nicer tees. She decided on the blue one. She
took it off the hangar and examined it. It was a V-
neck. She threw it on the bed. She shifted her
attention to the long sleeve shirts. She decided on
a blue plaid. She pulled it off the hangar and went
to her bed. She got dressed and glanced at her
watch again, twenty minutes. She went into the
bathroom and examined herself in the mirror. The
shirts looked okay, the hair looked awful, and the
jeans ... she did not like the jeans. They did not
look good with the brown boots. She went back to
her closet and analyzed every pair of blue jeans
she had. Finally deciding on the best looking
ones, again they were Bubba's outgrowns. She
really needed to do something about her wardrobe.
She laughed. "There's nothing wrong with the
clothes I have. I don't need dresses. I don't need
high heels. I'm just a cowhand. Jeans and T-shirts
are fine and there is nothing wrong with
secondhand, they still have plenty of wear left in
them." When she was finished berating herself,
she changed jeans and went back to the mirror.
She needed a belt. Fortunately, there had been
several in the box Bubba had given her. She went
back and examined them. There was a very nice
brown belt with a fancy Eagle belt buckle. She
tried it on. It fit nicely, though it was obvious she
did not use the same hole Bubba had, but one

tighter. There was a tap on her door. She jumped. "Who is it?"

"Aaron."

She looked at her watch. "You said four thirty, it's only four twenty-five."

Aaron pushed the door open. "Seriously? You left the stables forty-five minutes ago, what is taking you so long?" He looked around at the discarded clothes and rolled his eyes. "Seriously, what are you doing? Going on a date?"

"No, I'm going to dinner with your mother, and nobody told you to come in ... How do I look?"

"Fine." She put on her boots and went back to the mirror. He rolled his eyes. "Come on. I'm starving."

"Fine. You leave, I'll stay here. Everybody will be happy."

He sighed. "I will not be happy. My mom will not be happy. My dad will definitely not be happy, and I don't think you'd be happy either. You look good. Let's go."

"No, I haven't done anything about my hair. I'm not going with my hair like this, it looks horrible."

He groaned and threw himself on the bed and stared up at the ceiling. "Oh my God! Is this what I have to look forward to with Denise?"

She went into the bathroom and undid her hair and shook it out and started brushing it. "Who's Denise?"

"Our thirteen year old sister, and if you tell me I have to wait for you to put on makeup, I'm throwing you in the truck right now."

"I don't own any makeup."

"Hallelujah! Thanks be to God!" He held his arms out towards the ceiling.

She rolled her eyes as she tied her hair in a ponytail and then braided it. She decided she liked a braid, but she did not like this braid, it was too tight. She brushed and re-braided her hair, this time in a soft braid that she pulled to the right over her shoulder. Yes, she looked from side to side. She definitely liked that better, it made her look softer and a little more feminine which helped offset the clothes. She grabbed her watch. "Okay, we can leave now."

Aaron got off her bed and looked at his watch. "Look at that, twenty-five minutes late."

"Hey, I'm a woman. You should be grateful it's only twenty-five minutes."

He grabbed her by the arm and started pulling her out of the house. "My mom is always ready first."

"I'm not your mother. I'm not even related to your mother, which is more reason why this is a very bad idea."

Alejandro asked, "Where are you two kids off to?"

Aaron replied quickly, "Dinner if she'll move her butt."

Alejandro raised an eyebrow. "Really? A date? You two? I would never have guessed that."

Lenore said quickly, "Eww, gross, don't make me gag."

Aaron made gagging noises and said, "That is disgusting. Don't ever say that again."

Alejandro looked at them both in surprise. "Why? Besides the fact that she's two years older than you, she's cute, you're a good looking kid."

Aaron made gagging noises again. "Dude, she's my sister."

Lenore amended, "Half sister."

"Oh, I get it! That explains why Diego came to dinner. Interesting ... did not see that coming. Have fun."

Aaron pushed her out the door. They got in his truck and headed off the ranch. Lenore had to sit on her hands the whole ride. She wanted to bite her nails. She wanted to jump out of the truck. She just knew this was going to end badly.

XXIV

It was the longest hour car ride of Lenore's life, but finally they pulled up in the drive. He parked beside the Sheriff's work truck. The garage was open and she saw a blue minivan and another pickup truck. Aaron got out. He leaned on the door. She sat there examining the house. It appeared to be on a large plot of land, though there were neighbors to either side, but they were not particularly close and it was a very attractive well-maintained home. There were toys scattered on the lawn and on the front porch. There were some fall decorations out. It did not look like a house from a magazine, it looked like a home that was used. It also looked warm and inviting.

Aaron laughed. "You know, the longer you wait, it does not get easier. Come on, you'll like my mom. She doesn't bite. Everybody loves my mom, even her students like her."

Lenore sighed and got out of the truck. She headed for the house behind Aaron. She tried to remember how she had felt the first time she had gone on stage. She was not sure, but she thought she was more terrified now than she had been then. In fact, she thought for sure she was going to have a panic attack or maybe faint. Aaron opened the door and walked in. He hollered, "Mom, Dad, we're here."

The attractive blonde from yesterday came out of the kitchen. The Sheriff came from the other side of the house.

Diego opened his mouth, but before he had a chance, a herd of elephants came charging down the stairs. The littlest one screamed, "Aaron, I missed you! You've been gone for ever so long!" She jumped into his arms. He hugged her tightly.

The younger boy looked her up and down and demanded, "Is she your friend, Aaron? Never seen her before."

Lenore smiled. "I have been getting that a lot around here. I'm Lenore. I work on the Cartwright ranch."

He nodded and extended his hand. "Cool, I'm Lorenzo."

She shook hands with him. "It's very nice to meet you."

Natalia hugged her son. "You are late."

Lenore grimaced as Aaron jerked his thumb in her direction, opened his mouth, but she got there first. "Sorry Miss ... I mean, Mrs. Mendoza, that's my fault."

The little girl walked up to her and started patting her on the leg. "I'm Amelia and that's my big sister, Denise."

"Well, it's very nice to meet both of you."

Diego said, "Well now, if all of you kids are done chattering, let's go into the living room and sit down for a minute. Your mother and I need to tell you something." They all trooped into the living room and sat in their accustomed seats. Lenore hesitated. Diego indicated a chair. "Please sit down." She sat. He stood by the fireplace where he could look at all of his children. Natalia squeezed his arm. "I know this is going to be hard for some of you to understand, and maybe even accept, but it is what it is, and we all need to find a way to be okay with …" As Denise and Lorenzo started looking worried, he murmured, "… I am not handling this well. Look, it's not bad news. It's just news and it's gonna change things, but not in a bad way … Look, when I was young before your mother and I started dating, I let myself get involved with …"

Lenore frowned as she watched the Sheriff struggle, so she supplied, "A psychotic woman."

He pointed at her. "We'll go with that. And my involvement with said woman resulted in one Lenore. Lenore is my daughter. She is your sister."

Lenore added quickly, "Half sister."

He shook his finger at her. "No, I'm not playing that game. I have five children. They each have four siblings. I better never hear any of you calling each other half siblings. Siblings are siblings, is that understood?"

The younger four all replied, "Yes, sir." Lenore remained silent.

Denise raised her hand. Natalia said, "Yes, sweetie?"

"How do you feel about this, Mom?"

She sighed. "I am just as surprised as your father is by this. This kind of hit us out of the blue, but it was before my time. I have no cause to complain. I hope that Lenore will accept the opportunity to be involved in this family, because she is a part of this family, and I hope everybody will be happy about that."

Lorenzo raised his hand. Diego pointed at him. "So, did you like date her mom in college?"

Diego rubbed his hands up and down his face. He looked so miserable, Lenore decided she should field this one. "No, my mother wasn't smart enough to go to college. He and her just hooked up for one night because my mom's a tramp, okay? I was raised in California and I stumbled upon him purely by accident. I just turned eighteen, and I left home and I took the only picture of my dad with me and Mr. Cartwright saw it, showed it to your dad, and one DNA test later, it is what it is."

Aaron said, "Don't you mean 'Our dad'?"

Amelia asked, "What's a tramp?"

Lenore grimaced. "Sorry."

Natalia said, "Well, sweetie, it's not a very nice thing to call somebody, and I better never hear you do it, but nevertheless, sometimes it is a truthful statement, and it's something that is attributed to a woman who behaves inappropriately with men." The doorbell rang. Natalia looked at the door and smiled. "By the way, I invited company to dinner. I thought it might help keep things friendly. Aaron, if you'll get the door, I'm going to go start putting dinner on the table. Denise, you can help me."

Aaron got to his feet and went and answered the door. Lenore was sorely tempted to run out the back door, but when Aaron reemerged a minute later, he was followed by Bubba. She actually found his presence comforting and began to relax. Though to her surprise, he was carrying a bouquet of flowers and a grocery sack. He smiled and said, "Evenin' everybody." The kids all jumped for joy and immediately started clamoring for his attention. He whistled. "Chill, I'm here all evening."

Natalia laughed as she entered the adjoining dining room carrying a dish. "Well, if you would accept more of my dinner invitations, they wouldn't be so starved for your attention."

He smiled. "You are quite correct, ma'am, and I will be better about that, but at least I'm contrite and come bearing gifts." He offered her the bouquet of flowers.

She smiled and took them. "Thank you, Bubba. They're beautiful."

Lenore said out loud, "Dammit." Then she realized that she had actually spoken. She blushed. "Sorry."

Diego raised an eyebrow and asked, "And what was that all about?"

But it was Bubba who replied, "I don't think she believed me when I said even my teachers called me Bubba."

Natalia blinked and demanded, "You have another name?"

Lenore groaned and rolled her eyes. "Seriously?"

Diego laughed. "Welcome to the South."

Bubba offered him the sack. "The beer is for you and me and maybe ..." He jerked his head in Aaron's direction. "And the chocolate is for the brats. You can decide who are brats."

Diego laughed and took the bag. He tossed the chocolates on the hutch and handed the beer to Aaron, then he pulled out two as he said, "Put that in the fridge."

Aaron headed for the kitchen, but tossed over his shoulder, "Can I have one?"

Natalia replied before either of the men had a chance. "Not unless you're spending the night and getting up at four o'clock in the morning to be at breakfast at six AM on the ranch."

"Oh, come on Mom, it's just a beer!"

"And your father is the Sheriff, so you have my answer. However, I will compromise and tell Bubba he has my permission to give you one anytime he feels it is appropriate and you are sleeping in the bunkhouse."

Lenore stared in amazement. "You're discussing underage drinking in front of the Sheriff? Seriously? I guess the law doesn't apply to you?"

Bubba chuckled and replied, "Welcome to Texas. It is legal for a minor to drink in public if it is served to the parent and handed to the minor by the parent or custodial guardian, but most places don't want to have the insurance problem so they don't allow it, but on any private property, the adult responsible for the private property can serve alcohol to the minors if they are taking legal responsibility for the minor's actions. So in other words, myself or Pop can give you or Aaron alcohol and it's perfectly legal."

She looked at the Sheriff and demanded, "Seriously?"

He laughed. "Seriously. You know you say that a lot."

"Wow, you Texans are weird."

Diego and Bubba both grinned and said simultaneously, "And damn proud of it." They looked at each other and laughed.

Natalia laughed and smacked them both on the back. "Behave, both of you. Kids, go wash up for dinner, everyone else come to the table."

They all sat down. The two youngest joined them a couple minutes later. Lenore was not at all surprised that just like at Mr. Cartwright's table, they said grace before dinner. She examined her dinner options. There was a large dish of what appeared to be pork chops covered in a cream sauce, mashed potatoes, green beans, and what appeared to be a basket full of garlic bread. Natalia said, "Bubba, if you pass me your plate, I will serve you up some pork chops. One or two?"

He quickly handed over his plate. "Two, please."

Diego handed her the green beans. She took them and put a huge helping on her plate. Thank you." She passed them on around the table.

Natalia said, "Lenore, if you pass me your plate I'll get your pork chops."

Lenore felt a little embarrassed as she stared down at her plate. "No, thank you."

Denise said quickly, "What's the matter? My mother's cooking not good enough for you?"

Lenore played with the green beans on her plate. "I'm sure they're delicious, but I'm a vegetarian."

Natalia's mouth fell open and she stared at the guilty looks of her husband and son to Bubba's stricken face. She demanded with irritation, "And not one of the three of you thought to pass that on to me."

Bubba cleared his throat, but got there first. "My apologies, I assumed one of them mentioned it." He felt a little guilty. It was almost like lying to poor Natalia. Lenore had been edging slowly away from vegetarian. Alejandro had taken to making sure there was an alternative to beef just for her. Though, she had been eating a little more chicken every time and she had eaten a bit of ham, she had not yet ventured in to beef. He figured it was just a matter of time. She was working her way towards it.

Aaron followed up quickly with, "I don't usually pay attention to what she's eating. I mean, yeah, the guys keep teasing her about it, but she's a good trooper. She's happy with green beans. Don't even sweat it, Mom."

Natalia glared at her oldest son. "Next time be sure to tell me things like that, young man. I would've put more vegetables on the table." She shifted her gaze to her husband and glared at him across the table.

He finished chewing the bite of food in his mouth and swallowed hard. He said apologetically, "You are correct, my love. I totally dropped the ball. My sincerest apologies, Lenore."

Denise said quickly, "Why should we apologize because she's a picky eater? That's her problem, if she doesn't like what we have for dinner, she can eat somewhere else."

Diego looked at her and shook his head with clear disapproval. "Denise, be nice. She is a guest."

She smiled and asked, "Is she a guest or family? She can't be both."

Natalia said quickly, "On the contrary, she is family who does not live in this house. Therefore she is a guest, just like your grandparents are guests when they are over visiting. That does not change the fact that they are family, and I'd watch that smart mouth of yours, young lady, before it gets you in trouble."

Lenore took a deep breath, put her head down, and focused on eating her green beans. The dinner table was very quiet for a few minutes while everybody filled their plates, then fortunately the two youngest started clamoring for Bubba's attention. Lenore discreetly observed them all. She decided Denise definitely did not like her, she kept giving her dirty looks and looked moody all through dinner and mostly played with her food. Everyone else seemed okay with her. But finally dinner was over. Out of habit, Lenore got up to clear her place. When she turned to head for the kitchen, she bumped into Denise. She murmured, "My apologies."

Denise snapped, "Don't bother to apologize."

Natalia said, "Denise, a little less attitude."

Denise snapped, "Why? Just cause she's Dad's daughter doesn't mean I have to like her and it doesn't mean I have to accept her as my sister. She's not. She's just Dad's daughter. I mean, she as good as said her mom was a whore and Dad was drunk when he banged her mother. I mean, that was what you're hinting around at, right?"

Bubba whistled. "Damn that was harsh. When did she grow up?"

Diego got to his feet. "Denise, you're thirteen years old. I do not want to hear you talking like that, and you don't even begin to understand the circumstances, so don't pretend like you do. It doesn't matter what happened between Lenore's mother and I, that is no more her fault than it is yours. What happened between her mother and myself is our fault. Do not blame her, and she is your sister. Get used to it. I would've thought you would have been happy to have an older sister."

"Happy to have an older sister? Why would I be happy? She shows up on your doorstep fully grown and she's gonna get all of your love and attention, not to mention all of your guilt, because you're gonna feel guilty because you weren't there for the past eighteen years, whereas I've gotten the, you know, punishment, criticism, and now I'm going to go from the second oldest which was rough enough, to the middle child."

Lenore sighed and said very calmly. "Don't worry, Denise, you can have him. I don't want him and I never wanted to take anything away from you, but clearly I'm stepping on your toes. Don't worry, I won't." She turned to Natalia. "Thank you for dinner, Mrs. Mendoza, it was very good, and thank you for yesterday. I appreciate you trying to interfere." She dug in her pocket and pulled out some money and tossed it on the table. "That's for my groceries. Good evening, ma'am." She turned and headed quickly out of the house.

Diego tried to grab Lenore's arm, but she dodged. He turned his attention back on Denise and snapped, "What was that all about? I hope you realize how much trouble you are in."

Denise smiled and shrugged her shoulders. "The atmosphere has improved already."

Aaron snapped. "WOW! You are unbelievable! Did it ever occur to you that maybe I liked the idea of having an older sister? Did it ever occur to you that I like Lenore? She's a nice person, something apparently you're not. You're a jerk, and Dad loving Lenore doesn't take anything away from you! His love is not a cup of water that he runs out of or that he has to dole out sparingly, it's an endless river, and Lenore could use a little love right now."

Lorenzo said matter-of-factly, "I don't think her irritation has anything to do with Dad. I think it has everything to do with Bubba."

Natalia looked where Bubba had been sitting, then she realized he was gone. She looked back at Lorenzo and said, "Why Bubba?"

Lorenzo shrugged his shoulders. "Denise has a crush on him, has for a couple of years. Didn't everybody know, or did you think she got all of the bronco busting and bull riding magazines and promotionals just because she likes to read the articles?"

Diego looked at his wife. He was pleased to see she looked as surprised as he felt. Denise snapped, "You wretched little worm, I'm gonna get you!" She lunged in her brother's direction but Natalia grabbed her around the waist.

Lorenzo stuck his thumbs in his ears and wiggled his fingers as he blew a raspberry at his sister, then taunted her, "You're just pissed off because he has eyes for someone else. I mean, it's kind of obvious he's really interested in Lenore."

Diego whistled loudly. Everyone stopped and stared at him. He pointed at his youngest son. "Stop terrorizing your sister. Help your mother clear the table and then go to bed, and Amelia, wash up and go to bed. Denise, go straight to your room and get ready for bed. I will be up in a few minutes and you and I can have a lovely little chat about your very bad behavior and your very bad attitude. Aaron it's getting late, you should head back to the ranch."

Aaron asked quickly, "But what about Lenore?"

"I will make sure your sister gets back home."

Aaron nodded. "Yes, sir."

Diego turned and headed for the front door, grabbing something off the side table as he went. He was not surprised to see that Bubba's truck was still there. He started walking toward the ranch.

He was not at all surprised that he found them only about half a mile down the road, sitting on a low stone wall.

Lenore looked up when he approached. She laughed and shook her head. "Evening, Sheriff."

He sat down next to her. "You know, it wouldn't hurt you to call me Dad."

She shrugged her shoulders. "Maybe not, but apparently it's gonna hurt you badly. I told you this was a really bad idea, Sheriff."

He shrugged his shoulders. "So one person out of six has a problem with it, and I'm sure I'm gonna get an earful when I tell my parents, but that is my problem, not yours. You are my daughter, and I need you in my life."

She looked at him in surprise. "Your parents are still alive?"

He nodded. "Your mom's aren't?"

She thought about that for a minute, then she shrugged her shoulders. "Honestly, I have no idea. They were never talked about. They were never in the picture. I don't know anything about them. I guess I just kind of always assumed they were dead, but I don't know that."

"Well, you have my parents for grandparents. I debated about inviting them to dinner tonight, but

Natalia and I decided, that baby steps was a better way to go. But I'll probably call them tomorrow morning, and tell them before they hear from one of their friends, cause word of this will start getting around town."

Bubba supplied, "And you have met Natalia's dad."

She looked at him in surprise. "I have?"

He nodded. "Sam. You got your hat and boots from him."

She nodded and rubbed her face. "Oh, I'm sure they're gonna love learning about me. Man, I wish I could back my life up a few chapters."

Bubba chuckled. "Don't we all." He patted her on the thigh and got to his feet. "I think I'll go see if Natalia needs any help cleanin' up." He left them alone.

They sat in silence for a couple of minutes, then Diego said, "Lenore, I know this is hard, but I think you need to stop trying to undo it, or trying to cushion the blow, or whatever you feel you need to do to make this better for the rest of the world. Just tell me honestly what do you want, because sometimes in life you need to be just a little selfish." He swallowed hard. He was afraid of the answer, but he felt he needed to ask the question. "Do you want me to be your father?"

She swallowed hard several times trying to find her voice. A tear slid down her cheeks. She wiped it away. "I always thought it would be nice to have a dad."

He scooted a little closer and wrapped his arm around her. "Then stop worrying about everything else, I'll take my lumps." He tilted her chin to look at him. "But you don't have to take any. Don't let anybody blame you for what I did. You shouldn't apologize to anybody for existing. Somebody expects you to apologize because you're here, tell them to piss off."

She closed her eyes and took a deep breath, then she nodded. "Okay."

He smiled. "Good. Now that that's out of the way, I got you something. It's silly and you don't have to use them, but when I was a kid it was something people did."

Lenore raised an eyebrow. He handed her a small thin paper sack. She opened it and examined the contents. He pulled out his phone and turned on his flashlight. She smiled. There were several stickers. One of them looked like a Leaf Sheriff's Department badge, another one was a bumper sticker that said 'Mendoza for Sheriff'. There was also a Texas flag sticker. "For my guitar case, right?"

He nodded and shrugged his shoulders. "Like I said, people did it when I was a kid."

She smiled and hugged him. "We still do. They're great. Thank you."

"If you really like them, I will look into getting you a Mexican flag and Irish flag. If you're not interested just say so. I'll only frown a little if you ask for a California flag."

She laughed. "No, I think that'd be cool and I'm kind of done with California, at least for the time being. I might change my mind."

He laughed. "Good to hear." A thought suddenly struck him. He raised his eyebrow in her direction. "Out of curiosity, were you born in California?"

She laughed. "Something tells me you'll be pleased to know that I was born in Memphis, Tennessee."

He grinned. "That does thrill me to pieces, and I will happily buy you a Tennessee state flag." They both laughed.

XXV

Lenore sat staring at Bubba. As of yet he had only spoken once, and they had now been in the truck for ten minutes. "You know, you could've stayed and talked with your friends. You didn't have to give me a ride home right now. I could've started walking and you could've picked me up later."

He chuckled. "You do realize this is the country. It's dangerous, there are wild animals, and I'm not just talking about the four-legged variety, there are plenty of dangerous animals with only two legs, or no legs."

"You still didn't have to leave your dinner party early."

"It's not early, gonna be late by the time we get back, and I am an early to bed, early to rise kind of guy."

"You know, Bubba, I just can't understand you."

He laughed. "What's there to understand?" She shifted sideways in her seat to better look at him. "Please don't do that, it's dangerous."

"Well, it's difficult to talk and not look at you."

He nodded. "That I can understand. Give me just a minute." He made the turn off onto the ranch, pulled over and put the truck in park. He cracked the windows and shut it off. He unbuckled his seatbelt and shifted sideways. "There, now we can talk."

She unbuckled and shifted sideways. "You're so nice to me, even though all I've done is cause you trouble. Take tonight, for example, you were invited to a dinner party."

He interrupted. "Family dinner, not a dinner party, entirely different thing, but I interrupted, please go on."

She sighed. "When things turned ugly and I walked out, you left and followed me out. I'm walking down the road and all of a sudden you appear next to me. You don't say a damn word, you just walk next to me. Then I sit down on the bricks and you sit down next to me, but again you don't say anything. Why?"

He shrugged his shoulders. "You didn't seem in a talkative mood. You'd been unusually quiet all evening, not that you're a particularly chatty woman anyways. I guess I figured you'd had enough talk and just wanted a little peace and quiet."

She nodded and turned back in her seat. "Right, and I forgot you're worried about me throwing myself in front of a car or something."

He shook his head. "Honestly, that thought never crossed my mind. I was worried about you walkin' alone down the road. I was worried about wild animals, and I thought you could use a friend. After all, that was the number one reason Natalia invited me. She thought you could use a friend. She invited Pop too, but it's been very hard to get him to go out and do anything since Mama died …" He shrugged his shoulders. "At first I was a little worried about him, but he gets up, he eats, he works, he doesn't drink any more than he did before. I guess he just needed Mama to be social. I don't know if he was not exactly a social person before Mama. One of the things I keep meaning to ask the Sheriff, but I start to, then I tell myself maybe it's better if I didn't know. He's not hurting himself, he's not hurting anybody else, he's going on with life the best he can. I should be grateful for that, and I am. I figure one day maybe I'll give him some grandkids. Maybe that'll breathe a little life back into him, but until then, I guess we'll just keep on keeping on."

She smiled. "Has anyone ever told you you're incredibly smart for a twenty-four year old? You have a wisdom beyond your years, and you have an incredible outlook on life. If I could just harness one tenth of your outlook, man, I'd be the happiest person on the planet."

He laughed and shook his head. "No, I've never been told I was wise. Mostly I've been told I had shit for brains, but then again, that was in high school, and Mama always used to say you do a world of growing up between eighteen and twenty-one, but you don't really come into who you are until between twenty-one and twenty-five."

She nodded. "That sounds really good. So I guess your mother wasn't a believer in getting married young?"

He shook his head. "No, quite the contrary. She actually believed you should get married young before you got settled and set in your ways, when the clay is still soft enough to mold. After all, a husband and wife are just two halves of the same batch, and if you wait too long, they'll never quite fit together because it's gotten too hard." She sighed and looked sad. "Did I say something wrong?"

She shook her head. "No, I just think I would've liked your mother. Granted, she probably would have been like every other woman in this town. Get one whiff of the California girl and automatically think I'm a ..."

He cut her off. "Very nice girl. Has it occurred to you that part of your problem in this town might not be how everybody perceives you, but how you think everybody perceives you?" He grinned. "I have a perfect idea. I'm gonna take you to the Fall Festival Wednesday night. It's the biggest night of the festival. Practically the whole town is gonna be there, either selling or buying. We're gonna wander around and eat popcorn, we're gonna ride rides, and you are going automatically assume that every person you meet is gonna like you, and if I think you're not, I'm gonna start pinching you and you're gonna come home black and blue."

Lenore felt all warm and tingly. It sounded like he was asking her on a date, then she reminded herself, *He is your boss and you two clearly come from two separate batches of clay,* but it did sound like fun. After another minute she replied, "Sure, I guess we can hang out."

Bubba was sure he was grinning like a fool, but he had seen the glint of excitement on her face before she cooled. He knew it was a defense mechanism and he was okay with it, but it was hard not to laugh when she used the words 'hang out'. But he knew by Saturday or Sunday, it would be all over town that he was dating her. He had not taken a girl to the Fall Festival since high school. He was already planning it in his mind. "Awesome, I will let Pop know to not plan on us for supper then, because believe me, there is gonna be plenty of food to eat and it's all bad for you."

She laughed and shook her head. "Why does it sound like that's a turn on for you? And I thought I was supposed to be handling the meals?"

"Hey, don't judge. I eat healthy dinners ninety-nine times out of a hundred. I mean, it hasn't escaped your notice has it, that there is never a bite of fried food on our table, and all of the vegetables are either fresh or were fresh when Alejandro canned them. He does all of our own canning. There is not a bite of food that goes on that table that wasn't prepared by him and everything is bought local, or as local as we can get it. Some things just don't come local and we have to get them from out of state, but we get them from small businesses just like us. We don't order anything big box if we can avoid it. And usually when Alejandro goes away, Pop's the one who handles the meals. He can handle them for one night."

She smiled. "How very civic minded of you. And as long as Mr. Cartwright's okay with it, it sounds great." She shivered and hugged herself. It was getting cold.

Bubba said quickly, "Are you cold? Put on my jacket. You want me to start the truck and turn the heater on?"

She laughed and shook her head. "You do realize I'm just an employee. You don't have to give up your jacket. I mean, you're already wasting your time sitting here talking to me. You don't need to waste gas running your truck."

He rolled his eyes and shook his head. "Employee or not, you're still a woman, and I'm a gentleman. I will always give up my seat for you or offer you my jacket. It's what I do, and I'm not wasting my time sitting here talking with my friend, because you're not just an employee. You are my friend, and if you're cold, I will happily turn my truck back on, or come to think of it …" He turned around in the seat and reached over the back. Groping around, he came up with a blanket and tossed it over.

She happily wrapped it around her. It was nice and warm. She rubbed the fabric, the pattern looked familiar to her. "This looks like one of those blankets you see in one of those old pioneer movies."

He laughed. "That's because they haven't changed their pattern in three hundred years, maybe even more. It's a Hudson Bay blanket. They're very warm. It's what I have on my bed. You just haven't noticed because I have that cheap coverlet over it and there's one in every truck, along with a sleeping bag, two gallon jugs of water, two days dry rations, first aid kit, and a flashlight." She stared at him in surprise. He laughed. "When you work on a fifty thousand acre ranch, you have to plan for the worst case scenario, and that's you could end up stranded. The line shacks, those date back to before we had trucks and cell phones, but they still come in handy sometimes. It just don't make no sense to drive two hours back to the ranch house to just drive two hours back in the morning when you know you're going to be working out there for two to three days. Granted, when we do that, we usually plan better and have fresh food instead of dry rations." He shrugged his shoulders. "But sometimes even with the best plan in the world, you end up in the soup. Granted, in desperation most of us could hunt our dinner. Honestly, the only two I'd worry about being out on the ranch overnight would be you and Alejandro, though at least he knows how to use a gun."

She nodded. "That all makes sense, and I guess I just never thought of how much organization and coordination it takes to keep a place like this running, how much you have to plan ahead, how much you have to account for everything, the good and the bad."

He nodded. "Actually, what always surprises me about running this place is how little things have changed. With the exception of the incorporation of cell phones and trucks, I still pretty much do things the way my granddaddy did them, and he did them the way his granddaddy did them, and now thanks to you Californian yuppie types, there's a huge cry for grass fed beef. There's only one way to get grass fed beef, the old fashioned way, and that's where ranches like mine are cleaning up."

She nodded. "I can see that." She was really enjoying sitting, talking with him, but it was getting late. "You know, we should probably get back to the house, so we can get to bed."

He nodded, turned back in his seat, buckled up, and started the truck. She did the same, but after she was buckled, she covered back up with a blanket. After a few miles she realized Bubba kept glancing at her. She demanded, "What?"

He shook his head, not wanting to say what he was really thinking about. He said the first thing that came into his mind, "Look, I know it's none of my business, and if you don't want to tell me, go right ahead and say so. But I was just curious why your mother never married. I mean, if she's half as good looking as you, I would've thought she would have had men lining up."

Lenore sighed. She shrugged her shoulders. *Why not.* "Don't tell the Sheriff, I think he'd flip out, but when I was four my mom's music career went down the toilet because of polyps in her throat, and my mom being the kind of person that she is, she only knew one way to make a living, and that was off of men. But my mom's not smart, and yes, she's pretty and guys think she's sexy and all that, so it was easy for her to get guys who would pay her bills for a little while."

Bubba involuntarily stomped on the brake. The truck came to a squealing halt. He turned and said, "What? You mean like live in guys, right?"

She shook her head. "No, I mean like Sugar Daddies, though of course she couldn't always procure one of those, so she would have several different guys coming and going between Sugar Daddies."

"Please tell me you're exaggerating."

She sighed and shook her head. "No, my mom had sex with men for money. I mean, don't get me wrong, they were all really nice guys. Some of the more respectable ones were nicer to me than she ever was, and that's where I got my first guitar."

He put the truck in park and turned to stare at her. "So your mom would just bring these guys around you?"

She nodded. "Like I said, there would be the occasional one or two timers, but for the most part, they were regulars. She'd usually keep one for about six to eighteen months, the more upstanding guys usually stuck around less time." She shrugged her shoulders, trying to play off like it did not matter.

Bubba was a little afraid of the answer, but he asked anyways, "How did you get your first guitar?"

"So one of the more decent upstanding ones, Drake, he was much older, like sixty-five, very fit, good looking guy, way too good for my mother, other than of course the fact that he was married with kids and had a mistress. If you put that aside, he was way too good for my mother. He came over to spend some quality time with my mother, and I was sitting at the dining room table doing my homework. I guess I was about eight at this point in time. I did not understand that my mother was a prostitute, that knowledge came later. I just thought these guys were like her boyfriends, but I digress. I was sitting doing my homework and part of my homework was we were doing a Christmas concert and my grade was singing 'We Wish You A Merry Christmas' and I was practicing at the table. He paused and listened to me for a couple of minutes, and then he told my mother that I had real talent, she should encourage it." She gave a little laugh and shook her head. "My mom snorted and said something to the effect of 'That takes money' or something like that, and the next time he came over he brought a child's guitar, a really nice one and a couple of instructional DVD's on learning to play the guitar for children. I liked it. I enjoyed it so I actually worked at it. A couple months later I played him a song, and the next time he came over he brought me some music sheets and some more advanced DVD's." She sighed several times. "Then of course, he came over on a day he wasn't supposed to be over, and he found my mom stoned out of her mind and thus ended his relationship with my mom. But I continued to play the guitar and then my mom snagged a musician, not like, you know, a big name musician, but he was making a real living at it and he would play around on his guitar with me and taught me some tricks. But he got tired of my mom's drama. The drugs didn't bother him, he did drugs. I guess I was about eleven. Then one day after school this young guy shows up at the door saying that Jesse had hired him to teach me how to play the guitar, and he showed up at my door twice a week for the next two years, even after Jesse ditched my mom. He kept showing up saying Jesse was still paying for it. And for my twelfth birthday he brought me my first adult sized Yamaha." She sighed and looked very sad. "I'm sure Jesse paid for it, but it was special to me because Ricky gave it to me. Ricky, that was my music teacher. He is actually the one who's responsible for me becoming Persephone, not that he chose the name, Mother did that, but he came over one day with a flyer about a music competition and he convinced Mom that I should try out. It cost to enter, but he worked on Mom and he got her to agree to it. I won and Persephone was born, and I've been going full steam ever since. So there, now you know a little bit more about my mother, and like I said, I really don't want the Sheriff to know. I think it would upset him to know what a whore my mother was."

Bubba nodded, though he did not think her mother being a whore would upset him nearly as much as her doing drugs around a young child would. "That it would." He reached over and squeezed her shoulder. "Are you okay?"

She nodded. "Why wouldn't I be?"

He shrugged his shoulders. "Because you seem to think that you and your mother are synonymous. Seems to me like you think you're going to end up just like her. That's why you make all the decisions you do in your life, because you think that's your destiny."

She laughed. "Isn't it? I mean, don't we all end up our parents? I mean look at you, you are your dad."

He smiled. "That's the best complement I've gotten in a while, but what you're forgetting is I'm not my mother. I'm nothing like my mother, and don't say it's because I'm a guy. That has nothing to do with it. I've been around you for a couple weeks now. I see a lot of the Sheriff in you. It's a proven fact people don't have to be raised with their parents to end up like them, but then again, people can also choose to be nothing like them, and it seems to me in some ways you're actually going out of your way to end up just like your mother."

She turned and shoved him. "Excuse me, what the hell is that supposed to mean?"

"Your mother never married, never settled down, never laid down roots. She had a kid, but she wasn't a mother. You don't want a family. You don't want to be a mom. You don't want to put down any roots. You want to keep your bag packed under the bed. Sounds like you're trying to be her."

She opened her mouth to argue, but she closed it. She turned and stared out her window, pulling the blanket up over her shoulder, clearly indicating she was done talking to him.

Bubba grimaced inside. He hoped he had not just overplayed his hand. He started the truck and headed back to the ranch house.

When they pulled up outside the house, she neatly folded the blanket, set it on the seat between them, and then got out without saying a word and closed the door very quietly. He growled and smacked himself in the forehead. "Smooth move, Bubba." Deciding to be optimistic that their date was still on, he pulled out his phone to text the Sheriff. It took him several tries before he had a message he thought sounded right.

'Look I don't want there to ever be any hard feelings between us, so I just want to check to make sure that you're okay with me taking Lenore to the Fall Festival Wednesday after work?'

He read it three times before he finally hit send, then he picked up the blanket and was just setting it back where it belonged when his phone rang. He looked at it. It said Sheriff. He swallowed hard then answered. "Evening Sheriff, long time no talk."

Diego was glad he was not looking at Bubba, otherwise he would not have been able to conceal his amusement. He had never heard Bubba sound so nervous. He hesitated a moment, then asked, "Have you already asked my daughter out, or are you planning on asking her?"

He chuckled nervously. "Well, I already asked, but she thinks we're just hanging out."

"But you're not just hanging out. You want this to be a date?"

"Yes sir, I do."

"Bubba, I would never have a problem with you dating my daughter, so of course I don't have a problem with you taking her to the Fall Festival. I appreciate your checking. However, as the Sheriff, I do feel compelled to point something out to you. Under normal circumstances it wouldn't be a problem, and I would like to be very clear. I, Diego, do not have a problem with you giving Aaron or Lenore a beer every now and then. I do, however, as the Sheriff, feel I should strongly discourage you from giving your eighteen year old … female employee that you have gone out on a date with, any alcohol. Given the nature of your business, I would strongly discourage your father from doing it as well. Not that I think there would be any wrongdoing, but sometimes things are about perception. If it was just me and Natalia that

I was talking about, I wouldn't be at all worried about it."

Bubba considered all that for a long minute, then he said, "Right, I get you. You're worried about the town's perception, not just of me but of Lenore, but more importantly you're also worried about the psycho bitch."

"I am far more concerned about the latter than the former, but the former is definitely a consideration."

"Well, I'm not sure, but I honestly don't think that would be an issue. Lenore is very fastidious about what she puts in her body. She does not eat sweets. I can't see her getting behind alcohol, especially right now. Honestly if it were to come up, I would discourage her based on her current …"

"Rehabilitated state," added Diego.

"That's about right."

"Good, then we clearly see eye to eye on this, and have a very enjoyable date … but not too enjoyable."

Bubba laughed. "I will keep that in mind, Sheriff."

XXVI

Monday, November 20

Lenore had tossed and turned half the night, unable to get what Bubba had said out of her mind. She had never thought of it that way, but he was right. In her desperate need not to make the same mistakes her mother had made, she charged blindly down the same road just for different reasons. Fortunately, life's road has many turnoffs, some created by others, some you create yourself, and she intended to create one herself right now. She threw the covers back and got out of bed. Giving up any hope of sleep, she grabbed her box of mint tea and five dollars out of her drawer.

She crept quietly into the kitchen and put the kettle on, then she went into the office and flipped on the light. She paused to look around the office. Every room of the house had framed sketches hanging on the walls, some were simple charcoals, others were pastels. They were all incredibly well done. She crossed to one and examined it. It was a charcoal drawing of Mr. and Mrs. Cartwright. She shifted her attention to the one next to it. It was also a charcoal drawing, but this one was of the two boys, perhaps six and seven years old. They all looked so happy and full of life, it was hard to believe that half of them were gone now. She frowned as she examined the bottom of both drawings. She had yet to find a single one that had been signed. She wondered why Mrs. Cartwright did not sign her work. She shrugged her shoulders and crossed to the supply cabinet. Opening it, she grabbed one of the spiral notebooks, checked to make sure it was empty, and helped herself to a purple ink pen. She opened the notebook and scribbled off, 'Took a notebook and ink pen. Hope this covers it. Lenore'. She tore the note off and set it on the desk, along with the five dollar bill.

She went into the kitchen and retrieved a cup and made herself some tea, then sat down at the dining room table and began writing. The first several pages were an incoherent mess. She would get halfway through the page and decide it was crap, then she would flip to the next page. She got up to get herself another cup of tea. She knew she was going about this all wrong, but she had heard people talk about how journaling was therapeutic. She was not finding it very therapeutic. She sat back down at the table, flipped to a fresh sheet of paper, and wrote in large bold print, 'I am not my mother! I will not be my mother!' She nodded. That was the first thing she had written all night that made sense. She flipped to the next page. 'I can be somebody different. I am my own person.' She considered that for a minute. 'I am my father's daughter ...' She considered that for a minute. She did not know if it was true. She put a question mark at the end. 'I can be my father's daughter!!!' She nodded. She liked that. She leaned back in her chair tapping her pen, then wrote 'Hispanic

Irish English'. She stared at that for a little while, tapping her pen, then she drew a line through it. 'American!' She nodded. 'Rock star or cowhand?' She got up and got herself another cup of tea. She wrote in all capitals. 'NOT A ROCK STAR!!!' She circled it. 'Then cowhand?' She considered that. 'If I stay here, cowhand will lead to …?' She considered that, sipping her tea. Did she actually want to write it down? Was that a thought she was even willing to entertain. 'I am not my mother.' She tapped her pen. 'What do I know about being a mother?' She smiled and laughed softly at herself. 'You have had an excellent example of how not to be a mother.' She nodded. That was true. 'Okay, so back to if I stay here, eventually I will find somebody who's going to ask me to marry him.' She frowned. 'Is that Eventually or Hopefully?' She chuckled quietly to herself again. This was a very interesting way to carry on a conversation with oneself, but it seemed to be working, so why not keep going with it. She was starting to think there was a song in here somewhere. This is how she used to write music when she used to write music. Granted, none of the songs she ever wrote were Mother approved. She tapped her pen several more times and then wrote, 'Hopefully!' She smiled and nodded. That was it. She had found it, that one word made the difference. She was Diego's daughter. Diego was full of hope, always positive. Jane was negative. She never saw the bright side of anything. Lenore wanted to be hopeful, and when she was not under her mother's oppressive tyranny, when she was at school, she was always a happy, hopeful child, eager to help others, eager to be involved. It was not until she had started becoming famous and spent all of her time around her mother that she had found it more difficult to be hopeful. But here she had found it easier to see the bright side. If she made a concerted effort, she was sure the negative would drift away. Her mother was not the problem, not anymore. She was the only thing standing in her way, and she had no intention of doing that anymore. She got up and went into the kitchen and grabbed Alejandro's black marker. She returned and wrote across the notebook 'HOPE'. She returned the marker, turned off the stove, made sure the kettle was not going to be damaged if she left it on the burner, then went to her room and got ready for the day.

When she re-entered the breakfast room, everyone else was already at the table. She smiled, sat down, and said cheerfully, "Good morning, everyone." Everyone looked at her and smiled as they all returned her greeting. Mr. Cartwright quickly doled out their duties for the day and everyone had a quick breakfast.

She headed for the stables with a spring in her step. When she entered she heard an odd noise. She looked around, then heard it again. It was coming from the tack room. She headed for it without hesitation. When she entered, she looked around, then she stared wide-eyed. One of the ranch dogs was curled up in the corner with a litter of puppies. She asked in surprise, "How on earth did you get in here without anybody noticing you?" She moved cautiously to the mama dog, then held out her hand. The mama sniffed her hand several times, then licked it. She scratched her ears. "I wonder if you're supposed to be in here. Well, I'm in charge of the stables and everyone else pretty much just comes in and gets their horse and leaves, so if I move you and your pups to one of the empty stalls, nobody would ever know you were in here." She continued scratching the mama's ears while she considered the best way to go about it. The mama was too big for her to pick up and carry with the puppies. She would have to make two trips, but she did not know whether mama would allow that. She got up and went and retrieved one of the blankets. She returned and gently rubbed the mama down with it. When she was finished, she laid it on the ground still folded in quarters. She tentatively picked up one of the puppies. Mama did not protest. She carefully moved each one of the puppies onto the blanket. Now came the tricky part, she picked up the blanket like a basket, being very careful not to harm any of the puppies. There were a few little yaps and mama sat up, but again did not protest. She backed away slowly in the direction of one of the empty stalls. Mama got to her feet and followed her. She set the blanket in the corner. To her delight, mama went over, moved some puppies out of the way, and lay down on the blanket. The puppies immediately crowded around her. Lenore went and retrieved a bowl of water and some of the dry dog food they kept around. For the most part, they did not feed the dogs or cats. They were expected to find their own food, but there was a large shed which was for the animals to take refuge in if the weather was bad, and if it was unusually rainy or cold, they would feed them. She set the food and water near the mama, then proceeded to examine each puppy. There were eight in all, three girls and five boys. Mommy was a golden retriever; however, from the look of the puppies, Daddy was not. Two looked like golden retrievers, two looked like German shepherds, and the other three looked like a mix. There was one that had the coloring of the German Shepherd with the long fur of a golden retriever. He was the cutest thing on the planet. She kept picking him up and playing with him.

"Uh oh, why do I have the feeling you have a new bedfellow?"

Lenore jumped out of her skin and gave a little screech. She looked quickly over her shoulder to see Bubba standing there smiling at her. "G-man-ee Christmas, you scared ten years off my life! How long have you been standing there?"

"Standing here since after you brought them in, but I've been watching you since you got the blanket."

She got to her feet and dusted herself off as she demanded, "Well, why didn't you say something?"

"I was curious to see what you were up to. Any idea how they got in here?"

"No. I was going to figure that out after I got them settled." She hesitated, then asked, "I guess I should move them out to their shed?"

He shook his head. "No, it wouldn't be safe for them out there. They don't have any protection from other animals. Had I known she was expecting, I would have moved her in here." He crossed over to mama dog, squatted down on the balls of his feet, and held out his hand. After he went through the approval process, he picked up the one Lenore had been admiring. "He's a cutie. You've got good taste and it's a good thing he's a male, otherwise Pop wouldn't let you keep it in the house, but you won't be able to separate him from mama for about eight weeks."

Lenore smiled. "Seriously, I can keep him? But I live in the house, why would your dad let me keep him?"

He laughed and set him back down. "Dogs are as useful around the ranch as a horse. Well, not as useful, but dogs are very useful around a ranch. We've had hands before that their dogs slept at the foot of their bed."

"Yes, but aren't your hands usually in the bunkhouse, not in the house?"

He shrugged his shoulders. "Pop won't care, but we will have to put the word out to see if anybody else needs some dogs, cause we're not keeping eight of them. So what are you going to name him?"

She went over and sat down on the ground. She picked him up and examined him. He was so cute and fluffy. "What do you think of Razor?"

He nodded. "Razor, I like it, makes him sound tough."

"Are you sure I can keep him?"

He laughed. "Positive, but let's close them in here where they're safe and go find out how they got in here in the first place. After all, we don't want something else finding its way in."

They went into the tack room and Lenore pointed. "They were over there when I found them." She and Bubba started moving things around, looking. "Found it. Looks like she dug her way in. I can't imagine doing that while being pregnant, but okay, more power to you, mama."

Bubba nodded. "Yeah, that's actually quite uncharacteristic for an animal, something must've frightened her last night. The exertion combined with terror probably's what set her in labor. I think one of us guys should sit up the next couple nights, see what lurks in the dark. Looks like she tore up a couple of boards on her way in, let's fill in the hole and then I'll teach you how to replace the boards." She nodded and started to turn and walk away. He reached out and touched her arm. "Hey, I didn't just come in here to get my horse or anything. I wanted to say sorry about last night. I was out of line. It was none of my business and I should've stayed out of it. What you choose to do with your life is your business."

She smiled at him. "No, you were right, and you don't need to apologize. If anybody should be apologizing, it should be me. I mean, I think I called you a name and shoved you. That's not exactly the way you're supposed to behave with your boss."

"I thought we covered that last night. I'm not just your boss, I'm your friend, or at least I hope I'm your friend."

She smiled and tucked some hair behind her ear. "I'd like to be friends."

He smiled. "So we're good?"

"Definitely."

"Awesome, that means we're still on for Wednesday night?"

She smiled. "Looking forward to it."

"Come on, we better get to work before Pop jumps both of our butts."

She laughed and shook her head. She had yet to hear Mr. Cartwright raise his voice. "I find that impossible to believe. Your father keeps telling me as long as all the work gets done, he doesn't care how long it takes."

Bubba nodded. "This is true, but today's work does have to be done today." They both laughed and got to work.

XXVII

Diego sat in his office at home drumming his fingers on his desk, going over everything in his mind. His plan was solid and it operated within the confines of the law, something that was absolutely essential to him. He powered up his laptop and made sure he had all documents easily accessible. He could not remember the last time he was this nervous. He picked up the phone and dialed. A machine picked up and gave the standard lawyers' disclaimer, all calls are recorded for training purposes, but attorney client privilege would prevail, then the phone rang again. This time it was picked up on the second ring. "You have reached the law offices of Sanderson and Sanderson. This is Patrick, how may I assist you?"

"Would you inform Mr. Hector Sanderson that someone would like to speak to him in regards to Persephone."

"I'm not sure if Mr. Sanderson is in. Can you hold for a moment?"

"Yes."

Patrick pressed the hold button. He looked at his associate and said, "I have a man on the phone with a withheld number asking to speak to Mr. Sanderson Senior in regards to Persephone. What do I do?"

Delilah hesitated, then she shrugged her shoulders. "Transfer the call to Mr. Pratt, let him handle it."

He took a deep breath, then took the call off hold. "Are you still with me, sir?"

"Yes."

"I'm transferring your call to Mr. Pratt. He is Mr. Sanderson's personal assistant. He will be able to further assist you in this matter. Please hold the line."

Diego could not help it, he smiled. None of this surprised him. Though he had made the call to the investigating officer several days ago, nothing had been made public in regards to the Persephone's disappearance. The phone was picked up on the third ring. "This is Pratt, how may I help you?"

"Yes, I would like to speak to Mr. Hector Sanderson in regards to Persephone."

"Mr. Sanderson is currently in a meeting, can I take a message?"

"Is he really in a meeting, or is this just your gatekeeper's effort to keep me at bay, because I assure you what I have to say is very important and I think Mr. Sanderson's going to want to hear it. As I said, it does involve one of his more public clients at this time."

"As I said, Mr. Sanderson is in a meeting; however, I will see if he can take a moment to speak with you. Can you hold, please?"

"I can."

Pratt put the call on hold, got to his feet, and entered Mr. Sanderson's office. He closed the door and crossed to the desk. "There's a very determined man on the phone wishing to speak to you in regards to Persephone. His phone number was withheld."

Hector stroked his chin and leaned back in his chair. All he knew about Persephone's disappearance was what had been splashed across the rag mags and the Internet; however, he had his own thoughts on the matter. She had gotten her affairs very neatly in order. He thought she had walked away. He did not anticipate this being a phone call from a kidnapper. It had been far too long, such calls usually came within twelve hours. He nodded. "Transfer the call in here and turn off the recorder."

Pratt raised an eyebrow but did not argue. He turned and went back to his desk. He picked up the phone. "Are you still there, sir?"

"Waiting breathlessly."

"I do apologize for the long wait; however, Mr. Sanderson is now available to speak to you. If you will hold, I am transferring the call to him."

"Oh sure, what's holding again." This time the phone had barely begun to ring when it was answered.

"This is Hector Sanderson, how may I help you?"

"Good morning, sir. I apologize because I'm going to take more than a couple of minutes of your time; however, if everything I've been told about you is true, I think you're going to greatly enjoy what I'm going to ask of you."

Hector raised an eyebrow and leaned back in his seat. He was quite intrigued. "I must say you have my attention, sir, but since I have introduced myself, don't you think you should do so?"

"I'm getting to that. I have an account number for you. It's one of yours."

Hector raised an eyebrow. This was definitely becoming curiouser and curiouser. He leaned forward and held the phone with his shoulder as he opened up his computer. "Go ahead, I'm waiting."

"H497J422."

Hector typed it in and it popped up on the screen. It was a low-level retainer account, not something he usually wasted his time with. It was something for a junior associate. He leaned back in his chair and said a little bored, "All right, I see you have a retainer in place. You're losing my interest."

"Oh don't worry, I'm gonna grab it right back. Now that you see that we have a retainer in place, everything you and I discuss is attorney client privilege. Persephone is my daughter."

Hector sat up in his chair. "And do you have proof of this?"

"Do you have an email that goes straight to you, not through any little minions?"

"Hector Sanderson at Sanderson legal dot com."

Diego had the email ready to go. All he had needed was the email address. He entered it, then hit send. "You will be receiving an email momentarily from the Leaf Texas Sheriff's Department, that would be me. There's a copy of my daughter's California ID, a copy of my driver's license, my badge, and a DNA test. I think you should find that sufficient, and after you look at all that, I'm quite sure you're gonna run an internet search on me."

Hector quickly read through the file. It was thorough and he was familiar with the company that had done the DNA test. They were quite reputable, used by law enforcement. He checked the address and verified that it was indeed the office that that part of Texas would have used. It was then he went to his search bar and entered Leaf Texas Sheriff's Department. When he clicked on the Sheriff, the man's photo popped right up. "You were not kidding. You have my full and undivided attention. What can I do for you, Sheriff?"

"I want you, not one of your minions, you, to go to the address that I'm emailing you and you're gonna talk to a guy that I'm gonna email you a copy of his California driver's license, and you are going to explain to him very nicely that Persephone was seventeen years old and he was twenty-six years old when he bragged about having sex with her and deliberately leaked pornographic images of him screwing an underage girl. I do not need my daughter's consent to press charges against him. Now, he and I both know that he faked those videos, and the images of her in her bedroom were obtained without her knowledge. He will confess to his wrongdoing. He will name names of all of the people that were involved, because I know his dumb ass didn't do it by himself, and then he will write a statement and deliver it with you on the spot to the local news station. I don't care what network, and if he does not do these things, he will be seeing me in court, and he won't like me when he sees me. And before he tries saying anything about Persephone's mother protecting him, you can remind him that that won't fly."

Hector sat there considering. He ran over everything in his mind. It was a solid plan. It would work; after all, the last thing this little weasel wanted to do was go to jail for child porn and statutory rape. He nodded. Yes, he was definitely going to enjoy this, though his lawyer's mind required him to ask, "Are you absolutely positive that the images were faked? I know that Persephone's press agent gave a statement to that effect, but ..."

"My daughter says quite firmly that it is not her, and I have had the footage analyzed by a friend of mine. He says without the originals he can't say for certain that the image was doctored, but if he had to make a guess he would say it was, because any of the images involving the face are innocent, but when the face is turned away is when they're not. Again, he can't say for certain without the original footage, but he thinks there is a slight size difference between the two women, maybe as much as two inches in height. He says if I could get him any footage even close to ground zero he could give me more information, but everything he was finding online was three and four hundred thousand generation."

Hector nodded. "That makes sense. You know, it could be possible if we end up having to press legal charges to get an original copy. After all, it was first released through one of the internet rag websites. They might have a direct copy, and again, with the threat of child pornography, they would probably hand it over. If you like, I can get one of my associates on that."

"That might not be a bad idea."

Hector hesitated a moment. "How is Lenore doing?"

"I think she's doing good. She's had a couple of rough starts, but I think she's found her groove. She's a hell of a lot happier as Lenore than she ever was as Persephone. If you would like, I'll ask Bubba or Aaron if they can snap a shot of her. You would never recognize her."

Hector smiled. "I think I would like that. Is there anything else we need to discuss before I go see how amiable Mr. Taylor is?"

"No, I think that's all for the moment, though I am working on getting the names of those other three who also claimed to have sexual relations with my daughter. When I do, I'm going to want you to have a chat with them as well. I will not be happy until retractions have been printed from all of them. I know it will never fully repair the damage that's been done, but I think it will at least ease Lenore's mind."

"I couldn't agree more, sir. Though I should tell you, sir, by all rights I should discuss this with your daughter since she was my client first; however, I do have authorization to act in her best interest, and I do believe that this is in her best interest, but divas can be a bit temperamental."

"Lenore is a very reasonable young woman. If any heat comes down on this, I'll take it, and anyways you're working for me."

Hector laughed. "With all due respect, Sheriff, this has been a delightful conversation, but your retainer would not have covered this phone call. As I said, I'm doing this because it is in the best interest of my client, and I am also on retainer for her."

Diego swallowed hard. He had expected the attorney to be expensive, but he had not expected a three thousand dollar retainer to be used up in thirty-five minutes. "No, this is on me. This is me protecting my little girl."

"I do, of course, respect that, but I also must again remind you that this does involve your daughter, so if she and I end up in communication, I will, of course, have to make her aware of the situation."

"I can't see any reason why Lenore would contact you, but something tells me you're gonna finagle a communication, which I have to say will be fun to watch you figure it out."

"You mean figure out that Bubba is Bubba Cartwright, a bronco rider from Leaf, Texas? His father is the owner of the Cartwright Ranch, also located in Leaf, Texas. Small towns are so wonderful to work with, and the internet is such a beautiful thing, especially when somebody has the decency to be on some nationwide magazines. I have to admit, I didn't expect Bubba to be that easy to find, but cross referencing Bubba and Leaf, Texas, he popped right up. I wonder if I call the ranch house if I can get a hold of Lenore. I'm looking at the phone number."

"Mr. Sanderson, you officially impress me. I expected you to take at least three hours to figure that out. Granted, I forgot how popular Bubba was a couple years ago, but I'm assuming you will, of course, respect my daughter's desire for her mother not to know where she is."

"Tell Jane anything? You must be insane! I try to have as little communication with that woman as possible, especially right now. She really hates me right now."

"No, January first, she's gonna really hate you. Right now she's just mad at you."

"You know all about that? How interesting. Lenore must really like you. Good, she needs a stable parent in her life. He, he, stable. Sorry, I crack myself up sometimes. Well, Sheriff Mendoza, I will communicate with you as soon as I have spoken with the little weasel."

"Thank you, good day."

XXVIII

Hector hung up the phone and hesitated. He dialed the ranch house number. It rang and rang and rang. Finally it was answered by a man. "Hello?"

"Yes, I was wanting to speak with Lenore, might she be available?"

"She's in the stables. Give me a minute, I'll transfer the call."

He raised an eyebrow and tried to imagine the Persephone who had sauntered into his office in the stables. He could not. Again the phone rang and rang and rang, then another man answered. He sounded a little surprised, "It's a little early for lunch isn't it?"

"My apologies, this phone call has nothing to do with lunch. I'm calling to speak with Lenore."

Bubba pulled the phone away from his ear and stared at it. After a long minute, he looked over his shoulder as he put his palm over the receiver. He whispered, "There is an unfamiliar man wanting to talk to you."

Lenore cringed and bit her lip. She crossed to the phone and took it. "Hello?"

"I'm not sure what I'm supposed to call you. Something tells me you prefer me to call you one thing, but I think on my end, that would be a very bad idea. It's not that I do not trust my people, but we are human beings, we make mistakes. I do not want to get in the habit of calling you one thing and then slipping up in public, so how about we go with Persephone."

Lenore blinked. "Mr. Sanderson?"

"Oh, very nice. I wasn't sure whether you would recognize my voice."

"Oh no, how did you find me?"

Bubba gripped her shoulders. She reached out with her free hand and grabbed a hold of his shirt.

"I just got off the phone with your father. He asked me to take care of something actually rather ingenious. I'm not sure I would have thought of it, probably has to do with the difference between a lawyer's mind and a cop's mind. We are generally trying to get around the law, not use it to our advantage."

"The Sheriff called you?"

"Yes. I hesitated about calling you, but I decided I really could not do this without your consent, though I do think it's incredibly sweet that your father … he thinks he can afford to pay me for it."

Lenore could not help it, she started laughing. "Yeah, I think the Sheriff has a really wrong idea of what you charge." She patted Bubba on the shoulder, and took her mouth away from the receiver, and whispered, "It's okay. It's my lawyer." Then she looked stricken. "You're not going to tell my mother are you?"

"Why would I do a stupid thing like that?"

She sighed and patted Bubba on the shoulder again. "Okay then, what can I help you with?" She leaned against the wall.

"Well, Sheriff Mendoza would like me to get some retractions printed. He has a very nice plan to get that taken care of, and I can almost guarantee it's going to work; however, as previously stated ..."

"The Sheriff can't possibly afford to pay you to do it. Does this fall under my retainer?"

"It does, but in order to use your retainer I need your permission."

"Retractions? What kinda retractions?"

"Well, in all reality, retraction is probably the wrong word. What he wants me to do is get statements from the four little weasels who claimed to have had sexual relations with you to inform everybody that they lied. He has a very good plan for this. As I said, I think it's going to work, and quite frankly I'm going to enjoy doing it, but since you are my client first, I really felt I needed your consent."

"If this backfires, is my name gonna get drug through the mud again?"

"Doubtful."

"Is the other name going to come to light?"

"Absolutely not, nor will Sheriff Mendoza. I have no intention of using his name during any of this. Granted, if they call us on it, then he will, but they're not. Believe me, the last thing any of these guys want is a charge of statutory rape and child pornography on their record."

Lenore's eyes widened. "Is that a serious thing? I mean, I know that that's serious, but I mean, wasn't I too old for that?"

"You were under eighteen and under the law, no. And under the law, even if you were a consenting participant, your father can still have charges filed and there's nothing your mother can do about it. But as I said, it's not going to come to that. They will roll over."

"I trust you. I trust the Sheriff. Do it."

"Very good. While I have you on the phone, is there anything else you would like me to attend to?"

"Yes, actually there is. Can you set up some kind of endowment for the Leaf Texas Public School System for music and art? The music program costs sixty ish thousand dollars a year and I'm sure the art program costs that too. Three schools, so what is that? We'll say roughly about four hundred thousand dollars a year, so let's say we give each school two hundred thousand dollars a year for five years, but the total endowment is four point five million dollars, and the extra they get now to update instruments, supplies, whatever they need to do. That should also free up the funds they are currently using on those programs for other areas. That's all a good thing?" She looked at Bubba and asked, "Does that sound good?"

He crossed his arms over his chest and asked with a laugh. "Explain to me why we're paying you."

She laughed and shrugged her shoulders. "Technically, you haven't been. I haven't cashed any of the checks. I don't have a bank account."

Hector was smiling and laughing on the inside on the other end of the line. "You should probably open an account. If you would like, I can have a modest sum transferred into it every month to give you a little working capital. You know, it would make communicating with me a lot easier if you would create an email account and maybe buy a laptop or phone. Any of these things would make managing your funds a lot easier."

She shrugged her shoulders. "I survived this long without any of that. I have your number, I can call you. I was planning on calling you about the music endowment anyways. This is much easier, but you're right, I probably should open a bank account. I'll get back to you on that because you're right, having a little money put into it probably wouldn't be a bad idea. Okay, I got a great idea. Can you send me a check for a thousand dollars?"

"Of course, Madam, I have the address. I'll get it in the mail to you today, but I'll work up something very discreet. A check from a law firm might raise questions in a small town and I think the endowment sounds like a lovely idea. I will work something up and mail you the paperwork, and I'm assuming you want it to be one hundred percent anonymous. After all, you can't have Persephone doing things in your small little town. Somebody's bound to connect the dots." He began tapping his fingers on his desk. "Though I will have to come up with something very discreet; again, papers from a law firm are not good. Anything else?"

"Yes, just to make things easier in the future why don't you go ahead and add the Sheriff, his wife and their children to my family retainer, not that I ever expect them to need you, but again, cover the bases. Hey, and you know what? I was just thinking, make that endowment for five million and make sure that it specifies some pay raises for the music and art teachers. As I understand it they've had to take some pay cuts to keep the programs alive. I think they deserve it, and maybe some new assistant teachers. Let's create a little work." She made faces as she considered, then she added quickly, "And why don't you come up with a proposal for an art and music scholarship program."

"Of course, that's easily done. Also, do you want me to refund the retainer your father sent?"

"Refund? No, I think that would hurt his feelings, however, make sure that it doesn't renew or anything. Out of curiosity, what was it?"

"A standard retainer is three thousand dollars."

Lenore grimaced. "Ouch! I'll sort something out about that, though Christmas is coming up. I'll probably need more than a thousand dollars."

Hector considered that for a moment. "Probably true; however, why don't I still send you a check for a thousand dollars? You can use that to open your account, and then once you have the account open, you can contact me and I can wire transfer in money, which would cause less suspicion than you taking a very large check up to the teller window. The chances of them seeing a wire transfer is very slim."

"Okay, that makes sense. As always, Mr. Sanderson, you are the bomb. Thank you, I don't know what I'd do without you."

"I'm glad you think so. I will keep Sheriff Mendoza up to date on the situation, and he can fill you in. Is that satisfactory?"

"Yeah, that's great." She hung up the phone. "Sorry about that. Apparently the Sheriff's on the rampage."

"I gather that. The phone is not very quiet. I hope you don't mind, I kind of heard everything."

She shook her head. "I don't mind as long as you're not going to blab about the endowment."

He rubbed her back. "I won't blab. Are you sure you're okay? Looked pretty scared there for a minute?"

She laughed. "I was positively terrified. The last thing I want is my mother descending on this town, and believe me, she would find a way to make the Sheriff's life a living hell if she's given the chance."

He laughed and shook his head. "You know, Miss Stevens, you are something else."

She raised an eyebrow. "Miss Stevens? Really? And what makes me something else?"

He gestured to her appearance. "Here you stand in my old outgrowns and then you just give away five million plus dollars without blinking an eye."

She indicated her clothes. "I'm quite happy in these clothes, thank you very much, and I can't think of a better use for five million dollars, can you?" She turned and went back to work.

He smiled and watched her go. He had the overwhelming urge to pull her into his arms and kiss her. After a minute he replied, "Neither can I. I hated music, but I loved art."

She stopped and turned around. "Really? You're artistic? How interesting."

He nodded. "Did you see all the charcoal drawings in my Pop's office?"

"They're kind of hard to miss."

"I did them all."

"Really? Very impressive, you're very talented. I can draw too. I am an expert of deformed stick figures."

He started laughing. "That's awesome."

"You must've started when you were really young."

He shook his head. "No, middle school. I don't consider that young, really."

"But the one of you and Ethan, you can't be more than seven years old in that one."

He laughed. "I did that in high school. Mom had this photograph of the two of us, but it was kind of blurry, but it was one of the best photographs of us. She always bemoaned the fact that it was blurry, so when I was in high school I spent a couple of weeks drawing and redrawing and redrawing until I got it just right. I think it turned out rather well."

She nodded. "So all the sketches in the house, they're all yours?"

He nodded. "Mom and Dad were so impressed they framed them. Well, what I gave them. In the back of my closet, there are stacks and stacks of sketchbooks full of the stupid shit I drew for years."

She smiled. "Your parents should be impressed. You are very talented, and if I had a son as talented as you, I would frame his work too. Come on, we should be getting back to work." She turned to walk away.

He hesitated, then grabbed her arm. "I'd love to draw you sometime."

She smiled and laughed. "I don't know, I think the world has enough photos of me. I don't think there needs to be any more."

He shook his head. "No, the world has enough photos of Persephone, but I bet you there are not any of Lenore, and girls like Persephone are a dime a dozen."

She laughed. "Now, I know you're lying."

XXIX

Wednesday, November 22

Lenore ran through a quick shower, not getting her hair wet, then started drying off. She grabbed a clean pair of jeans, a long sleeved T-shirt, and a long sleeved flannel button-down. She quickly got dressed, then brushed and braided her hair. She glanced at herself the mirror. She wished she had a different shirt, then she told herself firmly, "It's not a date. We're just hanging out, just two coworkers enjoying the festivities." She exited her bedroom and headed for the main sitting room.

Bubba got to his feet. He held something out to her. "It's gonna be pretty cold tonight. I think you might want to use these. I think they will fit you. They were my mother's."

She hesitated as she took them. "Are you sure Mr. Cartwright will be okay with that?"

Wayne said from the doorway, "Val would love that they were being used. She didn't like anything to go to waste. She would hate that I packed them all up and put them in the store room."

She tried the gloves on. They fit very nicely. The other thing he had given her was a headband for covering the ears. She tried it on. Bubba supplied, "It'll make your hat feel little tight. If it's not comfortable, I could get you a wool cap. I actually have bigger hats for winter."

She tried the headband on with her hat. "Actually, I think it fits okay."

Wayne smiled. "Good. Now remember, children, no eating a big bag of popcorn and then riding the roller coaster, no drinking too much, no staying out too late."

Bubba laughed. "Like I'm going to drink too much and then drive the Sheriff's daughter home. I don't think so."

Wayne frowned and looked at Lenore. "Truth be told, I ain't worried about him drinking too much. Try to keep him off the bulls though. I can't afford to have him broken right now."

She looked a little worried. "Is that actually a possibility?"

He nodded. "There's always bull riding."

Bubba wrapped his arm around her waist and started pulling her towards the door. He grabbed her jacket and his as he shoved her out the door, saying, "Don't wait up." He closed the door behind him. He turned and held out her coat. She started to take it, but he shook his head. "No, put it on." She smiled and allowed him to assist her into her jacket.

She shivered. "Brrr, it's cold."

"Don't worry, once we're at the festival it won't be so bad." He went around to the passenger side and opened the door for her. She got in. He closed it and went around to the driver's side. He backed out of the drive and headed down the road then he stopped. "What am I doing? You need the practice." He put the truck in park, got out, and went around to the other side.

She sighed and slid over to the driver's seat. He hopped in and they adjusted the seat, and off they went. "I would think you would find this a nuisance, adjusting the seat, putting it back, all just so I can get a few minutes' practice."

"Well, you need a driver's license. Once you have one, we won't have to adjust the seat, you can just drive."

"I thought men didn't like women to drive them."

He shrugged his shoulders. "I guess that depends on the man. It doesn't emasculate me to have a woman drive me, and it doesn't make me feel like the big man to be the one behind the wheel. I usually only object to being the passenger when I don't trust the driver, like for example, don't ever ride with Travis or Justin."

She laughed. "Somehow I'm not surprised. I would think though, you would trust them more than you would me. They at least have licenses."

"You were a better driver after five minutes than they are."

She laughed. "They do seem to be a bit reckless."

"Reckless is a good word for them."

Lenore put the truck in park when they got to the edge of the property. She was about to open the door, but he popped out and charged around the other side. She scooted back across, he hopped in, adjusted the seat back, then they headed for the fairgrounds. Arriving, he parked the truck, then got out and walked around and opened her door. He held out his hand. She took it and got out of the truck. "I know you said you're a gentleman, but this does seem a bit above and beyond for hanging out."

He smiled. "I never used the words 'hanging out', that was you." He offered her his arm. When she did not take it, he sighed, reached down and gripped her hand and hooked it under his arm and placed it on his forearm. "By the way, Miss Lenore, you look very pretty this evening. I like when you wear your hair in a braid."

They got in line. She looked up at him and asked, "Mr. Cartwright, is this a date?"

"Yes, ma'am, it is." When they arrived at the gate, he pulled out his wallet and paid the admission fee. "Now, I don't know about you, but I'm starving and thirsty, so food first."

She shrugged her shoulders. "Something tells me they don't have anything vegetarian."

"Vegetarian? Really? I thought we got you over that."

She bumped her shoulder into him. "What is your problem with vegetarians?"

"I'm a cattleman. They're not clients. In fact, one might even say they're eating up my herd's dinner, taking food out of the mouths of innocent cattle."

She could not help it, she started laughing. "Well, I never looked at it that way."

He approached one of the vendors. "I will have two steak fajita tacos with onions and guacamole. She will have two chicken fajita tacos with onions and guacamole. I will have a beer and she will have ..."

She looked at the menu. "Unsweet tea."

They got their food and sat down at one of the tables. Lenore hesitated. She had been eating more meat. It was kind of impossible not to. Alejandro always looked at her like he was judging her when she did not eat his dinner, but this? She was not too sure about this. She took a bite. To her surprise it was really good. "Okay, I confess. I like it."

He smiled. "Good, I am succeeding at corrupting you."

"I thought I was already corrupted. After all, I am from California."

"Exactly, you're a California girl, so to convert you over to our ways, I have to corrupt you."

She laughed and shook her head. "You're terrible."

He smiled. "Thank you for the compliment."

She ate one whole taco, but only managed one bite off of the other one. "Okay, I'm stuffed."

He grinned. "Oh good, I was hoping you'd say that." He quickly finished off her second taco. "You want something more to drink?"

She shook her head. "No, I'm too cold to drink anything else cold."

They threw away their trash and started wandering. He was not exaggerating; every other vendor was a food stall. The other vendors alternated between craft goods and game booths. "Well, if you want, we can go on the hayride and then we can get some hot chocolate, or cider if you prefer?"

She smiled and gripped his arm. "I think the hayride sounds like fun provided it's pulled by horses and not a tractor. I've only ever been on the ones pulled by a tractor."

He laughed. "Well, this is horse country, so I think we can manage that."

After the hayride, they got some hot chocolate. Lenore was surprised at how much she was enjoying the festival.

They walked past a woman with a large mallet. She said, "Hey Bubba, you want to show your date how strong you are? Ring the bell three times, win a big teddy bear."

He looked at her and smiled. "You want a big teddy bear?"

She laughed and looked all the way up. "There is no way you can ring that bell three times. You'd hurt yourself trying."

"Ouch, I think she just dared me to. What do you think, Misty?"

"Sounded like it to me, Bubba."

He pulled off his jacket and handed over ten dollars. Lenore took his jacket and his cup of hot chocolate, glad they came with handles. She grimaced, then stared in surprise as he rang the bell three times in rapid succession. He took back his jacket and his hot chocolate. Misty handed him the teddy bear. He offered it to Lenore. She blushed as she took it. "I think I see why they charge ten dollars, it must be easy."

He laughed and shook his head. He wrapped his arm around her waist and pulled her along. "No, it ain't easy, we're just all country boys. I been swinging a sledgehammer or an axe since I could look over a fence. All the chopped wood on the property, we don't buy it like that, we make it ourselves, and I've driven a lot of stakes. It's all part of the job."

"I guess keeping to the stables I'll just see the easier side of the job."

"Well, let's see. You don't know how to drive, you don't know how to shoot a gun, and we haven't taught you how to ride a horse yet. It's not that you see an easier side, because believe me, taking care of the stables is not an easy job. You feed and look after the animals, clean the stables, help out around the house, that's hard work. You put in just as long hours as we do. In some ways, you work harder than we do because we have to drive out to where we're going, then drive back. You're workin' the whole time. Don't belittle your contribution. It's all work. It's all important and it's all gotta be done."

She smiled. "Well, I am glad to know you feel like I actually contribute."

"If you didn't contribute, Pop wouldn't have kept you around." He smiled and pointed at a booth. "Hey, why don't we fix one of those 'You don't know how to do's' right now."

She looked in the direction indicated. It was a little rifle range. She rolled her eyes. "Really, I'm going to learn how to shoot toy guns?"

He shook his head. "No, ma'am, those are pellet guns, not toy guns."

She shrugged her shoulders. "What's the difference?"

"You can still kill with a pellet gun." He pulled her in the direction of the booth, handed over some money, then picked up one of the rifles, and ran his eye it over, discarded it, and picked up another one. He discarded this one as well. He glared at the guy on the other side of the counter. "Really, Charlie? If you use these rifles again next year, somebody is going to get hurt. They're in bad shape. You have not been taking good care of them. I have half a mind to demand my money back and go and complain to the Sheriff."

Charlie said quickly, "Hey, they may not be the straightest shooting rifles around, but they're not dangerous."

Bubba finished examining the fourth rifle. "Finally one I'll let her touch, but I mean it, Charlie. I will check first day next year, and if these are the same rifles, the Sheriff will hear about it."

Lenore smiled and said, "He might hear about it anyways."

"Oh, come on Bubba, don't bust my balls. I'm just trying to make a little extra money. Tell your girl not to rat me out."

Lenore raised an eyebrow. "And what makes you think I'm his girl?"

He chuckled and sat down a tin of pellets. "Guys don't bring girls that they're not dating to the shooting range. That's a good way to get smacked."

She raised an eyebrow in Bubba's direction. "Oh really?"

He looked at her innocently. "I have no idea what he's talking about. Pay attention. I'll load it for you the first time, after that, you're on your own." He carefully showed her how to load it, then moved behind her and showed her how to hold the gun. "Now, see, you hold it like this."

She looked over her shoulder. "You have no idea what he's talking about, right?"

"Oh no, don't look at me. Look at the target."

They spent an enjoyable twenty shots at the shooting range. She rather enjoyed the lesson, and she thought she would not mind doing it again with a real gun. She did not like the little pellet guns. She thought their sights were off. She did not hit anything. She carefully lay the rifle down, then asked in a teasing tone, "Aren't you going to show me how it's done?"

He laughed and shook his head. He flipped his hand in the direction of the rifles. "Not with those pieces of crap. You couldn't hit the broad side of a barn with them. I just wanted you to shoot them a few times to get the idea, kind of ease you into a real gun."

"I thought you said those were real guns."

He shook his head. "That I would never have said. What I said was they were not toys, there's a difference."

She considered that for a moment, then nodded. "So now where to?"

He smiled. "Let's put the teddy bear in my truck and then off to the dance floor?"

"Are you sure you can keep up?"

He wrapped his arm around her waist. "I would be more concerned about whether you can keep up. I mean, do you know how to two step, waltz, and line dance?"

"I can waltz."

He grinned. "Then I would be afraid if I were you." It only took them a few minutes to get the teddy bear put away, then he dragged her onto the dance floor. Lenore was pleased to learn he was a very good dancer. It did not surprise her that he was a very strong leader. He moved with confidence, never hesitated. After several dances she said, "I'm dying of thirst."

He nodded and they went to a drink concession stand. They were just walking away when a man wearing a reflective vest, picking up trash in front of them, stood up. Jace glared at her, then he noticed who she was with. He looked back and saw that Bubba's arm was wrapped around her waist. He snorted, then chuckled and said lewdly, "Why doesn't that surprise me? So that's what it takes to get up between those pretty legs of yours. Is it the money or the land that attracts you? I mean, it's certainly not the man. He's an inferior specimen."

Bubba started forward. She darted in front of him. He bumped into her back, saying angrily over her shoulder, "Watch your damn filthy mouth."

Jace laughed. "Hey, I just think it's funny she wouldn't get friendly with me in my track, but she'd get friendly with you in your truck. After all, that is why you got a truck with a back seat, right? I mean, how many of those adorable little buckle bunnies did you bang?"

Bubba started to go around Lenore. Jace also started forward. Both men were growling and frothing at the mouth. She managed to stay between them, a hand on each chest, pushing them apart. "Stop it! Right now! Both of you!"

"Yeah, Bubba, you're not tough enough to take me on. You never were."

Lenore had to put her shoulder into Bubba's chest to push him back. She turned and glared at Jace. She said angrily, "I swear if you don't walk away right now I will scream, and I can scream very loudly, and where Bubba and I might get in a little trouble, you, who are already on probation, will get in a crap ton, and I just saw one of the Sheriff's men."

Jace glared at her and growled, "Bitch." Then he turned and stormed off.

Lenore turned around and grabbed Bubba by the arm and started pulling him in the opposite direction. When she felt they were a safe distance away, she demanded, "What is a buckle bunny?"

Bubba felt all of his irritation dissolve in a burst. He started laughing. "It's an unflattering nickname for girls who chase rodeo performers. You know, bull riders, bronco busters, things like that."

She nodded. "Got it. Kind of like fender lizards for car shows."

He laughed. "Guess so, though I've never heard that one before. I have heard of badge bunnies."

She nodded. "All the same thing."

He wrapped his arms around her waist and pulled her toward him. "Look, Lenore, you gotta believe me. What he said about me, that's not true. I was never that kind of guy. I never wanted the kind of girls who would screw me in the backseat of my truck."

She smiled. "I never thought you were. I knew he was just saying those things to get a rise out of you. The only thing that irritates me …" she popped him in the chest, "… is you were letting it work. Seriously, what is it between you two? He calls you a sanctimonious asshole and you were ready to punch out his lights."

He shrugged his shoulders. "Went to high school together. Had all the same classes together and we're in two entirely different worlds. He was on the football team, and I didn't do any extracurriculars besides bronco riding, which again, is not in his orbit. He was the one banging girls in the backseat of his truck."

She nodded. "Now that I believe."

He reached out and squeezed her hand. "But I just want to be clear as far as that petty high school bullshit is concerned, I couldn't care less. The only reason I want to punch his lights out right now is because of what he did to you and what he tried to do to you. That's all I care about."

She smiled. "That's very sweet of you, but don't get yourself in trouble over the likes of him. He's not worth it, and something tells me he's going to have a much rougher time in County lockup than the Sheriff was implying."

He pulled her against him. "So did that little run in ruin our evening?"

He was now holding her so close she had no choice but to press her hands into his chest. "I'm not in the habit of allowing his kind to ruin my time."

He smiled. "Good." He leaned forward to kiss her, but she put her hand over his mouth.

"You'll forgive me, Bubba, but I have absolutely no intention of allowing a man I call Bubba to kiss me."

He pulled her hand away from his mouth. "Nathaniel, my middle name is Nathaniel. Mama always called me Nat."

She smiled and gently rubbed his chest. "Nathaniel is a very nice name."

He smiled. "I'm glad you like it. Now may I kiss you?"

She stretched up on her toes and kissed him. He tightened his grip around her waist pulling her against him. She wrapped her arms around his neck. It occurred to her that she should be embarrassed, here they were standing in the middle of the fairgrounds kissing. She was not sure how long they had been kissing, when somebody walked past them and said, "Get a room."

Bubba pulled his mouth free and replied quickly, "Jealous much?"

The man who was walking away, turned around and laughed. "Just a little." He turned back around and went on his way.

Lenore was starting to feel a little panicky. She liked him. She liked him a lot, probably more than she should. She liked the peace and quiet here too, and she did not want to give it up. If she started dating him, and it ended badly, she did not know what would happen to her. He started to pull her into his arms again, but she pushed him away. "No, I don't think this is a good idea."

"Why not? I like you. You like me. What's the problem?"

"The problem is you are my boss, and if this gets out of control, I am going to end up getting fired, and I don't want that to happen."

He reached out to rub her arm. She pulled away. "Lenore, nothing's going to happen. It's just dating."

"Yeah, well dating turns to screwing, and screwing turns to screwed."

He shook his head. "It won't be like that." He tried to take her hand. She pulled away. She turned and darted into the crowd. He growled and smacked himself in the forehead. "Great job. Way to screw things up, Bubba."

XXX

Lenore charged blindly through the crowd, choosing her direction at random. Finally when she felt thoroughly lost, she paused and looked around. She saw an isolated wooden bench. She went over and sat. She rubbed her hands up and down her face, realizing for the first time that she had lost her hat. "Great, just great. As if the evening hadn't been a big enough catastrophe, now I lost my hat."

"I doubt seriously the evening was that much of a catastrophe."

She looked up and sighed when she saw the Sheriff standing there. "What are you doing here?"

He sat down next to her. "My job, the biggest night of the Festival. All but one of my Deputies is here. She prefers to be on patrol, and the rest of us don't mind being at the Festival, so it works out nicely. I thought you had a date with Bubba."

She looked at him and demanded in surprise, "How did you know that?"

"He asked me if he could take my daughter on a date."

She snorted. "Why am I not surprised?"

He shrugged his shoulders. "So am I allowed to ask you what happened?"

She sighed and shrugged her shoulders. "I don't know. Do you want to hear about me making out with Nathaniel?"

He chuckled. "So he finally told you his middle name. That is nice. So you and Bubba were kissing, what happened?"

She rubbed her face. "Please don't call him Bubba when you're talking about me kissing him. It just sounds so weird. 'I was making out with Bubba' sounds like I was making out with my brother."

He chuckled. "I never thought of it that way, but I see your point. So you and Nathaniel were kissing?"

She sighed several times, stuck her hands in her pockets, and watched the people go by. After a long minute she shrugged. "I screwed it up. I started thinking that he was great, that if we dated it would be great, but then what if it wasn't? Then I'd be out of a job and if I'm not here, I don't know where I'd go. So dating my boss is probably a really bad idea, so I told him I thought it was a really bad idea, and I said something kind of ugly, and he was his normal wonderful charming self, and I couldn't take it, and I ran away."

He nodded and frowned. "Yes, I have noticed that about you. Frankly, it's starting to alarm me a little, but don't think it's so bad that it's not correctable. At least not yet, but if you don't stop, it's definitely going to be a habit you can't break."

She laughed, but it was clearly without amusement. "Oh, so you don't know me but a couple of weeks and you already know all my personality problems. Fascinating, Sheriff, enlighten me." She crossed her arms over her chest and looked belligerent.

He smiled. "Good to see you still have a little fight left in you, because that's what worries me. Anytime things get rough, you run. I think almost any faith you had left in your fellow human beings has been destroyed, but I think if you give us a chance, there's a few of us left who will pleasantly surprise you, and Nathaniel is one of them. He is a good egg, honey, but if you're not interested, don't play with his feelings." He chuckled. "You know, when I think about it, there's something very interesting about you."

"What's that?"

"You're incredibly hard-working, but you're worried about a relationship between you and Nathaniel not working out. If you like each other, if you respect each other, all a relationship needs is work. Love, sex, all of those things, they take work. They come on easy, but they don't stay easy. Take it from a man who has been married for eighteen years. Marriage is hard work, and it is not for the faint of heart."

"If all a relationship needs is work, then why are there so many divorces?"

He laughed. "I think, baby girl, the answer's in the question, work. People don't want to put the time in. They don't want to work for it. They think it's going to come easy. They think that they can scream, holler, and throw a temper tantrum, and then just say 'I'm sorry' and their spouse's going to say, 'it's okay'. But if their spouse is the one who throws a temper tantrum and then says, 'I'm sorry', they don't have to forgive them. Feelings get hurt in a marriage. People fight, people do stupid things. But staying together, you have to work at that. To enjoy the good times, you gotta get through the bad times."

She sat considering that. "Nathaniel has already stood by me through some really bad times."

He nodded. "I noticed ... but if you're not willing to stand by him, then there's really no point in continuing this conversation. If you don't want the same things out of life, then there's really no point in having this conversation."

She looked at him and asked, "When did you know Natalia was the one for you?"

He smiled. "Our first date. She talked about college, and how it was nice to try it out, but she hated it and she was so grateful to be home, and how she thought it was nice to go other places and visit them, but this was her home, and this is where she wanted to be, where she wanted to raise her family, and that was how I felt. Most of the girls I had gone to high school with couldn't wait to get out of this one-horse town. Me, I already had my eye on being Sheriff. Bubba was the same way. Just like Natalia and like me, he put his nose to the grindstone and wanted to get back here as fast as possible."

She smiled and nodded. She wrapped her arms around his neck and kissed him on the cheek. "Thank you, Dad. Message received." She kissed him again. He wrapped his arms around her.

"Diego!"

Lenore started and pulled away.

Diego groaned. "Maybe I should put it in the church bulletin." He got to his feet. "Good evening, Mrs. …"

He was cut off abruptly. "And you, a Deacon in the church."

Lenore got to her feet and looked the woman up and down. "And your mind is clearly in the gutter."

"Don't smart mouth me, young lady."

"Why? You're being a bitch. I mean, seriously, I was sitting next to him, giving him a hug, and I kissed him on the cheek twice in front of whole town. Yet clearly we're carrying on an affair. I mean, seriously, he is the Sheriff and a Deacon, whatever that is. I'm a young woman his son's age, but no, you don't assume that he's giving me fatherly advice, or doing his job. You automatically assume he's cheating on his wife. Clearly somebody needs to get her mind out of the gutter. Maybe that's what's wrong with people today, they automatically assume the worst."

The woman crossed her arms over her chest and demanded coldly, "And exactly who would you be?"

Lenore held out her hand. "Lenore Stevens. I work for Mr. Cartwright on his ranch. I'm new in town, and Sheriff Mendoza is my father."

Diego smiled and wrapped his arm around her waist. "Maybe there's more fight left in you than I thought." He kissed her on the cheek."

She smiled. "Well, I'm not all Jane's daughter. I'm yours too, and Bubba keeps telling me there's more of you in me than I think there is."

The woman demanded, "Does Natalia know this?"

Diego rolled his eyes. "No, Mrs. Green, I thought I would tell the whole town first and leave my wife for last."

Mrs. Green said in a huff, "There's no need to be sarcastic." She turned and stormed away.

Lenore sighed. "Maybe what you said about putting it in the bulletin might not be a bad idea. I mean, seriously, how long is it going to take for everyone to get the message? I thought news traveled like wildfire in a small town."

He shrugged his shoulders. "Normally it does. I don't know what's going on."

She sighed. "Me neither, but I also don't know how I'm going to get back to the ranch."

"I should think the answer to that would be obvious. Bubba will take you back."

"Yeah, right. I stormed off like an hour ago and he's going to be just loitering around in the same spot waiting for me. No, he's gone back to the ranch. Hell, by now he's probably curled up in his bed."

Diego shook his head. "You know, young lady, you still have a lot to learn about gentlemen. Bubba brought you here, Bubba is not going to leave unless he knows for a fact that you have a ride back to the ranch and you are safe. And no, he will not be in the same spot because he's no fool, he'll be waiting by the gate because he knows there is only one gate in and one gate out."

"Do you seriously think after what I said he's going to take me back to the ranch?"

"Take you back, absolutely. Can I guarantee you he'll be the most talkative? No." He started pulling her in the direction of the gate. "But come on, kiddo. You gotta face the music eventually, and just remember, if you want it, fight for it. If you don't want it, be honest with him and with yourself."

XXXI

Lenore started feeling a little panicked as they approached the gate. She did not see Nathaniel anywhere, then a crowd of people moved and she saw him standing right next to the gate. He smiled, then he frowned. They approached each other. He held out her hat. "You dropped this." She took it and he shifted slightly and held out his hand. "Good to see you, Sheriff."

Diego laughed and shook hands with him. "Don't lie to me, boy, you've never been less happy to see me in your life."

Bubba shrugged his shoulders. "Reckon you'll be taking her back to the ranch."

Diego shook his head and gave her a little shove in Bubba's direction. "Nope. I told her she had to face the music eventually, and I've got to get back to work. I'll be here till the last dog dies."

Bubba perked up. "Well, I'll see that she gets home safely, Sheriff." Diego nodded and wandered off. Bubba indicated the gate. "Ready to go home?"

"Yes, thank you." As they walked to his truck, the tension between them was so palatable she could taste it, but she decided this was not the right moment to have this conversation. She would wait just a little. To her surprise, he walked around to her door, unlocked it, and opened it. He helped her in and closed the door, then he walked around, got in and started up the truck. She shivered. He reached behind him and grabbed the blanket off the back seat and handed it to her. "Thank you." She pulled off her jacket and buckled up before she wrapped up in the blanket and he started for home.

Bubba knew the longer he waited the worse it was going to get. Finally he decided if he did not say something, they might not ever speak to each other again. "Look, I'm sorry about earlier, I'm sure …"

Lenore interrupted him. "What do you want?"

He paused and looked at her. "I'm sorry. I'm not following you."

She hesitated. "What did you expect to get out of this date?"

He considered that for a minute. "I don't think I expected anything. Well, I guess that is not true. I expected to enjoy it."

"That's it? You didn't expect anything else?"

He shook his head. "No, I didn't expect anything else. I mean, there are things I was hoping for, but there's a big difference between hope and expect. Expect implies entitlement, that I feel I was owed somethin'."

She nodded. "Okay, I see that. What were you hoping for?"

He smiled. "I was hoping to get to hold you in my arms while I taught you how to shoot a gun. I was hoping to get to dance with you. I was hoping to get to know you a little better, and I was hoping for a kiss good night."

She looked at him dubiously. "You weren't hoping to get laid?"

He shook his head. "Getting laid wasn't even on the menu." He made the turn off onto the ranch, pulled over, put the truck in park and shut off the engine. "Lenore, I'm not one of your mother's special friends. My world does not revolve around getting laid. I'm not only happy to just kiss, I'm thrilled to be privileged enough to get to kiss a girl, because I do consider it a privilege when a woman allows me to kiss her, and frankly, it hasn't happened that damn often. I have spent most of my life busy running this ranch, and women don't appreciate that. They expect it to be a nine to five job that I can just walk away from on time every day. It doesn't work that way, and when I was in high school I was expected to be here after school, and I'm not complaining, because this is what I love. This is what I want to do, but girls didn't like that, and if we're going to talk about the girls from high school, I wasn't exactly sure where they had been. When I went away to college, I was there to get an education, not to party, not to drink, and not to screw. I dated a couple girls in college, but again, I was boring because I was there to get an education, not to party, not to drink, not to screw. As soon as I realized that their values and my values were not the same, I put my head down and focused on the books so I could get the hell out of there and come home."

Lenore unbuckled her seatbelt and shifted onto her knees on the bench and slid over and wrapped her arms around his neck and kissed him. His hat fell off in the back seat, but he did not seem to care and kissed her back. After a few minutes of kissing, she tentatively started running her fingers through his hair as the kisses became more passionate.

Bubba was finding it harder and harder to control his hands. They were squeezing her waist, rubbing her back, her sides. Finally he could not take it any longer, he tentatively started sliding his hand up the front of her shirt. His fingertips brushed up against her breast. She was running her fingers through his hair, rubbing shoulders, his chest, his arms. His right hand squeezed her breast gently. When she pulled her mouth free, he was convinced he was about to be slapped. He said quickly, "Sorry, I won't do it again."

Lenore blinked. "What?"

"Your breasts, I won't touch your breasts again. I get it, off limits."

"Okay, I'm confused. Why would you say that?"

"Well, as soon as I ... got overly friendly, you pulled away."

She blushed. "I was going to apologize. They're so small."

He shook his head and demanded, "What?"

"Well, my breasts. I know they're really small."

Bubba shook his head in disbelief. "You have got to be kidding me. What, guys have complained?"

"No ... I mean ... not exactly, well I mean, I never let guys touch my breasts. No matter how much my mom harassed me or lectured me, I would not kiss guys, and would not let them touch my breast, or my butt, or anything else ... you know what I mean."

He leaned forward and brushed his lips against hers. He tentatively reached up and caressed her breast. "Then why would you think they're small?

They're nice breasts for your size, or has it escaped your notice you're kind of tiny?"

"I'm not tiny. I'm five foot eight."

He laughed. "And weigh like a hundred and ten pounds."

Lenore was finding that her breath was coming a little quicker as he continued to gently rub her breast. "Mom said they were small and I needed to get them augmented."

He squeezed her breast a little harder and kissed her. After a long minute he said, "I'm very glad you didn't listen to her. There's nothing wrong with the way God put you together." His other hand slid around and grabbed her bottom. He went back to kissing her.

Lenore was very much enjoying making out, then all of a sudden a thought struck her right between the eyes. She jerked back and slammed into the steering wheel, hitting the horn. They both started. She said, "Oh my God! I just realized …"

He gripped her waist. "What's the matter?"

She started laughing. "Nothing is the matter. I just remembered why I refused to get my breasts augmented."

As one long minute stretched into another, he said, "Okay, I'll bite. Why?"

"When she took me to the plastic surgeon, there were bunches of pamphlets everywhere. I asked him about the risks involved and he gave me a pamphlet that covered all of the risks, and I remember the one that caused me to put my foot down and refuse to do it."

"And that would be?"

She put her hands to her cheeks. She could feel her face becoming very warm. "There was a chance that the implants could cause problems nursing, and if there were complications there was a possibility of not being able to nurse at all. Not to mention the possibility of losing sensation in your nipples altogether. I guess it was just so many years ago I forgot about it."

He narrowed his eyes and demanded, "How many years ago?"

"Oh, it's not worth going into. It was in England. It's legal over there, but it's not legal in this country."

"How many years ago?"

"I was fourteen, so four years ago, give or take."

He shook his head. "That is despicable. I'm very glad you stuck to your guns and refused. Besides, my mom said her breasts grew a size with each kid."

She laughed and shook her head. "Are you going to kiss me again, or we going to keep talking about my breasts?"

He shrugged his shoulders. "I don't mind talking about them. They're very nice."

She kissed him. They sat making out in his truck for a little while longer, then he groaned and pulled free. "It's getting late. We should probably get some sleep."

She sighed and went back to her seat. "You're right."

He started up the truck and continued to the ranch house. He had been driving for about ten minutes when he said, "Lenore, I really like you, but there's one thing that's a deal breaker for me."

"I know. That's one of the reasons I was trying to tell you us dating was a bad idea. After all, any girl who marries you has to understand that the third is a requirement."

"So does that mean you and me is a pipe dream?"

"Nathaniel, I really like you, but I think I need just a little more time to adjust."

He smiled and reached over and picked up her hand and brought it to his lips. "I'm not trying to rush you. I just think it's important we both know where each other stand."

XXXII

Thursday, November 23

Lenore was just in the process of deciding if the grated potatoes were ready when Aaron arrived for breakfast. She picked up a piece of potato and tasted it. It was done. She picked up the bowl of scrambled eggs and poured it over the potatoes. She would be so happy when Alejandro got back. Breakfast was the most terrifying part of the day, it required her to do the most cooking. Granted, Alejandro had chosen the easiest breakfasts for her to prepare. Today was breakfast tacos, which he said any idiot could do. She was not sure about this, but he was confident. She focused on making sure not to burn the eggs; then again, Alejandro had been adamant you have to work at burning scrambled eggs. She started them, then grabbed the bacon and the tortillas out of the warmer and headed into the dining room and placed them on the table. She hurried back and checked on the eggs. She stirred them again, then grabbed the cheese out of the refrigerator and took it to the table. Everything else was already on the table.

Aaron smiled, "Happy Thanksgiving."

She smiled. "Happy Thanksgiving." She dashed back into the kitchen and finished the eggs, then brought them to the table. She sat down and started helping herself to breakfast.

Stewart entered a moment later carrying a laptop. He sat it down on the hutch, opened it, and began fiddling with it. A moment or two passed before a female voice could be heard. He turned the volume up, then went and sat down. The woman went on to say, "And for any Persephone fans out there, looking for an update on the rock star's whereabouts …" Everyone at the table stopped eating and turned to stare at the laptop. "… A spokesperson for the rock star released a statement late last night. Persephone was never abducted and has been safe and sound the entire time. It has now come to light that a letter was left behind when she left her Hollywood penthouse, but that letter was suppressed by her mother …"

Aaron said firmly, "Turn that shit off, nobody cares about it."

Lenore snapped, "Shut up, I'm listening."

Stewart reached over and backed it up a few seconds. "… suppressed by her mother, but this reporter has learned that tension between mother and daughter had been running high for months. It was learned that Persephone walked in on her mother while intimately involved with one of her dancers and boyfriend, Davey Taylor, the dancer who was involved in the sex video scandal with Persephone, but my sources say that it was this incident that led to the rock star's attempted suicide in late August. We'll continue to keep you apprised of the Persephone scandal as more information comes to us, but for now, this is Desiree for America Rocks."

The video cut to another image of Desiree. "Well, Persephone fans, if you thought the tension between mother and daughter couldn't get any worse, and if there are any Evanjalevn fans still loitering around out there, hold onto your albums. Don't go smashing them just yet, but believe me, we are about to take you on a roller coaster ride of family drama, and quite frankly, I thought I had Mommy issues, but it turns out I ain't got nothing on Persephone. If I was her, I'd kill my mother. So as some of you may or may not have heard, yesterday at four o'clock, Davey Taylor walked into a major news network and handed over a notarized, signed confession with a formal letter of apology to Persephone and all Persephone fans for his involvement in the sex video scandal; because hold onto your hats Persephone fans, he not only states firmly that Persephone was in no way, shape, or form, the woman he is seen having sex with, it was none other than Persephone's mother, the once great Evanjalevn, but now just a jealous hack, because let's be honest, Evanjalevn was mediocre at best; whereas Persephone is a worldwide phenomenon with a net worth of nearly five hundred million dollars, but let's get down to the guts of the matter. He said he was paid by Mommy Dearest to do the sex video to try to get Persephone a bad girl image as she was just a little too cutie pie for Mommy, and Mommy thought it wouldn't hurt if she incorporated a little bit of the bad girl. I don't know who's clearing house, but somebody has got on the ball, because more confessions have come across. I bet you can guess who they were, all three of Persephone's former dancers who claimed to have sexual relations with her. All confessed that they were lying and paid to do it by ... ding ding, anyone? Anyone? ... That's right, Mommy Dearest, and as far as all those lovely naked pictures of her in her hotel room, I bet you can guess where this is going. It has also come to light that her Mommy Dearest is the one who arranged for those to be taken. I mean, seriously, this has to be the most evil woman on the planet. And I was able this morning to speak with a different representative of Persephone, her former head bodyguard JC, and he informed me that the letter that was left behind was actually addressed to him, and he delivered it to Mommy Dearest, who tore it up and flushed it down the toilet. And even though he informed the police of the existence of said letter, without the physical letter in order for them to analyze it, they were forced to continue to investigate it as a possible abduction. Sources close to the police say that based on all the evidence, they were never really working that hard, because they felt that she had just walked away. They did receive a phone call from an anonymous source, but it is a source that they verified. I don't understand how that works, but they're saying that Persephone is safe and where she wants to be and wants to be left alone. So I'm starting to think, Persephone fans, that's all bad news for us, because she is probably never going to come out of her hidey-hole, but let's be honest, after the couple of months she's had, who can possibly blame her? So I guess at this point, all that's left to be said is, Persephone, wherever you are, I hope you're happy. I hope you're safe, and I hope you have a wonderful Thanksgiving. We love you. We miss you and hopefully one day we'll get to hear you sing again, because I never got to see you in concert. So sad. This is Desiree for America Rocks."

Stewart reached over and closed the laptop. Lenore stared at him. After a long minute she said, "And exactly how long have you known?"

He smiled. "Since your first day here. When I got home that night, we were watching the news and there she was all over the television. You know, I've seen a lot of things in my life, but I ain't never seen a thoroughbred try to be passed off as a nag."

She rolled her eyes. "Gee, thanks, Stewart, I love you too."

Wayne hooted with laughter. "Silly girl." All of the guys chuckled.

Lenore felt her feathers ruffle. She opened her mouth to say something ugly, but Bubba got there first. "He wasn't calling you the nag."

She looked puzzled. "I don't understand."

Ramon smiled. "He's saying Persephone's the nag."

Wayne nodded. "Yeah, blonde was not a good look for you, kiddo."

She crossed her arms over her chest and looked around the table. None of them looked surprised. "Why do I get the feeling you all already knew?"

Ramon shrugged his shoulders. "It has kind of been all over the news, and I thought you were real edgy those first few times I worked around you, and then you got ..." he made quotes in the air, "... the flu, and then for a few days Bubba was watching your every move and then Diego came to dinner. Wasn't too hard to puzzle everything out. I mean, I have been around this ranch for a while."

She shifted her attention to George. He chuckled. "I have to confess I didn't figure it out on looks. You were working in the stables one day. I came in to get my horse and I heard a very familiar voice singing. I was halfway through saddling my horse when I finally realized there was no music. Peeked my head around the side of the stall. You were singing. When I got home that night, went into my daughter's bedroom and turned on her music, and there you were."

She grimaced. "So you're saying it's only a matter of time before the town figures it out?"

They all shook their heads. Stewart said, "No, the town hasn't really been around you, and I think if we keep you under wraps here for a few more weeks till this all blows over and something new takes over the news, nobody will figure it out." They all nodded.

XXXIII

Lenore was in the stables filling the wheelbarrow with hay when she heard snarling, growling, then yelling. She turned and ran out of the stables. Pausing, she looked around, then saw Mr. Cartwright on the ground, a large dog on top of him. She ran forward and impaled the large dog with the pitchfork. She heard growling to her right. She turned and another dog leapt on her, knocking her to the ground. It bit and clawed her several times. She managed to get onto her back and used her feet to scoot away. The dog charged in. She got her right arm up to protect her face and throat. The dog sunk its teeth into her arm, she screamed in pain, and using her left fist she punched the dog in the throat as hard as she could. It reared back and yelped. She struggled to her feet and started for the pitchfork, but the dog bit her leg, then she remembered her pocket knife. She grabbed it and flipped it open. The dog went to bite her leg again, she stabbed downwards, stabbing him in the back. He yelped and tried to bite her again. She stabbed him again and again. He fell to the ground dead. She backed towards the truck, looking around to see if there were any more. She bumped into the truck and dropped down next Mr. Cartwright. He was bleeding from several large wounds and appeared to be unconscious. She closed her knife and stuck it in her pocket. She felt his pocket and found his phone, relieved to see there was no lock screen. It opened. She started pulling off her long sleeve over shirt. She hesitated only a second between 911 and her father, she called her father.

Diego answered phone, "Hey Wa ..."

She cut him off. "Dad, I'm alone at the ranch and Mr. Cartwright was attacked by a dog. He's hurt real bad. I'm trying to stop the bleeding. He's unconscious and I remembered hearing one of the guys say something about the nearest hospital was in Amarillo and that if somebody got hurt, the best thing to do was meet the ambulance because the nearest rescue chopper was too far away as well."

Diego flipped on his siren. "Okay, do the best you can for Wayne. Get him into a truck. You know the road that leads back to town, not even three quarters of a mile down the road there is a dirt road that goes to the left. Take it, gun it down that road. Got almost forty miles that you are still on the ranch. You come off that road and you'll hit asphalt, hang a left and I will pick you up there."

While Diego had been talking, she had run inside and got the large first aid kit and a sheet. She dropped back down next Mr. Cartwright and did the best she could to bandage the wounds. "Okay, two lefts, I can do that."

"Good, what happened to the dog?"

"I got him with the pitchfork."

"Good girl. After you get Wayne in the truck, throw the dog's body in the back of the truck. The health department is going to want to look at it to determine whether it has rabies or not. You focus on the truck, focus on driving. I will call Bubba and get him to send somebody back to the ranch house to take care of everything. He will probably meet us at the hospital."

"Okay, I can do that." She hung up and stuck the phone in her back pocket, then focused on Mr. Cartwright. As soon as she had him bandaged up as best she could, she dragged him to the back door of the truck and opened it, glad they never left the trucks locked, and then struggled to pick him up and get him into the back seat. Fortunately, three weeks of cleaning out the stables and hauling fifty pound sacks of grain made it only slightly difficult, not impossible. She decided to use the middle seat belt to buckle him in, if nothing else it would keep him from getting tossed around the cab should the worst happen. She took a moment to bandage her arm and her leg, then she threw the first aid kit in the truck, shut the door, and started to head back to the house to get the keys when she saw them on the ground. Mr. Cartwright must have been heading to the truck. She grabbed the keys and stuck them in her pocket. She reluctantly grabbed both corpses and put them in the back of the truck. She was just turning to head for the driver's seat when she remembered she had not closed the door to the stables. She ran over and checked, everything was quiet. She closed the door and ran back to the truck. She knew it had to be the adrenaline, but as of this moment, nothing hurt. She got in the truck, buckled up, started it, and backed out of the drive, praying she did not hit anything. She had never used reverse in the driveway before, and she had never driven Mr. Cartwright's truck. When she made the turn off onto the dirt road, she recognized it. It was the road Nathaniel had brought her to the ranch house on that first day. She knew there was nothing down it so she put the pedal to the floor, then reached over the back seat and patted Mr. Cartwright. "Hang in there, Mr. Cartwright. I will get you to the hospital. We'll get you all fixed up." No response. She focused on her driving, but occasionally reached back and rubbed his arm or side, whatever she could get her hand on. She glanced towards the sky. "Okay, look, I know I've said I don't believe in you, but he does, and maybe with a little help so could I, so please don't let him die." She had no idea how long she had been going down this road, but it could not have been more than ten minutes when the throbbing started, then the shaking. She knew the adrenaline was wearing off. Every bone in her body ached and her back felt like the skin had been torn off of it, sections of her right arm were hurting so bad she could no longer move it. She had to rest it in her lap. She tried not to cry. Tears started down her cheeks. She told herself firmly, "Keep it together, Lenore. You can pass out when you get to the hospital."

Another ten minutes passed and then she saw a stopped truck ahead of them. Nathaniel was standing by the road.

She had barely brought the truck to a stop before he yanked open the driver's side door and said, "Scoot over." She reached over with her left hand and put the truck in park before she unbuckled her seatbelt and slid across the bench seat, then sagged against the door. She struggled to get her seatbelt. Bubba stared at her for a second, then he hopped in reached over to help her. When she was buckled, he buckled himself, threw the truck into gear and stomped on the gas, sending dust and dirt flying. Once he was on the move, he kept glancing at Lenore. She looked like hell. He tilted the rearview mirror so he could see his father lying across the back seat. He smiled when he saw that she had buckled him in, and then he reached over the seat and patted him. "Pop, stop your snoring and wake your damn ass up!"

Lenore started crying. "He's hurt really badly."

Bubba glanced at her. "So are you."

She sniffed several times. "I'll be fine."

Bubba snorted. He pulled out his phone and pressed it into the dashboard holder then hit the last received call. When it started ringing, he pressed speaker. Diego answered and demanded, "Are you with them yet?"

"Yes, I am behind the wheel. Did your daughter tell you that she was chewed up bad?"

Diego shuddered and the steering wheel jerked in his hand. "No, she failed to mention that."

"Quite frankly, if it wasn't for the fact that Pop is unconscious, I would say it's hard to decide which one is worse off."

Wayne said weakly from the back seat, "How bad is Lenore? Is she really that bad?"

"She sure as hell ain't good. Glad you're back with us, Pop. You must have been out for over half an hour."

Wayne groaned. "Dammit! Damn my stupidity! This is all my fault, girl. I am sorry."

Lenore was sure she should tell him not to talk, to save his energy, but it was good to hear him. "Stop it. It's nobody's fault."

Wayne chuckled. "Can't agree with that. The boy warned me about the mama dog. We knew there was something to be worried about. Shouldn't have gone to my truck without a gun." He groaned and coughed. "I know it's mighty personal, but please tell me you two ain't been sleeping together?"

Diego said on the phone, "Shit, that thought hadn't even occurred to me."

Bubba cringed inwardly, he did not like to think about it. "Well, you can both relax. We ain't been sleeping together."

Lenore demanded, "And exactly why does it matter right this minute? I think Mr. Cartwright should be our chief concern, not our sex life, or lack thereof."

All three men replied simultaneously, "Rabies."

She snorted. "Well, it's not like you can get it after the fact, so I don't see what the big deal is."

Bubba chuckled. "You know, Sheriff, your daughter's innocence is so cute sometimes. The concern is if you and I were sleeping together, there's a possibility you could be pregnant, which causes problems, because you can't be pregnant and have the rabies vaccinations. It causes a multitude of complications and a delay in rabies treatment, because they want to know to the best of their ability whether the dog had rabies or not before they would start treating you. Whereas since there's no danger, they'll just treat you and Pop both right off the bat, and then find out whether the dog has rabies. And if it is clear and they decide it's safe, you can just stop treatment."

Wayne groaned in pain then said, "Dogs, there were two."

Diego snapped, "Lenore, did you only see one dog?"

She sighed. "No, there are two dead dogs in the back."

"Why didn't you tell us there were two dogs?" demanded Bubba.

"Because I knew Dad would worry, and I was afraid if he knew, he would say that we had to stay there, and Mr. Cartwright needed help now. He couldn't wait an extra hour, hour and a half for somebody to get to us and then take us to the hospital."

Bubba growled. "I see your point, but you should have given us all the information. Sheriff, I'm about to make the turn off onto the highway."

"I'm just half a mile ahead of you. Get behind me and stay behind me, I'll lead the way."

The only conversation after that involved directions. When they got to the hospital, a team of doctors and orderlies were waiting for them. The truck had barely come to a stop before the doors were opened and the hospital staff began pulling them out. One of them demanded of Bubba, "Are you hurt?"

"No, I'm fine, just the two of them."

They were both quickly put on gurneys and rushed inside. Bubba got out of the truck and grabbed the remains of the sheet and threw it over the corpses. A nurse approached. She looked at Bubba. "If you'll come with me, sir, we can get you cleaned up then you sign them in. It's going to be a while. They both look pretty bad. Now we were informed that they had the body of the dog?"

Diego said with irritation, "Dogs, apparently my daughter was trying to downplay the severity of the situation."

She asked with concern, "But both attacking animals remains are in your custody?"

Bubba replied coldly, "Yes, in the back of my truck, which I'm sure you don't want in your parking lot. I covered them, but I'm pretty sure they're probably bleeding through as we speak, but I wanted to get the paperwork for my father and Lenore filled out first."

She nodded and looked him up and down. He was covered in blood. "Do you have any wounds on your hands or your legs?"

Bubba looked at his hands and slowly shook his head. "No, this is Lenore's blood, Pop's blood, and probably the dogs."

"Yes, but if you have any cuts on your hands or if you got any of the blood in your mouth or eyes, you might have to be treated for rabies as well. Let's go get you cleaned up and then I have an address for you to take the bodies. The sooner we get them to the lab so that we can get them processed and determine whether rabies is a factor or not, the better it is for everybody, but I highly recommend you come back here and start treatment yourself, just be on the safe side."

Bubba groaned. "Delightful. I don't see any point in getting cleaned up. I just have to go out to my dirty truck which still has blood everywhere. Let me go deliver the bodies, find out how they recommend I deal with my truck, and I will be back. Sheriff, you stay here, take care of all the paperwork, and keep me apprised of what's going on."

Diego nodded. "Yes, I will quickly fill out all the paperwork, but you stay here, you will have to answer some questions for me, then I will come with you. They will probably have us take your truck to a cleaning center that specializes in dealing with biohazard." She handed the paperwork to the Sheriff.

"Joyful. Joyful. This just gets better and better. Why do I feel like I'm going to end up in my underwear?"

The nurse smiled. "Don't worry, soap and hot water kills it, so even if they feel that you should bag your clothes, you can just take them home and wash them and they will be fine. Spray your boots down with some soapy water and give them a good scrub. But he's probably right, a professional cleaning job on your truck would probably be a good idea."

Bubba considered that for a minute then asked, "Would it be possible for somebody to bring Pop's and Lenore's boots?"

The nurse nodded. "Give me a minute, I'll be right back." She left and Diego and Bubba got started on the paperwork. They were just finishing filling it out when she returned. She held out a bag. "I regret to inform you that they felt the need to cut your father's boots off, but here is the young lady's boots and your father's jewelry. He didn't have a wallet, and the young lady had a knife in her pocket. It's in there too, apparently, it's really grody. And here is the address of the lab."

He took the bag, nodded, and headed for his father's truck.

Diego took the address and followed Bubba.

XXXIV

Diego pulled up outside a building, Bubba pulled in beside him. A small glass door on the far left said 'LAB'. Diego got out of his patrol truck and looked at Bubba who pushed open his door and gestured to the lab. "I don't want to go spreading the stuff around, why don't you go find out what they want us to do?"

Diego nodded and went inside. The woman behind the counter looked up at him and smiled, "Good afternoon, Sheriff. What can I do for you?"

He laughed and shook his head. "It's a terrible day, but I appreciate the sentiment. I have a friend of mine outside in his truck with two dead dogs, which could or could not have rabies. My friend is also covered in blood, which may or may not be contaminated by rabies. What do you want us to do?"

She grimaced. "Stay right there. I will call my supervisor." She picked up the phone and spoke quickly into it. When she was done relaying the information, she took the phone away from her mouth and asked, "Are we doing the cleanup, or are we just processing the remains?"

Diego groaned. He knew this kind of stuff was ridiculously expensive when done right. "What would it cost for you to clean the truck and my friend?"

"Did you get that, Sally?" She listened, then nodded agreement, pulled the phone away from her mouth again. "Pickup truck, four-door or two-door, inside and outside, and are we talking completely naked shower, scrub, the whole nine yards?"

"Four-door, inside and out, blood in the front seat, blood in the backseat, the truck bed is covered in blood, has two corpses in it, and yes, he was sitting in blood. I noticed his backside and down to his knee is covered in blood, and his hands and arms."

The woman nodded several times, clearly listening. She picked up a calculator and began punching numbers. "That's right. He's a uniformed officer. No, got it, Sally. Right, if their insurance does not cover the animal processes, the total cost is twenty-five thousand, four hundred and fifty dollars, right." She shifted the phone away from her mouth and punched a few more buttons on the calculator and spoke to the Sheriff. "My supervisor said that since this was a friend, we're going to give you the law enforcement discount which is ten percent. If the insurance does not cover testing the animals, the total will be twenty-two thousand nine hundred and five dollars. Now, if insurance covers the animal processing fees, the total will be one thousand, three hundred and five dollars, because sadly vehicle insurance never covers this kind of damage. They classify it as deliberate. If you know the name of the insurance company and the name of the victims, I can check really quickly, and have an answer for you about animal processing fees."

Diego shook his head. "Most ranchers have crappy insurance, but since the expensive part is what we have to have done anyways, will you bill me, or do we have to pay right now? And I appreciate the law enforcement discount, and one of the victims is my daughter. My daughter, her boss, and her boyfriend."

The receptionist sighed and looked sad. She shook her head. "That is rough, Sheriff. Don't worry, we will work with you, and Sally is pretty tenacious about finding loopholes to force insurance companies to cover these things. If you can give me a billing address and your name and the name of the people involved, we will have a team come out and start helping you and your ... sorry, what was that, Sally?" She looked back at the Sheriff. "She wants to make sure that you in no way have been contaminated."

Diego sighed and shook his head. "Quite frankly, I wish I had got a chance to hug my daughter, but by the time I got out of my patrol truck, she was already in the hospital. I did get a glimpse of her, and I've not come in contact with Bubba or the truck."

"I'm sorry, but that's good, because it's less contamination we have to worry about." She hung up the phone and he gave her all the information and she entered it into the computer. "Well, Sheriff, if you will go outside, Sally and her team are probably already out there with your friend or will be arriving momentarily."

Diego nodded and headed outside. He had just arrived next to the truck when a garage door opened, and a tiny little woman in a biohazard jumpsuit, hairnet, mask, and rubber gloves came out of the garage with two large men identically dressed, though each one of them was carrying a large cardboard box. They went straight to the back of the truck and began dealing with the bodies. The woman came around to the driver's seat.

She peeked around, then whistled. "Wow! What a mess! I don't think I've ever seen a rabies cleanup quite that bad. Why don't you do me a favor, sir, go ahead and pull the truck into the garage and then stay in the truck. Don't get out. I will meet with you in just a moment."

Bubba did as he was told. The Sheriff appeared next to him a minute or two later. He demanded, "What's going on, Sheriff?"

"You and the truck are going to get cleaned. You're probably going to be naked when they're all done with you. She said something about scrub down."

Bubba grumbled. "What's this going to cost? I know it's necessary, but I'm still worried."

Diego sighed. "Let's just say both of our savings is probably going to go up in smoke over this." Bubba started to bang his head into the steering wheel. Diego snapped quickly, "Don't do that!"

"Right, rabies, forgot. Somehow, someway, we'll find a way to get through it, not that it will cost you a damn dime. My ranch, my problems."

"My daughter, my responsibility, and besides, let's both cross our fingers and pray desperately to God that insurance covers the animal processing, because if it does, this is nothing, just thirteen hundred dollars. It's the animal processing fees that are going to kill us."

Bubba laughed and started to rub his face. Sally snapped, "Don't do that!"

He sighed. "Of course it would be the required thing that's expensive."

She smiled. "Don't worry, more and more insurance companies are covering the lab fees for it, thanks to the health department requiring it to be done, but for now let's get you cleaned up so we stop worrying about you infecting yourself. By the way, I'm Sally Newton, and you gentlemen are …?"

Diego responded, "I'm the Sheriff of Leaf, Texas, Diego Mendoza, and this is the son of a lifetime friend of mine, Bubba Cartwright. He's also my daughter's boyfriend."

She smiled. "Nice to meet you gentlemen, now …" She placed plastic backed paper on the ground and pointed. "Bubba, if you would please step out of the vehicle and onto the paper." He did so, then she handed him a little pair of shoe covers. "Take them carefully by the edge and slip one on and step off the paper, then put the other on and step off the paper."

He did so carefully. He murmured, "I feel like I have the plague."

She laughed and shook her head. "Oh no, if you had the plague, we would be in oxygen masks and the yellow biohazard suits and the whole area would be locked down and my front desk clerk would want to kill the Sheriff. This is just rabies. We are probably being way too cautious, but when infectious disease cleanup and biohazard cleanup is your business, you tend to be paranoid. I mean, in all reality, you probably could take your truck home, spray it down with bleach, hose it off, let it dry, and be fine, but with rabies being such a nasty death, is that really a chance you want to take?"

Both men replied simultaneously, "No."

"I thought you'd say that. And quite frankly, it wouldn't look as nice as when we're done. When we're done nobody will ever know anything happened. Now if you will follow me? And be sure not to scuff your feet, pick them up. If you tear up the little booties, I am going to yell at you." She walked over to a table that was covered in plastic. She indicated it. "Please, empty your pockets and remove all jewelry."

Bubba did as he was told. "I left the keys in the truck though. Also, Lenore's boots and my Pop's jewelry are in there too in a hospital bag."

"Not to worry, from bumper to bumper, inside and out, everything will be cleaned except the engine. I don't think we have to touch the engine, do we?"

"No, the engine's fine, and there's probably bunches of junk in the truck that can just be thrown out."

"Well, as soon as we have you cleaned and processed, we'll have you fill out the paperwork for us to clean the truck, and you can give us permission to throw away what we consider trash. We try not to throw away any important papers, like receipts, things like that, but sometimes there's just nothing for it."

Bubba laughed. "Other than the papers in the glove compartment, which you shouldn't have to touch the glove compartment, there won't be any important papers. Any time my Pop does anything that requires him keeping a receipt, he sticks it in his wallet, and he didn't have his wallet on him."

She nodded. "All done?" He nodded. "What size shoe do you wear?"

He answered somewhat hesitatingly, "Eleven and a half."

She nodded, crossed to large cupboard, opened it, scanned down and pulled out a pair of shoes. She closed it, crossed to another cupboard, opened it and pulled out a set of scrubs, a pair of socks and underwear. She returned. "Sheriff, if you will wait here." She stepped over to a door and opened it. She gestured for Bubba to enter. "Now this is going to be fun, never actually had to use this room before." She picked a plastic bag up off the table, shook it out and turned the edges down, then set it on the table. "Clothes that you want to keep go in this bag. If there are any clothes you don't want to keep, please put them in this bucket. Now in this room you don't have to worry about touching anything because if you look up, you will see that the entire ceiling is covered in showerheads because this entire room will be sterilized after you leave. If you would please go ahead and remove your boots, I will take them out with me and put them with the truck for cleaning. Everything that you put on the table I will get cleaned while you are showering. Here is a complete change of clothes for you, and in the shower you will find soap, shampoo, scrub brush, and washcloth. Use it all. There's also a back brush, use it. Try not to get any water in your mouth or eyes. Take your time, be thorough. I cannot stress that enough. Start with your hands and your arms, and then proceed the top and work your way down."

He sighed. "I'm so glad I left my hat in my truck."

"I know. It's rough, but everything will be okay. Remember, this is rabies in the United States, being treated on the day of infection. It's fine, annoying, but not deadly."

When she exited the room, she closed the door. Dan approached her. "The remains are in the lab being processed, can we get to work on the truck?"

"He has not signed off on it yet, so close the door and start processing the outside. Anything in the truck bed, set aside and don't do anything with it. Take these and put them with the stuff from the truck bed. Once we have his signed consent, then we can start processing that and the inside. Actually, wait a minute. He said there was a hospital bag of his father's effects. Go ahead and bring that to me, I will process it as a courtesy."

"Yes, ma'am."

Sally got to work on the personal items. She glanced at the Sheriff. "You know, just to be on the safe side, you should probably go over to that sink and give your hands a good scrub."

Diego nodded and did as he was told.

When Bubba came out of the room, he said with annoyance, "I feel like I'm going to jail."

She grimaced. "I'm sorry. I know it does rather look that way, but what else can we do?"

"I know and it's appreciated."

She indicated the other table. "Everything over there is already cleaned. Mostly it's just your jewelry, but I did get a few other things done, and I did go ahead and clean your father's jewelry. I hope you don't mind."

He shook his head, retrieved his cross and his father's wedding ring. He slipped the ring on the chain, then put his cross back on. He put his father's cross on, then put on his own watch. He started to slip his father's in his pocket, then he grumbled. The only pocket he had was a breast pocket. He put it on his other wrist. "No, ma'am, much appreciated. Pop wouldn't like the idea of that being left here. Not that he doesn't trust you, he's just had it a long time."

She smiled. "I understand." She looked back at the table in front of her and indicated it. "However, your wallet is very badly bloodstained. I can clean it, but my recommendation would be …"

He cut her off. "Toss it."

She nodded and indicated the other table. "Watch out, the money's still wet. I didn't have time to put in the dryer yet, but it's clean."

Bubba started laughing. He whispered, "Shush, I don't think you're supposed to talk about laundering money in front of a Sheriff."

They all laughed. "Well, Mr. Cartwright, Sheriff, now that you two are all nice and clean, you can go through that glass door and Alexis will help you process the paperwork, and then the two of you are free to go. You can pick up your truck anytime tomorrow after eight."

Bubba nodded. "On that note, one of my hands is flying in tomorrow morning. Can he pick up the truck for me and bring it back to the ranch?"

"Absolutely, just give his information to Alexis."

Bubba picked up his money, credit cards, ID, and stuck them in the breast pocket, and grabbed onto a cell phone and decided it was too heavy for the pocket, then he and the Sheriff headed for the office.

XXXV

Bubba shivered when they stepped outside and headed for the Sheriff's work truck. Once they were both in, Diego suggested, "I think we should go back to the hospital, get you your shot, check on our family, then we should run to a store to get you a sweater and get Wayne and Lenore clothes."

Bubba nodded. "Sounds like a plan. No, wait. Crap, it's Thanksgiving, nobody's gonna be open."

Diego sighed. "Unfortunately in this day and age there are a lot of places open. Sadly, we'll probably just have to deal with crazy lines, but I think it'll be better right now than if we wait until tonight or tomorrow. From what I've been seeing on the television, most of the sales don't start until six PM, so I think as long as we're in and out by then we'll be okay."

He nodded. "Good point." He looked at his phone and saw he had several missed calls. Three were from Stewart, two from George, and two from Ramon. Since Stewart was foreman, he called him back first.

Stewart demanded, "How bad is it?"

"Hard to say which is worse. Pop was unconscious for probably about an hour. He's real chewed up. Lenore's arm looked real ..."

Stewart cut him off and demanded, "Lenore? You didn't tell me anything happened to Lenore. You just said it was Wayne."

Bubba groaned. "Sorry, I didn't get a chance to tell you. She didn't tell us that she was attacked too. She also did not tell us that there were two dogs, not one. They were both covered in so much blood I can't really tell you how bad it was, or how superficial it was, but I'd say she lost a lot of blood. She was real pale."

Stewart closed his eyes and rubbed his face. "So I'm assuming you haven't heard anything yet, still waiting?"

"No, I haven't heard anything, and not exactly. I had to take Pop's truck to get cleaned up and get myself cleaned up. So until we know for certain, we have to treat it like it's rabies for all of us, since I was covered in blood too. Aww, shit! That reminds me, the ground around the truck, it could be contaminated. We have to keep the animals away from it and we need to find out what we have to do about cleaning it. It's two o'clock. Something tells me I'll be back to the ranch around five or six, and I'll get dinner on the grill then. Sorry guys, this ain't much of a Thanksgiving."

"The last thing on any of our minds is dinner. Cold ham sandwiches will be just fine. All we care about right now is Wayne and Lenore, and in regards to the ground, I already contacted the CDC and I've already cleaned it up. They said hot soapy water and we're good to go, and as far as the animals are concerned, the Vet is already out here. He's vaccinating the dogs and checking them over. None of them had any injuries that concern him. Only two of the dogs were behind a month on their vaccination, he apologized and said that was his fault. He didn't know how he missed it. He went ahead and vaccinated them, and as far as the others are concerned, he says if it turns out that the wild dogs had rabies, he'll give them boosters, but otherwise they're fine. He checked mommy and puppies over, says they're all healthy, and Ramon and Aaron went over the stables and the house with a fine-tooth comb. There are no boards that we need to be concerned about. The horses are safe. We checked the stables inside, everything is fine."

Bubba rubbed his hand up and down his face. "That's all a relief. What time were you and George gonna knock off for the day?"

"We're not going anywhere until you're home."

"Don't be stubborn, you both have families to get to. I mean, if you two aren't sitting down with your families at dinnertime, I will kick both your butts. Ramon and Aaron can hold down the fort."

Stewart growled and demanded, "Hey, George, what time is dinner at your house?"

"Five o'clock."

"He says five and dinner at my house is at six, so I'll see him on his way at four, and I'll leave here at five, but you damn well better call me as soon as you have word! I don't care what time it is."

"Roger that. Do I need to call Ramon or George?"

"George, you need to talk to Bubba? ... He says no, he was just checking in. ... Ramon, what about you? ... He said no, he was just calling you to tell you the stables were clear and he wanted a status report."

"All right, I will text or call you guys as soon as I have word. We're headed back to the hospital right now and I'm going to get my rabies shot. We'll see what we can find out and then we're to go get them some clothes, because their clothes are toast. And I'm holding out hope that I can take them home with me."

Stewart sighed and rubbed his face. He said gently, "Bubba, right now the best I think we can hope for is to bring them home tomorrow morning, but I bet they would rather have clothes than hospital gowns, so you take care of what you need to take care of, and I will call you after dinner, and if you need me you damn well better tell me, and I will be back. This is no boss/employee bullshit.

This is I am your elder and you will respect me on this one, kiddo."

Bubba closed his eyes and swallowed hard. It took him a moment before he was able to respond, and even at that all he could say was, "Yes sir." Then he hung up.

When they entered the hospital twenty minutes later, Bubba approached the nurses' desk. "Do you have any word yet about my father, Wayne Cartwright, or my hand, Lenore Stevens?"

The woman typed in. "Your father is in surgery, and Miss Stevens is out of surgery, but she is still not available to visitors."

Diego noticed Bubba was starting to look a little green. He reached up and squeezed his shoulder as he asked, "When will we be able to get more information about my daughter and my friend?"

"I don't know. Dog bites can take a very long time to treat. We had to clean them up first, and when I say surgery, I'm not meaning like what you normally think of as surgery. People go into surgery for a lot of very basic little things. She just needed a little more work than we were comfortable doing in an ER patient room. Unfortunately, the computer does not give me any more information, but it couldn't have been very big, she was only in surgery for twenty minutes.

Your father's only been in surgery for about forty minutes, and they only slated the room for an hour, and he probably just needed a little work."

Bubba swallowed hard and said, "When I was here earlier, the nurse that was here, she said I needed to get a rabies shot when I came back."

"Name please?"

"Wayne N. Cartwright the second."

"Yes, sir, I see she actually has everything all ready for you. If you will step into triage room number four, I will go ahead and pull that, and we'll get you all taken care of."

He stepped into the room and sat down. She came in a couple of minutes later with a little tray and a piece of paper. "If you'll sign that, I can give you the shot. You'll want to schedule an appointment with your primary care physician in three days for the second dose, and you'll want to setup a schedule for the next one. You have to have four shots over fourteen days and, of course, if they determine that the animal does not have rabies, then you can cease treatment, but that will be a conversation you have to have with your primary care physician. Usually they err on the side of caution and finish out the treatment anyways."

Bubba signed the paper and received his shot. She handed him a little card. At the top, it said rabies vaccines. Below that someone had hand written 'Wayne Cartwright Jr. DOB 11/15/1994'. Below that were four lines. The first box had today's date stamp on it and the name of the hospital. "You'll need to keep this on you until you finish treatments, and then it can just be added to your medical file. Any questions?"

"Yes, we're gonna run out and get them some clothes. Can somebody please call us when we can see them, or if they have more information."

"Of course, but it's only been two and a half hours. I really wouldn't expect any information for at least another three hours. Like I said, dog bites take a long time, and they might have to do some x-rays in addition to that."

He sighed with frustration, took the card, stuffed it in his breast pocket, then got to his feet and headed out. He stalked past Diego and snapped, "Let's go. No point in standing around waiting."

Diego followed quietly. Bubba slammed the door to the truck. Diego got in and headed to the store. He contemplated asking Bubba if he wanted to talk about it, but the look on his face told Diego he was in no mood for talk. They arrived at the store and headed in. Diego got a buggy.

Bubba grudgingly asked, "What do you suggest?"

"I was thinking slippers with plastic soles, larger than they normally wear, pajama bottoms, also much larger than they normally wear, long sleeved T-shirts, and they'll need some socks and probably underwear."

Bubba nodded and entered the shoe department. Slippers were quickly chosen. Then they headed for the men's department. As they walked past the women's department, Bubba paused. He stared at a nightgown. "You know, Lenore doesn't own anything feminine."

Diego was not sure how he felt about Bubba looking at the lingerie department talking about his daughter, but at least the nightgown in question was not a slinky little number. It was a long red T-shirt that said in cursive 'Santa's helper'. Bubba examined the sizes, grabbed one and threw it in the buggy, then he reached over and grabbed a blue one with white snowflakes on it, and threw it in the buggy too. He looked around then pointed. "You said underwear, and believe me, my underwear was not worth keeping and I wasn't bleeding."

Diego scratched his head, turned, and headed for the underwear aisle. He asked, "Are you sure we're up to the task?"

Bubba shook his head. "Absolutely not, but there's no one else here to do it." They stopped and stared at the wall of underwear packages. "G-man-ee Christmas! I had no idea there were so many different styles. I see high cut, bikinis, boy shorties."

Diego added, "I've got briefs, no lines, thongs – which I don't even want to think about – and hipsters. What the hell is a hipster?"

Bubba scratched his neck. He was just reaching for a package of underwear when a female voice, that clearly indicated that she thought they were perverts, demanded, "Can I help you?"

Both men turned and spoke simultaneously. Bubba said, "Yes, please."

Diego said, "God, I hope so, because I feel like I'm drowning here."

She crossed her arms over her chest and looked down her nose at them, which was quite amusing, since they were both over six feet tall and she was only about five feet tall. "And what can I assist you with?"

Again they spoke simultaneously. Bubba said, "My girlfriend."

Diego said, "My daughter." They looked at each other then back at her.

She asked, "Which is it?"

Again they replied simultaneously. "Both." Then they looked at each other again and back at her.

Bubba said firmly, "We've got to stop doing that. Only one speaks."

Diego nodded, pointed at him and said, "You go."

Bubba frowned and looked at him. "Nice way to hang me out to dry." He looked back at the woman. "We were trying to buy underwear for my girlfriend, his daughter, who's in the hospital. We live over two hours away and her clothes are ruined." He indicated himself. "As you can see, so were mine."

"Oh my goodness, what happened?"

They both sighed. "A vicious dog attacked my girlfriend and my father on our ranch."

"Dogs," amended Diego.

Bubba jerked his thumb in the Sheriff's direction. "What he said. In addition to being chewed up and scratched up, my girlfriend had to sit in blood while we drove to town, so believe me, she does not want her clothes back, and she doesn't strike me as a girl who wants to drive two hours' commando, so we thought we'd get her some new underwear. But we had no idea what we were undertaking."

She smiled. "That's very sweet. What kind of underwear does she wear? What do they look like?"

Bubba shrugged his shoulders. "Don't look at me. I haven't seen her in her underwear."

"Okay, how old?"

Diego said, "She's eighteen years old, five foot eight, weighs a hundred and ten pounds."

Bubba added helpfully, "And she can fit in my old size twenty-eight jeans."

"Then I would think you couldn't go wrong with bikinis in size fives. Most women own bikinis."

Diego glanced at the fixture, saw a package of them, took them off, and tossed them in the buggy. "Sold. Now let's grab her a package of socks and move on to the men's department."

Bubba looked back at the woman and pressed his hands together as he said gratefully, "Thank you so much. You made that much easier."

"Anytime. I will pray for them."

Both men said simultaneously, "Thank you."

The rest of their shopping was much easier. They checked out and headed back to the hospital.

XXXVI

Lenore felt violated. She had been pumped full of painkillers, antibiotics, stripped naked, scrubbed down, showered, poked, prodded, x-rayed, and forced to lie still while still mostly naked in a freezing operating room while she was stabbed repeatedly in her wounds, then subjected to multiple hands pinching, poking, and stitching all of her various wounds up. Then she had been covered in various forms of ointment and bandaged. She was pretty sure she had passed out at some point in time during all that. She did not exactly remember making it to the private room or having a gown put on, but now she felt very alert. She was laying on her left side with pillows pushed up against her chest and her left leg, with her right leg and arm propped up on the pillows. It took her a moment of careful maneuvering before she was able to sit up without hurting herself, because her entire right side of her body was killing her, but fortunately her butt seem to be okay. She looked around. Her right arm was in a sling and was splinted. That did not look good. Sitting on the table next to the bed was a cell phone. She picked it up. It was Mr. Cartwright's. There were a couple of missed calls, she did not recognize any of the names.

"Well, how are you feeling now that you're awake?"

She looked to see a man standing in the doorway, in scrubs, holding a clipboard. "Like I have been used for a pincushion."

He chuckled. "I'm Dr. Marks, and sadly that's not an inaccurate statement, but I have some good news. Your arm only has a very slight fracture, so we're going to keep it splinted for about two to six weeks. When it was all said and done, we ended up putting two hundred and thirty-eight stitches in you. We are going to keep you overnight for observation, and tomorrow we'll send you home with antibiotics, painkillers, and you get to sit back, relax, and take it easy for the next couple of weeks. Any questions?"

"Yes, how is Mr. Cartwright?"

"Unfortunately, he's not my patient. I can't tell you anything about him, other than the fact that he is still with the surgeon. However, he has been assigned the room across the hall, which is good news. If they assigned him a room, then they are getting ready to move him in. As soon as they do, I'll be able to tell you more because then he will be my patient."

She sighed. "When will I be able to get back to work?"

"Not until all of the stitches come out. You cannot be working in the mud and muck that is required of a rancher with stitches. I'm just not going to sign off on that. I grew up on a ranch, I know how filthy it is."

She sighed and shook her head. "Great. As if the holidays weren't rough enough with us being shorthanded."

He sighed. "I understand, believe me, but it's just too dangerous. There's just way too much bacteria out there to get into the wounds, and these are dog bites, which are already dangerous enough, not to mention the risk of popping stitches. And only half of your injuries got stitched up, the rest are still open wounds. I am sorry. Anything else before I leave?"

"Yes, since I'm being treated for rabies, when can I my kiss my boyfriend?"

"Would your boyfriend be the younger Mr. Cartwright?"

"Yes."

"I signed orders for him to be vaccinated for rabies as well. Apparently he was elbow deep in your blood, so with you both having received the first round, kiss away."

"Thank you." He turned and left.

A nurse came in a few minutes later. "Good afternoon, I am Nurse Jenny. I'm here to take your vitals and I will be looking after you this evening until eight o'clock. At that time, Cameron will be taking over."

Lenore sat there thinking while the woman checked her vitals. "Don't you have paperwork or something? Don't I have to sign myself in?"

"No, your boss signed you and his father in."

She said with more confidence than she felt, "Oh no, that can't be good. He probably gave the wrong billing address. He doesn't handle the paperwork. Mr. Cartwright and myself, we handle that. Could you find out for me?"

"Of course." Jenny picked up the phone and dialed the extension for billing. "Yes, Marcus, this is Nurse Jenny on the fourth floor. I have a patient here who is concerned that when she was admitted, her boss might have given the wrong billing address. Can we check that out for her? Lenore Stevens." Jenny offered her the phone. "He's going to look the file up right now."

Lenore took the phone. "I'm sorry to bother you. It's just Bubba doesn't handle the paperwork. Mr. Cartwright and I do. Is the address the Texas address or the California one?"

"The billing address on file is in Leaf, Texas …"

She cut him off. "That's what I was afraid of. That's the wrong address. The correct billing address should be four hundred Marketplace Plaza, Suite Two Hundred, Hollywood, California, and be sure to put it to Attention Hector Sanderson."

Marcus said a little bit uncertainly, "Are you sure about that address, ma'am?"

"Quite certain. After it goes through insurance, bill that address and I promise you it will be paid promptly, and be sure to send the bills for both myself and Mr. Cartwright."

"Which Mr. Cartwright? Junior, or Senior."

"The second, don't ever call him Junior. If your paperwork says Junior, it is wrong, and send all three bills to the California address."

"Yes, ma'am, I'm updating all that information right now, and I have removed Junior and corrected it to the Second."

"Thank you." She hung up the phone and looked at Jenny. "Thank you."

"No problem. I'm going to turn out the lights and leave you to get some rest, and they will be serving dinner here in a little while. Be sure to take it easy when you start eating, some of the meds they gave you might make your stomach a little wonky."

"I will be sure to keep that in mind. I don't like being alone. Can you leave the door open?"

"Of course, if that's what you want."

Lenore sat wondering when she had become such a liar. Since waking up, she had not said a single truthful word. Only about twenty minutes passed before she saw them wheel Mr. Cartwright into his room. She waited for them to leave, then she got off her bed, gripped her IV stand, and headed for the door. She peeked out. No one was looking. She moved across the hall as quickly as her aching body would allow. As she approached Mr. Cartwright's bedside, he raised an eyebrow. "You know, something tells me, girl, you ain't supposed to be out of bed."

She sat down in the chair next to him, careful to perch on the edge as the back of her right thigh was pretty chewed up. She reached over and tentatively touched his hand. He turned it over and squeezed her fingers. "I don't care. I wanted to come over and check on you. What did they say?"

"Torn up pretty good, muscle damage, concussion, apparently that's what knocked me out. When it leapt on me, I must've fallen back into my truck and hit my head. They are going to keep me for three or four days. Apparently they didn't like my EKG or my blood pressure when I came in, so they are going to be running some more tests on me, but that's enough about me. What did they say about you?"

She gave a faint shrug of her shoulders. "Scratches, a few stitches, a very slight fracture. Whatever that means, but that kind of puts my arm out of commission for a few weeks, and I can't go back to work until they remove the stitches."

He sighed. "That sounds about right. Looks like you and I get to sit and watch movies for a while."

"Don't that sound like fun."

"I would have to agree, but we're both just gonna have to suck it up and deal."

She nodded and hesitated a long minute. "Mr. Cartwright, you know that first week I was here, you told me to stay away from your son, and then back in the truck you said please tell you we weren't sleeping together. Was that just because of the rabies, or because you still want me to stay away from him?"

He smiled and squeezed her hand. "Lenore, I like you and I think you're good for Bubba. He definitely notices whenever you walk in the room, and I would be thrilled to pieces to have you as my daughter-in-law if it weren't for just one thing."

"Well, Mr. Cartwright, you don't have to worry, Bubba said the same thing. Well, he's said girlfriend." They sat there in silence. She smiled when she thought Mr. Cartwright had fallen asleep, but she was not eager to go back to her room.

Jenny entered the room, followed by Diego and Bubba. She demanded, "And who gave you leave to be out of your bed, young lady? Let's go back to bed ... actually, wait. I will get a wheelchair. You don't need to be walking around right now."

Bubba smiled. "Don't bother, I got this." He bent down and picked her up. "If one of you will bring that thing with you."

Jenny grabbed a hold of the IV and said, "Sir, I don't think that's a good idea." But since he ignored her, she had no choice but to follow.

He tucked Lenore into bed. "You look better than when I saw you last."

She cupped his cheek. "And you are as handsome as ever."

He leaned forward and kissed her gently. "You look very tired. They already told me they're holding you overnight, but they'll release you first thing tomorrow morning. That Dr. Marks promised that he would sign your papers about eight-thirty. I'm going to check on Pop, then I have to go back to the ranch. I will be back later tonight or first thing tomorrow morning. Get some sleep."

She wanted to argue, but she could barely keep her eyes open. She lay back against the pillows and fell asleep.

He pushed her hair off her cheek and kissed her gently.

XXXVII

Friday, November 24

Bubba had scarcely slept a wink all night. He looked at the clock, three thirty. He had had enough. He crawled out of bed, ran through the shower, got dressed, and headed down to the kitchen. He made coffee, then went out to the store room and opened the large freezer. He was relieved to see several boxes of the microwave sausage biscuits they kept on hand for emergencies like Alejandro being sick. He looked at his watch, he had plenty of time.

He went into the office, took a deep breath, and sat down at his father's desk. He began looking at the paperwork in front of him. He knew his father had a system. He was going to have to ask some questions. There was a stack of metal shelves on the corner of the desk that were neatly labeled. The one on top said 'Incoming mail', the one below it said 'Paid bills', the one below that said 'To be paid', the one on the bottom, thank God was empty, and said 'To be disputed'. The bucket for outgoing mail was by the front door, whenever someone went to town they took it. There was a single drawer to the left-hand side of the desk calendar. Bubba examined it. It said 'Orders to fill'. He went through it. Good, there were no surprises there. Everything in the drawer was already in the process of being taken care of, now he just had to make sure it actually happened. He groaned and looked at the computer. He had scarcely touched one since he graduated from college. It took him a minute to figure out how to turn it on. He sat twiddling his thumbs, wondering if this stupid computer was ever going to boot up. Finally it did. He sighed with relief. It looked like all of the important files were on the main screen. He clicked on their accounting file. When it opened, he looked at the bottom line. He groaned a little, their savings was not quite what he had hoped it was, but they had had a rough year last year. They had to make several major repairs to equipment and orders had not quite been as good previous years. This year had been much better, and they were anticipating next year being even better. They were already in negotiations for a large horse sale around February and several large beef contracts. He rubbed his hands up and down his face. "Chill out, Bubba, everything's gonna be fine. Pop will be home in a couple of days. He can sit here and handle the computer work and you can run the ranch. We can do this." He went through the little bit of incoming mail, struggled through paying two bills, and was just putting the last paper on a new stack when he heard sounds coming from the kitchen. He raised an eyebrow, grabbed his coffee cup and headed in. He smiled. "Betsy, what are you doing up so early?"

Betsy was just in the process of tying on an apron. She finished what she was doing, turned and crossed to him, hugging him tightly. "Hey, sweetie, how are you holding up?"

He hugged her back. "If I don't allow myself to think about it, I'm doing great."

She patted him on the shoulder. "Denial is never the best course of action."

"I'm not in denial, I just have ... stuff that has to get done. If I think too much about my fears and my concerns, it ain't going to get done, and you didn't answer me. What are you doing here, not that I don't love your company."

"I should think the answer would be obvious. I'm here to make breakfast and I'm going to get beef stew in the crock pots." She took his coffee cup out of his hand and crossed to the pot. "Still take it black?"

"Do I still ride?"

She rolled her eyes. She had never met a cowboy who took his coffee any way but black. She filled it, then crossed back to him. "Still a smarty pants I see."

He leaned down and kissed her on the cheek. "You wouldn't love me if I wasn't."

She smiled. "True enough. Now if you expect your breakfast on the table at six, you best get out of this kitchen and let me get to work." She turned to walk away, but tossed over her shoulder, "Susie went shopping this morning, of course, but she told me to tell you that she would be over tomorrow first thing and help tidy up around the house. She said she'd start in Wayne's room, making sure everything was ready for him to come home from the hospital. When is that new girl coming home?"

Bubba had to bite his tongue not to snap. He knew she did not mean any offense by it, but it really galled him to hear Lenore called 'that new girl'. "That's very kind of Susie, but not necessary. I'm sure we can manage, and her name is Lenore, and barring unforeseen circumstances, I'm going to have breakfast, get the boys started on their work for the day, and then head into Amarillo and pick her up."

Betsy turned and put her hands on her hips. "Don't be ridiculous. This is what we do in this part of the world. We come together when there are difficult times, and I'm sure Wayne will appreciate coming home to some clean sheets, and I will change the sheets on Lenore's bed and run the vacuum around her room and do any other tidying up I see. Though hopefully, she's not like a slovenly teenage boy." She looked at him very accusatory.

"I was never a slob, thank you very much. Mama wouldn't have allowed it, and I appreciate the offer to help around the house and with Pop's room, but I am going to have to say you can't go into Lenore's room. As an employee, she is entitled to a certain level of privacy. I cannot allow you to go into her room."

Betsy opened her mouth to protest, but Stewart, who had been standing by quietly drinking his coffee, interjected. "Now, Honey, I'm sorry, I have to agree with Bubba on this one. As ranch foreman, I do have to look after the employees and their employee rights, and though Lenore's bedroom is not in the bunkhouse, it is her bedroom, and as an employee, without reasonable proof of wrongdoing, we have no right to go into it, even to do something as nice as change the sheets. However, I can think of a compromise. If it is really that important to you, honey, you can make Aaron do it."

Bubba nodded. "Actually, I think that is an excellent idea, because it'd be really nice to have her sheets changed. I just don't feel any of us should do it, but Aaron is her brother."

Betsy shrugged her shoulders. "I think both of you are being silly, but if you think it's that important, Aaron can change the sheets and run the vacuum."

Bubba nodded. "Thank you. When we go over work for the day, I will make sure he knows that that is his number one priority." He turned and headed out of the kitchen and went back to the office.

Stewart followed him in and closed the door and asked softly, "Since I've never known you to give a damn about our privacy, is it safe to assume that there might be something Persephone related in there?"

Bubba shrugged his shoulders. "Truth be told, I have no idea, but I'm not willing to risk it. If this offends you, I'm sorry, but I'm worried about your wife running on at the mouth."

Stewart laughed and shook his head. "You got to be kidding me. Betsy's mouth is so big you could park a truck in it if she stopped talking long enough."

Bubba roared with laughter.

XXXVIII

Lenore was sitting up sideways in bed when Bubba entered and groaned. "I am so sorry I am late." He crossed to her and kissed her on the cheek, then he frowned. "You look tired. Did you not sleep well?"

She rolled her eyes. "It's very difficult to sleep well when nurses keep coming and going to check your vitals."

He grimaced. "That does sound miserable. Well, at least you'll get a good night's sleep tonight in your own bed."

She smiled. "I am definitely looking forward to it. How's Mr. Cartwright this morning?"

"I peeked in on him before coming over here, but he was still asleep."

They were interrupted by the doctor and a nurse entering. "Good morning, Miss Stevens, how are you doing this morning?"

"As well as can be expected for having been chewed up and spit out."

"I know, and hospitals are no place to get a good night's sleep, or to get better. You will get better much faster at home surrounded by your family."

She smiled. "Does that mean I can go home now?"

"Not quite, there's still a few things we have to discuss first. So all of your vitals from last night were good, all of your labs look good, other than your iron is a little low, so I recommend you start taking an iron supplement. Lots of bleeding wounds and anemia don't mix."

Bubba asked with a smile, "How about just stop being a vegetarian?"

"That would help, and I apologize. It was not noted anywhere in the file that you were vegetarian. Did they give you a vegetarian dinner last night?"

"No, and even the vegetables were disgusting."

He nodded. "Yes, if I don't get to go out to lunch, I eat the peanut butter crackers in my desk drawer, much tastier. Well, hopefully you can get a good breakfast on your way home. For now, I'm sending you home with antibiotics, a strong recommendation that you start taking iron pills, and when you go for your follow-up, to have your iron tested again. It's a simple little finger prick, no big deal, and I'm going to send you home with a pain pill prescription. Anything else I can do for you?"

Lenore said firmly, "I don't need that pain pill prescription."

Dr. Marks frowned. "You're going to be in a tremendous amount of pain for the next few days. I don't think this is the moment to be a hero."

Lenore bit her lip and looked down at her lap. She murmured, "I'm a recovering drug addict."

Dr. Marks stared in surprise. He had only been a resident for three years. Ninety-eight percent of drug addicts did not surprise him, but there was always that two percent that floored him. This was one of those cases.

Bubba said firmly, "Now wait a minute, I think you're being very unfair to yourself. She was not a recreational drug user, her mother had multiple doctors prescribing multiple kinds of drugs and messing her up. I'm not saying there's not cause for concern, but don't make it sound like you were just out to get high."

Dr. Marks groaned and shook his head. "I wish I could say that didn't happen, but unfortunately it happens all too often. Well, if you were not a recreational drug user and you weren't just out to get high, then we have a few options. I can give you a very small prescription and absolutely no refills, or I can give you a standard prescription, but have someone else be responsible for it if you don't feel strong enough to control it on your own. I could also split the difference and give you a light pain pill, something like ibuprofen, and then give you a half a prescription for something a little heavier for when the ibuprofen just isn't cutting it. If you're not willing to do that, that of course, is your prerogative, but it's going to be a miserable week."

Bubba reached down and squeezed her hand. "I think you're strong enough to handle it on your own, but if you don't, I'm more than willing to be responsible."

She bit her lip. "I haven't even been clean for two weeks. I don't think I can do it. I don't trust myself. Why don't we do the half-and-half and you be responsible, if that's not too much of a burden."

He squeezed her hand gently, and leaned down, and kissed her on the temple. "It's not a burden at all."

Dr. Marks nodded. "Good, and I feel very comfortable with this arrangement. Now before I discharge you, I do want to take a look under your bandages. There are some in some personal areas, so I don't know if you want him to step out or if you don't care."

Bubba quickly excused himself. He went in to check on his father.

Wayne was sitting up in bed when Bubba entered. "What brings you up here so early, boy?"

"Doctor's releasing Lenore. I'm going to take her home. How did you sleep? Lenore passed a miserable night."

Wayne smiled. "Oh, I see how it is. You go check on the girlfriend before the old man."

He snorted and rolled his eyes. "No, the old man was proving how old he was and was still asleep when I stepped in, so I went across and talked to my girl. You got a problem with that?"

Wayne chuckled. "Not at all. How is she?"

"Besides looking tired, she looks pretty good."

"What about business? What about my truck? Anything I need to know? Anything we need to discuss?"

"Well, I sat down at the desk, looked at our savings, looked at all the paperwork on your desk, everything looks good. Everything looks to be in order. I paid a couple of bills. I noted them in the accounting file, hopefully correctly. As far as your truck is concerned, I had to leave it to be professionally cleaned because you and Lenore bled everywhere, mostly you. Looks like that's only gonna end up costing us about seven thousand dollars, because it looks like the ranch health insurance covers seventy-five percent of the animal processing fee, but they'll call me on Monday after they verify that. So that's really good news, provided she's right, which they seem to be very conscientious. I don't think she'd say that unless she was pretty damn sure, and in addition to that, they're very kindly giving a law enforcement discount on the remainder which will help out immensely. It's ten percent. So now we're just waiting for the rabies result, which we should have those by Thursday or Friday, but that's after we've already gotten our second dose, and according to the doctor, they're probably gonna want us to run the whole gamut anyways, because the rabies might not be far enough along to test positive. Now we just have to worry about medical bills."

Wayne groaned and rubbed his face. "Yeah and if memory serves, our insurance only covers eighty percent of hospital stays; however, everything that was actually classified as ER will be covered except for the fifteen hundred dollar co-pay."

Bubba sighed with relief. That was actually better than he thought it was going to be. "Well, that ain't so bad. So we're looking at what, twenty thousand dollars, that's way better than what I was afraid it was going to be. That'll cut into our savings a little, but not so bad."

Wayne nodded. "And it will be even better if they only keep me a day or two instead of the four or five they're threatening."

Dr. Marks entered. He glanced at Bubba and said with a smile, "Oh, you again. What are you doing, wandering around bothering all my patients?" He glanced at Wayne and asked, "Should I call security?"

Wayne shrugged his shoulders. "Well, he is a crazy troublemaker but I'm used to him, so I guess I'll keep him."

Dr. Marks smiled. "Probably a good call, he seems like a good egg."

"So how is Lenore?" As the doctor hesitated, Wayne added, "Remember, she is my employee and was injured on the job."

Dr. Marks nodded. "Correct, I forgot that. She's doing really well. She needs to take it easy for at least a week to ten days until the stitches come out, keep all the wounds clean and dry, and change the bandages every day. When she goes in for her second rabies shot, the doctor will tell her if she needs to keep the wounds bandaged or if it's time to let them get some air, but she'll have to go back in a week for the doctor to make a decision about the stitches. He'll probably take some out at that time, others will probably be in for ten days. Y'all are probably going to spend a lot of time in doctor's offices for the next month. After the stitches come out she can return to light work, but she'll need to take it easy with the fractured arm and will probably be in a splint for about four to six weeks, just a guess. But I don't see a reason to cast it because of the stitches, just make sure she doesn't take it off to do work she's not supposed to be doing until after the stitches are out. Something tells me she is going to be a difficult patient."

Bubba chuckled. "I was starting to get that feeling too." He jerked his thumb in the direction of his father. "So what about this guy?"

"As far as the dog bites are concerned, he's pretty much in the same boat as Lenore minus any broken bones; however, he did suffer a severe concussion, so you can have the potential for dizzy spells, lightheadedness, and other issues involving his head for as much as three months. Six weeks is normal, but with a concussion, to say anything is normal is really a mistake. Now in regards to the EKG and the blood pressure, we haven't started on those other tests, and until we do, we don't know where we stand with that, but we will be doing that on you here shortly. It is a series of tests which will cause us to at least hold him through tomorrow, but I think we'll probably be able to release him on Sunday morning."

Bubba asked, "What is your gut telling you about those tests?"

"My instincts are telling me that he can go home with heart medicine and blood pressure medicine, other than that, he will be fine. But again he's going to have to have follow-up tests to make sure that the medicine is doing what we need it to do."

Wayne groaned. "So back to that get used to doctors' offices?"

He shrugged his shoulders. "I am sorry, but probably. Take a book, it makes it easier to wait."

Bubba nodded and got to his feet. He extended his hand to the doctor. "Thank you very much for your time and everything you've done for my family, Doc. I can't tell you how much I appreciate it."

"Anytime. That's what we're here for."

XXXIX

Lenore was amazed at how difficult and painful it was just getting into the truck. As she tried to buckle up, Bubba said gently, "Here, let me do that." He carefully buckled her up then went around to the other side, hopped in and buckled up before started the truck, then he said, "The nurse said the prescriptions wouldn't be ready for about an hour, so where do you want to have breakfast?"

"Anywhere is fine with me."

He nodded and headed in the direction of pharmacy. Lenore gritted her teeth and closed her eyes. Every bump was agony, and every time her back slammed into the seat was worse, and the seatbelt kept rubbing against her stitches on her shoulder.

Bubba found a quiet little diner, which was not easy given the Black Friday crowds. He said firmly, "Do not try to get out of the truck by yourself, I'll be over in a second and help you."

"You know, it just occurred to me, I'm in my pajamas. Are you embarrassed to be seen in public with me like this?"

"You just got out of the hospital, no. Now in a month or two, if I ask you to go out to breakfast with me and you tried to go in your pajamas, I would tell you no."

"I would never."

He got out and walked around to the other side. He opened the door and carefully helped her out. He was learning it was hard to find someplace to touch that did not hurt, or where she did not have stitches. She had scratches everywhere. They walked slowly into the diner. A woman grabbed two menus and asked, "Just the two of you?"

Bubba replied, "Yes."

"Table or a booth?"

"A table, and please, one in the back where people aren't going to be bumping into her, please."

"Of course, right this way." She led the way to the back of the diner and indicated a table. "Is this all right? I won't seat anybody at the next table unless we get real busy."

Bubba got Lenore seated comfortably as he said, "Yes, this is great, thank you." He sat down and they both perused the menus. The waitress returned a couple of minutes later. "Are you ready to order?"

Bubba looked at her. "Do you need more time?"

She frowned but asked, "That depends. If I order the chicken fried chicken, eggs and pancakes, would you please cut the chicken and pancakes for me?" She felt so embarrassed she wanted to cry.

Bubba looked at the waitress. "We will both have the chicken fried chicken. I would like my eggs over easy, and I'll have home fries instead of hash browns, and coffee to drink. Lenore?"

She murmured, "Scrambled eggs, home fries, and water. Thank you."

The waitress frowned. She felt really bad for the kid. She looked very pale and appeared to be in a lot of pain. She had limped in a very slowly and was still wearing a hospital bracelet. "I'll have your drinks right out for you. Give us just a few minutes on your breakfast."

Bubba reached over and touched Lenore's hand. "You got very quiet all of a sudden, something wrong?"

"Just a lot on my mind."

"You're not thinking about leaving us, are you? Deciding that working on the ranch is too dangerous, too uncomfortable, and you'd rather be doing something cleaner, not as smelly?"

"God, no! I love it. I don't want to leave. I just feel terrible. I'm not going to be able to do anything for a couple of weeks. I guess that's kind of what I'm thinking about. What good can I be around the ranch for a couple weeks? I might not have a job to come back to."

Bubba sighed and shifted to the seat on her left, scooting close enough their chairs were almost touching. "Okay, let's discuss the legal end first. You were injured on the job as a result of your job. Under the law we cannot fire you even if we wanted to, which we don't, and you can't come back to work until the doctor says you can come back to work, and we have to adhere to all restrictions that the doctor gives you until he signs off and gives you an all clear. That's the legal part. Personally, you got hurt working for us in a situation you should never have been in because I screwed up. I should never have left you alone without making sure you knew how to use a gun and had one on you. Pop screwed up too. He should never have gone outside without a gun, even if he was just going to get something out of his truck, he knows better. That's on us. You saved Pop's life. I can never repay you for that. You're really, really going to have to push me to get me to want to fire you, and that's before we even talk about what's going on between you and me, so please stop worrying about the ranch. Stop worrying about your job, and just focus on resting, relaxing, and getting better, because right now that's all I care about. It's all that anyone cares about, okay beautiful?"

She sniffed several times, fighting back tears as she pushed hair behind her ear. "I don't think I look very pretty right now."

Her shoulders started shaking and tears slid down her cheeks. She leaned towards him and he wrapped his arms gently around her, being careful of her injuries. He said gently, "I think you are as pretty as ever. Well, actually, the first time I ever saw you, you did not look pretty; in fact, I wasn't even sure there was a girl under there." She kicked him under the table. He laughed. "Okay, I knew there was a girl, I just didn't know what kind of girl." She kicked him again and sat up straight. He laughed harder. He opened his mouth and almost blurted something out, but he bit his tongue and hoped she did not notice. To his relief, she was looking off to the side. The surprised look on her face caused him to follow her gaze. He raised an eyebrow. He was just about to ask if something was wrong when she got up and walked slowly to a table.

Lenore felt a little self-conscious. After all, she was in pajama bottoms, slippers, and a hoodie, but at least it was zipped up, and the right sleeve was tucked inside. She and the nurse had decided it was better for her to wear the sweater over her arm with the sling, so only her left arm was out, and she did not think anybody could tell she did not have a bra on. She approached a table. The man and woman both looked up at her. The man raised an eyebrow and got to his feet. She held out her left hand. "I'm sorry, sir. I know we never exchanged names and you probably don't remember me …"

He interrupted as he took her left hand with his and placed his right hand over it, "Of course I remember you." He looked her up and down. She looked like hell. "Are you all right? Do you need to sit down?" A man appeared behind her. He squinted as he struggled to remember him. He looked familiar, he had seen him somewhere, but he could not for the life of him remember. He was a respectable looking cowboy, not a wannabe, a real working cowboy. The man stood directly behind her and put his hand on her left hip very possessively.

Bubba asked, "You two friends?"

Lenore smiled and glanced at Nathaniel, then back at the other man. "Not exactly. He gave me a ride from the sporting goods store to the farmers market, and I know I'm interrupting your breakfast, and I'm sorry. I'll leave you be in a second, I just wanted to tell you thank you."

The woman got to her feet and said gently, "Perhaps introductions would be in order."

Lenore smiled and gave a little laugh. "Of course, my apologies. I'm Lenore Stevens and this is my boss, Bubba Cartwright."

The older man snapped his fingers and extended his hand. "Right, Bubba Cartwright. I knew you looked familiar. I just couldn't quite place you."

Bubba chuckled and shook hands with him. "Not strictly surprising, Mr. O'Mannion."

It was Lenore's turn to ask, "Are you two friends?"

Bubba laughed. "In a manner of speaking. For about twenty seconds, he's the best friend a cowboy has. Lenore, this is Sean O'Mannion, one of the most famous rodeo barrel men, and since I know you have no idea what that means, it's only the most dangerous job at a rodeo. It's his job to keep the bull from goring the cowboy. He has saved my fat more than once and he has been pulling cowboy's fats out of the fryer for more than thirty years, but how do you two know each other?"

Sean indicated the woman with him. "And this lovely, patient, kind woman is my wife, Patty."

Lenore extended her left hand awkwardly and said, "Sorry about the awkward handshake, but my right hand is out of commission."

Patty said, "I know. I saw you limp over here. What happened?"

Lenore flipped her hand dismissively. "Just a dog bite."

Bubba rolled his eyes. "You have got to be the queen of understatement. What she's saying wasn't just a dog bite. It was two vicious dogs that resulted in her getting over two hundred stitches and my father getting over a hundred stitches. She spent last night in the hospital and my father is still in the hospital."

Patty grimaced and shook her head. "Dog bites are the worst. Hopefully they were a pet who had been properly vaccinated?"

Bubba said with irritation, "Wild dogs."

Patty sighed and crossed herself. "Good God! I'll pray for clear tests. Were you able to catch the dogs?"

Bubba grinned. "No need, this is one tough cookie. She killed both dogs with a pitchfork and a pocket knife."

Lenore grimaced and looked sad. "Please don't remind me. I feel just terrible about having to do it."

Sean snorted. "I would rather put fifty dogs in the ground than one human being, especially if they were vicious. They needed to go. I like dogs as much as the next person, but dangerous ones just got to go and I have to say, city girl, I'm pretty impressed. Looks like you're doing pretty well for yourself." He glanced meaningfully in Bubba's direction.

Bubba said quickly, "She ain't wearin' my brand."

Sean had to smile. Bubba seemed so disappointed, and Lenore looked over her shoulder and looked surprised, then a little sad. He decided to nudge slightly, "Oh, my mistake. I guess I misunderstood ... So we'll be seeing you in the ring this year?"

Bubba shook his head firmly. "I was originally signed up to do bull riding, but I'm gonna have to call this year's event coordinator and let him know I have to back out, and Pop won't be able to do his duties as a pickup man. So I will assume Pop's duties and handle pickup; after all, that's far more important than me riding another bull."

Sean smiled and looked thoughtful. "Your father's Wayne Cartwright, right?"

"That would be correct, sir."

"You know, it was just about twenty-five years ago when your father decided bull riding was too dangerous and he switched to bronco riding, and I think it was the next year he quit the circuit all together."

Lenore thought for sure she was blushing. One would have to be a fool to miss Mr. O'Mannion's meaning, but she decided it was a good idea if she changed the subject. She said quickly, "Well, I just saw you over here, and I wanted to thank you for talking me into buying that knife. I think if I had bought the one the clerk was trying to get me to buy, things would have gone very differently, so thank you." On an impulse she leaned in and gave him a kiss on the cheek.

He smiled. "I'm very glad I was of service. You take care of yourself."

Lenore and Bubba headed back to their table. Patty and Sean both sat down. She leaned across the table and said to her husband in a whisper, "If Bubba lets that girl slip through his fingers, he doesn't deserve to call himself a rancher."

Sean laughed, reached over, and took his wife's hand, and kissed it. "Wayne was never a fool and I doubt his son is. Grandpa was pretty slick too."

XL

They pulled up in the drive. Lenore looked around, only the two unused trucks and Alejandro's truck were in the drive. That was a relief, she would not have to deal with anybody right this minute. Bubba came around to her side and opened the door. He helped her out, then grabbed the bag from the hospital and the bag from the pharmacy. She walked slowly towards the house. After a minute she said, "Please don't wait on me, I know I'm just slowing you down."

He shook his head. "Maybe I like the view."

She snorted. "Yes, men's pajama bottoms are super sexy."

He shrugged his shoulders. "I think the woman in them is very sexy."

"You're such a charmer."

"So where do you want us to get you settled?"

"I'm kind of tired. I was thinking I was just gonna go to my room and go to bed, if that's okay."

"Of course it is. You've got to be exhausted. Why don't you go on down to your room? I'll get the portable phone out of the office and write down some numbers for you."

"That's really not necessary. I can take care of myself."

He shook his head. "You were just released from the hospital. You need a little looking after."

"No, I don't. They didn't even ask if I was going home alone or not. They told me how to take care of myself, and you've got work to do, so don't worry about me." She went to her room and sat down on the bed. She knew Nathaniel would be coming in in a minute. Sure enough, five minutes later he entered carrying a tray. He set it down on her nightstand.

"I brought you the portable phone, a notepad with everybody's numbers on it, two bottles of water, and a package of crackers. If you're sure you will be okay, there's a couple things I'll go check on, and then I will be back here to clean out the stables, but if you need me, you call me."

"I will be fine. I am just going to sleep."

He frowned and looked around the room. "Before I go, do you want me to bring a laptop in here so you can watch some movies?"

"No, I'll be great. I got my MP3 player if I want to listen to some tunes."

"Okay. By the way, when I bought you the pajamas and hoodie and stuff, I saw these and I bought them for you. If you don't like them, you don't have to wear them, but I thought they might be more comfortable under the circumstances. I washed them last night, so they're clean."

"Thank you, that was sweet of you. Now stop fretting and get to work. I will be fine by myself." She waited until he was gone. She was unbelievably warm. She unzipped the hoodie and threw it over the chair. The long sleeve shirt was warm too, as were the socks and flannel pajamas bottoms. She found getting her socks off was relatively easy, she could use one foot to take the other off; however, getting out of bottoms was tricky with only one good hand and bandages on her hip and thigh. She finally had to resort to taking her arm out of the sling. Using her right hand and arm, which was ridiculously painful, she finally got the bottoms off. Getting out of the shirt was relatively easy. She debated for a moment between a T-shirt and the nightgown Nathaniel had bought her. She laughed at herself. She was finding it harder and harder to think of him as anything but Nathaniel. It was such a nice name and he was such a sweetheart. She shook her head trying to shake those thoughts away and focus on the issue at hand. In the end, she decided on the nightgown because if push came to shove, she could go out into the main house wearing it because it went down to her knees. Since she was going to bed, she left the sling off and curled up in bed. It was hard to get comfortable as she had injuries on so much of her body, but finally she managed it, but sleep eluded her. After a half hour of trying, she decided to listen to music. She had been listening to music for three hours when there was a tap on the door. She removed the earpiece off her left ear and called, "Come in."

Alejandro entered and smiled. "Sorry to bother you, but it's time to take your antibiotic, and Bubba told me to ask you how you're doing. Do you need a pain pill?"

She sat up. "I'm a little achy, maybe an ibuprofen."

"No problem. What do you want to drink, and are you hungry? You want some lunch?"

"No need for you to put yourself to any trouble. I can get myself something to eat, and I'll get myself a drink. You just got back from being out of town, I'm sure you have other things you need to be doing, and I don't need to be waited on."

"No, you need to rest, and I'm the cook. It's my job. And I'm not waiting on you, I am looking after my friend. It's what we do, and don't pretend like you'd do any differently for me. So that being said, how does grilled cheese and tomato basil soup sound?"

She sighed. "I'm sorry. I just hate bothering people, but that sounds wonderful, and truth be told, I really don't think I could get up and get myself something to eat, just too tired, and can I have some orange juice?"

He smiled. "Then just let us take care of you for a little while okay? I'll be back in ten minutes."

He returned only a few minutes later with her medicine and her lunch. "Thank you, you're the best."

He smiled. "Now flattery like that will get you almost anything. How about some cookies later, and if you decide you want to come into the living room and watch a movie, I'll help you relocate and get comfortable."

"No, I'm just really tired. I just want to sleep."

Alejandro frowned. He did not think she was tired at all. He thought she was hiding, though he was not exactly sure why. He had not thought she was that vain, but maybe he was mistaken. "Okay, you have my number if you change your mind."

Shortly before dinner, there was a tap on the door. She closed her eyes, pulled her headphones off and under the covers as she flicked off her MP3 player, then she pretended to sleep. She heard the door open. After a minute she heard it close. She turned her music back on and went back to listening. By seven o'clock she had had all the music she could stand. She turned off her MP3 player and threw it on the floor, along with her headphones. At exactly eight o'clock there was a loud knock on the door. She knew there was no pretending to sleep through that. She pulled the covers up to her chin and reluctantly called, "Enter."

Bubba entered carrying a glass of juice and a plate. "Sorry to wake you, but you need to take another antibiotic, and it says you should take it with food, so I brought you some dinner."

Lenore was in so much pain, she thought for sure she was going to throw up, but she told herself firmly she did not need any pain pills. "Thank you, sorry to be so much trouble. I would've gotten it for myself."

"It's no trouble. I'm just worried about you. Can I get you something else, make you more comfortable?"

"No, I'm good. Thank you. I'll eat in a minute, and I'll take my medicine, I promise."

He frowned but nodded. "I'll be back in half an hour for the tray." He sat down the juice glass, picked up the plate from lunch, then set down the dinner plate and grabbed the glass from earlier.

"Thank you."

When he was gone, she pushed herself to a sitting position, and forced herself to eat some of the mashed potatoes and chicken, then she took her antibiotic, and drank all of her juice, then she lay back down. When he returned, she pretended to sleep. When he left she asked herself, "What is your malfunction, Lenore?" She frowned. She had no answer for that. She finally fell asleep around ten.

Lenore awoke with a start. She was shaking all over. She hoped she had not been screaming for real. She had definitely been screaming in her dream. She lay there listening for a long minute. Deciding she had not woken the whole house, she tried to go back to sleep, but she could not even bring herself to shut her eyes. Whenever she did, she saw fur, blood, and could feel teeth biting into her flesh. Just the thought of it made her want to scream again, and she was in an unbelievable amount of pain. She tried to calm herself down, but she jumped at every sound. Finally she could not sit there another minute. She pushed herself up and got out of bed. She exited her room and walked slowly to the living room. It was dark, cold, and creepy. There were several dead animals hanging on the walls. Normally they did not bother her, but tonight they did. Now in addition to being terrified, she was cold. She had forgotten to put her slippers on and standing on the wood floors made it feel as though the cold was seeping into her bones. She told herself over and over again, *You're being melodramatic. Stop it.* It was not working. In fact, the longer she stood there, the worse it was getting. She did not care if it made her look like a coward. She headed for the stairs. Fortunately, the railing was on the left side. She gripped it and walked slowly up them. She arrived at Nathaniel's room and knocked softly on the door.

Bubba awoke with a start, then he heard a knock and realized it had been another knock that had awoken him. He called, "Come in." He flipped on the bedside lamp and rubbed his eyes. Lenore opened the door and moved into the doorway but did not come any further. He blinked and stared for another minute. She was standing there in the light blue nightgown. "Lenore, what's wrong?"

"I know this sounds silly and childish, but ... but I had a bad dream. Can I stay here?"

"Of course you can, and that's not silly. You have every right to be afraid, but I'm in my underwear. If that bothers you, I can get up and get a pair of pajama bottoms."

She came into the room and closed the door behind her, then started moving slowly to the other side of the bed. "I'm okay with it if you're okay with it. I mean, really I'm just in a T-shirt and a pair of panties myself."

He said quickly, "I think you should come to this side of the bed. I'll scoot to the other side. I can't imagine it's comfortable to lay on your right side."

"No, it's really not. Actually, right now nothing is comfortable." She started sniffing.

Bubba got out of bed. "Okay, enough of this bullshit. I'm going downstairs and I'm getting you a cheese stick, a glass of juice, and a real pain pill. You can also take another antibiotic, and I'm not taking any arguments out of you, or I will put your ass in the truck and take you back to the hospital. Is that understood?"

She started crying. "I hurt too much to argue. Right now, I hurt so much, I think dying would be preferable."

Bubba hurried downstairs, grabbed the pills, juice, and a cheese stick, then on an impulse he opened the freezer and grabbed several reusable ice packs. He hurried back upstairs. He set everything down on the bed next to her. He opened the cheese stick and handed it to her. She ate it, and then he handed her the pills.

She took them. "Sorry I'm being such a baby." She sniffed and looked at the floor.

Bubba squatted down in front of her and tilted her chin up just a little. "Okay, we need to have a talk, because that shit needs to stop too. I don't want to hear you apologize again. You are not being a baby. You're not being too much trouble. You're not being any trouble, with one minor exception. I am not doing anything for you I would not do for any of the other guys who got hurt working for me, so stop. You deserve to be taken care of right now, so stop fighting and let us take care of you. You are not getting special treatment because you're a girl. We would all be taking care of each other under the same circumstances."

She sniffed several times. He reached over and grabbed a tissue and handed it to her. She blew her nose and wiped her eyes. "What's the one exception?"

"I would not let any of the guys sleep in my bed ... well, I'd let them sleep in my bed by themselves, but not with me."

She sniffed and laughed. "Okay, I'll grant you that one."

"Good, now let's make you comfortable. I brought up some ice packs. I thought we'd try them. See if maybe they'd help a little." It only took a minute to get her comfortably situated with the ice packs, then he went around to the other side and got into bed with her. After a few minutes he asked, "Is the ice helping?"

"Yes, actually it is, though I feel colder, and I don't feel as frightened now that I'm not alone."

He rolled on his side and tentatively wrapped his arm around her waist. "Well, let me see if I can warm the rest of you up."

She lay there thinking for a couple of minutes, then she asked softly, "Nathaniel, can I ask a question?"

"Of course?"

"Are we dating?"

"I would like us to be dating, but then I start worrying if we're going in different directions."

She thought about that for several minutes. "I don't think we are. In fact, the more I think about it, the more I think maybe we want the same things out of life. I'm just not sure I know how to deal with those things."

He started laughing. "According to my parents, children don't come with an instruction manual, and every one is different, so it's like starting all over every time."

"Well then, I guess if you're willing to see where this relationship goes, I'd like us to be dating."

He moved her hair aside and kissed her neck. "If I didn't want to see where this relationship is going, I would never have let you in my room, and I certainly wouldn't let you in my bed." He lay there listening to her breathe. After a few minutes, he knew she was asleep. He glanced at the clock. It had been twenty-five minutes since they had put the ice packs on. He carefully removed them, took them downstairs and put them in the freezer, and then he went back upstairs and crawled into bed. He snuggled up against her and wrapped his arm around her waist.

XLI

Saturday, November 25

Bubba awoke a few minutes before his alarm clock went off. He snuggled up against Lenore. He could definitely get used to waking up with her in bed. He pressed a kiss to the back of her head, then got out of bed, walked around to the other side, and flipped off the alarm. He quietly got his clothes and boots and went into his father's room to shower and dress. When he was finished, he headed downstairs and grabbed himself a cup of coffee off the side table then sat down. Most of the others had already arrived. He glanced at an empty seat. He was just about to ask where Aaron was when Aaron came out from the back hallway looking worried and demanded, "Where's Lenore?"

Bubba picked up his coffee and said, "Sleeping in."

Aaron shook his head. "No, she's not. I just checked on her and her room is empty."

Bubba took a drink from his coffee and said calmly, "I didn't say she was in her bed. I said she was sleeping in, there's a difference."

Aaron digested that for a minute then demanded, "Where is my sister?"

The table went very quiet. Bubba replied calmly, "Upstairs."

Aaron crossed his arms over his chest and said with irritation, "In a guest room?"

Bubba sighed. He realized there was no getting out of this, and Aaron had decided to be the overprotective little brother. This should prove to be an interesting morning. He got to his feet and turned to face Aaron. "No, she's upstairs asleep in my bed, and yes, I slept in it too, and before you ask, not that it's any of your damn business, but no, we are not having sex."

"Then what the hell is my sister doing in your bed?"

He sighed again. "Aaron, how old are you?"

He stood up straight. "Sixteen, but you know that."

"Exactly, you're sixteen years old. How old were you the first time you went hunting with your father?"

Aaron made a face as he considered. He had no idea where Bubba was going with this, but he shrugged his shoulders and said, "Ten or so."

"And how old were you the first time you killed something?"

Aaron frowned, "Second time I went hunting, so about ten."

"And how did you feel about it?"

He swallowed hard. "Kind of awful."

"And I'm sure your father explained to you, just like Pop explained to me, that there are only a few acceptable reasons to kill, for defense and for food." Aaron nodded. "And it made it a little easier, right? Because you knew you were going to eat the animal that you killed, it didn't die for no reason." Again, Aaron nodded. "Your sister was not raised by your father. She wasn't even raised in this part of the country. She was raised on the left coast where they teach killing is wrong for any reason, and eating animals is wrong too. Not only is she having to deal with the fact that she and my father could be dead right this minute had things gone even slightly differently, she is also having to struggle to come to terms with the fact that she killed not one, but two dogs. That's something you, me, and everyone else in this room could shake off pretty easily, but we were all raised differently. She is also trying to deal with a world of shit you and I and everybody else in this room can't even begin to understand because we were raised differently. So why don't you cut me and her a little slack, and understand that last night was about her not being alone."

Aaron looked down at the floor, then nodded. He asked softly, "Is she going to be okay?"

Bubba smiled, reached over, and squeezed his shoulder, forcing Aaron to look up at him. "She will be fine. She's tough. She just needs a little time to adjust. And she needs to see that we understand what she's going through, and we're here for her, and we love her. People don't come to our way of life overnight if they weren't born to it."

Aaron nodded and sat down. After a minute Ramon said with a laugh, "How disappointing, I thought we were gonna get breakfast and a show."

Bubba rolled his eyes as he sat down and said with extreme sarcasm, "Oh, yes, it would be really entertaining, Aaron and I kicking the shit out of each other."

Stewart entered, followed by Susie. He demanded, "Now why would you boys do a fool thing like that?"

Ramon supplied quickly, "Because Bubba and Lenore slept together last night."

Susie sat down at the unclaimed seat and said with forced annoyance, "Oh, I see how it is, Bubba. It's okay to sleep with an employee, but it's not okay to date an employee's daughter. Right? That makes perfect sense."

Bubba's elbows hit the table and he buried his face in his hands. He wanted to scream. After a minute he said through his hands, "You just gotta stir the pot, don't you, Ramon?"

Ramon laughed. "If you don't stir the pot occasionally, it gets stagnant."

Stewart demanded, "And exactly when did you two discuss dating or not dating?"

Bubba groaned. "Thank you, Susie. Nice to see you too, and this is exactly why I said it was not appropriate for me to date my foreman's daughter."

Susie added, "I made a play for him sophomore year. He shot me down cold, though I think what he said was something a little more along the lines of, 'Susie, you're a real sweet kid, but I'm a senior, you're a sophomore. Your father works for my father. I just really don't think it's appropriate for us to be pursuing a relationship.' But not to worry, Daddy, there were no hard feelings. I translated it correctly. 'Sorry kid, you're really nice, but I'm just not at all interested, so not gonna happen.'"

Bubba rubbed his hands up and down his face, then he ran his hands behind his head and tried to grab two handfuls of his hair, but unfortunately, it was too short. He said with annoyance, "If you're done picking on Bubba, can we have breakfast now?"

Alejandro said helpfully, "Everyone else is already eating theirs."

George suddenly shot to his feet. He said quickly, "Lenore, don't you dare come down the stairs by yourself!" He moved around Wayne's empty seat and headed for the stairs. Everyone had gotten to their feet.

Bubba ordered, "Aaron, go to your sister's room and get her pillows, her MP3 player and headphones. George, help her to the living room. We'll make her comfortable on the couch." He turned and headed for the laundry room to get extra linens.

Alejandro said, "I'll get a tray and bring her some breakfast."

Lenore sighed and stood at the top of the stairs waiting for George. When he arrived, she gripped his right arm tightly. "Sorry to be so much trouble, but I do have to say I appreciate the arm. With the railing being on the right side now, I'm not as comfortable going down without anything to hold onto."

"Understood, you set the pace."

"Thank you." She waited until they made it to the bottom of the stairs, then she said, "I know I was ordered to the couch, but I'd like to go to my room. I would like to shower, and I need to change the bandages."

He nodded. "Then I will help you to your room and we'll get the couch all ready for you when you come out. You gonna be okay by yourself?"

Susie said quickly, "I can lend a hand. I can tidy up your room while you shower and then I can help you with your bandages."

"Thank you. I'm sure I will feel more stable tomorrow, but for now, I just feel wobbly on my feet."

Susie smiled. "Totally understandable. I'm a baby if I sprain my ankle."

Bubba had retrieved a sheet and a blanket. He shook out the sheet and carefully covered the couch, then he and Aaron arranged the pillows and laid out the blanket. They folded the blanket back so Lenore could sit down and easily get under the covers. They picked up the coffee table and moved it closer to her head. Aaron retrieved the remotes from the television stand and set them on the table, then he asked, "Do you think there's anything else we should get her, Bubba?" Aaron chuckled to himself.

Bubba looked at him suspiciously and demanded, "What's so funny?"

"Nothing."

Bubba reached out and shoved him playfully. "Don't lie to me, Twerp. What's so funny?"

"Welllll, I was just thinking if you end up marrying my sister, Bubba's gonna bring on a whole new meaning."

Bubba reached out like lightning and wrapped his arm around Aaron's neck and pulled him down. He rubbed the knuckles of his other hand up and down the top of Aaron's head. Aaron screamed and squealed. Bubba laughed. "You mean like sibling rivalry." He let Aaron go and shoved him away.

Aaron ran his fingers through his hair. "Hey man, watch the hair. You're messing it up."

Bubba rolled his eyes and shoved Aaron in the direction of the table. "If you're done with your nonsense, eat your breakfast so we can get to work."

They were all just getting up from the table when Susie came out of the back looking green. Stewart demanded, "What's wrong?"

"I can't do it. I tried, but I can't. It's just too gross."

Bubba set his coffee down and headed for Lenore's room. He tapped on the door. Lenore responded, "It's fine. I got it. Go away."

Bubba looked away from the door and cracked it open. "It's not Susie. It's ... Nathaniel. Can I come in and help?"

She hesitated, then sighed several times. *The nurse said I need to keep my back bandaged, and my shoulder, and my hip, and my thigh, and my arm, and all of the major scratches.* "I'm naked."

"If that's a problem for you, you can cover yourself up to the best of your ability, but I'm not worried about it. This isn't about catching a peek, it's about helping you take care of your injuries. If you're not comfortable with that I can call ..." He hesitated. He was not sure Betsy or Luanne would be any better.

She sighed and then gave a little laugh, picked up the towel, adjusted it as best she could to at least cover most of her breasts, then she adjusted the towel so it covered her left hip and between her legs, but left all of her right leg and butt exposed. "There's really no way for you to help me without seeing something, so you might as well come in."

He entered, closed the door behind him, and went straight to the bathroom. He rolled up his sleeves then washed his hands thoroughly with soap and hot water, then he returned to her side. "Okay, so what am I supposed to do?"

She indicated all the bandages and tape. "Anything that's not stitched up is supposed to get ointment, and then everything has to be bandaged up. Some of the ointment might end up on the stitches, but that's not a problem she said. Are you sure this isn't too gross for you?"

He chuckled and sat down behind her and started carefully applying ointment to the scratches on her back. "Let's see, I've helped deliver horses and cows, I put stitches in all manner of animals – including a few humans. I've bandaged many a wound, assisted in setting broken bones, slaughtered chickens, cows, been forced to put down a horse or two, cleaned fish, skinned deer, rabbits – though not cows. We do not do our own skinning on our cows. We take those to a meat processing plant, they're too big and heavy. So believe me, a few little bite marks that have already been cleaned up and taken care of are not going to gross me out."

She smiled and looked over her shoulder. "Glad to hear it. I have to admit I didn't think it was that bad, but man, did Susie turn green at one glimpse."

He chuckled. "Not surprising. Though Susie knows how to use a gun, she's never actually fired it at anything but a target. Stewart tried on numerous occasions to get her to go hunting. She always flatly refused. Which, while we're on the subject, as soon as your arm is better, I will spend a good bit of time teaching you how to use a handgun and a rifle, and then you will go nowhere on the ranch without a handgun on your hip. Is that understood?"

She looked over her shoulder at him again and smiled. "Yes, boss."

Bubba had to shut his eyes and groan. Her hair was twisted up on top of her head in a bun, and every time she looked over her shoulder and smiled at him, all he saw was her hair twisted up and bare shoulders, bare neck, and her smiling at him coyly. He said firmly, "For the love of God, woman, stop looking at me like that."

She frowned and looked over her shoulder at him again. "What?"

"Better, that is way better."

She continued to stare at him confused and demanded, "What are you on about, Nathaniel?"

He groaned and started applying the bandages. "Please, when you are sitting naked on your bed, do not call me Nathaniel, and don't look at me like that."

She smiled. "What could possibly be appealing about me covered in stitches?"

He snorted. "There is more than enough of you not covered in stitches to be appealing, I promise you, but there, I'm done with your back. I'm going to move around to the other side, so I can do your arm." He got up and sat down in front of her. He frowned. "Can you easily take care of your leg yourself?"

"I don't think I can easily do it. I could struggle my way through it."

He nodded. "I was thinking it looked like it would be awkward to reach over your body to do it. I'll just take care of all of it." It did not take him long to get everything re-bandaged. "Well, I have to say everything looks real good. Don't see any signs of infection or irritation, so let's get you dressed, and then get you made comfortable on the couch, and you can take your meds."

She frowned. "I guess if I'm going into the living room I should put pajama bottoms on."

"I wouldn't think they'd be comfortable with all the bandages on your leg."

"You would be correct, but I don't think it's appropriate for me to be wandering around in my nightgown."

He snorted. "Girls wear shorter skirts to church. I don't think anybody was bothered by you comin' downstairs in your nightgown, and certainly nobody expects you to put on jeans, at least not until the stitches come out. Even then I'll give you fair warning, it'll take a few days for you to get used to the jeans rubbing on your scars, because they'll still be really touchy for probably a month."

"Well, if you're sure it's not inappropriate, if you would give me my other nightgown and give me a pair of panties. And that sounded like the voice of experience."

He chuckled, retrieved the items in question and handed them over. "Well, since you already saw me in my underwear, I'll show you few, if you want to see them."

"Go for it."

He turned his back to her and unbuckled his belt. He slid his jeans down and pointed to the back of his thigh. There was an odd crescent shaped scar about three inches long just below his boxers on the right side. He shifted to his left side a little more to her and indicated a long scar almost six inches. He pointed to the scar on the left leg. "This one I got when I was about sixteen. I was up on a ladder trying to fix a windmill. I was reaching too far, the ladder sunk into the mud on one side and I fell off and clipped a sharp piece of metal. Fifty stitches later I was back to work." He pointed to the other one. "That one I got three years ago when I got gored riding a bull."

She shuddered. "I am so glad you are not riding bulls this year. I don't think I could live through that."

"Riding a bull, no, I don't think it's your cup of tea." Keeping his back to her, he pulled his jeans up, tucked his shirt in, and re-buckled his belt.

Lenore discarded the towel and carefully pulled the nightgown on. "No, I mean I don't think I could survive watching you ride a bull. I think I'd have a heart attack just watching."

"Is it safe for me to turn around?"

She got to her feet and finished pulling her panties on. "Now it is."

He turned around and wrapped his arms around her, pulling her against him. He bent down and kissed her. He pulled his mouth free and demanded, "Is it safe to assume there are no bite marks on your butt?"

"Yes."

He squeezed her bottom with both hands. It was much nicer with only a thin cotton T-shirt and panties between her bottom and his hands. He went back to kissing her. Finally he groaned and pulled free. "If we don't hurry up and get in there, I am going to be in a fight with Aaron today for sure."

"Why would you fight with Aaron?"

He chuckled. "He's being an overprotective brother, and trying to make sure his sister's virtue stays intact."

She rolled her eyes. "And what makes him think I have a virtue to keep intact?"

He smiled. "He's a smart kid. He knows his sister's of good moral character."

She laughed. "And exactly how good can my moral character be when I'm standing in my bedroom in my nightgown, previously naked, with a man who is not my husband."

He tilted her chin up to look at him. "With the only man you've ever let get overly friendly, and a man who is only ever had his hands on top of your clothes, medical treatment aside, and I was strictly professional, until you had your clothes back on."

She smiled and kissed him on the cheek. "Yes, you were, and I was very proud of you."

He smiled. "You should be. It was hard. I wanted to nibble on your neck and do a lot of other things to you." She blushed deeply and looked away. "But neither one of us are ready to go that far just yet."

XLII

Lenore had spent the morning sitting with her feet propped up, watching television. She was about to go out of her mind. She was startled by the doorbell ringing. She raised an eyebrow and looked over her shoulder. Alejandro came out of the kitchen. He looked at her and raised an eyebrow. He demanded, "Did the doorbell just ring?"

She laughed. "So I'm not the only one who thinks that's weird?"

He shook his head. "Other than the Sheriff coming to visit earlier this month, we have not had a visitor in quite some time. I don't think the doorbell has rung in two years."

She laughed. "Well, I'd offer to get it but ..."

He cut her off. "You are injured and not dressed, I got it."

He crossed to the door and looked through the peephole. He opened the door and said with a smile, "Good afternoon, Sheriff, Natalia, and children."

Natalia leaned forward and kissed him on the cheek. "Good afternoon, Alejandro. I apologize we had to bring the kids, but we wanted to see Lenore."

"Of course I don't mind, in fact, I was just in the process of making cookies. So maybe if little people behave, they can have milk and cookies. If they don't behave, we can always go throw them in the stables. But as far as Lenore is concerned, let me go see if she's up to visitors. She hasn't been very social since she got home."

Lenore pulled the covers up to her waist and said with annoyance, "You do realize I can hear you."

He said without turning around, "Good, then you know I was telling the truth. So are you up for visitors, or do I have to take them the long way around to the kitchen like in the olden days?"

"I doubt seriously Dad would care whether I was up for visitors or not, but as it happens, I would be thrilled for any kind of distraction."

Alejandro stepped back and indicated the coat rack. "Please, feel free to hang up your coats, set your purses down, make yourselves feel at home." He removed his keys out of his pocket and locked the top drawer of the hall table.

Amelia removed her hat, coat, and boots. Natalia said quickly, "That doesn't mean you can take your shoes off."

Alejandro said with a laugh. "She's making herself at home, which is good. She's fine. Now if you'll excuse me for just a moment, I need to go lock the office."

Lenore said from the couch, "You'll forgive me for not getting up to greet you, but my boss gets bent out of shape anytime I'm moving about unnecessarily."

Diego smiled and said, "Good to know Bubba's keeping you out of trouble."

They all came in to the living room. She indicated the chairs. "Please, sit down."

Lorenzo and Denise sat down on the other sofa. Diego sat down in the big armchair. Natalia perched on the edge of the other armchair, setting two large paper shopping bags next to her feet. Amelia, however, came over and sat down on the edge of the couch next to Lenore. She reached up and put her hand on Lenore's cheek. "You look very tired. You should get more rest. When you're sick, you need lots of rest."

Lenore smiled. "That's very true, but I'm not sick, I'm just injured."

"Injured is like being sick. When you're injured, you need rest too. Your body heals best when it's sleeping. It allows our bodies to devote more of its energy to repairing the damage."

Lenore laughed. Amelia looked and sounded like a miniature adult, it was so cute. "You are one smart cookie. Are you ready for college? I bet you're going away to college next year, aren't you?"

Amelia laughed. "No silly, I'm only in the second grade."

"Oh, my mistake. It's just you're so mature I thought for sure you had to be eighteen or nineteen years old. So what do you want to be when you grow up?"

"I want to be a chef and make wonderful desserts."

Lenore smiled and nodded. "A pastry chef, that sounds pretty fabboo. Does your mother let you help in the kitchen?"

She smiled and nodded. "Yes, whenever Mommy is cooking, she lets me help. She doesn't let me do anything with popping grease or knives. She says I'm not ready."

"I would have to agree with your mother. That sounds very dangerous, and since you can barely see over the counter, I think you should wait until you're at least four and half feet tall." She shifted her attention to Lorenzo and asked, "How are you doing?"

"Pretty good, thank you. You look better than I expected you to. The way Mom and Dad were talking, I expected you to look all chewed up."

"I feel all chewed up."

"Well, you don't look it. You look rather pretty, other than the fact that you're in your nightgown."

She blushed. "I know it's not appropriate to receive visitors in your pajamas, but I wasn't expecting company."

Diego said firmly, "We're not visitors, we're family, and we're here to check on you."

"I know and I appreciate it."

Lorenzo demanded, "Aren't you going to ask me what I want to be when I grow up?"

She smiled and shifted her attention back to him. "My apologies, what do you want to be when you grow up?"

"I want to get my Masters in computer security, and then I want to join the military and fight terrorists using a computer."

"So I guess that means you're planning on going to MIT?"

He sighed and looked very sad. "Something tells me even if I get accepted to MIT, I won't get a full ride, and therefore won't be able to afford to go."

She smiled. "Well, you know, sometimes when you have big problems, it's best to share the responsibility. So how about this, you focus on getting into MIT, and I'll worry about paying for it."

Denise said with irritation, "Don't tease him. His only hope for MIT is a full ride. You're just getting his hopes up unnecessarily."

Diego said firmly, "Denise, I told you if you couldn't be nice to your sister, you are going to get in trouble."

"Why do I have to be nice to her? She's not my sister. She's your daughter. We didn't grow up together. We don't have to like each other, besides, having you spend my entire life talking bad about the left coast, and now you want me to get along with one of them?"

Natalia said firmly, "She is your sister. You will be respectful. You will be nice, or you will learn to go without your privileges, your phone, your computer. Those things can go away just like that." She snapped her fingers. "And I have never condoned that kind of attitude. We're one country, not north, south, left, right, conservative, liberal.

We're one country, and if more people acted like that, maybe there'd be less problems in it."

Denise stood up and stomped one of her feet. "Mom, how can you take her side? She's Dad's bastard!"

Lenore whistled. Everyone turned to look at her. "She doesn't have to like me. I want her to like me. I'd like to be friends with her, but if she wants to hate me for no reason, let her. It hurts her, not me. I can focus my attention and efforts on being friends with Amelia, Lorenzo, and Aaron."

Denise smiled and crossed her arms over her chest. "Yeah, they can have her empty promises and her fake smiles."

Aaron entered the room carrying a stack of wood. He demanded, "Whose empty promises?"

Denise said with a smile, "Lenore told Lorenzo if he got into MIT, she'd find a way to pay for it."

He dropped the wood in the box, turned around and said, "Now wait a minute. If he's going to MIT, can I go to State and get a new truck?"

Diego started laughing. Natalia said with irritation, "Aaron, that's not appropriate."

Lenore looked thoughtful. "What's wrong with the truck you have? It's a nice little truck, it's still in good shape."

"Yeah, but it was Grandpa's truck for like ten years, and then he gave it to Dad senior year of high school, so it's like thirty-five years old. I'd like a truck that's new to me. It doesn't have to be brand new."

"And what are you going to college to be?"

"I want to be a veterinarian, and before you go looking down your nose, vets are actually required to go to more school than regular doctors."

She shrugged her shoulders and laughed. "Awww, that really hurts. Remind me not to shrug my shoulders. Why would you think I'd look down my nose at you being a vet? I think it's a great idea. You're wonderful with the animals and I think you'd be great at it and I don't see any reason for you to restrict yourself to State. Granted, from what I've heard the State schools in Texas are pretty good. I think you should be looking into what schools have the best veterinarian programs, but as far as your truck is concerned, if you don't want Dad's truck anymore, I think I would like to have Dad's truck. So I think we can sort out something about a new truck." She suddenly realized the Sheriff might not appreciate this conversation. She glanced in his direction and asked, "This isn't upsetting you, is it?"

He shook his head. "We told the kids a couple of years ago that there was just no way Mom and I would be able to put them through college. We would help them out the best we could, but for the most part they were going to be on their own, so they better try to get scholarships. If big sister wants to put them through college, I think that's incredibly sweet, and I am not going to argue and I will eternally grateful."

Denise stood there stunned for a long minute and then she said with irritation, "Oh, you have got to be kidding me! She's skinnier than I am, taller than I am, prettier than I am, and she's richer than I am! That is not fair!" She turned to storm out.

Diego and Natalia both shouted for her to wait.

Lenore shot to her feet and reached out and grabbed the only thing she could get her hand on, Denise's hood. "Now wait a minute. I don't know who's been selling you that line of bullshit, but it is absolutely not true. There's nothing wrong with the way you look."

She jerked free, turned on her older sister, and shoved her hard. Lenore staggered back and cried out in pain. Denise felt momentarily guilty, but it faded quickly. She snapped, "If that's not true, then why do guys fall all over girls who look like you? Girls like you and Persephone have all the luck! Skinny, rich, beautiful, men throwing themselves at your feet! You've been in town a month, and you have Bubba, the most eligible bachelor in the county, sweet and good looking."

Lenore was really regretting taking her sling off. She cradled her injured arm to her chest. She glanced at the Sheriff and asked, "Can I tell her the whole story?"

Diego turned to Alejandro and asked, "Would you take the two younger kids into the kitchen and get them some milk and cookies?"

"Absolutely. Let's go kids, you can help me decorate more cookies."

Lorenzo said, "But I want to stay. This sounds like it's going to be interesting."

Alejandro grabbed his shirt and said, "Too bad, you're not old enough. Let's go."

Lenore waited until they were out of the room, then she indicated a chair. "Sit."

Denise crossed her arms over her chest and looked belligerent. Aaron grabbed her by the arm and pushed her in the direction of the chair. "I only know bits and pieces, but trust me, you're going to want to sit down for this."

Lenore looked at the Sheriff and asked, "No holds barred?"

He nodded. "I'd give her both barrels. She asked for it."

Natalia grimaced and sat down. "That sounds ominous. I think I need to sit down."

"I don't know where you got into your head that Persephone's life is all wonderful and charming. Trust me, it's not. Her life was hell, and you want to know how I know? Because I'm Persephone. I don't remember any good times in the first fourteen years of my life. Actually, that's not true. Getting my first guitar and my twice a week guitar lesson was the only part of my life I enjoyed, and my mom didn't even buy me the guitar or pay for the lessons. One of the guys who paid my mom to have sex with him, ..." Diego sighed and shook his head, "... because you're right, my mom was a whore, literally, not figuratively. As soon as my mom couldn't make a living singing anymore, she made a living off men. Fortunately, most of the guys were really decent, which means they didn't stick around, because it was only so long before my mom's shenanigans, drama, and drug use, became too much for them. Sometimes I would come home from school and find my mom snorting lines of coke ..." Aaron swallowed hard as any lingering doubt he had about his sister taking drugs from Jace dissolved, "... on the dining room table. Most of the time I had to fend for myself. Fortunately drug use leads to the munchies, so there was usually food in the house, but I had to learn to cook at a young age. No help from my mom, she was usually too stoned to be of help or too busy with her Johns. My mom didn't even enter me in the competition that ended up launching my career. My guitar teacher did, but he browbeat my mom into paying for it and signing the papers. Then I spent the next four years with my mom telling me everything I did was wrong. I was not pretty enough. I needed cosmetic surgery to make me look like better. I needed to get my breasts done because they were too small. I needed to shake my booty more because I needed more male fans. I needed to lose ten pounds. Since I was fourteen, my weight, no matter how low it got, was never low enough, and I hated being a Rock star. I hated everything about it. So she just kept getting me on more and more pills, anything to keep the dancing monkey dancing ..." Natalia put her hand to her mouth and stared in horror, "... and bringing in the money so she could keep snorting it up her nose; and of course, screwing nineteen year old dancers who were only sleeping with her to be on stage with me, because they would do anything to further their career. I had to fight hard against the choreographers, the dancers, and everybody who wanted to have these guys putting her hands all over my body. To keep guys I couldn't even stand having close to me, from touching me in places I really didn't want them touching me, which according to my mom, gave me too much of a nice girl image. So my mom decided to totally ruin my nice girl image, which trust me, I don't think my image was that nice, by leaking naked pictures of me and editing a video so it looked like I was having sex on set with one of my dancers. So that was all just too much for me, so I decided the best option was to swallow a bottle of sleeping pills. Fortunately, my bodyguard found me ..." Diego said, not the first time, a silent prayer of thanks to God for JC being there, "... and gave me the verbal kick in the ass I needed to get the hell away from my toxic mom and the toxic world which was destroying my heart and soul. So when I turned eighteen, I ran away and I somehow ended up here through a series of bizarre events, which basically ended up with someone suggesting I go back to my roots. So I thought why not? Let's go back to your roots, to try to find something in my life that wasn't toxic, which the only roots that I knew weren't, you know, poison ivy was maybe my dad. So I went in a bizarre way in search of him, without actually looking for him, but yet I found him anyways. And at some point in time during all of this, I went through a really nasty detox to get all the prescription drugs out of my body. So if you think it's glamorous to be Persephone, then think about being curled up to a toilet puking up your guts for a week and tell me that's glamorous. So the next time somebody tells you that she's better looking than you are, tell them to go to hell; because you are beautiful, and you have wonderful parents who love you and think you're beautiful just the way you are. You have a bright future. Of course, that would require you to take your head out of your ass and see your self-worth." Lenore looked from one stricken face to another. After a long minute she asked, "Too much?"

Diego demanded, "She had Johns around my daughter?"

She grimaced and made faces as she said, "They were nice, nicer than her."

He rubbed his hands up and down his face. "I can't imagine having ever been drunk enough to see that woman as appealing, but you know, twenty years ago she didn't seem that toxic."

Lenore sighed and said gently. "According to her managers, she wasn't that bad until she couldn't sing anymore. That's kind of when she went downhill. I forgot I hadn't wanted to tell you that part, sorry Dad."

Denise got up and moved to the armchair where her mother was sitting and dropped down next to her and wrapped her arms around her mother and buried her face in her mother's chest and started sobbing. "I'm sorry, Mommy. I won't ever complain about you being a bad parent again. I promise I'll be nice to my sisters."

Diego got to his feet and crossed to his oldest daughter. He gently pulled her into his arms. "Don't apologize. I'm glad I know. I'm just sorry I didn't know to be there for you. I would never have let you stay with that horrible woman. I wish I would've known about you sooner."

She pulled free and raised and lowered her left shoulder. "Trust me, I learned pretty quick in my life, that's the problem with one-night stands."

Diego pointed at his oldest son. "Learn from my experience. Keep it in your pants until you're married."

Lenore nodded. "I had never planned on getting married, but it seems like I'm changing a lot of plans these days."

He frowned at his daughter. "Hopefully that means you're thinking about getting serious with Nathaniel and not playing the field?"

She smiled and patted him on the shoulder. "Don't worry, Dad. I have no intention of playing the field and do not want to end up like Jane. I really need to stop calling her my mother, even if it does irritate the shit out of her."

XLIII

Natalia was more than a little nervous. She got to her feet and held up the shopping bags. "I know this might be a bit presumptuous of me, but when your father was telling me about your injuries, I thought maybe some different style clothes might be a good idea, so I went shopping this morning and bought you a few things ... if you don't want them, you won't hurt my feelings."

Lenore was quite certain that last part was not true. She smiled and said, "That was very sweet of you. Is this something I should try on, or just look at?"

Natalia shrugged her shoulders. "Whatever you want to do."

Denise wiped her face on the arm of her sweater and got to her feet. "You should go try at least one of them on. Mom and I can help."

"Sure, if you don't mind. My room is a little messy, I think." She turned and walked slowly towards her room. The other two women trailed behind. Entering, she looked around. Actually, it was quite clean.

Natalia crossed to the bed and began pulling out clothes. "I picked you up three very nice ankle length knit skirts, and I picked you up two short sleeve knit dresses. If I guessed right, they should be one size too big because I didn't think you wanted anything too clingy on your bandages, and I thought you might be more comfortable in nightgowns for a while, so I went ahead and bought you two of those."

Lenore slowly walked to the bed and picked up one of the skirts. There was one brown, one blue, and one gray. "I like the color choices." She carefully held it to her waist. It looked like it was the right size. She started to step into it, then swayed. Natalia reached out and put her hand on her left hip to steady her.

Denise stepped forward and said, "Here, wait. Why don't I hold the skirt, you step into it, and you can hold onto my shoulders to keep your balance while I pull it up."

With both of their help, she was able to the pull the skirt on over the bandages and get it properly situated on her waist. She looked down. "It fits really nicely, thank you. Do you two think we are up to trying on one of the dresses?"

Denise said with confidence, "I think we can manage."

Lenore looked at her suspiciously, "Okay, I know this sounds like a complaint, it's really not, I'm just curious, but why the sudden change?"

Denise blushed. "Okay, I know I was a bitch."

Natalia reached out and smacked her daughter in the back. "Denise, language."

Denise flinched and laughed. "Sorry, Mom. Okay, so I know I was a brat, but knowing that you're Persephone and hearing you say that you think I'm pretty, well that really made me feel good. And seeing how she was kind of my idol and hearing her saying she thinks I'm pretty, so you could say I'm kind of on cloud nine right now. But I guess when I think about it, my idol being my big sister, that's kind of cool too."

Lenore blushed. "I would love to just be your big sister, and please don't go spreading it around that I'm that other person. I'd really kind of like her to disappear and never come back."

She looked very sad. "After what you told us I can understand, and don't worry, I won't betray my sister, at least not about that. Might stab you in the back later, but not about that."

Natalia rolled her eyes. Lenore laughed. "I look forward to that, but remember revenge is a dish best served cold, and I will get even."

Denise shrugged her shoulders. "Isn't that what sisters are supposed to do? Now come on, let's try on a dress."

Lenore asked, "Which one, the red one or the blue one?"

Mother and daughter replied simultaneously, "Red." They looked at each other and laughed.

Lenore was surprised at how easy it was to put the dress on. It was basically a longer version of the nightgown, though shaped slightly different. She glanced at herself in the mirror through the open bathroom door. It looked rather good on her. "Well, Mrs. Mendoza, thank you. It really looks nice. You know, you didn't have to do this. I'm used to fending for myself."

Natalia smiled. "Well, just remember, you're only eighteen, you don't have to fight all your battles by yourself yet. It would probably do you good to let your father have a few rounds, and don't ever hesitate to ask me to step in and fight one for you. I would be honored to do it."

She started to protest, then she remembered her conversation with Nathaniel last night. She bit her tongue and counted to three, then she forced herself to say, "I will be sure to keep that in mind. If one of you wouldn't mind cutting off the tag, I think I'll just stay in this dress."

Natalia quickly removed the tag, then she picked up the sling and held it out. "Here, let me help you put this on, you're probably supposed to be wearing it."

After they were finished, Lenore asked a little hesitantly, "You know, it occurs to me, maybe I should ask what I'm supposed to call you. Maybe you don't want me to call you Mrs. Mendoza."

"If that's what you prefer to call me, I will answer to it, but I think it's a little formal. You're welcome to call me Natalia."

Lenore suddenly started tearing up. She was surprised to discover she was incredibly jealous of Denise. She tried to blink the tears away, but it was not helping.

Natalia stepped forward and wrapped her arm gently around Lenore's waist. She said, "Oh, sweetie, are you okay? Was this too much for you? Do you need to lie down? Do we need to get you something?"

Lenore sniffed several times, wiping her eyes. "No, it's stupid. I just suddenly realized how jealous I am of Denise. I guess that just goes to show we're never happy with what we have."

Natalia looked very sad and hugged her gently. Denise stared at her in surprise and demanded, "What could you possibly be jealous of me about?"

"You have a nice mom that everybody likes."

Denise smiled and hugged her older sister. "Well, if that's the problem, there's no need for tears. I will happily share her, so just call her mom, because believe me, I definitely wouldn't mind watching her lecture somebody else for a change, then maybe you won't think she's so nice."

They all laughed. Lenore said a little hesitantly, "That's very sweet, but I don't think Mrs. Mendoza wants her husband's daughter calling her 'Mom'."

Natalia rolled her eyes and said firmly, "Don't be ridiculous. I would be thrilled. I just didn't suggest it because I knew it took you a little bit to warm up to Diego. I didn't want to pressure you. You are more than welcome to call me 'Mom' as long as you understand I will jerk you up short when I think you're screwing up."

Lenore started crying again. "I can totally handle that."

XLIV

Monday, December 11

Lenore and Bubba were working on cleaning out the stables. She was glad to be back to work now that all of her stitches were out, though her arm was still in a splint. She had a follow-up appointment with the doctor in twelve days and was hoping he was going to tell her she could do away with the splint.

Wayne entered the stables. He looked around. "Oh good, it looks like you two are done."

Bubba looked up from what he was doing and asked, "Something wrong?"

"I don't know. I just got a call from Hank. There's an emergency town council meeting."

Bubba hurled the pitchfork into the hay. "That don't sound good. You know what's up?"

"All he said was it has to do with the rodeo, so why don't you two get cleaned up and we can all go and find out what's going on."

Lenore asked, "Why do you want me to go?"

Wayne demanded with a smile, "Have you ever suffered through a town meeting before?"

"No, but with a ringing endorsement like that, who could possibly refuse to go?"

Bubba walked up behind her and grabbed her around the waist and pulled her against him. He kissed her on the neck. She giggled. Still holding her tight, he started marching her forward as he said with great amusement, "We can sit on the back row and if it gets boring we can start making out."

She laughed and pulled free. "I don't think so. I don't relish the idea of being a spectacle before the entire town."

He sighed and looked sad. "Killjoy. What time's the meeting?"

"Seven, so I figured we'd grab a late supper in town, unless, of course, Lenore objects to dining out with the two of us."

She smiled and wrapped her arm around Nathaniel's waist. "Never, but since you're forcing me to suffer through a town meeting, you're buying."

"I think I can manage that, but everybody has to suffer through a town meeting at least once in their life. Best to get it out of the way early."

Lenore went to her room, showered, and changed. No surprise, she was the last one in the living room.

Wayne said with amusement, "Well, if you two slow pokes are finally ready, we'll get going. I don't want to be late." They all headed out the door. Lenore started to get in the backseat. He said with a laugh, "Bubba's truck, Bubba's girl rides in the front seat. I'll ride in the back."

Lenore opened her mouth to protest, but Bubba said firmly, "Get in the front seat."

"Yes, boss."

Wayne waited until they were in the truck and headed down the road, then he asked, "Lenore, sweetheart, you wouldn't happen to know anything about our missing medical bills?"

"I didn't know they were missing. Would you like me to help you look for them after the meeting?"

"No, there's no point in looking in the house because they never arrived, apparently somebody gave them a California mailing address, and when I tried to get them sent to the ranch, I was informed that they were already paid, so that was unnecessary. Then I tried to get the bill from Diego for the truck, and he said it was already paid. When I asked him how much I owed him, he said it never arrived at his house, and when he called to check on it, it had already been paid. You wouldn't know anything about that, now would you?"

She sighed. "I don't see any point in dancing around this, arguing over it, or anything of that nature. It's paid. What does it matter who paid it?"

Bubba said with irritation, "Because you're our employee, those bills were our responsibility."

"Well, I guess we'll just have to agree to disagree about it."

Wayne sighed and added, "And while we're on the subject, are you ever going to cash your paychecks?"

"What for? I am content to work on the ranch for room and board. I don't need money as compensation. I like what I do. I like living here and I'm grateful that you allow me to continue to live here. This is why you brought me along, isn't it? You just wanted to ambush me in a truck where I couldn't get away. It had nothing to do with the town meeting?"

"Maybe, but who knows, the town meeting might actually be interesting. We haven't had an emergency town meeting in like nine years."

They chatted amiably until they arrived at the Town Hall. They all went in. Bubba indicated two seats on the back row, "We can sit there."

She shook her head and indicated some empty seats on the fourth row. "I think we should sit there." Not waiting for a reply, she went and sat down.

He grudgingly sat next to her. He leaned over and whispered in her ear, "Back row is better."

She shook her head and whispered back, "Will you behave."

"I have been on my best behavior for two weeks, and my contact with my girlfriend has been rather limited."

"You call sleeping four nights in your bed limited?"

"Yes, because you went back to yours. I was just getting used to it."

She elbowed him. "We can argue about this later."

The Town Council trooped in and the head of the Council, John, sat down. Lenore found the nameplates very helpful, it allowed her to identify who everybody was. John banged his gavel. "As you all know, Hank has called an emergency meeting of the Town Council in regards to the rodeo. I suggest we immediately hand the meeting over to Hank."

She shifted her attention to Hank, the sign in front of him read 'Event Coordinator'. "Well, ladies and gentlemen, we have suffered a tremendous blow. Here we are, only fifteen days until the start of the rodeo, and our largest performer, our biggest draw, none other than Mr. Allen Ford, responsible for opening the rodeo and for five performances at the rodeo, two of which are on the first Saturday, has backed out for reasons unknown. Now I cannot get a straight answer out of his manager, other than a firm he will not be here, which means not only do we have to scramble for a new performer who we hope can fill the Colosseum five times, but we also are going to have to be prepared to refund all of the money for the people who don't want the new performer."

Melissa, the Council treasurer, said with exasperation, "But the money from advance tickets sales is already spent. That's how we pay for the rodeo. We don't really come into profit until the last few days. The concerts really just allow us to have the rodeo, what actually gives us our profits are the concession stands, the rides, and the game booths. That's where we really make our money, but if there's no concerts, there's no rodeo."

The room was dead silent. Lenore sighed and rubbed her hands up and down her face. She looked at Nathaniel and asked, "Would you date a girl who danced half naked on a stage?"

"I would date you, but you know if you do this, you are so screwed."

"Do you hear any alternatives being mentioned?"

He sighed and shook his head. "I still say it's not your problem. You don't have to do this."

"And that would hurt the town, and I live here. This is my town now. If I can help, I should, right?"

He smiled. "I love you." Then he kissed her.

Lenore enjoyed the kiss for a moment, then she pulled free and stood up. "How many seats are we talking about?"

John looked momentarily confused, then he said, "I'm sorry, young lady, I'm not familiar with you, but if you are not a voting resident of the town, please sit down."

Lenore opened her mouth. Diego shot to his feet. "John, I strongly recommend you do not want to make her mad, and just a suggestion, you might want to remember that the teenagers of yesterday are tomorrow's voters. She has been a resident of the county for almost two months and will be voting in the next election. She is of age, and I repeat, I don't think you want to piss her off." He started to sit down and stood back up. "Oh, and by the way, for anyone who hadn't learned as of yet, that would be Lenore Stevens, my oldest daughter."

John sighed and said, "I'm sorry, I didn't understand the question, ma'am."

"My apologies if I was unclear. What I was trying to ask is how many seats does the Colosseum hold, so how many tickets do you have to be able to sell?"

Melissa responded, "The Colosseum holds fourteen thousand five hundred people, and all five performances are almost sold out. I think we have a total of four hundred tickets left between the five performances."

Lenore quickly calculated, then she said, "So you only need to re-sell seventy-two thousand, five hundred tickets so that you can refund the money. Do all performer tickets cost the same, or different performers' concerts cost different amounts?"

"A little bit of that depends on the entertainer. Some entertainers do require a larger cut, which causes prices to go up. We try not to do business with those entertainers because we try very hard to make sure that the most expensive ticket in the Colosseum is thirty dollars. We want this to be an experience that people can bring their families to."

"That's awesome. I love that. So if you didn't have to pay the performer a cut, could you lower ticket prices to pass that savings on to the audience, and maybe still increase your cut just a little? I mean, surely, since he is backing out, he is refunding whatever you have already paid him?"

Everyone looked at Hank. Hank cleared his throat and tugged on his collar. "Yes, I was informed that his retainer fee would be wire transferred back to us immediately. We should have it in the next day or two."

Melissa said, "We're not gonna get an entertainer who can fill the Colosseum for five performances to work for free."

Wayne laughed. "I'd tread lightly, Melissa. You're about to have to eat your words."

Lenore ignored that and moved on. "And I'm assuming that performers take ninety percent of the merchandise?"

Hank replied, "That is the standard contract."

Lenore calculated in her head, then she nodded. "Okay, here's the deal I am willing to offer the town. Everybody in this room helps keeps my anonymity, and in exchange, I will fill your Colosseum five times. I will purchase all performer merchandise and I will split the profits with the town. Fifty percent goes to the town with all of the other rodeo profits, and fifty percent goes to the Leaf County Food Bank. If there isn't one, create one and I will work for free, but ticket prices will not be one dollar higher than what you charge for this umm …"

Wayne supplied, "Allen Ford."

She nodded and pointed at Mr. Cartwright. "Yes, him, and I will do all of this for free because of the fact that it's not exactly what I think you guys are used to having at a rodeo, and I promise to be very family-friendly."

John demanded, "And exactly what makes you think, young lady, that's even a reasonable bargain for us?"

"Because if you don't sell fifty thousand T-shirts, I will be floored. That's in addition to any of my other merchandise, though I am going to have to rebrand a little bit, even if it's just for fun." She turned sideways and propped her boot up on Nathaniel's shoulder. "After all, I don't think Persephone's ever been photoed in Cowboy boots."

Bubba smiled and said quickly, "Can I suggest black boots, white Daisy Dukes, and a black tank top? I can get behind this."

She smiled and nodded. "I think Dad would probably agree with you."

Melissa leaned forward and demanded, "Diego, did your daughter just say she's Persephone?"

"Yes, I believe she did, and for the record, I fully support the tank top."

Lenore snapped her fingers. "Oh, yes, and there's one other condition. Everything has to say 'farewell performance', but y'all don't really have time to think about it because if this is going to happen, we need to get the ball rolling, because I don't even have the band. Don't look so worried, I mean, I can totally get a band, I just need to get one. And as far as the town having to refund ticket costs to people who don't want to see Persephone, I'm sure we can work something out about fronting all the money for that."

The Council all got out of their chairs and went to confer, then they returned to their seats. John asked, "We just want make sure we understand one thing correctly. You are asking that everyone present at the meeting, right now, not let it leak out that Lenore Stevens and Persephone are one and the same?"

"In an ideal world, yes. I don't expect it to stay that way, but if you can all help me out, that would be fabulous. It would also be nice if nobody mentioned that Persephone was living in this town. It is as much for your benefit as it is mine."

"The Town Council feels that these are more than fair terms and asks if the citizens present are willing to agree to it. Please indicate, by raising your hands." It appeared as though the entire room had raised their hands. "Against." Not a single hand was raised. "In that case, the Town Council agrees to your terms, Miss Stevens."

She nodded. "Very good, I will have my lawyer get in touch with Hank, or Melissa?"

"Melissa. Hank only handles coordinating all of the events."

"Awesome. If I can get Melissa's information, you will be hearing from him tomorrow, and I will get all of my balls rolling."

XLV

Bubba put the truck in park outside the ranch house. Lenore started to open her door, but he reached over and grabbed her thigh. "If you're not in a hurry, there's something I'd like to show you."

She smiled at him and nodded. "Of course."

Wayne got out of the truck. He said with a laugh, "Just remember, all employees are required to be at the breakfast table at six AM, that includes upper management." He closed the door and headed into the house.

Bubba waited until his father was inside, then he backed his truck up and headed away from town. Lenore asked, "Am I allowed to know where we are going?"

He smiled. "It's a surprise."

She unbuckled her seatbelt and slid over to the middle seat and buckled back up. He wrapped his arm around her, she rested her cheek against his shoulder. "I like surprises."

They sat in companionable silence for ten minutes. Bubba took a turn off the main road. Lenore raised an eyebrow and sat up. She could just see the outline of something in his headlights. He pulled up in a drive. Motion sensor lights kicked on and the area lit up. She looked at him and then back at the house. He smiled and put the truck in park, shut it off, and got out. She slid over and got out his door. He wrapped his arm around her waist and pulled her in the direction of the front door. She asked, "What's this place?"

Bubba unlocked the front door, then entered and turned off the alarm. He flipped on the lights. He gestured. "It's the old Foreman's place. He was still alive when Stewart came to work for us, so Stewart took the house that he and his wife live in. When Jake died, his wife decided she didn't want to live here anymore and she moved to Georgia to live with the grandkids. This place is bigger, so Pop offered it to Stewart and his wife, after all, it goes with the job, but they didn't want to move. So we cleaned it out, closed it, and it's sat empty for about seven years. Needs a little work, definitely could use a new paint job, could stand to have a swing set in the back, there's a tree that just longs for a tire swing, needs a new deck, but I think it'd be a real nice house for a family, for our family. Would you like to live here?" She stared at him, her mouth a little open, her eyes wide. After a long minute he chuckled nervously. "I know an engagement ring is more customary, and if you're going to tell me I'm rushing you and you need more time, I guess I can understand that, but Lenore, I'm crazy about you, and I've never met another woman I wanted to ask, but I would count myself fortunate to call you my wife." He got down on one knee reached out and took both her hands in his. "Miss Lenore, would you do me the honor of consenting to be my wife?"

She stood there still feeling stunned. Finally she realized she had to say something. "Nathaniel, there's nothing I would like more than to be your wife ..."

He shot to his feet and wrapped his arms around her and kissed her. They kissed for several minutes, then he pulled free and gestured to the house. "So what do you think?"

She frowned. "Is this where you want to live?"

He frowned and shrugged his shoulders. "When Mama was alive, she always talked about taking the cabin when I got married, and I'd live in the big house with my family. She said that the house was just too much upkeep for old people, and she and Pop would be happy in the cabin. That's where they lived when they first got married, then when I was on the way they moved to the house where George and his wife live. But they didn't even live there a year before Ethan was on the way, and Grandpa said enough of this moving around, and told them to move into the big house, and he went and lived in the cabin, and that's where he lived until he died."

"So you want to live in the big house?"

He shook his head. "I'm not asking Pop to move out. He's had to deal with too much change, I'm not …"

She put her fingers over his mouth. "You know, I think it was after that horrible first dinner with the Sheriff and his family you said something that really moved me. You talked about grandkids breathing life back into your father. The big house, it has eight family rooms. Unless your father just hates the idea, I don't see why we can't all live there. I'd be happy there, you'd be happy, and let's be honest, I don't think he wants us to go."

"You'd be happy living with my father?"

She wrapped her arms around his neck. "I have been the happiest of my life living with you and your father. Why would I want to change that? Well, I do want to change it just a little, after all, I don't want to support the English aristocracy's concept of married life."

He gripped her bottom with both hands and pulled her against him. He kissed her on the lips and then said firmly, "If you wanted separate rooms, I would refuse to marry you."

She rubbed her cheek against his chest. "Definitely not, I've missed sleeping in your bed."

He ran his fingers into her hair and demanded, "Then why in the hell did you go back to your own room? I sure as hell didn't want you to."

"Lots of reasons."

He pushed her away just a little and said, "Name three."

"Well, I didn't want there to be any difficulties between you and Aaron; after all, until I went back to my own room, he was giving you dirty looks over the breakfast table. And you said you didn't want to go too far, so I thought I was encroaching." She blushed. "And being that close to you was getting very difficult. I started wanting more than just kisses. I realized I was longing for you to get more amorous."

He rubbed her cheek with the back of his hand. "As long as you were all stitched up and bandaged up, that was not going to happen, but I will not lie, had you been in my bed these past few days, it probably would've been very hard for me to keep my hands to myself."

She started rubbing his chest and kissed his neck. "So does that mean if I come to your room tonight, you'll make love to me?"

He laughed. "If you don't stop kissing my neck, I'll make love to you right here, and as enjoyable as that would be, that's not exactly how I want to lose my virginity."

She giggled and rubbed her cheek against his chest. "I thought so."

He wrapped his arms around her. "Thought what?"

"Well, after that little rant about you weren't in college to screw, I was a little suspicious that you had never had sex either. So does that mean you would rather I didn't come to your room tonight?"

"I do not know what I could've said to give you that idea. I most definitely want you tonight, and I think tomorrow you and I should talk to Pop and sort out living arrangements, and then hopefully from then on you'll be in my room."

"Don't you mean our room?"

XLVI

Tuesday, December 12

Bubba came downstairs just a couple minutes late. He had had a hard time dragging himself out of bed this morning, the company was just too good. As he entered the breakfast room, he said, "Ramon, slide one chair to your left. Stewart, you scoot over one to the left as well and get used your new seats, boys." He sat down in his usual place and began helping himself to breakfast. Both men did as they were told but looked curious.

Wayne got to his feet and walked to the other head of the table. He sat a small box down next to Bubba, then went back to his seat. "It was your great grandmother's, maybe even older. My father always said he thought it dated back to the Civil War, but my grandmother had very tiny hands. Something told me you were going to need that this morning."

When Lenore entered from the wrong side of the room, she was sure everyone was staring. She started towards her seat, and then realized Ramon was in it, but Nathaniel got to his feet and pulled out Stewart's old chair. He indicated the seat. "This is your place from now on."

"And what was wrong with my old chair?"

"It wasn't next to me. I will not sit next to one of them when my wife is at the table."

She sat down and so did he. She said with a smile, "We're not married ... yet."

He opened the box and removed the ring. Examining it carefully, he nodded with approval, then reached over and took her left hand and slid it on to her finger. He wiggled it. "That fits pretty nice. It was my great grandmother's. If you don't like it, I will get you another one."

Lenore looked at her hand and shifted it from side to side. It was clearly an antique ring. The center stone was a ruby so dark in certain light it appeared black, surrounded by six small diamonds. She sniffed and felt herself getting teary-eyed. "No, it's beautiful. I will remember to take it off when I am working in the stables."

Wayne snorted. "Don't be ridiculous. The only time I ever remember my grandmother taking that ring off was when she was making bread, and that was because the bread dough got in the stones and was a bear to get out."

She nodded and smiled as she reached under the table and squeezed Nathaniel's thigh. He placed his hand on top of hers. "You're right, this is nicer."

Bubba took a deep breath then said, "Pop, do you think you might have a few minutes this morning? Lenore and I would like to talk to you about something."

Wayne smiled, positive he knew where this was going. "Of course, right after breakfast."

Lenore was on pins and needles the whole meal. It seemed like an eternity, but it could not have been more than twenty minutes before they were alone at the table with Mr. Cartwright. He looked around and said, "Well, it seems we find ourselves alone. Is here all right, or do you insist on having this conversation in my office?" he asked, taking a swig from his coffee.

Bubba shook his head. "Here's fine as far as I'm concerned." He looked at Lenore and raised an eyebrow in question. She just nodded. He smiled. She looked positively terrified. He knew it was probably cruel, but he could not help it. He chuckled, picked up her hand and brought it to his lips. He kissed her knuckles. "Are you gonna be sick?"

She punched him in the shoulder. "Jerk."

Wayne laughed. "You two can flirt later. What's this about?"

Bubba indicated Lenore. "Well, I think Lenore should tell you, it's her idea. I mean, she shot down mine, after all." He frowned at her.

Lenore swallowed hard and turned to glared at him. She demanded quickly, "What? Me? No, he's your father, you should talk to him about it."

He smiled. "But it was your suggestion." Lenore kicked him under the table.

Wayne said with exasperation, "Oh for heaven sakes, woman, spit it out. I get it. The two of you want to live in the big house. I will happily move to the cabin, when ... before Nathaniel's mother died it was always the plan to hand the big house off to him and us go back to where we started. I'm fine with it. I don't understand why the two of you are making a production out of this. Oh, wait, my mistake. I forgot, singer, is that anything like an actress?" Wayne was having a really hard time not laughing. Lenore turned on him. She was glaring daggers at him. He could not help it, he started laughing. "Man, if looks could kill I would've burst into flames already."

Bubba said laughing. "Hell, with that look, I think the house would've caught on fire."

"I'm not an actress and I don't like drama! I just don't think it is appropriate for me to discuss living arrangements with you. I think that Nathaniel should be doing it. He's your son. I'm just a hired hand, but since clearly neither one of you want to make this easy on me, I guess I have no choice. Neither Nathaniel nor I want you to go anywhere, but we also don't want to go anywhere.

There are six empty family bedrooms and two guest rooms. What I mean is ... unless it would drive you absolutely crazy, there's more than plenty of room here for all of us, unless the idea of living under the same roof as your grandchildren is more than you can handle."

Wayne hesitated, then asked, "At the risk of setting you off, so there will be grandchildren?"

She blushed deeply. "God willing, lots. We haven't exactly discussed how many, but something tells me he wants a half-dozen."

Bubba smiled and reached over and squeezed her hand. "Four or six. I could be okay with either number, God willing. But I'll take what I can get and be grateful I have them."

Wayne smiled. "I would love living here with my grandchildren, and of course I don't want y'all to move out, but in my mind, as soon as Nathaniel ..."

Bubba cut him off. "Oh, hell no! You people better not get used to using my name. Lenore is the only one that can call me Nathaniel."

Wayne shot his son a dirty look. "I'm your father, I'll call you anything I damn well choose, but you're right, it doesn't roll off the tongue naturally. But I'd always figured as soon as Bubba married, I'd skedaddle on out of here and let him and his family have this place. It's not meant for just an old man."

Lenore got to her feet and picked up her dishes. "Well, like I said, I'm just a hired hand, but as far as I'm concerned, I'm the only one who needs to relocate."

Bubba slapped her across the bottom. "Dammit, woman! If I hear you say you're just a hired hand one more time, I'm going to put you over my knee." He got to his feet and grabbed his dishes. He bumped his shoulder into hers. "Like it or not, when you're my wife, that will make you the mistress of this household, and there's going to be times when even Pop will yield to your judgment."

She opened her mouth to protest, but Wayne cut her off. "No, ma'am, he's right. There are certain things that are dictated by the woman of the house, and as far as I'm concerned, that's already you."

She sighed several times. "Fine, clearly I can't fight both of you." Wayne nodded, got to his feet and picked up his dishes. They all went into the kitchen as she asked, "Is there anything I need to know right this minute that is under my domain?"

To her surprise it was Alejandro who responded. "I could be wrong, but I think you're my new boss. Ah, damn! That means I can't order you around anymore." He laughed.

She looked at Mr. Cartwright and said, "Surely not, he is one of the …"

But Wayne was already shaking his head. "No, ma'am, he's right. The kitchen and the house fall under your domain. If we decide to hire another housekeeper, they'll answer to you too, but don't worry, I still pay the bills. But you get to discuss menus with Alejandro from now on, not me. Now, of course, you could always take things back to my mother's day, and decide that you want to do the cooking and fire him."

She looked from one face to the other. They were all laughing. "Y'all are teasing me."

Bubba finished putting his dishes away and said still laughing, "Actually, that's what's so funny. We're not."

Wayne decided to take mercy on her and change the subject, but only slightly. He asked, "When are you going to tell your folks, and when do you kids want to get married?"

Lenore grimaced and asked, "We don't have to make an ordeal out of it, do we?"

To everyone's surprise it was Alejandro who replied, "That depends on your definition of ordeal. If you mean the big white church wedding with hundreds of guests, probably not. But I don't see you getting away with getting married at the courthouse. Something tells me I'm not the only one who's going to protest. Diego would have kittens. Diego won't be happy with anybody short of a minister marrying y'all."

Wayne nodded. "Got to say I agree with him on that one. I don't think Bubba would be happy with a Justice of the Peace either."

Bubba scratched the back of his neck. "Realistically, I don't see how we are going to get out of having to invite at least a hundred guests, probably more like three hundred. I mean, whether you admit it or not, there is probably a handful people you are going to want to invite. I've got a list. The Sheriff is gonna have a list. Pop, I know, is gonna have a list. I think Amelia'd be devastated if she wasn't a flower girl. I figured you'd ask Denise to be your Maid of Honor. You, Natalia, Denise, and Amelia are going to want to go dress shopping." He chuckled at the look on her face and amended what he said. "Okay, they are going to want to go dress shopping. Alejandro is gonna want to flex his culinary muscles, which will probably result in us having to hire outside help to cater it, but figure he should easily have food under control. There is the question of whether we need to order a cake, or whether he's got that covered …"

Alejandro interrupted him. "You tell me whether I'm serving dinner, or cake and punch, and I've got it covered, but you want to know the funniest thing about this? Something tells me us three guys are going to be doing all the work, because the bride's gonna be the one who just wants to stand there and hold up the dress for pictures."

Lenore sighed several times. "I have to wear a dress?"

All three men replied in one voice, "Yes."

She sighed again. "Fine. We're getting married on the ranch, and it has to be an outdoor wedding, and an outdoor reception, so I suggest you choose a time when it's cool."

Alejandro nodded. "And probably sooner rather than later, if you two are going to be sharing a room."

Bubba nodded. "How about we decide on mid-March. Shouldn't be too cold or too hot, and we can rent tents if we are worried about rain, and I say let's go all out. Let's do dinner."

Lenore sighed again, then nodded. "Sounds fine to me. Whatever makes Nathaniel happy."

XLVII

Lenore waited until they walked out of the kitchen, then she said, "Okay, now that that is settled, we have bigger problems we have to discuss."

Wayne shrugged his shoulders, "Like what?"

She sighed and said, "Persephone."

He nodded. "Oh right, I forgot about your alter ego. What about her?"

She sighed several times and shrugged her shoulders. "To begin with, I have about a dozen balls I need to get rolling if I'm going to get all this rodeo stuff sorted out, and I know that as a result I'll be getting fired, but at least I don't have to worry about being homeless, but I'm afraid probably for the next three or even four weeks, I'm not going to be able to work on the ranch regularly." She hesitated and rubbed her face. She knew as soon as she said what was on her mind Nathaniel was going to flip out, and the Sheriff was probably going to be right behind him, but she was not sure it could be helped. She sighed several times and then added, "And I think it might be better if I fly to San Diego as Lenore Stevens, then either have a limo or a friend pick me up and drive me to Los Angeles. I get a hotel and I set everything up from Los Angeles, and then I fly back as Persephone. I work the concert. I go back to Los Angeles as Persephone, and then Persephone disappears again and is never heard from or seen again, and Lenore Stevens comes home."

Bubba began shaking his head vigorously. "Not only no, but hell no! If you have any care or concern from my feelings, you will not leave the state of Texas!" He gripped her by the waist. "Please, Lenore, I am begging you, do not go back to California."

She sighed and leaned forward and pressed her cheek against his chest. After a minute she said, "Look, I understand your feelings. Believe me, I do not want to go back there either, but I can't do what I need to do from the ranch, or I will lose what happiness I have found here."

He tilted her chin up so that she had to look at him and said firmly, "Hey, I understand, and I understand you don't want to risk people finding out that you and Persephone are one and the same. I'm not asking you to conduct your business from the ranch."

Wayne said gently, "May I interject myself here for a moment?"

Bubba wrapped his arms tightly around Lenore and said, "Go ahead, Pop."

"What exactly are we talking about here? I mean, I know last night you said you needed a band, but what else do you need?"

Lenore pulled free. Nathaniel grumbled but did not protest. She rubbed her face as the sheer weight of everything she had to do washed over her. She could not imagine what she had been thinking not only to agree to this, but actually be the idiot who suggested it. Two weeks to do what was normally done in months. She knew it could be done, but it just terrified her. She rubbed her face and sighed several times. After a minute she said, "I need a band, I need to get the merchandise sorted out, I need to get ahold of my lawyer to get with the Town Council, I need to hire somebody to handle wardrobe, I need a manager, bodyguards. I need to find out what happened to my tour bus, my equipment, I need to find out what we actually owned and what we rented, I need to hire somebody to handle my makeup and my hair ..."

Bubba accidentally said out loud, "Shit!"

Wayne demanded, "What?"

"She's going to go back to being a blonde."

Wayne shuddered. "Sorry, sweetie, but blonde is not a good look for you, at least not in my opinion."

Bubba nodded and pointed at his father. "What he said."

She sighed and wrapped her arms around Nathaniel's neck and kissed him on the lips. "I know you don't like me as a blonde, and I promise you I will have a bottle of hair dye standing by to go back to this ..." She grabbed the end of her braid and trailed her hair along his neck as she said, "I don't like being a blonde either, but it's a key element in separating me from her. I thought about a wig, but I think it's too dangerous and hot."

He grumbled. "Whatever makes you happy."

"I'm happy the way I am."

He smiled. "Good, because I like you the way you are. I like the real you." He only barely managed to stop himself before he said he did not like the sex idol. He knew it would upset her and she was already upset enough. He kissed her on the lips, then said, "But I interrupted, go on."

She pulled free, sighed, and said, "I need a photographer, I have to do a photo shoot. I need to hire dancers, a choreographer, I need to get back in shape. I probably need to lose twenty pounds ..."

Bubba cut her off. "The hell you do! You look fine just the way you are, and at the risk of getting myself hit, in my opinion you could stand to put on a couple more pounds. I mean what, since you've been here you went up one pant size maybe?"

Lenore wanted to protest. She closed her eyes and took a deep breath, then she nodded. She opened her eyes and smiled at him. She took another deep breath, then said, "You are right. I do not have to maintain my mother's standards of beauty, just my own. I mean, honestly, what's the worst that can happen? I end up on fifty magazines coast-to-coast saying that I was looking fatter than ever." Nathaniel looked at her very disapprovingly. She cupped his cheek and kissed him on the lips. "That may have sounded like I care, but I actually don't. I really don't. I swear. Their opinion doesn't matter. My opinion matters. Your opinion matters." She blushed slightly then kissed him on the lips again. She whispered softly, "After all, you saw me naked last night, and if you still don't think I'm fat, then that's all that matters."

All three men said firmly, "You are not fat."

Lenore pulled free and peeked around the corner into the kitchen. "Is somebody eavesdropping?"

Alejandro did not even look up from what he was doing as he replied, "It is not eavesdropping if you're talking loud enough I can hear you. After all, there is no door from the kitchen to the dining room, and not that anybody asked, but I agree with Bubba, stay away from California."

She laughed, sighed, and then said, "We can argue that in a minute, but as I was about to say before I was so rudely interrupted, I also have to make sure whoever I hired to handle my makeup can airbrush all of my scars so nobody can see them when I'm on stage. I have to make sure that the photographer I hire can touch up the photos so that there's no texture issues so they can't be seen in the promotional photos, and that needs to be done like now, because the rodeo needs to get down all of that guy's stuff and get mine up. I think that covers everything."

Wayne let out a whistle. "Well, I hadn't even thought of a bunch of that stuff, but I agree with the boys, I don't think California's an option. However, I think I can solve a few problems pretty quick. Didn't I hear you say your bodyguards are still under contract to you? Call them, get them out here. I bet you that lawyer of yours knows where all your stuff is. That sounds like that's right up his alley. Find out what that lawyer of yours can do to whittle down this list. I bet you he can recommend a good manager, and tell him you need to hire somebody in the D/FW area. Get those bodyguards of yours to come pick you up here. They can take you to D/FW. D/FW is about three hundred miles away, that'll get you some distance from the ranch and yet still close enough somebody can sneak over and say hi." He jerked his thumb in Bubba's direction. "And the D/FW area is huge, you should be able to get everything you need there. If you still got your fancy bus that has Persephone painted on the side or whatever, it can pick you and your team up in D/FW and bring you out to the rodeo grounds, though sadly you'll probably be going back and forth to Amarillo. That's usually where the big stars stay, it's the nearest place with big hotels. And as far as Persephone making her next great disappearing act, I'll bet you Lenore has made enough friends around this area we can make her disappear in a puff of smoke and never reappear. We just have to time it right, and between the Sheriff, the Town Council, and the boys here on the ranch, I think it should be no problem whatsoever."

Bubba snapped his fingers and pointed at his father. "Say, she's got some friends you don't even know about!"

Wayne demanded, "Who?"

Bubba replied with a laugh, "Sean O'Mannion, and with O'Mannion on her side, that puts every rodeo clown and pick up man on her side. Nobody would dare cross him."

Wayne raised an eyebrow and demanded, "How the hell did city girl meet up with him?"

Bubba laughed. "I still haven't gotten the whole story on that one, but I say we table that discussion for dinner tonight. She can give us the whole story then and we can see what everybody can come up with on disappearing act number two."

Wayne nodded. "Well, you and I got work out on the ranch to get done, boy. I suggest Lenore goes into my office and gets to work on those phone calls. If the boys start coming back and she hasn't gotten the stables done, they can either help her finish or do it all together."

Bubba nodded, peeked his head around the corner into the kitchen, and demanded, "Hey, what's the chances of you makin' a run in to Amarillo for me today?"

Alejandro looked up from what he was doing. "As soon as I get this roast into the oven, I'll be free for the rest of the day. What do you need me to do?"

"Go buy Lenore a cell phone."

Alejandro chuckled. "Well, she doesn't have any credit, so they're gonna gouge her two arms and a leg, so it would probably be best if one of us puts her on our account, so I'll go ahead and take care of it and the kid can owe me."

XLVIII

Wednesday, December 13

Alejandro was in the kitchen working on dinner when he started hearing a beeping noise. He looked around, then realized it was coming from the refrigerator. He groaned and shook his head. He had forgotten about the three new additions stuck to the refrigerator. They were small white boxes, about two inches by two inches and one inch thick with a red light that blinked when it started beeping. One said front porch, one said driveway, the other said road, this was the one that was blinking and beeping. After Bubba had left yesterday, he had texted Alejandro to find some kind of motion sensor that would alert anybody in the kitchen that somebody had pulled up. It had taken several phone calls and texts back and forth with Bubba before they had agreed these were the best options until they could come up with something better. Bubba had not said it, but Alejandro had gotten the distinct impression Mr. Cartwright was looking into upgrading their security system. He knew that though none of the guys had said anything, they all had different concerns. Things were probably going to be a little tense around here for a couple of months until they were sure that none of Persephone's psycho fans discovered her whereabouts. Ramon and Bubba had set up the motion sensors last night while Lenore was working on laundry. Alejandro knew it was silly that they were all trying not to worry her any more than necessary, because it was obvious she was terrified. He quickly washed and dried his hands and headed out of the kitchen.

He paused by the front entryway table, opened a drawer, and pulled out his gun holster. He hooked it on his belt, then he pulled out his gun, and triple checked that it was loaded. He had checked twice already today. They were definitely all on edge now. Normally weeks would go by without him touching his gun. Though Mr. Cartwright required quarterly gun evaluations, he or Bubba would go out with a couple of the guys to the shooting range set up on the property where you were required to fire twenty pistol rounds and twenty rifle rounds. As long as you shot well, you were good for another three months. Shoot badly, you got to do it once a week until they felt you had improved. Fortunately, since they had taught Alejandro how to shoot a gun, his marksmanship had never fallen that far, but he also had never been forced to shoot at anything but a target. They actually all enjoyed going shooting, so it was unusual for more than a month to go by without a group of them going out to the range.

He peeked out front. Parked on what they called the road directly in front of the house was a big black SUV with tinted windows. He did not think anyone had gotten out and he could see the profile of the driver. He reluctantly opened the front door and stepped out onto the porch. Normally he would not even hesitate, but having already been on edge, this was making him more nervous. He had scarcely closed the front door behind him when the driver's side door opened and a tall, muscular black man stepped out. His age was difficult to determine, and he was in very expensive black and red sneakers that did not belong around here, baggie designer black jeans, and a red designer T-shirt. He had on a very expensive looking gold watch, a few gold chains, both of his ears were pierced, and he had on a few bracelets and rings. He definitely did not look like he belonged here. Alejandro looked at him suspiciously and said, "I don't think you belong here."

The big man laughed and held his hands up towards the sky. "Thank God, a person! Do you know I haven't seen a person for like fifty miles? Where I'm from, that's like unheard of. You're probably right, I am probably absolutely lost, but all I had to go on was a photograph of a hand-drawn map, and do you realize you ain't got no names on your streets out here?"

Alejandro was just opening his mouth to reply when he heard a squeal of delight. Both men shifted their attention to see Lenore come running from the stables. She shouted, "JC, my man!" When she was a few feet away, she leapt into the air, throwing her arms around the man's neck and hugging him tightly.

Alejandro, who could see the man's face clearly, did not think him wrapping his arms around her had anything to do with recognition, but more to do with the fact that he now had a woman dangling from his neck. He grabbed her by the waist and pulled her free and set her on the ground.

JC quickly separated himself from the woman and stepped back. Then his eyes widened and he let out a wolf whistle. He grabbed her by the hand and spun her in a circle. He whistled again, then said with a laugh, "Damn, girl, you look fine, even if it does look like you're dressing out of your little brother's closet."

Lenore laughed and hugged him again. "Man, I never thought I'd be so happy to see anybody from the past, but I sure am happy to see you. Did you have any trouble finding the place, because if you did, you have to blame Bubba, he drew the map."

JC started laughing and slapping his thigh. "Dude, you know somebody named Bubba? Holy shit!"

She rolled her eyes and slapped him on the shoulder. "Stop your nonsense, and by the way he's a pretty cool guy, thank you very much. I think you two will get along great." She wrapped her right arm around his waist and turned him in the direction of the house. She gestured with her left, "That's my friend and coworker Alejandro, and Alejandro, this is my former head bodyguard, soon-to-be temporary head bodyguard, JC, and for the longest time, the only friend I had." She whistled and then demanded, "What's with the piece? Since when do you walk around carrying a gun?"

Alejandro lied smoothly, "Since somebody killed two rabid dogs."

She shuddered, then said a little unsteadily, "I thought we all agreed to stop talking about that."

"You asked about the gun, sweetie."

JC pulled free and turned to face her. He crossed his arms over his chest and said, "And quite frankly, I don't even know where I am supposed to begin. Am I supposed to ask about the clothes first, the cast, the knife on your hip, or the rock on your finger, and since I know how graceful you are, the cast really isn't that interesting, which really means that I'm torn between the knife and the rock, though rabid dogs are also interesting." He turned back to Alejandro, crossed to him, and extended his hand. "Forgive my bad manners, but I'm so excited at seeing her again and confused, but it's real nice to meet you, man."

"Likewise. I have heard a few good things about you, not that she talks that much about the past, but you did come up a couple of times."

He chuckled. "I'm sure whatever the brat said were all lies."

Lenore rolled her eyes, but was not given a chance to respond because Bubba pulled up in his truck. He parked, got out, and crossed to the group, walked right up to their visitor, and extended his hand. "You must be JC. I'm Bubba Cartwright. Real nice to meet you. Heard a lot of good things about you, and to merely say I owe you one is a monumental understatement."

JC caught his meaning immediately. He shook hands with him as he said, "So the rock is yours. Very nice. You hurt her, I will kill you and they will never find the body, I promise you."

Bubba laughed. "Not to worry on that score, you would have to stand in line because there are a lot of people who would beat you there and we all carry guns, not least of which is my father, all of my hands, my cook who is standing behind you, and her father." He chuckled and added, "Though come to think of it, that rock ain't the only thing she's got on that's mine. In fact, with the exception of the boots and hat, everything she's got on is mine."

Lenore made a face and decided to get even with him. She said quickly, "You know, Bubba, I don't think you should go around advertising that you wear bras ..." Alejandro started laughing so hard he thought he was going to fall down. "... but I'm pretty sure you couldn't fit into mine; however, I do believe the underwear I am wearing you did buy ... let me check ..." She unzipped her jeans, pulled them a little to the side. "Yep, these are the ones you bought me."

Alejandro quickly turned his back and said with irritation, "Dammit, Lenore, I did not need to see that!"

JC just laughed and rolled his eyes.

Bubba put his hand over his face. After a long minute he said, "Okay, I will admit it, I asked for the thing about the bra. I won't lie, I walked right into that one. However, Lenore my love, please do me the courtesy of never unzipping your pants in front of another man again."

She looked at him innocently and said, "But Bubba, I thought they were your pants."

He shook his head. "I yield. It was a stupid thing to say. You can torture me for it tonight, especially since I won't be seeing you again for a few weeks, and please don't call me Bubba, it feels like a punishment."

She sighed, walked up to him, and wrapped her arms around his neck. "Nathaniel, I love you, but you are going to have to understand, at least for the next few weeks, there's probably going to be quite a few guys who are going to see me in my underwear. Provided JC hasn't had to hire any new bodyguards, it will be nothing new to them. They will have seen it before; however, my makeup person could be a guy. It's very likely the photographer will see me in my underwear and could be a guy, and wardrobe could be a guy, not to mention managers, band members, dancers, it's all part of the stage performer life. Privacy and modesty aren't high on the list of things we get in life."

Bubba growled several times, wrapped his arms around her waist, and held her tightly. "As long as you don't expect me to like it."

"No, I want you to hate it. I hate it, but it's just one last time, I swear."

He nodded and shifted his attention in JC's direction. He said firmly, "And I know it goes without saying, but she's runnin' the show, and nobody puts their hands anywhere she doesn't like, or you better flatten them. That's your job, and I expect you to do it, or you will answer to me."

JC smiled and said quickly, "In a New York minute."

Bubba nodded, pulled free as he said, "Then we'll get along just fine, but while we're on the subject ..." He pulled out his phone and went to his text messages. He clicked on a photo and turned it so JC could see it. "Know that face. He comes within fifty feet of her, you flatten him. He doesn't speak to her, he doesn't look at her."

JC held out his hand. "May I?" Bubba handed it over to JC, who began typing as he said, "I'm forwarding it to myself, so I can forward it to the other guys. What's his name, and why does this look like a mug shot?"

"Jace Walker, and that's because it is. He is currently serving thirty days in county lockup for selling drugs and trying to rape my fiancé. I don't like him. And they're letting him out two days early because of Christmas, so he gets out on December twenty-three."

Alejandro demanded, "He did what? And when the fuck were you gonna tell us?"

Lenore put her hands over her face and said with irritation, "Thank you, Bubba."

He said firmly, "Don't you Bubba me. Like it or not, his job is to protect you, and since I can't be around you to protect you, he needs all the facts. He can't do his job if you're only giving him half the information he needs to know. It's not just psycho fans he has to worry about, but Jace is a potential threat, and I'm sorry if I said something in front of Alejandro, which is good, because the other guys need to know. Quite frankly, in my opinion, they need to because I've already made it very clear to Deputy Baxter, and I made it very clear to Jace's father, he steps one foot on my property, I will shoot him dead. I ain't playing with him, Lenore."

She sighed, rubbed her face, then nodded and said, "I agree with you and I understand your point of view, but that doesn't mean I have to like it."

He reached out and cupped her cheek. "I know the Valley girl rebels against killing, but sometimes some things need killing. If he stays away from you, I don't got no problem with him. I hate him, but I don't got no problem with him. He comes near you, he steps on my property, and we've got a problem." She sighed and nodded.

JC handed back the phone. "Can I ask just one question?" They both looked at him and nodded. He asked, "Her father?" pointing at Lenore.

Lenore laughed. "Oh, yes, you're gonna love this, my father is Sheriff Diego Mendoza."

JC started laughing. "Hispanic? I told you there were some mix in the batter!"

She laughed. "Yes, apparently on my father's side I'm Mexican, Irish, Catholic. Oh, and by the way, despite your crack about me dressing out of my little brother's closet, Aaron is way too big, there's no way I could wear his clothes. And Lorenzo is too small, and my little sister Denise might be able to wear some of my clothes, but probably not, and for Amelia wearing my clothes would be like playing dress-up."

He whistled. "Oh damn, are you the oldest?"

"Yep, I'm big sister."

He smiled, then sighed, and shook his head. "Jane is gonna love that."

XLIX

Thursday, December 14

Lenore snuggled up against Nathaniel, wrapping her arm around his waist. He reached back and rubbed her thigh. She lifted her head off the pillow. The alarm was going to go off any second now. He reached over and turned it off, then got out of bed and started getting dressed. Lenore sighed and did the same. She was nearly dressed when he reached over and grabbed her by the arm and pulled her towards him. He bent down and kissed her on the cheek. "I will see you in two weeks, but you'll probably not see me, and in three weeks you will be back here in my arms and we will never be apart again."

She smiled and hugged him tightly. "Agreed."

He finished getting dressed and grabbed his hat. He stood there fiddling with it for a minute, then he said, "Don't take this the wrong way, my love, but you won't see me at breakfast." He picked the phone up off the dresser and handed it to her. "I programmed everybody's numbers into it. If you get homesick you can call any of us. I put a few extra numbers in there for emergency's sake, and that fancy lawyer of yours, his number's in there too, and after JC texted himself that photo I had his number, so I added him too."

She took it, nodded, and stuck it in her backpack. "Please tell me you're not planning on coming to one of the concerts."

He smiled. "Already got my ticket. After the Town Council meeting, the Sheriff told the Council that there was an off the record requirement, he got everybody tickets, all the hands, their families, even Pop wants to go. Of course, as far as any of the families are concerned, the Sheriff just called in a personal favor, they don't know ... so like I said, I'll be seeing you." He pulled her into his arms and kissed her passionately.

Lenore pulled free and looked up at him. She pulled her engagement ring off, took his left hand, and pressed the ring into it. She curled his fingers around it. "Just so we're clear, I am not giving that back. I'm just asking you to hold onto it for a little while. I will be back for it and its owner, understood?"

He gripped the ring tightly. He reached out with his right hand and gripped the back of her neck. He bent forward and pressed his forehead into hers, then he rubbed his cheek against hers. He said softly, "You damn well better." Then he let her go, turned, and headed out of his room before he lost his nerve. He headed down the stairs. He stuck the ring in his left pocket. He would put it up later, but not now. He could not do it now, just like he could not face the guys now, which was why he headed through the front entryway, down the back hallway, and into the kitchen, avoiding the dining room. He grabbed his lunchbox, coffee thermos, and opened the cabinet. He found a bag a trail mix, grabbed it, opened the refrigerator, grabbed two cheese sticks, and headed out the way he had come, slamming the front door.

When Lenore entered the dining room a few minutes later, everybody looked grim. JC asked, "Are they usually this cheery? I mean, they were grumpy last night."

Stewart, who had not been at dinner last night, but had already been introduced to their guest, said, "We're just gonna miss the kid. I'm not looking forward to Friday night."

They all grumbled their agreement. JC asked, "What happens on Friday night?"

They all sighed, but it was Wayne who replied, "Aaron comes to work over Christmas break, which means either myself, Alejandro, or Stewart get to tell him that his big sister left without saying goodbye. Hopefully Diego has already told him that Persephone will be giving a farewell performance, because if he learns it at school, there's gonna be hell to pay, and none of us are gonna be very popular for a while. Speaking of Diego, have you told your daddy that you're leaving town yet, girl?"

She looked down at her plate and played with her fried potatoes. After a long minute she murmured, "No, and I'm pretty sure he doesn't know we're engaged either." No one else said a word. When she noticed JC was finished, she got to her feet and reached for her dishes.

Alejandro said quickly, "Leave them. I will clean up."

"But ..."

He snapped, "I said leave them."

She sighed, clearly everybody was going to be mad at her today. "Look everybody, I'm sorry, I didn't mean to make you all mad."

Wayne shook his head and said quickly, "Baby girl, the only thing I'm mad at you about is that you haven't told your daddy and you haven't told your brother. I'm not mad at you for what you're doing, but I am gonna miss you. We all are. Been kind of nice having you around, so just remember to come home where you belong. Don't decide you like being her again."

They all got to their feet. She turned and hugged Stewart tightly. "No danger of that. I promise you I will be back here, with any luck by the fifth." She walked around the table hugging them all goodbye. They all murmured their farewells and walked her and JC outside. She tried very hard not to roll her eyes as they all shook hands with him and made various threats if he failed in his job.

JC waited until they were in the car headed back the way he came before he said, "That is a very nice family you found for yourself, kid. I'm very happy for you."

She smiled. "Thank you, I love them all so much. I'm gonna miss them like crazy."

He nodded. After a couple of minutes he said, "You should probably close your eyes and try to get some sleep. We got a forty-five minute drive to the airport, then we got an hour and twenty minute flight. Your new manager is supposed to pick us up outside the airport and then life is going get a little crazy. Oh, and by the way, all your bodyguards will be familiar faces. They all dropped everything they were doing to come back. I didn't even have to remind them they were still under contract."

She smiled as she pulled off her splint and shoved it into her backpack. She said with a laugh, "Good to know at least somebody liked working for me."

He smiled. "Miss P, you were the only thing any of us liked about that gig." He glanced at her arm and asked, "Were you supposed to take it off yet?"

"No, but Persephone can't be seen in public in a cast. That would cause questions, questions I do not want to answer."

He nodded but said firmly, "Okay, but take it easy. And behind closed doors, you need to wear it."

She smiled and asked, "Who's the boss?"

He looked at her and grinned. "You are, as long as your health and safety aren't involved."

Not quite an hour later they arrived at Hereford Municipal Airport, where the pilot and mechanic quickly loaded their baggage and a representative from the car company reclaimed the keys. Ten minutes later they were airborne, and an hour and twenty-five minutes later they landed at Grand Prairie Municipal Airport. They taxied to a hangar bay. Lenore twisted her hair into a bun, then pulled a wool cap over it, pulled her hoodie on, zipped it up and pulled the hood up to cover her head, and pulled it down low. She put a pair of sunglasses on, then turned to JC and asked, "How do I look?"

He looked her up and down. She was wearing a brand-new pair of cheap sneakers, but at least today's jeans were actually made for girls, and she was wearing a cheap black hoodie. He said with a laugh, "Like a dime store hoodlum."

She glared at him. "Thank you, you really have a way of making a girl feel good about herself."

He chuckled. "Well, I think this should really knock your socks off then. I think you look fifty times better right now than you're going to in a couple of hours."

She smiled. "Actually, yes, thank you."

The plane came to a stop. A moment later, the pilot came out and opened the door. She grabbed her backpack. JC grabbed his bag, then reached over and took her backpack. He leaned down and whispered in her ear, "Remember, Persephone does not fetch or carry. That's what you have minions for."

She sighed several times, nodded, and said, "You're right. I will remember that."

JC pulled out his phone and said, "Hold on, wait a minute, would you repeat that so I can record it."

She laughed and shoved him. "You big jerk."

They disembarked. A man in a business suit was standing off to the side. He approached and extended his hand as he said, "Miss Persephone, I do apologize for the small airport, but I thought under the circumstance it would probably be better for you not to make a big appearance at the big airports. When I spoke to Mr. Sanderson, he gave me the distinct impression that you didn't look like yourself and should not appear in public until you did, so I thought we would go from here to a small hotel where we already have makeup and wardrobe people standing by. We'll get you back to where you want to be for this performance, and then I thought we would make our grand arrival at a big hotel in Dallas where we have already set up shop for a few days while we get things in order. If you come this way, we have a car and driver waiting, in addition to your other bodyguard, Sonny, who I believe you are already acquainted with."

She took his hand and shook it. She grimaced slightly.

JC said quickly, "Careful of the arm, it's injured, but we'll discuss it later."

Lenore rolled her eyes. "Yes, Sonny and I are old friends, but you didn't introduce yourself."

He grimaced. "My apologies. I'm Max Grover. Mr. Sanderson hired me to be your temporary manager, and quite frankly, ma'am, I've never worked for a client as big as you before and I'm a little nervous, but I promise you I will take care of everything. You have nothing to worry about and everything will run smoothly. I already have some band auditions lined up for you. I had three different teams going through thousands of auditions, weeding them down so you only see the top. Quite frankly, I think you should be able to pick your band in the first twenty groups. If I'm wrong, fire me. I have cross-referenced everybody. You have never worked with any of these people before. Mr. Sanderson was very adamant that you did not want to work with any of the same people, except your bodyguards, who he sent to me. Everybody else has never worked for you before on anything, and I have made sure that none of the hotels we are going to be using you have stayed at before, and I've even gone so far as to make sure that none of the management staff are the same. I can't guarantee maids, cooks, dishwashers might not have been at some of the same hotels at the same time. But chances are they had little to no dealings with you."

She smiled and jerked her thumb over her shoulder. "This is my head bodyguard, JC. He tells you whether he likes places or not. He has the final word on anything security-related." She reached over and patted Max on the shoulder. "Chill, Dude, you're sweating bullets. I'm not going to fire you on the first day."

Max extended his hand. "Nice to finally meet you, JC." He shifted his attention back to Persephone and said, "Mr. Sanderson had already made that quite clear, so JC and I have been in communication and he has approved all of your transportation, the routes we're going to take, the airlines we're going to use, planes, buses, hotel, and all of the staff that I have actually hired to date, though of course, that's all pending your approval, ma'am. His guys are still running background on some of the potential band members you're going to be meeting."

JC said quickly, "Let's not keep standing around here. The last thing we need is for somebody to catch us. Let's get in the vehicle and get to the hotel, we can discuss more of this en-route."

Max turned and led the way to the limousine. Sonny got out as they approached and said, "Nice to see you again, Miss P."

She smiled and gave him a hug. They all got in. After a minute's consideration she said, "Okay, let's be very clear about something. This is my last gig, but just because I'm going out doesn't mean I want to take anybody with me. I want to make sure we look very carefully at where people are in their careers. People who are already a little dicey being connected with my farewell performance could tank their careers. I would rather launch somebody's career than bury it."

Max nodded, pulled out his phone, and began typing away. "I will let my teams know to keep that in mind."

Five minutes later they were pulling up outside a nice little hotel that had doors that opened onto the parking lot. Max got out and pointed. "We have one sixty-five and one sixty-six. They have a communicating door and they're both doubles."

Sonny pulled out the key and opened the door to one sixty-five and held it open. They all entered. Max said, "This is Carlotta, she's going to be doing your makeup and hair, and I'm told she is a whiz with the airbrush. From some of the photographs I've seen, and what I have been told, I would agree with that. And this is Heather, she will be handling wardrobe, and quite frankly, talk to her first as she needs to go shopping."

Lenore smiled and looked from one to the other. "Nice meeting you both. Sorry about the time crunch, but if you guys get me through this, I assure you I will give you impeccable references. Sorry this gig is only a couple of weeks, but it means a lot to a lot of people."

They both started talking simultaneously, then they looked at each other and laughed. Carlotta said, "Heather, you go first. I have everything I need, but I ... but I ... do want to just say really quickly, it is so awesome to be working with you even if it was just for a day."

Heather pointed at Carlotta and said, "I'm with her. This is an awesome opportunity. I'm thrilled to be a part of it as well."

Lenore smiled. "I'm very happy to be working with you as well, and I do apologize for having to ask, but Max, they have all signed the confidentiality agreements, and that includes you too, right?"

Max nodded and opened his leather case. He pulled out a piece of paper and handed it over to her. "Here's a printout from Mr. Sanderson verifying everybody he has received the confidentiality agreements for. He said you'd want to see it. I was surprised. Usually stars don't actually want to see those." He looked at her puzzled.

She smiled and unzipped her hoodie. "That's because most stars don't want to hide these. They either have surgery to reduce them or come out and show them off, but for reasons of my own, I don't want to do either. But this is part of the uphill battle Carlotta is going to have to fight, and Heather is going to have to help her." She pulled up the sleeve of her shirt all the way to her shoulder, then she turned around and pulled up the back of her shirt. "There's also some scars on my thigh, but I think they should be easily dealt with by tights or nylons. We'll probably have to play around with it a little."

Carlotta said, "Holy shit! Can I see your arm?"

Lenore stepped forward and held it out. "Be my guest."

Carlotta took it and carefully turned it over examining it. Lenore grimaced and JC said quickly, "Careful, it's still broken. She's supposed to be wearing a splint, but something we all need to keep in mind, she can't go picking up anything heavier than a glass, and when she's out of sight of press and not being made up, she needs to have her splint back on."

Lenore looked over her shoulder and gave him a raspberry. "Somebody's overprotective today."

"Only always, baby girl."

Carlotta finished examining it. "Visually I can cover them up and conceal them. They won't show on photos or anything like that, but somebody standing here talking to you, they're gonna see the texture difference and there's really not a lot I can do about that. So probably for public appearances we're gonna want to shift that over to Heather and have her conceal it with wardrobe. For stage and photos, I've got you covered."

Lenore nodded. "Awesome, ladies. Thank you."

Heather nodded. "Between the two of us, nobody will ever see it, so let's talk wardrobe. I went ahead and picked up a few things. I was able to get some information from Mr. Grover, so I picked up a few things in some different sizes. It doesn't look like you've changed an ounce, so everything should be able to be made to fit. This is just to get us through the next day or two. Now, Mr. Grover said that you wanted to change your look for this performance. What am I looking for?"

Lenore sighed. "I assured the Town Council that I would be very family friendly, there can't be anything too sexy. They were very open to the concept of Daisy Dukes, and maybe something like tank tops. We're doing five performances, but I don't know if I'm going to be asked to do any other kind of appearances, photo shoots, so we probably need a bit of a variety. It is December, so I might end up standing out in the cold, and this is Texas we're talking about, so we need to kind of look at the weather and probably be prepared for it to be hot and cold. It is a rodeo, so I think we need to be very respectful of that and keep that in mind. Quite frankly, I'm thinking boots and hats. It's not unheard of for a pop performer to be seen in these kinds of objects, so I want to show them that I can fit in in their world. Mr. Grover might have a better idea of what I'm going to be required to do outside of the five performances." They all turned to stare at Max.

He opened up his tablet and said quickly, "Okay, I have not accepted anything on your behalf; however, the Leaf Town Council has been inundated with requests for special considerations regarding Persephone. You have hundreds of requests for signed objects for silent auctions and charity events throughout Leaf, Texas for the entire year to come. Most of them are just merchandise requests, signed T-shirts. Some of them are just requests for anything that you are willing to donate. However, there have been some special appearance requests as well. The Leaf County Fire Department has asked if you would come and take a photo with the guys and the fire truck. The Leaf County Youth Rodeo Association has asked if you would be willing to do some kind of charity fundraiser. What has been suggested is somebody with a digital camera standing there snapping photos and handing out tickets, a dollar apiece to get your photo taken with Persephone, and then they'll email them the photos later. So all you have to do is stand there and smile. The Town Council has asked if it is possible for Persephone to make herself available for a little bit of time one day before a performance, for any of the rodeo performers to have their photos taken with you, maybe you can sign a few autographs. The head of the rodeo clowns has specifically requested a photo with you, the rodeo clowns, and the pickup men for the rodeo. I don't understand any of these terms, I'm not from Texas. If this is stuff you are not willing to do, tell me to stop. I could literally go on for hours. The Amarillo Children's Hospital has asked if you would be willing to come and maybe perform a few songs for some of the children. You have received requests for as far-flung as a hundred miles in any direction."

Lenore sat down on the bed hard. She put her hand over her mouth. After a long minute she asked, "JC, are you aware of me ever receiving requests like this before?"

He sighed and shook his head. "If you ever did, I never heard about it, but now that I am hearing about it, I can guarantee they were probably all turned down unceremoniously."

She sighed and rubbed her hands up and down her face. "Okay, requests for merchandise? Anything high school, food bank, church related, anything that's good and has no immoral or political undertones, agree to it, even if it means I'm signing merchandise for years. As we have time, start running any of the other requests for merchandise past me. Once we get an idea of the types of places, hopefully you can stop running them all by me and just agree to them or don't agree if we've already determined it's something I'm not willing to do. Appearances, I really don't want to tell the children's hospital that I'm not gonna come and visit the kids. We'll see if we can find a way to squeeze that in. I can't tell firemen no either." She smiled and said quickly, "But I will not do the fire department and not the police department, so why don't you reach out to the Leaf County Sheriff's Department and see if they're interested. Tell the rodeo clowns yes. Tell the rodeo commission yes. Tell the rodeo commission and the rodeo clowns that they're gonna have to coordinate with the Youth Rodeo Association and tell them yes too. As far as all the other requests, we'll tackle them as they come in. Unfortunately, I don't think I'm gonna be able to do any of the farther flung stuff, except I will do the Amarillo hospital request, maybe we can do that on Christmas Eve. Get with the hospital and see if that can work for them. I don't know when you were planning on arriving, but let's look at maybe arriving in Amarillo on the twenty-third, staying the twenty-fourth, and arriving in Leaf on the twenty-fifth. What days are my performances? I don't even know."

Max replied, "The rodeo kicks off Thursday the twenty-eighth with the pancake breakfast. You are not required to attend but you are most welcome. Apparently all out of town staff and people who are going to be helping them arrive sometime late afternoon on the twenty-sixth into the evening, so the twenty-eighth is really kind of when everybody comes together, except people who are performing later in the rodeo generally arrive later. It does last a whole month, but there are no concerts on the twenty-seventh. The first concert, and it's yours, is the twenty-eighth. You open. You have one on the twenty-eighth, one on the twenty-ninth, with two on the thirtieth. You only have one on the thirty-first, which is your last one."

Lenore stared at him wide-eyed, her mouth hanging open. After a long minute she said, "I'm performing on New Year's Eve?"

Max looked stricken. After a long minute he said, "I have no control of the dates. The dates had already been agreed upon before I was hired. I was under the impression you agreed personally to the dates."

JC said quickly, "Give us about ten minutes. Everybody go into the other room." He waited until they were alone, then he sat down on the bed next to her and asked, "What's wrong?"

She rubbed her face and said, "If you ever repeat this I will never forgive you."

"Never in a million years."

She said softly, "Jane performed at that rodeo on New Year's Eve and met my father, got drunk, and got pregnant. They have never spoken to each other again and he didn't even know of my existence until he ran into me accidentally on the ranch."

JC let out a whistle. "Talk about creepy déjà vu. You gonna be okay with this?"

A thought struck her, and she grinned from ear to ear. She hopped up and ran over to the door, yanked it open, and said, "Tell the Youth Association it has to be on New Year's Eve or not at all."

L

Sunday, December 24

Lenore stood in the bathroom of her penthouse suite in Amarillo, Texas, looking at herself in the mirror. Though Persephone had gotten a definite makeover, Lenore still saw her as Persephone, of course that was what she wanted. She wanted everybody to see Persephone. She did not want them to see Lenore. She looked herself up and down. She was in high-heeled black leather boots, skintight white jeans, a snug fitting black long-sleeved blouse with a turtleneck collar, but from her throat to her cleavage was cut out showing her collarbone all the way to the top curves of her breasts. Her hair was again blonde with lots of extensions making her hair look even fuller than it was, and it hung all the way to her waist with the big thick curls that were popular right now. They had wanted to shorten her hair, but she had told them firmly, no, they could trim it, but not really cut it. She now had on way too much makeup, but at least for this she did not have to wear body makeup. Hopefully she would only have to do that for stage performances and a couple more photo shoots. The rest of the time she could wear pants and long sleeve shirts to hide her scars. There was a knock at the door. She sighed and asked, "Who is it?"

"It's Max. If we don't get going, you're going to be late to the hospital."

She sighed several times, then mentally kicked herself. She wished she would never have opened her big fat mouth and gotten herself involved in this. She could have just given the Town Council an anonymous donation to get them through this, but no, she had opened her big fat mouth and now here she was, but at least it was on her terms and almost half over. Sadly, the easy half was done, now was the hard stuff. She turned and opened the bathroom door saying, "Sorry, I'm ready." She exited the bathroom and they headed out of her room, down the hallway, and arrived at the freight elevator. She had been mobbed by reporters everywhere she went. She hoped when she left Amarillo this would stop. They boarded the elevator and headed for the ground floor. When the elevator came to stop and the doors opened, the hotel manager was standing there.

He smiled and said quickly, "Good afternoon, Miss Persephone. Your vehicles are waiting at the loading dock, and if you'll follow me, I will show you the quickest route out of here."

She smiled. "Thank you, lead the way." As they walked through the bowels of the hotel, staff got out of the way and stared at her. She smiled at all of them and said, "Hello." Most of them looked surprised and murmured back at her. She loved that nobody scolded her and told her to just keep walking. It was nice not having her mother breathing down her neck.

They turned off the main corridor and headed through the kitchen. As they walked past a row of sinks, a busboy was just setting down a heavy plastic tub. He looked up at her, clearly recognizing her. He hesitated, then deciding it was worth the risk, and asked with excitement, "Could I snap a photo of you?"

The hotel manager responded quickly, "Certainly not, and you're not supposed to bother the guests."

The young man looked stricken, and the manager gave him a cold stare. Lenore patted the manager on the back and said with a smile, "No, he's cool. I don't mind posing for a photo."

JC said quickly, "You can't post it online until after she's out of the hotel."

The young man grinned and said quickly, "Awesome, you're the best, and no worries, big man. I won't. I promise. I just want to gloat over my brother that I saw her in person." He pulled out his phone and snapped a photo.

Lenore pointed to him and flicked her hand in the direction of Carlotta. She said, "Why don't you give Carlotta your phone, and she can snap a photo of the two of us together."

He passed over his phone quickly, saying, "No shit, that's awesome!" The photo was quickly taken and then a half dozen more kitchen staff asked to have their photos taken. Lenore happily posed with all of them.

Max looked at his watch and said softly with irritation, "We're going to be late."

JC shot him a warning glance and said coldly, "We're not gonna be that late, and let her have a little fun."

As another half-dozen people asked to have their photos taken, Lenore gripped JC's wrist and looked at his watch. She sighed. "Look, I would love to stand here and take photos with all of you, but I can't let the children at the hospital down, but I should be back here by eight. So my manager and your manager will come up with a room and a time, and let all of the hotel staff know that I will be there, and I will take pictures and sign autographs, I promise. I probably won't have a lot of time for chatting because I do have another engagement this evening, but I promise I will do my best to be obliging. Right now we gotta bounce." She turned to Max and said, "Make that happen."

Max sighed and nodded. He looked at the manager and said, "Once I get the ball rolling at the hospital, I'll give you a call and we'll sort something out."

The manager nodded and led them to the loading dock where three black Chevy Suburbans were waiting. They got in and headed for the hospital. Max was flipping through his schedule. He looked at her and asked, "I don't have anything on the schedule for this evening, did I miss something?"

Lenore sighed and looked very sad. After a long minute she said, "Since I can't spend Christmas with the ones I love, I decided to spend Christmas Eve as close as I could get to them, which left a barbecue or Mass, so JC and I will be going out this evening."

Max raised an eyebrow. "I didn't think Persephone was religious."

She shrugged her shoulders. "I'm not, but some of the people I care very much about are."

JC pulled out his phone and texted Max. 'Dude, shut up. If you make her cry, I will hit you. She misses her family so she's going to midnight mass, and if you repeat that I will hurt you. Let it go.'

Max looked at his incoming text message. He replied. 'Sorry, just trying to do my job.'

They arrived at the hospital to a mob of cameras and media. It took her five minutes just to make it into the building, but finally she and her team were on the other side of the hospital doors with the media outside. A group of people in suits and doctor's coats approached her. An older gentleman said, "I am terribly sorry, Miss Persephone, we thought we had a better handle on the crowd and media, but apparently our efforts to keep this under wraps failed miserably. I'm so sorry. My name is Dr. Foreman. I'm the Chief of Internal Medicine, and this is Sylvia Deighton, she will be with you for the duration of your visit. She's the hospital Press Secretary, and again, I just can't begin to express how excited we are to have you here. The children have been looking forward to it all week."

Lenore shook hands with everybody. Sylvia said, opening her leather notebook, "I just wanted to run over the schedule that we received last night with you again. I'm not complaining, it just sounds a little odd, and I wasn't sure whether there was some kind of miscommunication."

Lenore smiled. "I'm pretty sure there's no miscommunication, but I mean, if some of my suggestions don't work for you, I understand. I just thought it might be a little more fun for some of the younger children."

Sylvia laughed. "Okay, so I really did read nursery rhymes sing-along?"

Lenore blushed. "Okay, let's be frank. I've never done this kind of thing before. My manager's never organized this kind of thing before. What you initially requested was just for us to do a couple of songs if possible, and maybe do some elbow rubbing, which I'm totally cool with. And it said we could spend as much time as we wanted, or could be in and out as fast as we needed to be, so I was thinking my band and I could do five songs, all family-friendly, I promise, not a swear word in sight. My drummer and keyboard player have both requested to stay in the performance area, and they both thought it would be fun if some of the more mobile children could come and bang a drum, bang some keys, have a little fun. Maybe learn a couple of notes, but I'm not going to hold my breath. My guitar player and my bass player are both more mobile and thought that they could do some room visiting for children who couldn't come to us. I would also like to do that and I brought a guitar too. We thought it might be fun to get some of the smaller children together, and you know, do Itsy-bitsy spider. Do a little bit of fun sing-along. Carlotta is my makeup wizard and she brought a makeup kit, and thought maybe she and some of the kids could do some makeup. Heather says she's no expert, but she brought a whole bunch of face painting stuff and thought she could do face painting, tattoos on arms. Basically, we have set aside six hours of our day today and we are prepared to wreak massive havoc on your hospital. Oh, and I hired a woman to come in and do balloon animals. She's gone through all of the school background checks and my man JC here has all of her information, which you should have received in an email as well."

Sylvia was having a hard time not crying. Though they had lots of people who would come in and give up their valuable time in an effort to cheer up the children, and lots of performers who were willing to open their check books and write them checks, they had never had a group like this converge on them. Fortunately she did not have to reply, Dr. Foreman did it for her. "Miss Persephone, that all sounds fabulous, and we are beyond grateful to you and your staff. The only thing is a hospital employee must be with each individual person or each group, but we have plenty of staff. We will get you enough escorts."

Lenore smiled and held out her hand to Max, who handed her a piece of paper. "Awesome, there's just one more thing."

Dr. Foreman was not sure why, but he was suddenly a little nervous. He asked, "Yes?"

"So as you can tell, music and the arts are very important to me, and since I know a lot of your patients are stuck here for weeks and months, I would like to give the hospital an endowment, I think that's the right word, for ten million dollars. Most of that you can use on new equipment, helping patients who can't afford to pay their bills, whatever you want, but I do want a small portion of that to go to setting up a music and art room, where patients can come and learn about those things. I would like you to hire two teachers, one music, one art, who work forty hours a week. I would like their schedules to be a little bit flexible because I would like them to sometimes cover the weekends, and I would like for your hospital to try that for three years and to pay for it out of the ten million dollars that I'm giving you. If this program works and you like it, contact my lawyer and I'll give you another endowment, provided I haven't bankrupted myself."

JC could not help it. He snorted. "Yeah, baby girl, I don't think that's possible."

She shrugged her shoulders. "I could always go crazy and give all my money to the animals."

He looked at the doctor and shook his head. "Don't worry, her lawyers will commit her before it comes to that."

She elbowed him in the side and held out the papers. "I'm sure you have a legal team or somebody who needs to look at this and verify it. If you agree to it, contact my lawyer and he will hook you up."

Dr. Foreman finally found his voice. "Wow, Miss Persephone! That is incredibly generous of you and I can guarantee that the hospital will be contacting your lawyer first thing Tuesday morning to get this ball rolling, because that sounds like a fabulous idea, and I am always in favor of anything that will boost the morale of the children."

She smiled. "Awesome, let's get this party started."

Four hours later, Lenore's feet were killing her. She was hot and hungry but forged on. She looked at the nurse and asked, "Where to next?"

"Well, that's everybody on this hallway who agreed to have a visitor."

Lenore nodded, gestured and was just opening her mouth to speak when she saw a woman approaching nervously. She changed what she was about to say. "Something the matter, ma'am?"

"Yes, I know my daughter said she didn't want any visitors, so she is probably not on your list, and you probably don't have time, but I was wondering if maybe you'd just step in and say hi. My daughter's a huge fan, but she's refusing all visitors right now."

Lenore frowned. "That doesn't sound good. Why doesn't she want visitors?"

The woman sighed and started getting teary-eyed. "I don't know if you were in the area, or if you even watch the news, but on Thursday morning three high school students who are on the high school track team were out running. It was actually a group of nine out running to stay in shape, and a man on his phone ran a stop sign and struck three of the students. Two of them, fortunately, only received very minor injuries. My daughter, however, wasn't as lucky. She's alive and she's going to survive, but they had to do surgery on her knee, her shin, and her forearm. She was never a particularly vain girl, but she decided to be very vain and she's very upset about the scars, there's some facial bruising in addition to a lot of road rash and some minor lacerations, and she's in a very bad humor."

JC bumped his elbow into her shoulder. "Fifty bucks says you have her smiling and laughing before you leave the room. You got this one in the bag. This is gonna be the easiest one of the day."

She snorted and rolled her eyes. "If you think I'm betting on myself to fail, you are out of your mind." She looked at the mother and said, "You are? And your daughter's name is?"

"I'm Angie, and my daughter is Mary."

"It's very nice to meet you, Angie. Why don't you lead the way, and I will see if I can't cheer Mary up a little."

Angie smiled. "Thank you, it's right over here."

They entered the room. Mary was sitting in her bed, looking moody, a set of headphones on, clearly listening to music, but not actually enjoying it. She shifted when she saw the door open and pulled off her headphones, and said with exasperation, "Mom, I said I didn't want any visitors."

Lenore ignored her and walked over to the right side of the bed. She indicated the edge. "Do you mind if I sit here for a minute? My feet are killing me because these boots are just awful."

Despite herself, Mary looked down at boots. She sighed with envy, then her eyes alighted on the black suede jacket with fringe. It was gorgeous. She sighed again, then she forced herself to say moodily, "Since clearly I'm not getting rid of you, suit yourself, though I do have to say I wouldn't care what they did to my feet cause those are just gorgeous, and the jacket..." She sighed with envy.

Lenore perched on the edge of the bed, then stuck out a leg and admired the boot. "Okay, I'll grant you that the boots are really nice; however, I disagree with you on the jacket. I think it's too small for me." She stuck out her arms.

Mary frowned and nodded. "Yeah, the sleeves do appear to be a little too short on you, that's a disappointment. I would think your clothes would fit you perfectly."

Lenore laughed. "Yeah, the problem is, unlike you, I'm five nine in my bare feet, so I'm really tall and gangly."

Mary frowned. "I would rather be tall and gangly than short and fat and now scarred."

Lenore rolled her eyes. "Oh my God, you sound like my sister! You're not fat, you're not even chubby, and as far as scars are concerned, so what? The right guy isn't going to care anyways."

Mary stared at her and said quickly, "Wait a minute. You can't be Persephone. Persephone's an only child."

JC, always helpful, laughed and said, "Oh, oh, baby, busted!"

She glared at him. "I thought bodyguards were supposed to stand off to the side and be silent. So why are you always breathing down my neck?"

He grinned and crossed his arms over his chest and looked intimidating. "Because there is no love in indifference, and the only time your mother ever showed you love is when she was holding out her hand full of bills. I figured somebody needed to give you a little love."

Lenore snorted and looked back at Mary. "So painful, yet so true, and that was what is called a Freudian slip, so I would really appreciate it if you wouldn't go bandying that about. Jane, oh sorry, Evanjalevn only has one child. My father, however, has other children, so I guess technically she's my half-sister, but Dad gets very vocal if we start throwing the half around. And quite frankly,

I kinda like having siblings, so I don't like using it either, but can that just be between the five of us please?"

Mary looked very interested. She pushed herself up a little and said, "Well, I guess I never thought about Persephone having problems like normal people. I thought all of your problems were like big ones like ..."

Lenore sighed. "Like somebody leaking naked photos of me? Yeah, that was pretty big, terribly embarrassing and humiliating really, but I'm here to cheer you up, not talk about my scandals. So your mom says you don't want visitors. That's not fun. You should see your friends. They probably miss you."

Mary frowned. "I don't want them gawking at my scars."

Lenore sighed and nodded. "That I can totally understand. Couple weeks ago, I got hospitalized and when I came home, my current boss, he had to pick me up and take me home, because we all know I'm in hiding. A female friend said she'd help me take care of my injuries, but they kinda grossed her out so my boss, he ended up having to do it. I thought he never would look at me again after seeing them. They didn't faze him a bit."

Mary frowned and started removing her splint. When she finally had it open, she shifted and pointed. "I bet it didn't look like that."

Lenore and JC both looked, but it was JC who spoke first. He shook his head and said with a laugh, "No, Miss P's look way worse."

Lenore stood up, pulled off her jacket and laid it on the foot of the bed, then pulled her right sleeve up past her elbow. "Don't rat me out, but I'm supposed to still have a splint on this arm. Dog bit my forearm so hard he cracked the bones, and while he was doing that, his buddy was doing this." She turned around and pulled the back of her shirt up just a little. "It goes from below my waist band all the way up my shoulder and down my whole right arm. One of them also got my right leg. All told, two hundred and forty stitches and two cracked bones, and of course rabies treatment, let's not forget that."

Mary stared. Suddenly her scars did not look nearly so bad. "So that's why all the photos of you that have been seen online the past couple days, you're always in jeans and long sleeves, but those concert promotions, you're in shorts and a tank top."

Lenore fixed her shirt, then sat back down on the edge of the bed. "That's because all those promotional photos were done by my photographer with my whole team of makeup people making me look beautiful. You think looking like that comes naturally? Nobody looks like that naturally, and after they're done with me and he photos me, he then touches up the photos to make them look even more perfect. When you look at a singer or movie star, never forget the amount of work it takes to make them look that good. Rita Hayworth used to say, 'Men go to bed with Gilda, but wake up with me.' There are a lot of things to take away from that sentence. What I've always taken away from it was make sure that the man you're chasing wants the woman you really are, not the one he thinks you are." Lenore got to her feet, then shrugged her shoulders. "Which I guess for girls like you and me that means, don't hide your scars. Put them out there for him to see. If he keeps looking, then I guess that means he's the right one, or at least he's in the running." Not waiting for a reply, she turned and headed for the door.

Mary said quickly, "You forgot your jacket."

Lenore flipped her wrist dismissively in Mary's direction. "You keep it. It suits you better than it does me."

LI

Thursday, December 28

Lenore looked at herself in the mirror. She found she was doing that a lot lately. They had arrived late last night. She had decided she was not staying in Amarillo and spending three hours in the car every day round-trip, so they were staying in a hotel about ten miles down the road from Leaf. Though it was small and not up to the standards she was used to, it was clean, it did not smell, and was surprisingly quiet. They had been able to secure the entire West wing downstairs, not like this was a great feat, it was only ten rooms. She smiled to herself when she wondered what Nathaniel would think of the fact that she and JC were sharing a room. This hotel did not have communicating doors and he was firmly against her in a separate room by herself. Mickey and Sonny had the room on her right, and Bobby had the room on her left. Her thoughts were interrupted by Carlotta asking, "Are you not happy with it? Do I need to change something?"

Lenore laughed. It was freezing cold outside so she had to bundle up for this morning's outing. She had decided to forego wearing a Cowboy hat and Cowboy boots in favor of warmth. She was wearing thermals, jeans, and a long-sleeved T-shirt. She had a wool cap, earmuffs, and a Sherpa lined jean jacket standing by. She was also wearing Uggs. She sighed and decided that she looked quite presentable for five o'clock in the morning. She turned to Carlotta and smiled. "No, everything looks great. You can get all your stuff loaded in the car. If you need any help, make one of the guys help you."

Carlotta smiled. "Sonny already has all my stuff loaded except for what I have right here, and I can take that out myself."

Lenore nodded and turned to face Heather. "How many changes of clothes are you taking?"

Heather grimaced. "Don't freak out, but I'm taking eight. Four different kinds of footwear, six different hats, and of course, the option is always available to go without any kind of headgear. Both the fire station and the police station say that they have rooms where you can change and do whatever you need to do. The police station is significantly smaller, so the best that they can offer is either the interrogation room or the Sheriff's office. The fire department, however, you can have one of the bunk rooms to yourself, well, to us, but unfortunately that's the best we're going to be able to do without having to come back here. Is that going to be okay?"

She smiled. "Of course, we'll make it work." She hesitated a moment, started to turn to speak to JC, and then turned back to Heather. She pointed at her, "Actually, as I come to think about it, go ahead and let the Sheriff's Department know that if the Sheriff's office does not have video cameras, I would prefer to take over his office. I know interrogation probably has cameras and I'm a little camera shy after, you know, my hotel room."

Max grimaced and said quickly, "As soon as we're on the move I will contact the Sheriff's office. Our go-between is a Deputy Baxter, apparently he's like second-in-command, but apparently this pancake breakfast is a real big thing, and the Sheriff is there in an unofficial official capacity. I didn't fully understand. It was something to do with the rodeo business, but I know that this is kind of a swan song for you, but any impromptu photos we can get of you with officials, like the Mayor, the Sheriff, some of these rodeo performers, they could really help your image if you decide to do a comeback."

Lenore rolled her eyes and said firmly, "There will be no comeback. The only careers that might be getting launched out of this is all of yours, and for which I wish you all the absolute best of luck, and if you need any job references, refer them to my attorney, who will give you all glowing recommendations."

Max shrugged his shoulders. "Hey, I'm a manager. It's what I do, always got to be thinking ahead."

She decided to ignore that and grabbed her stuff off the bed and turned to JC and asked, "Are you ready to go?"

He grumbled but got to his feet. "If one has to go out in freezing cold temperatures, I guess I'm ready to go."

She looked at his watch. "I seem to recall seeing something about the breakfast started at six AM. We're twenty, twenty-five minutes away, and it's already five twenty, so let's get going." They all headed for the rented Chevy Suburban. Her band had unanimously decided that it was too cold and too early, but to her surprise, Carlotta and Heather had thought it sounded like fun, though she thought for sure it had a little more to do with the concept of all the handsome, real cowboys. They were, after all, both single.

Arriving, Heather climbed into the far back and stretched out. "You know, if you get banished to the kid's table, at least the kid's table is roomy."

Carlotta snorted and rolled her eyes. "Nobody banished you to the far back. I would've gone back there."

Lenore laughed. "For that matter, so would I."

Surprisingly enough, they arrived at the fairgrounds a little early. Though the food tents were set up and there were plenty of workers bustling, getting things ready, there was not a single cowboy in sight. A man walked past with a sledgehammer over his shoulder. Lenore turned to him and said, "Excuse me, sir, are we in the wrong place?"

He smiled. "You ain't never been to a rodeo before, have you?"

She laughed. "Do I look like I've been to a rodeo?"

He chuckled. "No, ma'am, you don't, but at least you pronounce it correctly. We don't do the cattle drive anymore. Most of the ranches around here think it's more trouble than it's worth, but if you head that direction just a little bit you'll see the crowd, and then you can watch all the cowboys arrive on horseback. They meet up just outside of town and ride in together. Usually the people from out of town will saddle their horses, go out and meet them, and ride back with them. It's social and fun for them."

She smiled. "Thank you." She turned to her entourage and asked, "Shall we go watch the cowboys arrive?"

JC snorted and said with a chuckle, "As long as I'm not looking for the football team, I'll go."

She rolled her eyes and they all wandered down to watch them arrive. She was surprised at how quickly an audience formed. JC was making sure everybody was staying at least arms reach away from her. As of this moment nothing was happening, but then something caught her attention. Somebody said, "Good to see you out and about, Wayne." She looked quickly to see Mr. Cartwright approaching. He shook hands with the man who had spoken to him. The man asked, "How you healin'? I heard you had a pretty near thing."

Wayne snorted. "Damn stupidity was what it was. Guess I just got lazy and comfortable. Thought I could go get some papers that were in my truck without taking a gun with me. Damn fool thing. I'd be dead if it wasn't for that new little girl I got working for me. That's one tough little cookie."

The man chuckled. "Yeah, heard Mrs. Adams on a rant about you hiring some outside city slicker. How's that working for you?"

"Don't knock her till you meet her. She's as tough as they come, and I plan on keeping her around for a long time, so you'll meet her sooner or later."

"What? You mean you didn't drag her to this?"

Wayne chuckled and shook his head. "Nope, she's the new kid on the ranch, she pulled the short straw to hold down the fort while the rest of us fulfill our rodeo duties, and of course, Bubba's had to take over mine, but I still got roped into doing some judging. Anything I can do sittin' on my backside."

The man chuckled. "I think you've earned a little bit of rest. Let Bubba hold down the fort for a while. Hell, if I had a son as efficient as yours, I'd just give it to him and let him take it over. I'd sit on my rump all the time, play a little cards, go on vacation, go on one of them fishing cruises, take up golf."

Wayne shuddered and shook his head. "I love what I do, but I do think Bubba is ready to settle down. I wouldn't be at all surprised if he takes over my pickup duties from now on. That's a young man's job anyways."

The other man snorted. "Not the way Bubba loves ta ride them bulls. Take my word for it, next year he'll be back to bull riding and bronco busting."

Wayne knew it was wrong of him, but he could not resist. He chuckled and said, "I'll bet you a hundred dollars next year he's riding pickup, and that's the only thing he's riding."

"You're on. That kid of yours ain't ready to settle down just yet."

Heather leaned forward and said softly between Carlotta and Persephone, "With a name like Bubba, he is either absolutely gorgeous or a dog faced boy. I look forward to finding out."

JC started laughing. "Dog faced boy."

Fortunately, Lenore was saved from having to defend Nathaniel by the cowboys coming into sight. She was staring in surprise. Nathaniel and the Sheriff were the first two riders. The Sheriff was carrying the United States flag and Nathaniel was carrying the Texas flag, but it was not just that that surprised her. The Sheriff was wearing blue jeans and a red, what she had learned was called a Calvary bib shirt, with his badge pinned on his breast. He was wearing a dark brown hat, a brown leather slicker that appeared to be Sherpa lined, and a belt buckle she knew was very familiar, even though she could not see it clearly from this distance. Instead of his usual handgun, he was carrying an old fashion six shooter in one of those leather holsters you always saw cowboys wear in the movies. Nathaniel was wearing jeans, a blue bib shirt, an old fashioned six shooter and holster, a black leather slicker that also appeared to be Sherpa lined, and a black cowboy hat, with a most ostentatious silver Concho band and what appeared to be a very familiar belt buckle. As she stared a moment longer, she realized that they also had rifle scabbards attached to their saddles. Though she had seen the guys on the ranch with their horses and their rifles on many occasions, she had never seen them take guns like this out. They were gorgeous. They must be purely for show.

She was startled from her observations by JC saying, "I'm sorry, sir, but I'm go to have to ask you to stand back, sir."

She turned to see Mr. Cartwright standing there. She looked from one face to the other. She could tell instantly that JC did not like it, but he felt he had to since he had run everyone else off. Then a thought struck her. "No, JC, he's cool. I heard him say he's working for the rodeo, maybe he can tell us what's going on."

Wayne reached up and tipped his hat. "Be my pleasure, ma'am."

She extended her hand. "I'm Persephone, and this is my makeup artist Carlotta and my wardrobe expert Heather, and my head bodyguard and main man JC."

He smiled and shook hands with all of them. "Wayne Cartwright, rodeo judge, and it's real nice to meet all of you." He shifted so he was standing facing the same direction. He indicated the riders, "In about thirty seconds they're gonna reach the center and then everybody's going get real quiet. Then they're going to ask if everyone will please rise for the national anthem. Then all of us gentlemen are gonna remove our hats, you ladies of course don't have to. Only the color guard will keep their hats on, that would be our Sheriff Diego Mendoza, and this year I'm pleased to say that my boy Bubba Cartwright was asked to carry the

Texas flag. It's tradition for the Leaf County Rodeo that the Sheriff always carries the United States flag, and he decides who carries the Texas. It's considered quite an honor to be asked. The Sherriff doesn't choose just anybody."

Carlotta said, "Well, I'll say this. The Sheriff and Young Mr. Cartwright are definitely excellent representatives for the look of the Texas gentlemen."

Lenore decided it would not be out of character, so she reached over and gripped Wayne's arm, looked up at him and smiled as she said, "Mr. Cartwright Senior is not very bad either." She winked at him as she said 'senior'.

Heather asked quickly, "So why did your son get chosen?"

Wayne chuckled. "Well, there actually was a better candidate but they left town real sudden like, so the Sheriff asked my boy because a little while back we had a drifter come through town. Bubba got that drifter a job and helped them straighten out their life, stood by them through some really ugly times. Sheriff figured it was worthy of recognition."

They were interrupted by an unfamiliar female voice over the loudspeakers saying, "Ladies and gentlemen, if you will please stand for our National Anthem, followed by opening prayers, and then we will say Grace, and then we will declare this rodeo officially opened and dig in."

Wayne removed his hat with his right hand and held it over his heart as they all sang the National Anthem. Opening prayers were brief, but with emphasis on a safe and prosperous rodeo, then they said Grace together. As soon as Grace was over, a male voice came over the loudspeaker. "All right, ladies and gentlemen. If everyone will please line up in two separate lines, we have two separate buffets going so that we can get you all served as quickly as possible, and then we can sit down, and we can all socialize and enjoy our breakfast."

Lenore got in line to get her breakfast. She thought everything smelled wonderful and she desperately wanted some of the sausage gravy and biscuits, but unfortunately Persephone was publicly known as a vegetarian and she knew if she was going to maintain her Persephone image, she had to watch what she ate in public. So in the end, she only got one scrambled egg. She really wanted a pancake. They looked wonderful, so thick and fluffy, but Persephone would never have eaten pancakes or biscuits. After she ate her egg, she hobnobbed and socialized. Sadly, Wayne was the only one of her friends who dared to approach her, the others all turned tail and ran at sight of her, literally. She wondered if they were mad at her or were afraid that they could not keep their stories straight. She hoped it was the latter rather than the former. She reached over and turned JC's watch so she could read it and realized it was almost ten o'clock. She was just about to make her excuses when Max approached.

He looked at the person she was speaking with and said, "I'm terribly sorry, but I'm going to have to drag her away. She has an eleven o'clock photo shoot with the Leaf County Fire Department."

LII

Lenore was a little more than nervous as they pulled up outside the Sheriff's station. The fire department had gone remarkably well, now she just had to get through this and a few photos with the rodeo clowns and pickup men. Then hopefully she would be on the downhill slide, headed for home. After all, concerts were easy for her. It was this pretending to be somebody else in front of her friends that was killing her. She wanted to walk up to them, she wanted to talk to them, ask how things were going. She wanted to know what Christmas had been like. It had killed her to miss Christmas. She had cried herself to sleep on Christmas Eve and Christmas, but she promised herself next year she would find a way to attend every Christmas party they got invited to, and she would find a way to eat two Christmas dinners and two Thanksgiving dinners. A voice in the back of her head that sounded disturbingly like Jane said, *Aren't you getting a little ahead of yourself? What if you're not invited to anything? What if you're not welcome? What if nobody wants you around after they see you like her? After they see that you are her, maybe the Sheriff won't want you around his other daughters after he watches you shake your booty on stage.* She cringed inwardly.

JC opened the car door and held out his hand. He said flippantly, "Tired already? Do I need to carry you inside?" Then he saw the stricken look on her face, he reached over and squeezed her hand. "Hey, what's the matter?"

Lenore did not know what was coming over her, but she suddenly felt like she could not breathe.

JC grabbed her shoulder and gave her a little shake. He said firmly, "Hey, snap out of it. Do you need to lie down? Do I need to take you back to the hotel? We can reschedule this or cancel it altogether."

That finally did it. She shook her head. "No, I'm ... I'm fine. I just ... I just need this to be over with. Next Saturday can't come fast enough." She hopped out of the car, stood there for a moment re-assuming her Persephone persona and told herself, *I am Persephone. I am a rock star. I am loved and adored by everyone. There is no Lenore, only Persephone.* She repeated this in her head several times until she felt like she could actually believe it, then they headed for the Sheriff's station. JC opened the door and she entered.

The Sheriff, who was now in uniform, was standing at the counter talking with a female deputy. They both stopped talking and turned to stare at her. The Sheriff frowned. The female deputy crossed quickly to them. She extended her hand. "Persephone, it is so awesome to meet you. I'm Deputy Carol McFarland. We were all so excited to get your request for a photo opportunity, and Deputy Baxter did receive your manager's email this morning, so the Sheriff is already aware that you would prefer to use his office. I went ahead and put down all the blinds so you can have some privacy."

Diego murmured under his breath, "Not all of us."

Lenore could tell that he was really not happy with her. She told herself again firmly, *I am Persephone. Everybody loves me.* She shook hands with Deputy McFarlane and said, "Thank you so much for having us. I'm sorry for any havoc that I'm wreaking in your small town and I'm sorry if some of the deputies aren't as excited about the opportunity as I am. I just thought that it wasn't fair to do the Fire Department and not the Sheriff's Department." She crossed to the Sheriff and extended her hand.

He grudgingly took it and shook it. After a moment he said, "Try not to disarrange my office too much and I'd be much obliged if you wouldn't spray any perfume in my office."

She did not know why, but the Sheriff's attitude was putting her back up. She said with a smile, "If it is an inconvenience, Sheriff, we can use interrogation, or for that matter, why don't I just change in the street? I mean, it's not like everybody hasn't see me naked anyways. I mean,

I'm sure you and your deputies dug out the images. I mean, everybody else has, why wouldn't all of you, or is that the problem? You don't want to be photographed in uniform standing next to a woman who's had naked pictures of her splashed all over the Internet? Bad for politics. Might interfere in your next election."

Diego took a deep breath and let it out slowly. He reached into his jacket pocket. "That's a real nice attitude you have there. By the way, I have something I think belongs to you." He pulled out an envelope and handed it to her.

She took it, puzzled, and opened it. Inside was the letter she had written the Sheriff and Natalia and asked Aaron to put under the Christmas tree, telling them that her Christmas present to them was a vacation anywhere they wanted to go, plus two thousand dollars spending money and free babysitting at the Cartwright ranch, courtesy of Lenore and Nathaniel. She stomped her foot and glared at him. "Dammit! Really? You know, if you're pissed off at me, just say you're pissed off at me! If you've got something to say, just say it! It's really not fair for you to be torturing me like this! Look, I know I'm not exactly the daughter you wanted, but damnit Dad, I'm tryi …" She stared wide-eyed at him as she gasped and put her hands over her mouth. She started tearing up. She said through her hands, "Dammit! This is exactly why I told you to stay away from me, I'd only cause you problems."

Diego sighed and reached out and grabbed his daughter and pulled her into his arms. He held her tightly. He jerked his head in the direction of the door. "McFarlane, would you make sure nobody comes in without a warning."

"Roger that, Sheriff." She crossed to her desk and pulled up the security camera for the front door. "Parking lot's clear right now."

Diego held his daughter until she pulled herself together and pulled free. She started to wipe her face, but Carlotta stuck a tissue in her hand, and said, "Watch it or your mascara's gonna run everywhere."

She sighed with exasperation. "Right, I forgot. Oh no! I didn't get any on your uniform, did I?" She started patting dry her face as she examined his shirt. "No, it's good."

"I don't care about my uniform shirt. I care a lot about my daughter, who I'm very angry with."

She held her hands out to the side and demanded, "What did I do?"

He snorted. "Oh, let's see. Where do we start? You left town without saying goodbye to your family. Your siblings are really not happy with you. You didn't come home for Christmas. Everybody's mad at you about that, and as far as that stupid thing is concerned, I don't need expensive presents. The only present I want is time with my daughter, and don't think I didn't realize that your whole point is paying me back that three thousand dollar retainer. I'm a cop. I figure things out."

She sighed several times. "Okay, I shouldn't have tried that underhanded way to pay you back, but I did really want to give you a nice vacation. You deserve it, and it would give me time with my siblings to bond. I already cleared it with Mr. Cart ... Shit!"

At that, JC could not hold it any longer. He started roaring with laughter. "Dammit, woman! It's no wonder your mother never let you talk to the press, you can't keep a secret for shit."

She buried her face in her hands and shouted, "Damn it!" as she started crying again.

Diego said with annoyance, "Language."

"Great! He's right, I can't keep a secret. How the hell am I supposed to get through the next five days?"

McFarlane said with a laugh. "I didn't hear anything." The other two deputies murmured their agreement.

Diego reached out and gripped his daughter by the shoulders. "My deputies will not betray your secret, or trust me, they won't have a job. As a small-town Sheriff's department, we learn a lot of things we're not supposed to know, things that aren't criminal, just things that people would rather aren't public knowledge. We couldn't do our jobs if we blabbed about everything we see and hear. Discretion is a key element of our work. Okay, baby girl? Truth be told, I'm a little more worried about all of them." He jerked his head in the direction of her associates.

JC smiled. "Not to worry, Sheriff, I made sure all of their contracts are full of gag orders. They won't say shit." He shifted his attention to the other four, smiled and asked, "Now will you?"

All four of them shook their heads vigorously, but it was Max who said, "I don't have thirty million dollars just lying around. Hell, I've never even earned thirty million dollars if you total up every penny ever!"

Lenore's eyes bugged out of her sockets and she said, "Thirty million dollars?"

JC smiled. "Well, we had to make sure the sum that they would have to pay you for blabbing was more than somebody'd be willing to pay for the information. It's a nice round number."

She crossed to him and hugged him tightly. "JC, if I haven't told you recently how much I appreciate you, I appreciate you and I don't know what I would do or where I would be without you."

Diego grimaced and said, "Sadly, I do, and believe me, sir, I am forever in your debt."

JC hugged her a moment longer, then pushed her to arm's reach. "No, sir, Sheriff, it's all part of my job, but we do have another engagement with a rodeo crew, so somebody needs to get changed, since apparently she can't stay in the same clothes for all of this. I don't know who decided that, but whoever it was is crazy."

Max held up his hand. "That would be me. It would look bad for the pancake breakfast, the firemen photo shoot, the police photo shoot, and the clown photo shoot for her to be wearing the same clothes. It would look like she just lined them up like they weren't special. You got to make everybody feel special. No offense, to you and your Deputies, because believe me, you are special and I respect what you do, which is why we have to go to the extra effort."

Lenore rolled her eyes. "Well, Sheriff, if you'll give me five minutes to get changed into my other clothes, you can come harass me while they put my face back on."

He smiled. "That I would love, and I'll even share. My deputies can harass you too."

McFarlane said quickly, "I know I said I didn't hear anything, which I didn't. I promise I won't repeat it, but I don't exactly feel comfortable cutting into father/daughter time. I don't know when you're gonna get more of that, sir."

Diego smiled. "Not to worry, McFarlane. I will be getting plenty, I promise. So you are more than welcome to harass her. She's a good kid, you'll like her."

Lenore blushed and asked, "So does that mean I can use your office, Dad, or do I have to go to interrogation?"

Diego grinned from ear to ear. "When you call me 'Dad' you can even spray that nasty smelling shit in my office."

She laughed. "I think my perfume smells very nice, thank you." She turned and headed for his office. She looked over her shoulder and gave him a raspberry.

Diego, without thinking, swatted his daughter across the backside.

Lenore burst out laughing as she turned on him and pointed. "Dude, if that leaks you are so screwed."

Diego put both hands over his face and shook his head. "You are right." Everybody started laughing.

LIII

Lenore sighed several times. She looked at herself in the mirror. Since these were more official concert photos, she was wearing black cowboy boots, nylons to hide her scars, white Daisy Dukes, a black tank top, her arms had been airbrushed to conceal any scars, and a black cowboy hat. She kept telling herself that she just had this one last little thing to do and then she was on the downgrade. It was going to be clear sailing from here on, but she was not sure if that was true. Something told her from the first concert to the last concert was all going to be an uphill battle and she still did not know how she was going to disappear. Everything she kept thinking of would not work. Maybe she would just fly back to Dallas, disappear from her hotel room, go to another hotel room and change her look back to Lenore, then catch a bus to Amarillo and call Nathaniel to pick her up. She was not sure. She would cross that bridge when she got to it. For now, her audience awaited.

She exited her little trailer and headed for the main arena. She was surprised by the level of controlled chaos. She was used to the chaos of a concert, but this was like a concert on steroids. Ten times the chaos, but far more controlled. She felt momentarily panicked when she realized that the fun and games were about to begin. As she entered the large dirt arena, she was surprised to see how many men were standing there. She quickly counted six rodeo clowns and twelve men who were all in black boots, black hats, different colored shirts, all Western-style though, and they were all wearing black leather chaps that had the Dodge symbol on them multiple times and said 'Ram' at the bottom. They were all chatting and clearly enjoying spending time together. One of the clowns broke off and approached. He was halfway to her before she was certain it was Mr. O'Mannion. He removed his hat and extended his hand. "It's a real pleasure to meet you, ma'am. I'm Sean O'Mannion. I'm in charge of the rodeo clowns and pickup men. I can't tell you how excited my boys and I are to have this photo opportunity with you."

She smiled. "The pleasure's all mine, Mr. O'Mannion."

"That's kind of you to say, ma'am. If it wouldn't be inconvenient, we'd like a couple of different shots. We'd like one of the whole group, one with just the clowns, and one with just the pickup men."

She smiled. "No inconvenience at all, and I will happily take individual photos, or if there are other groups in the group, whatever I can do for you. My time right now belongs to all of you."

He smiled. "Well, if you'll come on over here, I'll introduce you to everybody and then we can get started." He offered her his arm.

Lenore smiled and she took it and he escorted her over. She was surprised to discover that all of the clowns were wearing sneakers. As she studied their wardrobe, she realized that everything about it was designed for maximum range of movement. Though their outfits looked big and clunky, in reality they were not. Everything about them was very practical, especially given how dangerous their line of work was. She shook hands with all the men. Sadly, she was introduced to them so quickly she did not remember any of their names.

Sean said, "Well, gentlemen, Miss Persephone has most kindly offered to take individual photos as well as some group photos, and she says if there any groups within the group. Yes, I'm looking at you, Jerry and Johnny." He shifted his attention back to Persephone and said, "In case it escaped your notice, they're twins."

She smiled and shook her head. "No sir, I caught that right off the bat."

Johnny said with a laugh, "Does anybody else detect a touch of country in her accent or was that just put on for our benefit? Where you hail from?"

She looked at him and smiled. "I was born in Memphis, Tennessee."

Bubba had been involved in another conversation. His head whipped around and he said, "Seriously? You little liar, you said you were a California vegetarian." The words had barely left his mouth before he realized what he just said.

Artie, a former classmate, pounced. "Bubba, aren't you a little old to be crushing on the teen pop star? I mean, she's barely legal."

Sean chuckled and said, "Legal's legal, it don't matter how legal, but if all you young bucks are done flirting with the pretty doe, maybe we can get a few photos taken."

Jerry chuckled and said, "I'm sure she's spoke for."

Bubba had to bite his tongue not to say, 'Yes, she is.'

Sean said, "How about we take the clown photos first, and then the pickup men can come in and join us, then us clowns will clown out of here, and leave you pickup men to clean up the mess, and then we can take our individuals." Everybody either laughed or rolled their eyes.

Bubba was glad he had a minute to watch her. He frowned. She looked tired and her smile seemed forced. A voice at his elbow said very softly, "If you're worried about her falling in love with the life, she's miserable. She wants to come home. Today's been pretty rough on her. I think she's afraid you're not gonna like seeing how other men react to her."

Bubba shrugged his shoulders. "I don't give a damn about them. She's mine and that's all that matters to me." He chuckled then added, "I also think she's afraid she's never gonna see you again, so I hope you come to visit. There will always be a place at our table and a spare bed for you."

"I'd like that a lot." JC watched Miss P for a minute, then a thought struck him. He said, "You know I don't exactly blend into your town, not with my eight hundred dollar kicks. If I keep popping up, somebody's bound to recognize me and get suspicious then put two and two together. I wouldn't ruin this for her for anything."

Bubba nodded and considered for a minute, then he chuckled and said, "Then I suggest you and I run into each other a few times make it obvious we're becoming friends. Then nobody will bat an eye if you come and visit me."

JC nodded. "Sounds like a plan."

Sean called, "All right, pickup men."

JC said quickly, "Just be sure none of you pickup men get any ideas about picking up my client. I'd hate to have to hurt any of you before the rodeo started."

Sean laughed. "That would be mighty embarrassing."

Bubba stood back watching the guys take their individual photos. He thought it was interesting how even the older guys liked to stand a little too close to her. She had a definite sex appeal like this. He thought it was interesting. Though he felt it, it did not do it for him. It did not draw him in like Lenore did, but at least he was glad to see JC was doing his job. He cautioned a couple of the guys for getting a little too close, and one of the guys for the way he grabbed her hip.

Sean asked, "Has everybody gotten their turn?"

Bubba seriously contemplated saying he did not want his photo taken with that woman, but he decided it might hurt Lenore's feelings, so he said, "I think I'm the last."

Jerry said, "You know, the way he's obviously been stalking her since he knows she's a California vegetarian, I would've thought he would have been the first."

Sean did not like the sharp look Bubba gave Jerry. Jerry was known for being a shit stirrer, and it occasionally got his nose busted. He decided it would not be good to have two of the pickup men at odds. He said with a laugh, "No offense to Miss Persephone, but I don't know why Bubba would even give her a second glance, not with that handsome filly he's got of his own."

Artie demanded, "When did Bubba get a girl?"

Lucas, who had been at the town hall meeting, said with a laugh, "I don't know how it ain't all over the town. Bubba was trying to get his girl to sit on the back row of the last town meeting so they could make out. She's a mighty pretty little thing, but before any of you guys get any ideas about trying to steal Bubba's girl, watch out. She's Sheriff Mendoza's oldest daughter."

Lenore was finding it very uncomfortable being talked about behind her back to her face. She decided to see if she could divert the conversation by saying with a laugh, "No offense taken, Mr. O'Mannion. I have to travel with a team of makeup artists to look this good."

Bubba moved to stand next to her. She stepped in close, forcing him to put his arm around her, but he was careful to place it on her waist. He smiled and said out of the corner of his mouth, "Don't you mean it takes a team of makeup artists to make you look this bad?"

Lenore was sure it was just stress and nerves, but that irritated her. She stepped on his foot hard. "Overgrown jackass." She turned and headed for JC.

Bubba grimaced and growled. He murmured, "Okay, I deserved that." All the other guys were laughing even though they did not know what he had said. He ignored them.

Sean demanded, "Is there anything else we need to discuss.?" He looked around. No one responded. "All right then, everybody get your chores done, get some rest, get ready for a long month. Though of course, some of you aren't working the whole rodeo and I will see you when I see you. If something comes up and you can't make your shift, call me. Do not leave me in the lurch, because I need to get somebody else in the saddle to cover your shift." They all waved and murmured various replies which all amounted to 'We'll be there', but he knew at least a couple of them were going to leave him hanging. They always did. If he was lucky, it was only for one shift. Sometimes there was one who just never showed to work, always drove him up the wall. Fortunately, he had worked with most of the guys before, there were only two or three he had never worked with. Sadly, two of the ones he had worked with previously he knew were going to leave him high and dry a couple of shifts. He looked at Bubba, one of the ones he had never worked with before, but his father was reliable and never left them hanging. Something told him like father like son.

Bubba approached Sean and said, "Just like with Pop, if you get left high and dry, give me a call, I'll be here quick as I can. Takes me about forty-five minutes to get from the ranch house to here, depending on where I am on the ranch. Could take me three hours, but I'll keep my gear in my truck so I can drop everything and come if I have to."

Sean looked around. They were alone. "Good to know. I appreciate it, but what did you say to make her so mad?"

Bubba sighed and rolled his eyes. "I made a stupid remark that the makeup made her look worse, and sadly, I didn't put it that tactfully."

Sean shook his head. "Look, I know this can't be easy on you, but that was a fool thing to do. You got a good little girl there, don't go losing her."

Bubba growled and rubbed his face. "I know. I know."

LIV

Friday, December, 29

Diego sat in his patrol truck outside the hotel, a Manila envelope in each hand. It was just a question which one he wanted to deal with first. One involved something he looked forward to and dreaded. He wanted it done, but he also hated that it had to be done. The other had involved a lot of sleepless nights, but finally he had decided it was what he wanted. He folded one and stuck it in the inside pocket of his uniform jacket, then he looked at the room number on the other and got out. He gestured for McFarlane to follow him. He led the way to the stairs.

McFarlane decided that this was probably the best time to broach a subject. She said, "So Sheriff, before you find out on your own and get really mad at me, I wanted to let you know I've violated one of your standing orders."

Diego stopped and turned to stare at her. She was his second best Deputy and his third in command. He found it impossible to believe that she broke a rule without good reason. He asked, "And you did this why?"

She laughed. "You would ask why before asking what. I erased that twenty minutes of footage from the station, well, not exactly twenty minutes, but roughly, and believe me there will be no recovering it and the reason is though I trust all of my fellow deputies implicitly, I don't one hundred percent trust other people. So I figured it was better if just certain innocent video disappears, and I double checked, there is no law that says we have to store that footage since there were no prisoners in the station or people making complaints. For all intents and purposes, it was just staff and visitors. We're well within our rights to scrub all of that footage, and since all routine station footage goes away every thirty days anyways, it probably won't even come up."

He sighed several times. "I appreciate the loyalty, but I'm not exactly happy you did it, but I'd be lying if I said I wasn't a little relieved. I had already decided in thirty days to fully scrub that footage. Let's get back to business and never speak of this again."

"Roger that, Sheriff."

When Diego neared the door, he indicated she was to stand back a little. She did. He knocked and waited. He was just about to knock again when the door was answered. The woman laughed and said, "If somebody sent me a stripper, they sure have good taste, though I will say this, it's not my birthday."

Diego looked her up and down. All right, it was painful to admit, but she was still an incredibly good looking woman. Granted, he was sure it was plastic surgery, liposuction, and a boob job. Unless he was mistaken, they were all contributing factors. "Evanjalevn?"

She laughed. "Oh goody, you're definitely here for me. Why don't you come on in and take a load off?"

He smiled to himself. She definitely had not had that predatory eye the last time he had seen her. He nodded and removed his hat. "Don't mind if we do, more private that way." He entered, followed by McFarlane. She closed the door behind her.

Evanjalevn sighed with annoyance and dropped down on the bed. "Oh dear, you're a real cop, and what are you doing here?"

He opened the envelope and pulled out a stack of papers. "Let's be very clear. I'm not doing this exactly of my own free will, but since our daughter asked me to do this, I didn't feel I could exactly say no. If it was up to me, I would say publish and be damned, but Lenore doesn't feel that way, and since you have tortured her for eighteen very long years, I will not be a party to you doing it again. So if this is what she wants, if this is how she wants it to go down, then I will see that it happens. But understand this, I am supposed to tell you this deal expires when I walk out that door, so there's no calling your lawyer, there's no renegotiating, take it or leave it." He held out the papers.

Evanjalevn snatched them out of his hand and demanded, "What do you mean 'our daughter'?"

"Well, surely you don't think you're the Virgin Mary. I mean, I know I was drunk, but even I remember. I'm pretty sure you remember, and since I don't recall observing you do any drugs, and according to our daughter you didn't do drugs back then, I would like to think that you haven't fried all of your brain cells. Remember that it takes a man and woman to make a baby, which means I'm Daddy, and you, unfortunately, are Mommy."

Evanjalevn stared up at the ceiling. "Oh Jesus Christ! Are you telling me that is what brought my daughter to this little shithole town? She came looking for Daddy? How pathetic! I thought I raised her tougher than that. Actually, I was never capable of making her tough, she was always weak and pathetic, always whining, though I don't understand how she thinks she found Daddy. There are so many options for who Daddy could be, because believe me, if I slept with you, I don't remember because there were just so many of you. So I would prefer it if you do not call my daughter your daughter. Besides, even if, which I doubt, you are, you are nothing but a sperm donor. I mean, you were just a one night drunken romp and clearly not even good enough to remember. But back to my daughter, because if you think I'm going to let you take any credit for her, you are out of your damn mind, and so what does sweet little Lenore want now?" She began flipping through the papers. She started laughing. "Oh, that's laughable. She wants to pay me one and a half million dollars a year to stay out of her life for the next twenty years."

Diego sighed several times. "It's not just about you staying out of her life for the next twenty years. You cannot publicly speak about her, you cannot divulge her real name, you will not discuss that you had a one night stand in Leaf, Texas, you will not disclose that her father is a Sheriff, you will not disclose that her father is from Texas, you will not even mention Texas and her in the same sentence ever, at any time. You will in no way, shape, or form, draw the media's attention to Lenore, her family, me, or my family. It's all in the contract. It's basically a complicated gag order. Sign it and you get one and a half million dollars a year. You pack your bags and there's a private plane waiting for you at Hereford Municipal Airport to take you back home to Los Angeles. It's a simple agreement and you make a lot of money and you leave me and my family alone. As far as you're concerned, for the next twenty years, we don't exist. Let's be honest, do you really want to be a grandmother?"

Evanjalevn cringed and got to her feet. She gestured to her body as she spun in a circle. "Does this look like the body of a grandmother? So what are you telling me, that Lenore is knocked up by one of your stupid little cowpokes? What do they do, put fertility drugs in the water?" She dropped back on the bed, crossed her legs, crossed her arms, and glared at him.

"No, my daughter is not pregnant. She has more sense than her mother."

Evanjalevn laughed. "Don't bet on it. I always found her to be a stupid little girl. I mean, she has to be an idiot if she'd rather be your daughter than my daughter. I can make her rich."

Diego could not take it, he saw red. He snapped angrily, "You almost made her dead! I would rather her be poor and happy than rich and dead or addicted to all the drugs you had her on! And as ashamed as I am to admit that I slept with you, there's not a doubt she's mine! And I'm damn proud of Lenore. She is a good kid despite everything you did to her, and before you argue with me, I did a DNA test. She's my little girl, and you will stay away from her whether you sign those papers or not! So you better sign them, because it's the only way you're getting anything out of the deal."

Evanjalevn got up and crossed to the little table. She picked up an ink pen and signed and initialed it everywhere she was supposed to, then pointed. "I'm assuming your officer is the witness." McFarlane crossed to it and signed it. Evanjalevn demanded, "When do I get my first check?"

"I'm overnighting these to Lenore's attorney. I'm supposed to tell you he'll direct deposit the money into your account on January second, provided the bank doesn't put a hold on it. After all, that is a power beyond his control. After that, you will receive your deposit on the first of every month provided it does not fall on a holiday, then you will receive it the day before. Pack your bågs. A car will be waiting outside to pick you up." Diego picked up the papers and verified the signatures. She had actually signed them Evanjalevn, which Lenore had warned him to watch out for because Jane Stevens was no longer her legal name, and she had initialed everything EJ which is how she always initialed things. He put it back in the envelope, turned, and exited the room, followed by McFarlane.

McFarlane waited until they were on the stairwell before she said, "Okay, I see what you saw. She is smoking hot. It's actually kind of unfair. She's almost old enough to be my mother and she looks way better than me."

Diego turned and glared at her. "The difference, McFarlane, is your beauty is natural, and hers is surgically augmented, trust me. I could spend twenty minutes telling you everything I noticed that is different, but we're not going to do that."

She held out her hand. "Truth be told, not interested. When I'm eighty I will still look good and she'll look like a patchwork quilt. Why don't you give me the papers, sir? I saw the envelope on your front seat. I will take these and mail them while you deal with that other envelope. The one I'm not supposed to know you have."

He grudgingly held it out to her as he asked, "Are you sure you don't consider it beneath you to mail my letter?"

She snatched the envelope out of his hand and rolled her eyes. "It's not your mail, it's Persephone's mail, and given how much money she is donating to the rodeo, I will deliver her mail any day of the week."

Diego smiled and went to the other end of the hotel. He knocked on Lenore's door. He raised an eyebrow when JC answered. "Morning, Sheriff, come on in. She's in the shower, but she'll be out in just a minute. I'll let her know you're here." Diego frowned as the man crossed to the bathroom, opened the door a little, and said, "Hey Miss P, the Sheriff's here." He could hear Lenore say something but he could not tell what she had said. JC turned around, closed the door and said, "She says she's just rinsing shampoo out of her hair, give her ten minutes." JC indicated the armchair. "Not a lot of seats, but please sit down, Sheriff." He crossed to one of the beds, sat down, and picked up his book.

Diego looked from his bare feet to shorts and T-shirt. He asked, "Are you staying in the same room as my daughter?"

JC nodded. "This is not the Marriott. They don't have suites and I was not allowing my client to sleep in these crappy hotel rooms with those crappy locks by herself. If that bothers you, Sheriff, I'm terribly sorry. Besides, at the risk of making you blush, it's not like she's got anything I haven't seen before, and no, I don't go out of my way to see it. Seeing her without her clothes on is just as bad as seeing one of my sisters naked. After all, I've been her bodyguard since she was fourteen, and despite any videos you saw online, no, she does not generally wander around naked. I always considered her a quite modest young lady."

Lenore came out drying her hair. "I do try. Morning, Sheriff, what bring you out so early?"

He crossed his arms over his chest. "So now I'm Sheriff?"

She sighed. "Just for a couple more days. I don't want to get into the habit of calling you Dad and then slip up in front of a bunch of people who aren't going be nice and keep their mouths shut."

He sighed and looked her up and down. She was in sweat pants, and a T-shirt and a pair of crocs, still drying her hair. He smiled. "I have to say, sweetie, I prefer you like this, but I was here this early for two reasons. One, my source in the hotel lobby informed me that Jane arrived last night so I went to deal with her promptly this morning. And I figured while I was here, I'd ask you how you felt about this. I expect the answer is no, but it would mean a lot to me." He pulled the envelope out of his uniform jacket and handed it over.

Lenore frowned and took the envelope, opened it, and began reading. She turned and sat down on the bed. After a long minute she said, "You can do this?"

He smiled and sat down next to her. "Yes, already checked. They will agree to it. I also already filled out all the paperwork. Everything just needs your approval. It'll be a little bit of a pain in the butt. It will require you to change some things, but that fancy lawyer of yours says he's ready and waiting."

"So if I agree to this, my name on my birth certificate is gonna change. I won't be Lenore Stevens anymore, I'll be Lenore Mendoza?"

"That is correct."

She turned and wrapped her arms around his neck, hugging him tightly. "Of course! What made you think I wouldn't agree to that? I mean, I don't know how long I'm gonna keep it, but ..."

Diego shut his eyes and held his daughter tightly. After a long minute he said, "I know. I figure it's just a matter of time before Bubba asks you, but I figure if I'm lucky, you'll keep it for a year."

Lenore pulled away and looked at him surprised. "Nathaniel didn't talk to you?"

Diego groaned and threw his head back. "So he's already asked. Okay, I can take it. Have you guys picked a date yet?"

"The guys were all talking about mid-March, and by guys I mean Nathaniel, Alejandro, and Mr. Cartwright. I have to say I'm really surprised he hasn't talked to you, but then again, since I gave the ring back, he's probably a little torqued with me."

Diego frowned at his daughter as he asked, "Now why would you do a damn fool thing like that? You're nuts about him."

"Because Persephone couldn't be photoed wearing an engagement ring. I told him I was only giving it back to him to hold on to. I was coming back for it and its owner."

He smiled. "Come to think of it, Bubba did ask me before the pancake breakfast if I could spare a few minutes, but we had a few little problems and I didn't get a chance to talk to him. Maybe I should be loitering around when the pickup men arrive tonight. I think he's got tonight's shift. If not, I'll drive on out to the ranch and have a word with him."

She smiled. "Are you okay with this, Dad?"

He hugged her tightly. "I'm more than okay with it. I couldn't ask for better son-in-law and as long as it's Lenore Mendoza on your marriage license, I'll be happy."

She grimaced and pointed at the papers. "How long does it take those to go through?"

He grinned. "As soon as we have a court date, and we don't even have to show. Your lawyer can represent you and me, but as soon as the judge signs it, it's legal. I've been told we should get a court date within a couple of weeks, so by the middle of January you will be a Mendoza."

She wrapped her arm around his waist and leaned her head against his shoulder. "I'm already a Mendoza." After a minute she started laughing. "Hey, you want to really get up Jane's nose?"

He looked at her and raised an eyebrow, "What?"

"Do you think Natalia would adopt me?"

He grinned. "In an LA minute."

LV

Sunday, December 31

Lenore was standing in front of the fairground sign having her photo taken over and over again. It was bitter cold, but she did not mind because it was snowing. Every time a photo was going to be taken, she told herself just a couple of days and she could be curled up in front of the fire in Nathaniel's arms. That thought kept her smiling. She had been surprised at what a large turnout they had had. She thought the cold weather would keep people at bay, but it had not, though from what she had heard, the turnout on the fairgrounds had been better on the two days it had gotten into the seventies. She just could not understand Texas. Wednesday the temperature had been in the teens, Thursday and Friday had gotten to almost seventy. Yesterday the high had been thirty, and today they were again in the teens. She guessed there was just no predicting this Texas weather. She looked at JC's watch, she had half an hour before she had to go get ready for her concert. She had taken another dozen photos when she saw two familiar faces in line. Now she did not have to think about Nathaniel to smile, she just had to look at the line. Finally they got to the head of the line.

Diego said, "I know I had my picture taken the other day with you, Miss Persephone, but a very long time ago a very dear friend of mine and I had our photos taken almost on this exact spot, and though he's no longer with us, his older brother Wayne and I thought maybe we could catch a little shadow of that photo. Would you mind?"

She had to fight back tears. After minute she shook her head. "No, Sheriff, I think that sounds pretty great. It would be an honor." She wrapped an arm around each one of their waists and had their photo taken.

Wayne leaned down and whispered, "Tonight as you're heading back to your trailer, keep an eye out for familiar faces."

She looked at him sharply. "What?"

Diego chuckled. "You heard him."

Before she had a chance to say anything else, they both turned and walked away. She wondered if it classified as assaulting a police officer to hit him in the back of the head with a snowball. Sadly, she had no more time to think about it. She turned to the youth group and said, "Well, I hope y'all made lots of money for your organization. As soon as you all have a total, get with my manager and he will cut you a check. I am going to match dollar for dollar what you earned."

The two parents looked at her in surprise. One of them said quickly, "Thank you, Miss Persephone, that is so generous of you! I can't tell you how much we appreciate it. I will be sure to come and find your manager here in just a little bit. It won't take us long to add it up. I think we did really well. My camera says we took three hundred and eighteen photos, but we were really blessed, a lot of people paid us more than the five dollars we were charging. The Sheriff and Mr. Cartwright each gave us a hundred dollars."

Lenore smiled. "That's awesome." She headed for her trailer and her quick change. As soon as she was done, she headed for the main arena. When she got there, the pickup truck, which had been there every night before, was not there. She looked around. The Wrangler who seemed to coordinate all the backstage stuff was standing there. She asked him, "Am I early or late?"

He grinned. "You're right on time, Miss Persephone, but we thought since this is your last performance, we'd do something a little different."

She looked at him dubiously. "Should I be worried?"

He shrugged his shoulders. "I don't think so. I've been told you're a good sport and you're not afraid of big animals, you should be fine."

She immediately began shaking her head. "If you crazy people think I'm getting on one of those bulls, you are out of your minds! I'm a good sport, but I'm not that good."

Bubba said from behind her, "But are you a good enough sport to take a ride with me?"

She turned around quickly to see Nathaniel standing there with a gorgeous black Clydesdale. She caught her breath and held out her hand. "Oh my God, he's gorgeous!" He sniffed her hand and immediately began nestling it. She rubbed his neck. "I'm sorry fellow, I don't have a treat for you. I wish I did."

Bubba chuckled. "Fortunately, I came prepared." He pulled out a carrot and offered it to her.

She smiled at him. She took it, broke it up, and began feeding it to the horse. The horse scarfed it up. She demanded, "What's his name?"

"Storm." He leaned in close and whispered, "I just bought him."

Her face lit up and she rubbed his neck. "You did not. He's incredible. What are you going to do with him?"

He shrugged his shoulders. "I don't know, use him to pull a sleigh or maybe just carry a rock star around an arena." Without waiting, he reached down and grabbed her around the waist and set her sideways on the saddle. "Shift a little and hook your right leg over the saddle horn."

She quickly did as she was told and grabbed the saddle horn with both hands. She wanted to yell at him, but she was afraid it would attract unnecessary attention, then she remembered she had been introduced to him. "Mr. Cartwright, I'm not sure about this, I've never ridden a horse before."

Bubba chuckled and mounted up behind her. He wrapped his arm around her waist. "Then I think it's long past time for you to learn." He shifted his attention to JC. "We can scare you up a ride if you'd like."

"No thank you, Bubba, this is one of those you gonna crawl before you walk, so I think I'll walk to the stage. It ain't that far."

Bubba shrugged his shoulders. "Suit yourself, city boy. But if you ever change your mind, come on out to the ranch. We'll scare you up something to ride."

JC chuckled and said, "Watch it, I might just do that."

Bubba laughed. "Anytime, city boy." He turned his horse and headed for the arena. He bent down and kissed Lenore on the neck. He whispered in her ear, "God I miss you."

She snorted. "Really, I hadn't noticed from the way you've been treating me or ignoring me."

He knew they would be out of sight for another moment or two, he ran his hand along her thigh. "I'm sorry, but it was hard being around you and not being with you. I was afraid if I tried to be nice it would give away the whole show, so I found myself being a jerk ... and we're in public view."

She sighed and focused on her audience, waving at them. She said with a smile. "Believe me, that I can understand. Both times I saw you, I wanted to run into your arms."

He laughed and pulled his hat down so nobody could see what he was saying, "Now that, I love to hear. By the way, I officially have permission to marry you, Miss Stevens."

She laughed and said without moving her lips, "Mendoza."

Bubba groaned and looked down at the ground. "Okay, we need to talk about something else or I'm going to shock everybody and kiss you."

She sighed but asked, "So how many laps do we have to take?"

"Three."

"But we normally only do two and that's in a truck, that goes much faster."

"Oh well, it was agreed, none of us care. By the way, hold on." He tightened his grip around her waist and before she had a chance to protest, they were galloping.

Lenore gripped the saddle horn with one hand and with her other hand she reached back in gripped his chaps. "If you drop me ..."

He laughed. "Never in a million years." They finished their third lap and he approached the stage. He dismounted, reached up and grabbed her around the waist, and lowered her to the ground. She stretched up on her toes and kissed him on the cheek. The crowd was cheering. He leaned forward and hugged her and whispered quickly in her ear, "Keep an eye out for friendly faces." He pulled free, grabbed the saddle horn and swung himself easily into the saddle, then tipped his hat to her.

Lenore desperately wanted to call him a showoff, but she smiled and wanted to demand to know what that was supposed to mean, but he was already riding away. She quickly climbed the steps and grabbed the microphone. She laughed. "Whoa! That was a first. Apparently a bunch of the rodeo staff decided that the city girl needed to ride a horse at least once while in Texas, so thank you, Mr. Cartwright. That was an excellent ride and you are an excellent chauffeur. I don't think I'd want to drive myself just yet." Everyone laughed, so did she. After a minute she said, "But I think you folks came here to hear some music, right?" Everyone cheered louder.

Lenore had ended up doing three encores, but finally her ride was there to pick her up. Fortunately, this time it was a Dodge Ram pickup truck, the one she had usually been driven around in. She and JC got in the back and held onto the bars that were specially installed for the purpose. She waved goodbye to the crowd and then they drove out of the arena. As they were climbing down off the pickup truck, the Wrangler approached.

"Miss Persephone, we're gonna have to take you out a different door. There is a mob of people out there waiting for you, so unless you want to take the next three hours pushing your way through it, we're gonna take you through the animal pens."

JC suddenly felt nervous. He said quickly, "I'm not sure about that. We never discussed that route and I've never walked it."

Lenore reached over and gripped his arm. She said firmly, "I think it will be okay."

JC started shaking his head. "No way! We have three other routes that I have walked. We've never done the animal pens. I will choose the alternative route, not you guys. I'm the Head of Security."

The Wrangler shook his head. "You may be the Head of Security, but I'm in charge here, and I'm telling you, all of your other routes are being mobbed and they're getting bigger by the minute. The animal pens are the only safe way out of here. I've got two security guards here to help you and your team. Follow them and do as you're told, or I will not be held responsible for what happens, and don't forget the rodeo is setting off fireworks at midnight, so none of this crowd is going anywhere. Besides the fact that a bunch of them are staying to say goodbye to her, they're also staying for the fireworks."

Lenore said firmly, "JC, if you want to go the other way, you go the other way. I'm going through the animal pens, trust me."

JC growled. "Fine, but I give you fair warning, anybody gives me any shit, I'm shooting them."

Lenore and the Wrangler replied simultaneously. The Wrangler said, "With my blessing."

Lenore shook her head. "You are not shooting anybody just because they annoy you." She turned to the two security guys and gestured. "Lead the way, gentlemen." They nodded and started off.

One of them she was certain did not look familiar, the other one did, but she could not quite place him. They walked through several long tunnels and then came out in the animal pens. Lenore could smell them before they got to it. A couple of months ago she would have said it was disgusting, now it was normal, almost even familiar and comfortable. When they entered the animal pens, she was surprised at how many people were still working and it was almost midnight on New Year's Eve. Then she smiled. There was not an unfamiliar face in the place. They turned and walked along the side of the building past the animal pens. They were just approaching a small tool shed when the door opened, and a woman gestured her in.

JC grabbed her arm, but a voice to his right said, "Sorry, JC, but for the final curtain call, the part of Persephone is going to be played by Angeline. She'll be going back to the hotel with you tonight, then she'll be going with you to Amarillo, and she will board the plane as Persephone. A private jet has already been arranged for."

JC had turned as soon as someone said his name. He extended his hand. "Ramon, right?"

"That is correct. You have a good memory."

Lenore had not waited for the men to speak. She had slipped into the storage shed. She looked the woman up and down. She was identically dressed from head to boots. The only thing that was absent was her jewelry.

The woman extended her hand. "Hi, I'm Angeline, and I'll be taking over your role. Your disappearing act is on me. Quickly give me all your jewelry." Lenore started pulling off her jewelry and setting it on the little shelf. Angeline started putting it on and she gestured. "These are some clothes that Bubba brought you. You and the boys are gonna finish cleaning the pens, which should not take you but a half-hour. They are almost done, and then you'll be home free."

Lenore grinned from ear to ear. "That sounds fabulous. It's great to meet you, Angeline."

"Likewise, but I have to get out of here. Take your time getting changed." She slipped out.

Angeline turned and said, "Well, if you boys are done catching up, it's late. Get me back to the hotel before the fireworks are over."

JC grumbled but shook hands with Ramon. He said firmly, "Anything happens to her, I'll hunt you all down." Then he gestured for her to go on.

Lenore grabbed the long-sleeved T-shirt and pulled it on over her tank top. She pulled off her boots, her shorts, and grabbed her pair of jeans. They felt so nice to wear, they were not skintight. She grabbed her old brown boots and stuck her feet in them. She picked up a jacket and inhaled deeply, it smelled like Nathaniel. She slipped it on and zipped it up. She ran her fingers through her hair and quickly braided it, then twisted it up on top of her head and pulled the wool cap on, pulling it down over her ears, glad it was a little cool in the pens and she would not get too warm. There was an empty grain sack, clearly intended for her to put her stuff in it. She started stuffing her clothes into it, then she saw a package of baby wipes. She grabbed them and started wiping off the makeup. She threw all of her trash into the grain sack. She probably looked a fright, but she did not care. She grabbed the grain sack and a shovel and exited the tool shed. She asked, "Where to next, boss?"

Ramon paused in what he was doing and indicated one of the pens. "That's the last one and then we can call it a night."

She quickly got to work. It did not take them long to finish up and start putting away all the equipment. She was hot and sweaty, both from the performance and from the long-sleeved shirt and jacket, but she did not care. She could take a shower when she got home. When everything was done, they walked out as a group. She was just about to ask where Nathaniel was when his truck pulled up. Ramon took her by the arm and escorted her over. Nobody was watching them. He opened the door and she got in the front seat.

He tossed the sack in the back, then closed the door.

Bubba asked, "Somebody call for a getaway driver?"

She laughed, turned in the seat, hugged him tightly, and kissed him. "Yes, take us home."

The End

Made in the USA
Middletown, DE
16 November 2024